D0347063

The Silent Ones

Also by William Brodrick

The Sixth Lamentation
The Gardens of the Dead
A Whispered Name
The Day of the Lie
The Discourtesy of Death

The Silent Ones

William Brodrick

Little, Brown

LITTLE, BROWN

First published in Great Britain in 2015 by Little, Brown

1 3 5 7 9 10 8 6 4 2

Copyright © William Brodrick 2015

The moral right of the author has been asserted.

All characters and events in this publication, other than those
clearly in the public domain, are fictitious and any resemblance
to real persons, living or dead, is purely coincidental.

All rights reserved.
No part of this publication may be reproduced, stored in a retrieval system,
or transmitted, in any form or by any means, without the prior permission in
writing of the publisher, nor be otherwise circulated in any form of binding or
cover other than that in which it is published and without a similar condition
including this condition being imposed on the subsequent purchaser.

A CIP catalogue record for this book is available from the British Library.

Hardback ISBN 978-1-4087-0491-2
Trade Paperback ISBN 978-0-349-00036-7

Typeset in Bembo by Palimpsest Book Production Limited,
Falkirk, Stirlingshire
Printed and bound in Great Britain by Clays Ltd, St Ives plc

Papers used by Little, Brown are from well-managed
forests and other responsible sources.

MIX
Paper from
responsible sources
FSC
www.fsc.org   FSC® C104740

Little, Brown
An imprint of
Little, Brown Book Group
Carmelite House
50 Victoria Embankment
London EC4Y 0DZ

An Hachette UK Company
www.hachette.co.uk

www.littlebrown.co.uk

In memory of Clare Hawks
And for James, Basil and Phoebe

Acknowledgements

My gratitude goes to Ursula Mackenzie, Richard Beswick, Iain Hunt, Her Honour Judge Moreland (any errors of law or procedure remain mine), Françoise Koetschet, and Damien Charnock, with whom, many years ago, I first discussed the inner workings of this story.

Secret guilt by silence is betrayed

Dryden

Part One

'What's the matter? Tell me what happened?'

Ignoring his mother, Harry Brandwell jumped from the car and ran the short distance home. Kicking open the iron gate he shoved past Fraser and made for the front door. Once inside, he scrambled up the stairs. He didn't have long. His stomach had turned. Bile was rising.

'Harry?' called his father, leaving the kitchen; then, in a lower tone to his wife: 'What the hell is going on?'

'I don't know. He won't say.'

Harry made it to the bathroom just in time. When he'd finished heaving and spitting, he yelled over his shoulder, 'Don't come up. Leave me alone.'

'But Harry—' His mother was on the landing.

'I said let me be, now go away.'

After she'd backed off, Harry undressed, shaking off his clothes as if they were crawling with lice. He stepped into the shower and turned on the hot tap. Gradually the temperature increased. When he couldn't stand the heat any more, he moved away and reached for a towel, dabbing his red skin as if he was bleeding from every pore. He was eerily calm. The flush of pain had cleansed his mind.

'Harry?' His mother was outside. She'd knocked gently. 'Please talk to me.'

He didn't reply. He let the silence drive her away. Then he went to his room and lay down, listening to the soft scrape of the garden rake. Fraser was gathering up the fallen leaves.

A month back Harry had refused to speak to Geraldine, the counsellor. So his mum had suggested he talk to Father Littlemore instead. He was new on the scene. An American. Came for Sunday lunch with presents. Flowers for his mother. Wine for his dad. Most recently − for

Harry — a ship-in-a-bottle. But Harry hadn't been fooled. Right from the start, when he first introduced himself as Father Eddie, Harry thought him a bit too nice, a bit too helpful. He tried too hard. Harry had seen these kinds of desperate measures before — at school when someone new turned up. He'd learned to read the signs. And the biggest of the lot was when Father Eddie changed the subject when asked where he'd been before moving to London. Harry had tried to tell his mother that there was something odd about the guy but she'd refused to listen.

'And what about Gutsy Mitchell?' she'd asked, a hand on each hip.

It was a fair point. When Gutsy had arrived not wanting to talk about Dover, Harry had thought he must have something to hide, and he hadn't. His parents had split up that's all. And so thinking of Gutsy, he'd given Father Eddie a break. And anyway, he hadn't liked Geraldine's rules about open doors and not keeping secrets . . .

'You can trust him,' Harry's mother had said, moving a few strands of black hair behind an ear. 'You can tell him anything.'

Father Eddie promised to teach him the chess moves that had never appeared in a book. Stuff the Russians would kill for. Tricks handed down by Bobby Fischer.

'Who's Bobby Fischer?'

'You'll have to come along to find out. You don't have to speak. I'll do all the talking.'

Meetings had been arranged at Father Eddie's place. They played chess. Harry found himself relaxing and then smiling but he just couldn't open his mouth. And so Father Eddie played a clever trick. He told him a secret, the answer to where he'd been before coming to London: Freetown in Sierra Leone. He'd gone there to get away from his own problems, only it hadn't worked. He'd had to come back. 'We can't escape who we are,' he said. And he taught Harry a Krio phrase, ohlman de pan in yon wa-ala: 'everyone has his own troubles'. In the end, Harry took the plunge and opened up.

The gentle raking had come to an end. Which meant that Fraser would now be in the back garden with the tray of seedlings, waiting for Harry.

They'd sown spring cabbages in little pots a month back and now it was time to plant them outside. It was their autumn project.

Harry would have trusted Gutsy Mitchell with his life. Once you got to know him, Gutsy was Gutsy. Whereas Father Eddie had turned out to be two people. Once he got Harry telling him the stuff he wouldn't tell Geraldine, once he got him at ease with assurances and promises – once he'd established a bond between them – he changed. With the recollection of their third and last encounter – the one that had made him retch and take a shower – the nausea returned to Harry's stomach; he thought he might be sick again. Swinging his legs off his bed, he reached for the ship-in-a-bottle and gripped it by the neck. After opening the door he walked down the stairs, coming to a halt when he reached the door to the sitting room. His parents exchanged bewildered glances, their eyes finally coming to rest upon the object in Harry's hand, raised high in the air. When his accusing stare had brought his mother to tears, Harry threw the bottle against the wall above her head. The gift from Father Eddie exploded, showering his parents with splinters of glass and balsa wood as they crouched, whimpering with fear. After a few moments of shared disbelief, Harry went outside . . . to carry on with the rest of the day, and tomorrow and the day after.

'Are y'all right there, laddie?' asked Fraser.

The old man was on his knees making pockets in the soil with his gloved hands. His movements were slow and deliberate, his voice soft. Harry didn't answer. He took the tray of seedlings off the garden table and laid it on the ground between them.

'Canna give ye some advice, son?'

Again, Harry said nothing. His eyes were on the dark earth. He was trembling with rage and self-disgust.

'Sometimes things happen in life that we don't like. D'ye follow me?'

Harry nodded.

'And we think we'll never forget what's happened. D'ye get my drift?'

Harry nodded again.

'Well, you can take it from me, son, that's just not true. Not — true — at — all. And I should know.'

Fraser had once been one of those hunched homeless figures who haunted the streets around the Embankment. He'd seen no point to living, but thanks to Uncle Justin and the Bowline Project he'd been given a second chance. The man who'd once eaten out of dustbins had become Harry's friend and adviser. He'd let slip words that were wise and consoling.

'I'm not sayin' life's a piece of shortbread, all right? I'm not sayin' everything's rosy in the garden. Because we all know that's just nonsense. But what I can tell you is this' — Fraser fixed Harry with an anguished stare, the look of a man who'd been there and bought the T-shirt — 'no matter what's happened, we get over it, in time. It's hard to believe, I know, but it's God's honest truth. Everything'll fade away, eventually. You've just got to wait, laddie. In the meantime, how about we enjoy oursels a wee bit? Help me plant these cabbages. Okay?'

Harry nodded.

'Good lad.'

They set to work, filling up a patch of ground by the wall, Fraser remembering his mother's boiled bacon stinking out the tenement, Harry listening from a distant place. The fact is — and Gutsy Mitchell agreed — there were certain experiences that were burned into your memory; they'd never disappear. Fraser knew that as well as anyone. He just daren't say it to an eleven-year-old.

1

Anselm shuffled along the North Walk while his brothers continued west towards the refectory. Opening an arched door he slipped out of the cloister and presently came to the reception area where, a hand on each hip, his reproving gaze fell upon Larkwood's Gatekeeper. The aged yet ageless Sylvester, lodged behind his desk, ignored the looming presence. Wide, sunken eyes glanced up from a book onto the bank of telephones and then returned with ostentatious concentration to the page under consideration.

'You missed Vespers again,' began Anselm.

'No one bothered to warn me.'

'There was a bell. It rang repeatedly. In fact there were *two* bells . . . a small one to tell you that a big bell was going to ring . . . and then, five minutes later, the big bell itself – the one you'd just been warned about. It rang and rang. You can hear it a mile away. And, from where you're sitting, I'd say you're about two hundred yards distant. Hard to miss.'

The old man snorted. He didn't quite run with time any more. Its movement was strangely parallel to whatever he might be doing. He'd always turned up flustered and late for every Office, but recently he'd begun to miss some of them completely; he frowned when reminded of things he'd known all his monastic life. The shift in behaviour had begun to worry Anselm. Larkwood's Night Watchman was too important to fade away; too much loved to die. He had to live for ever.

'It's a disgrace,' said Anselm. 'This sort of thing would never have happened in the old days . . . when monks were monks. When we used our hands for speech. When the sound of a bell meant something.'

In fact, unable to master monastic sign language, Sylvester had invented his own. The problem was that no one else had understood it, persuading a visiting philosopher from Harvard that Wittgenstein's argument against a private language had been forcefully contradicted. The old man turned a page.

'You're mentioned in here,' he said, archly.

'Me?'

'Yes.'

Anselm smiled modestly. He'd been in the papers, but never in a book. Having quit the London Bar many years ago, he'd come to Larkwood Priory in Suffolk intent on the Silent Life. Made a beekeeper, he'd thought his days serving the interests of justice were well and truly over. But then, in one of those mysterious decisions reserved to monastic superiors, he'd been sent back to the world he'd left behind, instructed to help those forgotten by the law. A number of high-profile investigations had ensued, bringing with them – paradoxically – the recognition that had eluded him at the Bar.

'Really? I'm mentioned by name?'

'In the old days, we never repeated ourselves,' snapped Sylvester. 'Once said was enough. But, yes, he knows all about you and your kind and what happens when you come near a holy man.'

Sylvester held up the cover so Anselm could read the title: *Athanasius: The Life of Anthony.*

'I'm reading that bit about discerning good from evil. He's on about demons in the desert but it works for people round here, too. When the good turn up, he says, joy and delight and stability enter the soul; whereas, when the bad come round the corner' – Sylvester grabbed his gnarled walking stick, prodding Anselm's midriff with each word – 'there's confusion and disorder, dejection, enmity towards ascetics, and fear of death. So there. That's you nailed and sorted.'

The old man grounded his stick and leaned back in his seat, examining Anselm with his watery blue eyes. He'd held every job in the monastery except that of Prior. As Cook he'd made more apple crumble than mashed turnips. As Cellarer his donations had outstripped Larkwood's income. As Guestmaster, he'd thrown open the door to every shadow on the ground. He claimed never to have met an evil person in his life.

'You're not a bad lad,' he said, reluctantly. 'Come and get me next time, will you? I've heard the bells so often, I've forgotten what they're for. They're just part of the air I breathe, do you know what I mean?'

Anselm did. Sylvester had reached that hallowed state which is so easily overlooked, where an elder's every action, even answering the telephone, becomes a profoundly recollected activity. His every gesture was steeped in significance. Although he didn't recognise it, Larkwood's Lantern Bearer was on the edge of this life; he pottered about blithely on the cusp, catching the light of the next, reflecting lost grace back into the corridors he'd almost left behind.

'Let's go,' he groaned, struggling with bony hands out of his chair. It was time for supper, a communal gathering for which the old man was habitually and mysteriously early. 'I could eat a horse. Oh yes . . . I forgot to say. There's someone here to see you. Just turned up out of thin air.'

'Who?'

'I can't remember. But he looked a bit shifty.'

'Fair enough. Where is he now?'

'I suggested he might go to Vespers.'

'Really?'

'Yes.'

'And when was that?'

'After the bell rang, you goose. When else do you think?'

9

Anselm couldn't find words for the occasion. He just watched the old man hobble off to the refectory, bemused and maddened by the trappings of holiness.

2

The man on the other side of the parlour table didn't look shifty to Anselm in the least. His eyes simply flickered while he spoke, which Anselm took for intelligence, as if he had some difficulty processing his many thoughts and insights as they passed before his mind's eye. Curiously, he didn't introduce himself and he didn't reciprocate after Anselm had taken the initiative – a quite useless step since this composed, purposeful visitor knew exactly who he was talking to.

'There's a great difference between who a man is and what he does,' said the visitor. 'A man can be constrained by his place in life . . . by his responsibilities to other people. He can find himself trapped by his public role. There are things he would like to do that he can't do. I find myself in such a position and so I've come to you in a private capacity. Can I rely upon your discretion?'

'Absolutely.'

'Good. You must keep this meeting between ourselves. It's better for me that way.'

'How can I help?'

Anselm placed the man in his early sixties. He had dark hair, silvered lightly above the ears. His speech was measured, his accent polished, his tone persuasive. Pushed to choose an occupation, Anselm would have said the CEO of a company with a strong listing on the stock exchange. Away from the office, he was dressed in an open-necked blue shirt and badly ironed beige trousers: a bachelor waiting to get back into his Savile Row three-piece. Satisfied by Anselm's unqualified assurance he reached into a tatty briefcase and produced a brown envelope. He placed it carefully on the table, folding his hands on top as if to defeat a sudden gust of wind.

'I'd like you to find someone, Father. Someone who's gone missing. As far as the police are concerned, he's vanished off the face of the earth. I'd have thought that to be a highly improbable eventuality.'

Anselm liked the man's sardonic humour, though the hard smile underlined the seriousness of his purpose.

'The situation is complicated by the fact that there are vested interests involved. There are people occupying positions of considerable trust and influence who do not want this man to be found. They want him to remain hidden. Let's say that they, too, in their own way, are constrained by their responsibilities to other people. Someone, however, must intervene, regardless of such misguided . . . sensitivities.'

Anselm nodded. A potential whistleblower had gone into hiding. Unlike the other board members, this CEO had a conscience. He wanted the truth out.

'This much is certain,' said the man. 'He must have feared for his life. His home was wide open. The lights were left on. He took no money, no clothing and no passport. He simply ran into the night and never came back.'

'When did this happen?'

'Seven months ago. October the second.'

'Did he leave a message of any kind?'

The man shook his head in such a way that Anselm didn't bother to ask all the other preliminary questions that had no doubt been raised ad nauseam by the police. At the same time – and to his mild astonishment – Anselm could feel that the interview was drawing to a rapid close. His guest had opened the envelope and taken out a photograph. Spinning it around, he slid it slowly across the table.

'This is the man I'd like you to find.'

Anselm looked at the sombre, clean-shaven features and made a frown. There was something familiar about the facial expression. That hint of sadness. And disappointment. Anselm stared hard, trying to tie down the recognition. Mentally, he sketched in a rough beard and then trimmed it back. After adjusting his glasses, his gaze settled on the white clerical collar.

'His name is Father Edmund Littlemore,' said the visitor, standing up. 'He's a member of the Lambertine Order. From what I understand, some of his confrères are glad he's disappeared. And they aren't alone. As I said, there are vested interests, and they extend beyond his immediate circle.'

'What has he done?' asked Anselm.

'Nothing wrong, of that you can be sure.'

'Then why did he run away?'

'That is the most important question. Which is why I insist upon one preliminary step: find out *why* before you find *him*. What you discover can only help you. This is what he needs more than anything else . . . your assistance.'

Anselm was struck not so much by the adamant tone as by the dogged hope in his eyes. This man lacked the detachment of an interested bystander. His engagement was altogether personal. Anselm couldn't help but wonder . . . was he a relative? Could he be Edmund Littlemore's father? Whoever he might be, he was now by the door. He'd clipped shut his briefcase and shrugged on a cream raincoat.

'Two final points,' he said. 'First, I would ask you to treat this matter with considerable urgency. Enough time has been lost. There is much at stake.'

'And second?' asked Anselm.

'I am going to rely upon your discretion. Should we meet again in whatever circumstances, I won't show a single sign of recognition. And if for any reason you break your word and refer to this meeting, I'll deny it took place. I'll deny I ever met you. Is that understood?'

Anselm gave a nod but his visitor had already opened the parlour door. Turning to the window, Anselm watched him stride along the gravel path that led to the car park among the plum trees. It was a lovely spring evening. A shade of green was emerging in the distant woodland, still hatched brown from a hard winter. The birdsong was intense. Larkwood's mysterious guest had paused as if to allow himself a fugitive moment of recollection. Then he brusquely set off. As he rounded a corner Anselm picked up the photograph, blinking stupidly at the face on the page. What was he to do? Anselm had recognised him. He knew him. More than that, he considered him a member of the community. He was John Joe Collins, Larkwood's handyman . . . a wanderer from Boston, Massachusetts, in the US of A.

3

On a cold November evening only six months previously, a homeless man in his early forties had arrived at Larkwood. He'd been soaked to the skin, filthied by the road and shivering. Such men often turned up. They left the big cities and made their way through the countryside seeking a change of horizon and often the continuation of a conversation begun months and sometimes years previously. The monks called them wayfarers. Providing for their comfort was one of Anselm's responsibilities.

'I'm John Joe Collins,' he'd mumbled through a ragged beard, revealing a distinctive American accent. He'd been grateful for the offer of a bed. 'I'll be on my way tomorrow.'

Anselm had watched him with pity. They spoke of London night shelters. The Archway. The Viaduct. Anselm brought him some clean clothes. The next morning, dressed in the designer cast-offs of the late Mr Justice Phillimore, John Joe helped Anselm repair a broken fence, and then he'd made to go.

'There's no rush,' Anselm replied, shaking hands. 'You don't have to leave.'

'Then let me earn my bed and board.'

After a week the odd jobs were lining up – jobs that none of the other monks wanted to do. Every morning John Joe was ready to go; every morning Anselm told him to have another coffee. And yes, Anselm was compelled to agree: the honey was exceptionally good. That alone was a good reason to linger. As if daring to settle down, he trimmed his beard. He spoke of his past in snatches.

Born in London, he'd moved to Boston aged two with his American mother who'd left his English father behind to ponder the meaning of divorce. It was there, in the capital of Massachusetts, that John Joe had acquired the telling dialect with the broad 'ah' which, to Anselm's ear, displaced the letter R almost completely. John Joe had confirmed the observation, giving 'pahk the cah in the Hahvahd yahd' as a classic example. Long before the ahs had slipped into place, his mother married a man with a refined aversion to things English, or perhaps it had just been John Joe. Either way, by the time John Joe became a true son of New England, he'd dropped out of school, drifting here and there until he finally crossed the Atlantic once more, seeking a father who, it transpired, had developed a crude aversion to things American.

'Sometimes the Special Relationship ain't that special.'

John Joe had teetered on the edge of a disclosure but then changed his mind. Anselm filled the gap with a pleasantry. But pleasantries, easing pressure, also open doors, and in due course Anselm discovered that he and John Joe shared common ground, from a dislike of mobile phones to an enthusiasm for jazz . . . all the way back to Papa Jack Laine, with a soft spot for the fifties revival. Bobby Hackett et al. Anselm felt he'd known him for years. And then John Joe started turning up for the Offices: first Lauds, then Vespers and finally Compline. He made a bench his own, towards the back of the nave. Their conversations shifted towards deeper water. While splitting wood, John Joe asked Anselm if he'd ever lost his faith; if he'd ever thrown it away.

'Frequently.'

John Joe was surprised. 'How do you find it again?'

'I don't,' replied Anselm. 'It returns like a boomerang. You have to watch out.'

Anselm expected a laugh but John Joe didn't oblige: it was as though the subject was too serious for joking. Later, constructing a flat-pack wardrobe, Anselm had scorned the instructions. He had to start all over again, removing all those screws and dowels before the glue could dry. John Joe checked the drawing and said, 'What happens if there's no going back?'

Anselm used a solemn voice: 'There's always a way back.' But then John Joe flashed either anger or regret – Anselm couldn't distinguish one simple emotion:

'But what if there ain't? You're left with what you've done.' John Joe was staring at the instructions with the faraway look of someone who'd sought greener fields and learned something unexpected. He calmed, like water taken off the boil: 'I wonder where you went wrong?'

It had been these brief excursions into depth – all of them carrying the mark of unfinished business – that led Anselm to table a proposal at Chapter. A novel situation had developed (he ventured). Mr Collins would never ask to linger and it didn't make sense to ask him to leave. Something good had been happening. Something unprecedented. 'Why not let him stay for as long as he likes? We could do with a handyman.' One by one, the monks voted, dropping a wooden bead into a linen bag. The proposal was easily carried. But among the black beads of assent the Scrutator, Father Damien, found two white murmurs of opposition.

The first had to have been cast by Dunstan, 'the Weaver'. He rarely approved of anything and he'd voiced his disagreement in trenchant terms (legend had it that he'd once voted against a motion before it had even been debated). So Anselm was more concerned by the second. As a lone voice, it had grown strong in his imagination.

Gazing now along the empty path that led to the plum trees, another conversation came to Anselm's mind. He'd been testing his Advent mead on a connoisseur.

'Do you get those haunting notes?' Anselm had asked.

Sylvester rounded his lips and breathed in deeply.

'The roast goose and bread pudding . . . the mince pies and brandy butter of lost youth . . . Christmas cheer, far from the madding Zulu hordes?'

Sylvester placed his glass on the table and fixed Anselm with a determined stare.

'Well, Prowling Wolf?'

'It was me.'

'What was?'

'The other white bead.'

Anselm thought for a moment, shifting his mental standing, and then said, 'Anyone can make a mistake.'

'I didn't make a mistake.'

Anselm put down his glass. 'You didn't?'

'I know the difference between black and white. It's you that's got yourself confused.' Sylvester pulled up the old army blanket that had almost slipped off his bony legs. 'I've been a monk for a long time and there are only two types of people who want silence and seclusion: those who seek to *find* and those who seek to *hide*. We're meant to work out who's who. Read the Rule, Anselm. It's all there in black and white. If anyone wants to join us, we're meant to test 'em. We're meant to discern the good from the bad. And we haven't done, not this time.'

Anselm didn't know what to say. Finally, he blurted out, 'For God's sake, he was in Curlew Patrol. What else do you want?'

'I'm not so sure he was.'

'What do you mean?'

'He doesn't know how to tie a reef knot.'

'You're not serious.'

'And he doesn't know north from south.'

'Neither do I.'

'But you were never in the Scouts. And it shows.'

'Eh?'

'You'd do an awful lot better solving things, young man, if you'd learned some proper field craft.'

'What the hell are you on about?'

'Learned to read signs in front of your nose.'

'Dear God, this isn't happening.'

'Baden-Powell used to say, "Be Prepared", and you're not. Never are, never have been and never will be.'

'Amen. Now why didn't you speak out in Chapter?' Anselm was baffled. The Gatekeeper always spoke his mind, even to show that he'd lost it.

'I should've done. But I didn't want to upset you. And Dunstan likes to think he's the only one who can spot the rotten apple.'

'Rotten apple? You've always said that a wayfarer should be treated like the Lord himself.'

'Yes, I know, but what did the Lord do after he'd been feted and fed? He cleared off.'

Anselm could no longer contribute.

'I just hope things don't end badly,' said the old man, pouring himself another snifter. 'Now, speaking of finish, the mead. For a man who tends to pick up the wrong end of the stick, you've surprised me. It's good. Chocolatey. Reminds me of Easter . . .'

Anselm turned away from the window.

The mechanics of that election were troubling him, now. He'd started persuading people even before he raised the matter at Chapter. He'd nudged the jury towards the verdict he wanted and now the jury would find him wanting. It was axiomatic. And very monastic: when a vote went wrong everyone turned on the proposer. Leaving the parlour, Anselm sensed his life was about to become a little complicated. To start the ball rolling, he went to tell the Prior that there was more to John Joe Collins than met the eye.

4

'A what?' drawled Dunstan.

'A Lambertine,' repeated Anselm.

'Never heard of them. Sounds like a kind of orange.'

Which was odd, because the Order had a long history, beginning in France at the end of the eleventh century. Anselm said so as if to gain a point in the ring because the Prior had narrowed the argument down to the views of its two most vocal protagonists. It was a way of flushing out the right thing to do. They were sitting in the Scriptorium, Anselm and the Prior facing Dunstan's desk, which was completely bare save for an old Sainte Croix typewriter, a relic that, when used, made work in the adjoining library impossible. In his late nineties, the old man had lost most of his white hair. The hard lines on his oddly greying face had become smooth of late, like a stiff shirt that had lost the tightness of its weave. He was wearing light-sensitive glasses and the lenses had turned a dark brown. He was smiling.

'My view is kick him out right now.'

Dunstan's accent had been refined by family, Eton and inclination. Dismayed by the austerity of monastic dress, he wore a silk cravat. He had a large and colourful selection, the choice for the day always worn with patrician flamboyance, the ruff clearly visible above the frayed black collar of his habit. His manner was debonair, though Anselm always sensed an element of tension, as if he was itching for a pink gin. One elbow rested on his desk, the open hand seeming to hold an invisible decanter. A sort of monastic Wilde, often ignored, he was enjoying the importance of being relied upon.

'Can't say I'm *entirely* surprised,' Dunstan continued. 'I won't repeat what I said in Chapter' – but he did – 'we knew nothing about him. We didn't ask. We should have done. And now we're entangled in the dirty laundry of some half-baked outfit with links to the French. I never liked his accent, frankly, but I kept that to myself.'

'You didn't,' said Anselm. 'And you appear to have forgotten our Order owes its existence to the French . . . and that my mother was French.'

The Prior was patient. 'Don't you think we ought to ask some questions first?'

'God, no.' If he hadn't been a monk, Dunstan would have added 'old boy', but it hung in the air, unsaid.

'Why not?'

'We know enough. I'd say too much as it is.' He reached for a pencil and began rotating it between the fingers of one hand – a trick learned to add tension during an interrogation. 'You appreciate I've considerable experience handling people who can't be trusted. Bent coins.'

'I do.'

Dunstan never tired of hinting at his wartime credentials: how he'd done risky stuff in Belgium with the Special Operations Executive; how, transferred to Military Intelligence, he'd devised intricate plans to capture Nazis on the run. 'In the Service I was known as "the Weaver".' No one took him seriously. Except the Prior, who said:

'But I'm inclined to learn more. Why shouldn't we?'

Dunstan seemed to speak to one of the slower undergraduates who'd made his later academic life a grinding chore. 'Occam's razor. Keep things simple. We already know he must have done something seriously wrong.'

'How?' interjected Anselm.

19

'Let me assist: the false name, the concealed occupation – if it had ever been a vocation – and the curious fact that his own Order . . . these Clementines . . . want him out of the way. It's fairly obvious, isn't it?' – again, the 'old boy' hovered between them. 'They don't want him found because he's made some dreadful hash of things. Something embarrassing. I'd *rather* not know what he's been up to. Thing is, you see, the more you *know* the more you're *involved*. Not what we want. Involvement brings responsibility.'

'Any other thoughts?' asked the Prior.

'Oh *yes*.'

'Well?'

Dunstan's dark glasses flashed at Anselm. He was in his element. It was like the old days, debriefing the credulous in a safe house off the Brompton Road. 'He's used you.'

Anselm sighed. 'How?'

'Made you pity him.'

'Nonsense.'

Dunstan rotated the pencil again. 'I wouldn't be too sure. He tells you absolutely nothing about himself but lets you know he's lost his faith' – Dunstan could have been talking about an umbrella – 'and that he'd like to get back to the Garden of Eden where every mistake's a nice mistake. And then he turns up for Lauds to join in the singing. *Oh come on*. It's all so *amateur*. Thought him bent then and I think him bent now. He made you his advocate. He wanted you to offer him a job. So he pulled the right levers and you did the asking. No shame in that. You lack my experience.'

Like the Prior, Anselm was patient, but part of him wanted to snap that pencil. He said, 'Why on earth would he do all that?'

'I *really* don't know,' intoned Dunstan, insouciance itself. He turned to the Prior as if to get his glass filled. 'And we don't want to know. The sooner you show him the door the better.'

Anselm could have been annoyed but he wasn't. Dunstan's

days under the sun were almost over and he was making the worst of what was left to him. Between pointless visits to the hospital where he looked down on consultants of various disciplines, he picked silly fights in Chapter, like opposing the offer of a job to a man whose vowels weren't right. So Anselm wasn't inclined to argue. He spoke about someone he'd come to know.

'Maybe I lack Dunstan's experience of duplicity. But I'm not surprised a man lost his faith. I'm not surprised he came to a monastery. I'm not surprised he chose a new name to escape his past. I'm not surprised that seeming friends have turned away. He has my pity' – Anselm looked at Dunstan – 'he had it then and he has it now. I've nothing else to say. But I do have a proposal.'

'Tell me,' said the Prior. He'd been watching Anselm intently.

'If anyone has been deceived, it's me. And I'd like to know the answers to the questions Dunstan doesn't want to ask. I understand you' – Anselm nodded at the Weaver – 'you're not involved. I am. I'm already responsible.'

The Prior showed a readiness to quibble but he said, 'What do you want to do?'

'Let me find out why John Joe Collins left Edmund Littlemore behind.' Anselm glanced a challenge at Dunstan. 'I've been told that he's done nothing wrong. If he has, then I'll ask him to leave myself. But if it turns out he just needs our help . . . then we take it from there, step by step. I think that accommodates Dunstan's caution. I also think it's fair.'

'To whom?' enquired Dunstan over an imaginary glass.

'Me. The stooge with the levers. And the man you'd show the door without a hearing.'

The Prior went to the window and opened it. The sounds of spring came on a breeze. A distant tractor. The scuff of sandpaper on dry timber.

'How long do you want?' he asked.

'Just a day.' Anselm sought Dunstan's support. 'What could go wrong in a day?'

21

Dunstan reflected. 'Burgess and Maclean . . . Philby . . . the Arnhem drop.'

'Take the time you need,' said the Prior. He came back from the window. 'Just one matter that we might as well clear up now. You think the man who came here was Littlemore's father? The man he tracked down when he returned to England?'

'It's possible.'

'Well, he isn't. You described wit and intelligence but no father could speak of his missing son without anxiety. This man is not a parent. And if I'm wrong, then either his son isn't missing or he knows the secret of where he is.'

Part Two

'You've got to go back to the police,' said Gutsy, passing a cigarette to Harry.

'I can't.'

'You can. What was his name again?'

'Sanjay.'

'Well, this time you have to give him the facts. You can't just sit there and say nothing.'

They were leaning on the barrier of a wooden walkway built on a lake, one of the filled-in gravel pits on Wandsworth Common. Some ducks were thrashing about in the rushes. Two swans looked over, curious.

'Do you want me to tell him?' offered Gutsy, manfully.

'Just give us a light.'

To be healthy Gutsy had nicked a packet of Rothmans menthol, which were disgusting. But they were better than nothing. Having lit up, Harry dropped the burning match into the water. He listened for the hiss, but Gutsy was talking again.

'It doesn't matter who he is or how important he is, he can't get away with it.'

'I know.'

'Then spit it out.'

Gutsy didn't understand. You can't spit things out without thinking where your glob is going to land.

'I'll come with you,' said Gutsy, tapping ash into the lake.

'Just let it go.'

'I can't. We're brothers.'

They'd tried to cut their thumbs with a bread knife and mingle some blood, but neither of them could face the pain. In the end they'd joined scratch to scratch. It still meant something.

'I know. That's why I trust you.'

Harry stared into the cloudy green water, his attention drawn away like a leaf on the surface of the sky.

Back in October – after Harry had spent twenty minutes in the hospital interview suite staring in silence at Sanjay's Reebok trainers – the policeman had gently pulled the plug. As a last resort he'd invited Father Eddie down to the station but ten minutes into the confrontation the priest had done a runner. The next morning Harry's mother had called Uncle Justin. Like Geraldine, he was a specialist in trauma. Only his methods were different. And so Uncle Justin came round with his holdall full of crampons and clips and all sorts of stuff Harry had never seen before. They went into the garden.

'He's out of reach, now,' said Uncle Justin, taking a thick yellow rope out of his bag. 'He hasn't gone back to the States because that's the first place anyone would look. I bet he's in Spain, sunning himself. And as long as no one says anything, no one's going to chase after him.'

Uncle Justin was lean and muscular. His blond hair had been ravaged for years by the wind and rain. He was the Marlboro Man. All year he'd been denying he was forty.

'This Littlemore will start a new life. And so must you. And that means learning how to get away from the things you can't forget.'

Harry didn't respond so Uncle Justin placed a hand on each of his shoulders, looking at him as if they were brothers in arms. His eyes were green and cloudy like the water in a lake.

'You have to trust me,' he said. 'Climbing is all about trust. And trust is all about knowing you're secure. And being secure is all about the knot around your waist. So that's where we begin, with learning your knots. And the first and most important knot is the bowline.'

Uncle Justin had climbed every dangerous rock face in Britain. He'd founded the Bowline Project for the homeless. The BBC had produced a documentary showing how he'd worked wonders for people with nowhere to turn. He hadn't just taken people off the street, he'd given them experiences that changed how they saw things. They'd conquered mountains, restored a shepherd's cottage in Wales, gone on holidays together.

He'd just been one of them, another man making his way through thick and thin. Harry had always adored him. Now things were different.

'To learn the bowline, all you've got to do is think of a rabbit coming out its hole,' he said, uncoiling the rope.

He'd said the same thing to Fraser and Kenny and Jock. The three of them had appeared in front of the camera to explain how Justin Brandwell had used climbing as a means of helping them turn their lives around. They'd all escaped life on the street, beginning with the safest knot in the business.

'It's like a bedtime story,' he said, giving the rope-end a shake. 'A rabbit comes out of its hole, takes a wander round a tree and then goes home again.'

Uncle Justin made a loop and fed the tag end through the hole. His hands worked expertly, taking the rabbit on its little outing. When he'd finished, he untied the knot and threw the rope at Harry.

'Your turn.'

The programme had ended with Kenny, a former glue-sniffer from Scarborough, twitching at the base of a windy outcrop in North Yorkshire. 'Once you're down,' he'd laughed, 'there's only one place to go, and that's up.' Which was a depressing moment, in retrospect, because after the broadcast, Jock was arrested for theft in Marylebone High Street and Kenny was found dead, fished from a canal in Birmingham. He'd been seventeen years old.

'Remember what I said, the rabbit comes out of the hole.'

Harry kept trying, but the rabbit was confused, going round in circles, unable to make its way home. Truth be told, Harry wasn't thinking about any kind of bedtime story. He was thinking of that scene in Jaws *— Uncle Justin's favourite film — where Quint is teaching the same knot to Police Chief Brody on the* Orca. *'The little brown eel comes out of the cave, swims into the hole, comes out of the hole, goes back into the cave again.' And that's the beginning of the end, really, because seconds later the fishing reel is whizzing and that great white has got them hooked.*

'Try again,' said Uncle Justin.

But Harry had stopped playing the game; he'd let the rope fall and he was staring at his uncle, searching for words that might even begin to express his anger and confusion. But nothing came out of the black hole in his mind, just more self-disgust, slithering into his consciousness. Uncle Justin was watching him – just like Quint when his spool began to click.

'What's up, Harry?' he said, coming close, tears of grief suddenly appearing. He knew the adoration had gone. He'd seen it die. 'You're not frightened of me, are you?'

'No,' replied Harry, thinking rage must look like fear.

Uncle Justin's green eyes turned dark. 'I think we'd better get you on a rock face,' he said. 'It's the best place to understand what I'm trying to teach you.'

Harry gathered the spit in his mouth, forming a sort of liquid ball. He was looking down at the water while Gutsy struck matches, letting them fall and fizz. A breeze sent a shiver across the lake and the reeds began to sway.

'I'm going to keep on twisting your arm,' said Gutsy.

Harry's cheeks and tongue carried on working.

'I'll stop when you finally spit out what happened.'

Gutsy waited for a reply, bringing the thrill of tension between them, but all at once the air held its breath and the ripples vanished among the reeds. Harry could see the dark outline of his head resting on the wooden barrier, his features browned like a corpse and speckled with flies.

'Well?' asked Gutsy.

Harry didn't stir, save to suck at the walls of his cheeks. When he'd filled his mouth, he released the heavy glob of spit, letting it drop on to the reflection of his face.

Gutsy backed away, frightened. 'You're disgusting,' he said.

5

Robert Sambourne still couldn't feel anything. His dad was dead
and he couldn't feel a thing. When he got the call ten days back
from his mother, he almost burst into tears but didn't want to
break down in the office with everyone watching. He made his
excuses and went outside into Balham High Street thinking he'd
explode as soon as his feet touched the pavement, but nothing
happened, the emotion got trapped somewhere frighteningly
deep, leaving its hand on his throat as a warning that one day it
would rise to the surface and squeeze the life out of him. There'd
been an upsurge only a few hours ago when, at the end of the
funeral, he followed his dad out of the church. He raised his eyes
to the coffin, aware of the faces looking on with pity, but all his
attention lay on the pine box on the shoulders of strange men,
used to the graft of grieving for a wage. And all at once he felt
abandoned, cut off from someone absolutely vital and irreplaceable. The big strong man had gone. It simply wasn't possible, but
he was lying in that heavily varnished box. Robert had wanted
to turn aside and bury his face in someone's lapels, escape the
pain and the brutality of the moment, but he couldn't. He was
a man, now, walking down the aisle on his own, two steps behind
his mother. By the time he'd reached the porch the emotion had
subsided again, once more leaving its thumb pressed against his
throat, threatening to return. For a moment he almost believed
in God: the depth of feeling, its content and power, was simply
terrifying – it was greater than the Bomb: it couldn't spring from

some biological connection alone, a chance ordering of atoms in a here-today-gone-tomorrow world. There had to be something else. But there was only one brute certainty: the bond between father and son had been severed as if it meant nothing. Robert's dad had been lowered into the ground. He'd been covered in clay

'Have a ham sandwich.'

Robert hadn't heard the French windows open. Crofty had turned the handle quietly and was now at his side with a plate in his chubby fingers. They were standing on decking in a small neglected garden that backed onto a railway line. This was Robert's parents' home in Raynes Park. His mother's place, now. At the end of a short flagged path, beneath trees, was his dad's old workshop; the place where he'd made magic out of wood.

'There's cheese, too.'

'No thanks.'

'Go on. I made them myself.'

Alan Croft was more than Robert's boss, editor of the *South London Chronicle*. He was a part of Robert's childhood, an amateur magician who'd messed up all the well-known tricks. A Les Dawson of the Magic Circle, his party piece was to try and cut his wife Muriel in half, breaking the saw instead. He'd also been Robert's dad's closest friend. They met on stage in 1964 after the young Lenny, fresh from Western Australia, came to England on the *Fairsky* seeking a new life among the Poms. He'd joined the Wimbledon Light Opera Society, drawn by a production of *The Sorcerer* in which Crofty landed the title role. Robert's dad, on account of his accent, was consigned to the male chorus. They became drinking partners, Crofty forging a career in journalism, Robert's dad working as a carpenter on various construction sites throughout London. By the time of Robert's birth, Crofty had become an editor and Lenny the master of his own business. The drinking was replaced by more enlightened pursuits and when Robert failed his degree – the natural result of a predilection for failed relationships with haunting older women – Crofty offered him a job on the paper. He'd schooled him in the craft.

'Your dad was a good man,' he said, as if making a point of order. 'He fought the good fight and now . . . well, I'm going to miss him.'

'Me too.'

A train thundered along the line, shaking the trees and the shed.

'Are you sure you don't want a sandwich?'

'Yes, I'm sure.'

Crofty tucked in, guilty to be hungry; guilty – Robert imagined – because he hadn't found any tears either. The loss was too sudden for both of them, too great to be managed by a sudden outburst of grief. They were both dry-eyed like gate-crashers at a wake. Neither of them felt they belonged.

'But of this you can be sure,' said Crofty, finishing a speech he hadn't made, 'your dad thought the world of you. He'd have walked on nails to make you happy. There aren't many sons who can say that about their father.'

'There aren't.'

'And that's his legacy.' Crofty sniffed. He was looking at the envelope in Robert's hands, curious to know who it was from. It had arrived at work that morning. After reading it several times, Robert had slipped the letter into the pocket of his black suit and then rushed to the church. He'd taken it out for another reading just before Crofty appeared with the sandwiches, leftovers after the well-wishers had said goodbye.

'Take some time off,' said Crofty, glancing over his shoulder back into the house.

'No thanks.'

'The news can wait.'

'No, I want to work. I'll take a break when I finally feel something.'

Crofty sniffed again and nodded at the envelope. He was curious – it was written all over his ample freckled face – but on this day of bereavement he imagined it was from an old friend of Robert's father . . . maybe someone he knew.

'Words of comfort?' he asked, tentatively.

'Not really. Do you remember that American priest who vanished last year?'

Crofty made a start as if he'd just heard a mild profanity. If they were going to talk at all, it had to be about Lenny Sambourne, Robert's dad, but Robert pressed on. His mind and heart were numbed. What else could he do?

'I was in the police station when he ran off. Don't you remember?'

Crofty said he didn't – which was inexplicable, because Robert had wanted to follow up the story but Crofty hadn't been in favour. They'd argued the merits and Robert had lost. But now, looking at the envelope, Crofty frowned, inviting a rehearsal of the particulars he couldn't seriously have forgotten. So Robert went back to the beginning.

He'd gone to a police station to check up some details on a local murder when a Catholic priest came striding out of an interview room, practically knocking him over. It turned out that an allegation had been made against the priest in relation to a young boy, but once the boy had sat down in front of the video gear, he just clammed up. So the police had invited the priest down to the station, hoping for an admission. When they quizzed him about his past, he'd taken off.

'That's right,' said Crofty, with another backward glance. 'And you wanted to chase after him.'

'No. I did chase after him. I practically camped outside his window, saying I wouldn't go until he gave me an interview.'

'Yes . . . and one night he slipped out of the back door leaving the place wide open.'

'Exactly.'

Suddenly, there were raised voices from inside. Robert turned round. His mother was squaring up to Muriel, Crofty's wife. Tears were streaming down her cheeks. She'd been crying and confused for days, though she'd managed to pull herself together for the service and burial. Against Robert's expectations, she'd been incredibly dignified in public . . . like a statue, no emotion on her face, cold even, looking beyond the ritual to something visible only to her. But now she'd cracked again and Muriel was nodding slowly like a nurse trained in palliative care. She was stroking her friend's arms, calming her down. Everything was going to be all right, her manner said, everything was going to be fine . . . she was unfolding a tissue now, she was gently dabbing those quivering cheeks. Robert frowned because Muriel almost looked as if she was acting. She'd played Aline in *The Sorcerer*.

'And I said there was no story because no allegations had made it onto a charge sheet,' said Crofty, raising his voice.

Robert turned from the window, disorientated. 'Sorry . . . what?'

Crofty stepped off the decking and brushed some crumbs from his paunch. Abruptly confidential, he went towards the end of the garden, drawing Robert with him along the flags, repeating what he'd said about the priest who'd done nothing wrong.

'Except run away,' resumed Robert. He couldn't bear to watch his mother in distress. In part it was because she'd never been one to show much feeling. She'd been absorbed in a world of her own, emptying the dishwasher, wiping the kitchen table. Doing something that should have been done yesterday. She can't have meant it, but in Robert's memory, her back was often turned. Seeing her distraught was a brutalising experience. 'And if you run away,' he said, reaching the trees, 'the chances are you've got something to hide.'

'That's right,' said Crofty. 'I remember everything. But why bring all that up now?'

'Because I'm not the only one who thinks it's wrong when

a guilty man stays free just because a kid is too scared to open his mouth.'

Robert took a letter out of the envelope and passed it to Crofty. When he retrieved the sheet of paper, Robert gave it another puzzled look:

Why have you given up?
Victims always need help to speak out.
Otherwise they get silenced by private agreements.
Don't let that happen.
The American is hiding at Larkwood Priory.
Do not delay. If he leaves, you'll never find him again.

Crofty took the last sandwich off the plate and said, 'Who the hell would write a letter like that?'

'It has to be someone who knew I was there, in the station.'

'The police?'

'No. Why would they want me to track him down if they already knew where he was?'

Crofty nodded. 'Well, that leaves the priest himself. What was his name?'

'Littlemore. But why would Littlemore want me to come and find him? It doesn't make sense.'

Robert looked at the misaligned print, because that was another anomaly. The author had used an old-fashioned typewriter. The ink was smudged and there were heavy indentations in the paper. No one used that kind of machine any more. Crofty broke the reverie:

'What's the postmark?'

'Glasgow.'

'*Scotland?*'

'Yes.'

Crofty drew a hand through his thick, rusty hair. 'Forget the geography. Whoever it is knows the kid's a victim even though he hasn't made a statement. We're talking about a member of his family.'

'But they'd go to the police, not write to me. And anyway, how would they know that Littlemore was hiding in a monastery?'

Crofty gave a conceding nod. 'They wouldn't.'

'Exactly. The only people who'd know are the monks themselves.'

'Only if he's told them who he is . . . and what he's done.' Crofty sniffed. 'You know who lives at Larkwood Priory? Father Anselm . . . that Sister Wendy in the world of crime.'

Robert had heard of the name. 'That's too much of a coincidence. What's Littlemore doing in the same building as a detective? That's the last place he should hide.'

'Go find out,' said Crofty. 'This might be a bigger story than you realised.' He looked at the sandwich as if it was the last of its kind. 'By the way, I've got a new hand on board. Andrew Taylor. A late starter. Interesting guy. Show him the ropes, will you? This might be a good story to break him in with.'

A train rushed along the lines, thumping the air into the trees. By the time Robert and Crofty reached the house, the garden was quiet again. They went inside, wondering how to act out the grief you couldn't yet feel.

When Robert went home that night to his flat in Tooting Bec there was something bothering him, but he couldn't chase it to ground. He prowled round the likely territory finding nothing but pity: on entering the sitting room with Crofty, Robert had found his mother completely composed. You wouldn't have known that, minutes before, she'd been on her feet, leaning towards Muriel, fists clenched like someone fighting her corner. Then, having calmed down, she'd been crouched on the edge of the settee, looking terribly alone. No one could reach her. She'd been contemplating the rest of her life, knowing that the greater part of it lay buried in Wimbledon Cemetery. It was only when Robert woke up next morning, head aching from the Chianti, that he knew at once what had been troubling him. As he had sat beside his mother, Muriel had moved towards Crofty as if to pat him on the back . . . a gesture that didn't happen, but whose preamble disclosed a baffling certainty, only seen with the clarity bestowed by a hangover: when Crofty had turned up with that plate of sandwiches, his reason wasn't to show compassion or chance his hand with a few fine words. And he hadn't forgotten about the priest who'd run away. That was all playing for time. The magician's trick had been to keep Robert in the garden.

The next morning Robert rang Sanjay Kumar, the officer who'd interviewed Littlemore. He said nothing of the letter. But he let Sanjay know he wasn't the only one who was looking for the American. Mid-flow, Robert made a sudden request. Perhaps it was because they'd established a rapport; or, more likely, because the case was hopeless, but Sanjay agreed to a minor breach of protocol.

6

Anselm's attempts to make contact with Father George Carrington, the Lambertine Provincial – the person responsible for the English Province of his Order – proved fruitless. He was never available when Anselm called and none of those calls had been returned. Not to be brushed aside so easily, Anselm took the train to London. By late morning, he was knocking on the door of a large Edwardian building in its own grounds ten minutes' walk from Ealing Broadway Tube station.

'Can I help you?'

Anselm was dumbstruck. The man who opened the door was looking at him quizzically – if anything, with the slight irritation that comes from being disturbed when busy – showing no trace of recognition, while Anselm, unable to reply, instantly found himself back in the presence of the stranger who'd asked him to find Edmund Littlemore.

'If you'll forgive me I have a great deal to do and I can't remain here wondering if you've lost your voice.'

Anselm had to go along with the charade. He asked if he might have a brief interview. Carrington reluctantly agreed. But he didn't invite Anselm into his study or offer coffee. He brought him into the hallway and no further. At the far end someone was on their hands and knees waxing the floor.

'And you are?'

Anselm, still bewildered by the pretence, introduced himself and then went straight to the point.

'I'm trying to find Edmund Littlemore, I understand that—'

'The matter is in the hands of the police and that is where it should stay.'

Anselm nodded, wondering what the script ought to look like next. But he was also impressed by Carrington's performance: it was magisterial.

'Might I ask what's prompted your interest?'

Anselm did his best. 'I was approached by an interested party.'

Impatient with the wordplay, Carrington walked towards the door. 'I appreciate your concern but I fear it's misplaced. This is a deeply worrying and I must say private matter for our community. Might I suggest you return home and leave a delicate problem to be handled delicately?'

The door was already open. Turning round, Anselm could see the cleaner at the end of the corridor. His head was down, one hand moving in a slow circle as he applied wax to the tiles with a large orange cloth. Anselm made one last-ditch attempt:

'Could you tell me why he might have run away?'

'No.'

'Where he might have gone?'

'I can't tell you anything. And at the risk of offending you, this conversation is over. Forget about Father Littlemore. With the deepest respect, his circumstances are none of your concern.'

The door clipped shut and Anselm began a slow walk back to Ealing Broadway. He couldn't understand the conversation that had just unfolded. The man who'd come to Larkwood refusing to give his name was deadly serious; so was Father Carrington, this second, parallel personality. No one would behave in such a manner unless the issues at stake were serious . . . and so delicate that they required subterfuge to bring them into the open. Just then, he heard a voice call his name. Turning around, he saw the cleaner running towards him. He was still holding onto his orange cloth.

'I haven't got long,' he said, panting. 'But maybe I can help you.'

7

The cleaner was, in fact, a former mergers and acquisitions tax specialist with PwC, PricewaterhouseCoopers. In his late thirties, Kester Newman had joined the Lambertines two years previously and was still getting used to doing the sorts of job he'd forgotten existed. For him, floors were simply things you walked on. And he'd been on that tiled corridor for a week, now, what with the stripping and washing and the three coats of wax. But Kester couldn't hang around. He'd slipped away and his absence would shortly be noted.

'When I was an accountant I had to deal with people running companies who wanted to hide significant transactions. Not just from the taxman, but me, their adviser. You can feel it in the air. You can tell that behind an honest explanation there's a strategy at work, and you just can't imagine what it might be, or why the man across the table doesn't want you to know what he's really doing. And I've got that feeling now as regards Father Carrington. Something strange is happening.'

By the time Kester had caught Anselm, he'd just reached the tennis courts in Lammas Park. They were standing by the fence watching a father and son practise their groundstrokes.

'He's genuinely concerned about Littlemore's disappearance but he's not cooperating with the police. He's not giving them the kind of information they need.'

Kester was leaning on the high fence with one arm, his fingers locked into the wire netting. Those years behind a desk had given a certain generosity to his frame, and he was no more used to running than he was to waxing floors. But his eyes were a sharp, bright brown. This man's athleticism was intellectual and he'd lost none of his form. Anselm could imagine him chairing a conference, listening to his clients while preparing questions to make them squirm. Only, you couldn't do that kind of thing to a reverend Provincial.

'What sort of information?' asked Anselm.

'About Littlemore's past. It's not straightforward.'

Strictly speaking, Littlemore and Kester were exact contemporaries. Littlemore had come to the Lambertines two years back, having already been ordained by the archdiocese of Boston. No clear reason had been given for his departure from the US, but he'd been accepted into the Order by Carrington's predecessor, Owen Murphy, who'd sent him to Newcastle – Kester's birthplace, as it happened. Carrington had been elected shortly afterwards, following Murphy's death, and one of his first decisions was to move Littlemore to Freetown in Sierra Leone . . . that's right, West Africa. A long way off. The rumour was that Littlemore had a serious 'personal difficulty', something 'fundamental', and Carrington was keeping trouble at arm's length. The ploy, needless to say, didn't work. Littlemore was summoned home after some sort of complaint.

'I was here when he returned and Father Carrington grilled him for over three hours.'

Kester – draining a radiator in the room next door – couldn't catch the words, but he'd caught the tone. Littlemore had been angry, hitting back it seemed at a reprimand.

'What he'd done I don't know, but I think we can work backwards from what happened next. He was sent to a parish in south London and that's where things finally unravelled.'

The father had gone up to the net for a volley, carefully aiming his shot to compel his son to use a specific stroke. The boy dashed right, stretching on the run. Kester watched him enviously. Then he said:

'None of this information has been given to the police. Because it's sensitive. Because Littlemore has crossed a line . . . either in the States, here or in Sierra Leone. Maybe everywhere. I've felt compromised ever since. Which is why I'm speaking to you.'

Anselm was perplexed. 'What line?'

'It's obvious, isn't it?'

'Not to me.'

Kester took Anselm's avowed ignorance for diplomacy so, in a changed tone, he referred to the subject no one in the Order wanted to talk about: 'Father Carrington said nothing to the police because it has to be linked to why Littlemore ran away in the first place. He doesn't want the publicity and I imagine he doesn't want to harm Littlemore's defence, if he has one.'

Anselm came clean as the boy broke out of training and lobbed his father. The kid wanted to take control for once. 'Kester, I'm looking for a man without knowing anything about him save his name.'

'Are you serious?'

'Absolutely.'

'You don't know why he vanished?'

'Any more than you know why he left the States or why he was sent to Sierra Leone.'

Kester glanced at his watch. Stepping closer to Anselm he spoke as if he were dictating a minute to his former secretary that would blow the reputation of a major client. 'Edmund Littlemore sexually attacked an eleven-year-old boy named Harry Brandwell. He's the grandson of Martin and Maisie Brandwell, longstanding friends of the Order. When the police confronted him, he ran from the station.'

Anselm was stunned but he showed nothing. His eyes followed the ball from racket to racket. Despite that show of nerve from the son, the father knew what he was doing. He'd returned the lob and got his son back into the groove.

'The day after the interview Littlemore came here,' said Kester. 'He had a conference with Father Carrington. I assume he owned up. What else could he do? Three days later he vanished. No one has any idea where he might have gone.'

Anselm reflected for a long time upon that last observation. But he still listened. Kester had his own worries.

'I pity Father Carrington. He's out of his depth . . . I mean, he reads Middle English for fun. He's an academic. Eighteen months ago he gets elected only to find he's got Littlemore on his hands. He's a good guy trying to preserve an institution's reputation. It's what he'd call "a delicate matter that has to be handled delicately". To be honest, I thought I'd left that kind of manoeuvring behind.'

Anselm noted the reply, watching the father and son. The father wouldn't let up. He kept hitting the ball to his son's weaker backhand. Anselm said, 'What do you suggest I do now?'

'If anyone knows anything, it's Martin Brandwell. He was here shortly after Littlemore went missing. He was with Father Carrington for most of the afternoon. They had a row as well, only I didn't catch anything. But it's safe to assume he was angry because he'd found out about Littlemore's past . . . that there'd been complaints or whatever in Boston and Freetown and, because nothing had been done to deal with this "personal difficulty",

41

his own grandson had been harmed. I've brought you his details. And now I really have to go.'

Kester handed over a piece of paper and then began his run back home with the uncertain vigour of someone committed to taxis. Insofar as Anselm could think clearly, given what he'd just learned, he felt sorry for him. Kester was young enough to retain strong ideals and old enough to think that he was – at long last – beyond the sort of disillusionment that plagues coming of age. The problem, however, was this: he'd yet to learn that those deeper, more costly ideals – the ones that can lead a man to abandon his professional career – are, in fact, the most brittle. It takes time to make them supple, able to bend with the otherwise shattering discovery that those who led you out of the desert haven't always left it themselves.

Anselm turned back to the tennis court. Father and son were shaking hands over the net, smiling and chatting. The son had made all the right moves, executing each stroke with considerable talent. But – and this was no criticism, just a natural outcome of the balance of power – the boy had only done what his father had wanted. His father had made all the decisions from a commanding position at the net, determining the reactions of his trusting son.

Just like Father Carrington.

8

'Late starter' was an understatement. Andrew Taylor was in his mid-forties. He had thinning black hair and rimless glasses. The three-day growth made him conventionally handsome, in the sense that he was the sort of good-looking guy you see everywhere: in wine bars, outside the theatre, standing at the bus stop, hailing a cab; smart, but lacking originality. He'd picked potatoes in Ireland, washed dishes in Marseille, been a barman on a ferry, swept platforms on the Underground, imported wine from Portugal . . . the list was endless, which, to Crofty, had been the perfect CV for a man whose new piste was to report on the odd things people do. He was, in effect, one of Crofty's vagrants, people he'd met and given a job when they'd found themselves in a hard corner: the same thing had happened to Robert.

Only Robert wasn't entirely enthusiastic about his mentoring role. Andrew was a bit too keen. He leaned forward, ready to do anything Robert asked: make coffee, do the photocopying, fetch the mail. If there'd been dishes to wash, he'd have washed them. He sat at a facing desk like a willing pupil who'd won a scholarship. It was pitiful. He'd made notes on the Littlemore case in a brand new reporter's pad, nodding as if he'd heard it all before, wanting to be an equal.

'I want to search where he lived,' said Robert, reaching for his coat. 'The police looked in vain. I'm hoping they missed something.'

Littlemore's last place of residence was in Mitcham, a grey stone building attached to a church, the spire of which rose like a blunt sword between two mock battlements. A cat slinked along a shadowed wall heading towards a pool of sunshine. Sanjay was sitting on the bonnet of his car, fumbling with a roll-up. He hadn't quite got the technique.

'There's no point,' he said, nodding towards the house.

Robert shrugged. 'We just want a quick look around. Get a feel for the guy.'

Sanjay licked the wrinkled paper. 'I know what you mean. But you'll still find nothing. Never seen anything like it.'

Taking the offered keys, Robert looked quizzical.

'Most people leave a sort of fingerprint where they live,' said Sanjay, searching for his matches. 'They leave something of themselves in the air. This guy left nothing because when he came he brought nothing. And I mean nothing.'

Sanjay was right.

Littlemore had made the premises available for general parish business, reserving one upstairs room for his exclusive use. Even that restriction seemed pointless, however, because it showed no signs of having been lived in. A bare desk faced a couple of faded yellow armchairs arranged on either side of a gas fire with plastic coals. A grey filing cabinet had been shoved into a far corner. All the shelves were empty. A bed, stripped by the police, stood upended by a wall lamp without a shade. There were no pictures, no cards propped on the mantelpiece, no ornaments or mementoes. There was no TV, CD player or radio. The only object, like something left behind inadvertently, was a small wooden cross, lost on a pale expanse of scuffed woodchip wallpaper. Sanjay had said that buildings speak and for the first time in his life he'd heard nothing.

Robert and Andrew checked all the remaining rooms, not quite knowing what they were looking for, each of them sure that Littlemore had left the place clean of anything remotely personal. This was no decision, thought Robert. It's instinctive. Littlemore was hiding from everyone, including himself.

'Let's go,' he said, frustrated, heading down the stairs. 'The man we're looking for was never here.'

'Every door is unlocked except for one.'

Robert turned on the bottom stair. 'And?'

Andrew pointed back the way they'd come. 'Well, the door's in the middle of an adjoining wall. The church wall. But it's on the first floor, which means the door must open into thin air. And that's impossible.'

Robert pushed by his bright-eyed apprentice, taking two steps at a time. Coming to the door, he felt along the top of the frame, hoping to find the key; disappointed, he turned the handle, pushing in vain until Andrew's voice came from behind.

'Allow me.' He'd taken a credit card out of his wallet and

was bending it into shape. Moments later, after jiggling the plastic against the lock, the door snapped open. Robert was impressed.

'Where did you learn to do that?'

'YouTube. I can do old cars as well. With a coat hanger.'

In fairness, Sanjay had probably worked out that the one locked door led to a tiny balcony visible from the inside of the church. But he hadn't bothered to call a locksmith. And as a result he'd failed to discover that this was the place where Littlemore had concealed the key to his future intentions.

The balcony was only large enough for a wooden chair and small desk. Finding a switch on the wall, Robert flicked it down, bringing a soft light onto a blue folder.

He was intrigued.

The folder contained faxed newspaper cuttings relating to a 'recluse who abjured the term detective', preferring – for the interviewer in question, at least – 'a bewildered cleaner in the basement of justice'. The recluse in question was Father Anselm, a man with a reputation for 'solving cases beyond the reach of the law'. His work had attracted the attention of several broadsheets, though no commentator had been able to secure an interview of any substance. Brief replies to unsolicited telephone calls had provoked reflections on the nature of the individual who couldn't stay on the line. Two of them had been marked with black lines:

> For a man who has confronted extreme evil he remains surprisingly buoyant about the human condition. Something good remains within reach, a particle, perhaps, that can be salvaged from any heap of moral wreckage. I venture to call him naive and he agrees, almost happily. I ask why help the perpetrator? Sadly, our conversation ended there.

The second took up the same theme but went one step further:

I wonder if his capacity to trust is almost blinding. It's a breadth of vision that most of us lose as we grow older, as we confront pretence in those we once admired. We acquire – at some cost – prudence. Has he found a cheaper route? Unfortunately he has to go. It's only after I've put the phone down that I'm left contemplating a paradox, which is surely the secret to this monk's success: it's this large outlook which permits him to glimpse what another observer might easily miss: the wickedness at our elbow.

Apart from these two passages, random details – insights into the monk's character – had also been underlined: a 'disciple of the fifties trad jazz revival', a 'horror of mobile phones', 'a monk more familiar with doubt than certainty'. He had another job, too: he was 'a sort of guestmaster for the homeless'. The last word had been circled twice. Using his mobile phone, Robert photographed the marked passages, along with the fax number and date of transmission printed along the bottom of the page.

'These were sent two days after Littlemore stonewalled the police,' he said to Andrew, who'd stood back to watch. 'Three days later he vanished.'

'They're linked to where he went?'

'I'd have thought so.'

Robert then photographed the only other document in the folder: a sheet of yellow paper containing notes about the history of jazz, from Papa Jack Laine's Reliance Brass Band onwards. Written on the folder itself, on the back cover, were a couple of phone numbers and addresses of London night shelters: the Viaduct in Paddington and the Archway, Victoria.

'He went homeless,' said Robert, more to himself than Andrew. 'And then he went to Larkwood Priory. They don't know who they're sheltering.'

Robert looked again at the fax number on the cuttings. *Someone else* had done the research. They then faxed what they'd found to Littlemore.

'They effectively *sent him* to Larkwood Priory,' Robert said quietly, realising that Littlemore's sudden departure hadn't been that sudden after all, and certainly hadn't been forced by Robert's persistence. It had been the first step of a more complex operation.

'But why run away at all?' said Andrew, uncertainly.

'What?' Robert had forgotten he was there.

'If the boy was too scared to stand by his story, why would Littlemore run away? All he did was draw attention to himself.'

Andrew was right. Crofty had picked a winner: diffidence aside, this late starter was in his element. He had nous. And he was looking at something on the floor, something that must have fallen off the desk: a postcard. Robert leaned down to pick it up.

It was from Sierra Leone.

Young boys were splashing around on a golden seashore. They were leaping and laughing among the breakers. Further out to sea, men cast their nets from long boats. Robert turned over the picture. There was no stamp and no address, just a phrase in red ink:

YU KOHBA SMOK SOTE, I MOHS KOHMOHT

Robert tried to pronounce the words. He turned to Andrew: 'You didn't work in West Africa, by any chance?'

'No, just with street kids in Lusaka . . . That's Zambia, in the south.'

'Ah.'

Andrew nodded at the file and postcard: 'You'll show this lot to Sanjay?'

'No. For now they're leads, and we keep leads to ourselves. If they produce anything we go first to Crofty. He's the one who decides. That's the chain of command.'

Robert photographed the picture and the text and then left everything as he'd found it, closing the door behind him.

They went back downstairs. On stepping outside, Robert tossed the house keys towards Sanjay, making him juggle for his matches and roll-up. The cat watched from behind some railings, its long tail curling in the sun.

'Well, did you find anything?' asked Sanjay.

'Like you say, you wouldn't believe he ever lived there.'

'Told you.'

'Have you got a photo?'

Sanjay opened the car door and reached in for a file, flicking through the papers until he found a Missing Persons profile.

'Can I see a transcript of his interview as well?' added Robert, pushing the boat out. 'Off the record.'

Robert read the document, making notes, and then they shook hands all round. After Sanjay had pulled away, Robert wasn't quite sure what to say. He didn't want to patronise Andrew by complimenting him and he didn't want to lose face by letting him think the teacher had been taught a lesson by his pupil. But he had to say something and Andrew was keeping half a step back, not wanting to lead the way back to the office.

'Twisted guy,' he said, eventually.

'Yes, very.' As if granted permission Andrew went further and ventured a thought. 'That cross.'

'Yes?'

'It was exceptionally small.'

Robert waited for more.

'He must have put it there and then left it behind.'

Robert had noticed the same thing. Pinned to the scuffed wall, it seemed to be floating like wreckage after a storm, detached from any meaning.

'I think we've just seen into Edmund Littlemore's private world,' said Andrew.

Robert agreed: even God was adrift. But his stronger thought was about the magician's apprentice. Where on earth had Crofty found him?

9

Martin and Maisie Brandwell lived in Leyborne Park near Kew Gardens. When Anselm dialled he got Maisie not Martin, and she suggested a meeting early that afternoon, to be followed by another with her son Dominic in Clapham. 'He'll want to see you,' she insisted, promising to make the arrangements. 'He'll be so pleased. We feel completely abandoned by the police. They're doing nothing.' And so, near the appointed time, Anselm rounded a corner and practically walked into a man standing in the middle of the pavement. Anselm tried to step past him twice but the man just mirrored Anselm's movements.

'You're going nowhere near my wife. Now listen to me.'

There was something silver about Martin Brandwell. His hair was silver, his glasses were silver and his eyebrows were silver. He was dressed formally: a white shirt, a red silk tie, a light brown and maroon checked jacket. There was perspiration on the high, lined forehead.

'This is our affair not yours,' he said. 'I've had enough of priests. But *you* can do me a favour. You can do our family a favour. You can make up for some of the harm. You're looking for that American, Littlemore?'

Anselm felt caged. This wasn't the place to explain that John Joe Collins was an employee of Larkwood Priory.

'Well, when you find him, give him a message.'

Anselm opened his mouth to speak but Martin Brandwell had no interest in discussion.

'You tell him to stay hidden, do you understand me?'

Anselm frowned. He seemed to hear Kester. *If anyone knows*

anything it's Martin Brandwell. He was here shortly after Littlemore went missing. He was with Father Carrington for most of the afternoon. They had a row . . .

'Hidden?' echoed Anselm.

'That's right. Tell him to keep out of our lives.'

'But—'

'I'll pay him if need be. But I want him out of circulation for good. It's the only way we'll ever get to the other side of this hell.'

'What do you mean?' Anselm flinched at Martin Brandwell's eyes. They were raw, like flesh when you peel back the epidermis.

'Don't you know? Have you forgotten what happens when these things end up in court? Harry will be pulled to pieces.'

'Not if—'

'I'm not asking your advice, right? I'm telling you what to do. My grandson's beginning to get over what happened to him. I don't want policemen and lawyers opening it up again. They don't have to live with the memory. He does.'

Anselm didn't know how to handle the transferred hostility. He opened his mouth to try and calm him, but again, Martin Brandwell intervened:

'Look beyond the crime. Isn't that your special gift? Try and understand that sometimes the right decision is a horrible decision. If Littlemore is arrested he'll only deny what he did, and then things will only get worse . . . far, far worse. For Harry. For Maisie. For everyone. Now go and give him that message. You'll have a father's blessing.'

Martin Brandwell waited. He wasn't going to leave until Anselm had turned round and gone. Obediently, Anselm backed away, finally retracing his steps beneath the shade of tall trees.

Anselm went to Clapham Common by bus. The route was tortuous but it gave him time to think. In principle – given Martin Brandwell's instructions – he ought to have simply not turned up at his son's home. But an appointment had been made by Maisie. They'd felt let down by the police and he didn't want to add to their disillusionment. More to the point, he didn't want to be controlled by Martin Brandwell: given his unthinkable request, Anselm thought he ought to meet Harry's parents, if only to demonstrate his refusal to cooperate with the boy's grandfather. It would be a delicate meeting and he didn't know how best to handle it. Hopping from bus to bus, seemingly on the run from Kester Newman's disclosure, Anselm let his mind play upon trivia: why had Martin Brandwell isolated Maisie from the long list of people who'd only be harmed by a future trial? Why had he made that slip of the tongue about a father's blessing?

He'd meant a grandfather's, surely? Unless he meant himself in relation to one of his own children.

10

Andrew chased down the meaning of 'Yu kohba smok sote, I mohs kohmoht' as soon as they got back to the office. It was a Krio proverb variously translated to mean 'A person's bad character can't be hidden for long.' More literally: no matter how much you try, you can't cover up smoke. He'd handed over the page, torn from his reporter's notebook, and then announced that Crofty had just asked him to cover a gas leak in Bromley, which was annoying, because Robert was warming to his trainee; he wanted him there when he doorstepped the monks at Larkwood Priory. He'd just organised the transport, borrowing the car from his mother, when Andrew appeared with his chit of paper.

'That's unfortunate,' said Robert. 'Because there's a chance I'll find him. You ought to be there.'

'Crofty says he's short-staffed.'

'Short-sighted, more like. Never mind. I'll let you know what happens.'

Robert glowered at Crofty and then went to Raynes Park, where he found his mother in the back garden. Passing through the house, he could tell every room had been cleaned from top to bottom. Cushions had been plumped, surfaces wiped. There was a smell of disinfectant. All the windows were open. The kitchen floor was wet. And, as if ambushed, Robert felt a stab of grief. Without realising it, his mother had removed all trace of his dad. Stepping through the French windows, he said:

'How are you doing?'

His mother hadn't heard. The tiny electric mower was whizzing over the grass. She was smiling to herself, like someone rehearsing a conversation. Back and forth she went, still wearing the flowery apron from when she'd blitzed the house. On seeing Robert, she came over, untying the strings.

'How are you doing?' she echoed, gathering in her features with concern.

'Fine.'

Robert had expected to find his mother in a heap, not fizzing with energy. He stalled for a moment, noticing the shocking difference in her appearance. She had the glow that comes with a second wind. A blush of colour lit her skin. There was a lightness about her movements. She was ready for the second half of the game. Glancing over her shoulder he saw a few plants in plastic pots. His mother had been to the garden centre. Their eyes met and Robert experienced his first taste of dust: life without his dad; neither Robert nor his mother wanted to talk about him. They were each of them on a road of their own.

'Where are the keys?' asked Robert, stepping over an abyss.

'The usual place. In the bowl by the door.'

He hadn't noticed because the house was no longer the usual place. His mother flicked a leaf off the garden table. 'How long do you want the car for?'

'Tomorrow morning. Probably towards lunchtime.'

'That's fine. Do you want something to eat before you go?'

Robert declined. He just wanted to get away from this incredibly clean and proper house that he no longer fully recognised. It was as though he didn't quite belong any more. He turned at the door to look at his mother and he felt abruptly sad. She was watching from the end of the corridor, but she seemed so much further away: at the end of a longer passage that reached right back into his childhood. She'd loved him, he knew that; but she'd been remote, too. She'd been *trying*. Doing her best. And now there was a distance that they couldn't even talk about because it was part of a history patched over time with the smallest of careful stitches. None of them could be unpicked. He waved, wondering if he'd ever really known Janet Louise Sambourne; wondering why it had taken the death of his dad to realise something so tragic.

A person's bad character can't be hidden for long.

Robert mulled over the insight while motoring through rural Suffolk. It turned out to be an exquisite phrase for the moment because, after parking in a country lane near the entrance to Larkwood Priory, he walked around the grounds, camera in hand, finally spotting Father Edmund Littlemore in the sun-trapped paradise of a walled orchard. He was piling cuttings from the apple trees onto a fire. At times he flinched, turning his head swiftly to one side as the breeze blew the smoke into his eyes. It took Robert a while to be sure. Littlemore had grown a beard and his hair was longer, and he looked different out of his clerical garb, but it was him all right. After another gust or two, and having taken several photographs, Robert moved away from the leaning gatepost. Now seemed a good time to put a few questions to the monk who sought 'justice beyond the reach of the law'.

'I'm sorry, he's away,' said the old monk at the reception desk. 'The Prior is occupied – God himself doesn't know where. The

Guestmaster can never be found' – he waved vaguely towards the world beyond his cluttered table – 'so that leaves me. I know the place backwards. Built half of it and thatched the rest. And that was *after* I met Baden-Powell. That'll give you some idea about the length of these old teeth. Anyway, sit down and tell me what's wrong.'

'Nothing's wrong . . . I never said there was.'

'Come off it.'

'What do you mean?'

'Well, I hope you don't mind me saying, but you don't look too well.'

'I'm fine, absolutely fine.'

The wiry monk's kind blue eyes appraised him like a father. Then, as if he'd found an ointment for a cut to the knee, he said, 'Sit yourself down and I'll tell you about a string of wooden beads worn by a king of the Zulus. How he lost 'em, we don't know. But they were found by my old friend . . .'

Before long Robert was under the heat of a South African sun during the late 1880s. The old monk, thumbs tucked into a frayed rope around his waist, spoke as if he'd been there. But those ancient eyes were like an open door, inviting Robert to talk of things he couldn't possibly know about . . . his dad . . . his mother's spring cleaning . . . those potted plants: they'd brought change and colour, upturning the familiar. Robert had wanted to hurl them over the fence.

'Do you want a glass of water?'

'No, thanks.'

'A soft-boiled egg?'

'No.'

The old man returned to King Dinizulu's necklace and the man who'd found it, Baden-Powell, but the effect of the story was altogether different. It was as though the old Scout was carefully unscrewing the lid on a jar. It was almost open. Robert felt the stir of rising emotion. Politely he cut the monk short:

'How long can someone stay here?'

'Seven days.'

'Why the limit?'

'Sometimes people want to run away from themselves.'

'Are there any circumstances when you'd make an exception?'

'Oh yes.'

'When?'

The old monk seemed to have finally understood what was wrong with Robert. He spoke a fraction more slowly: 'When the circumstances are exceptional.'

Robert had recovered. The lid was tight and secure.

'But you'd have to explain yourself? Say why a week wasn't long enough?'

'You're getting ahead of yourself, young man. If you want to stay, you can. But don't bother thinking any further than tonight. Things always look different in the morning.'

He winked but then his ancient features became absolutely still.

'Have you seen this man before?' Robert pushed Sanjay's photograph of Littlemore across the old monk's desk. 'He's an American priest. He may have grown a beard. I'm trying to find him.'

'Who are you?'

'Has he stayed here recently?'

The old man was studying the clean-shaven features and then he began reading the brief summary beneath the portrait. Robert pressed his enquiry: 'He's not turned up asking to stay longer than seven days?'

'Why do you ask?'

Just then an arched door flew open and a short, round figure stomped towards them. Like the older monk, he was dressed in black and white, but his face was a shining beetroot red. Blood pressure seemed to have stiffened his eyebrows. He glowered down at the receptionist.

'Didn't you hear the bell?'

'What bell?'

'For Vespers. The summons to pray. You're meant to come running *"mox auditus fuerit signus"*. As soon as you hear the signal. Chapter Forty-Three, Verse One.'

Robert intervened: 'Have you seen this man?'

The round monk gave a start as if a genie had just appeared from an oil lamp.

'Terribly sorry. I'm Brother Bede. Larkwood's Archivist. Member of the ARA.'

'I'm trying to find someone,' said Robert, retrieving the Missing Persons profile sheet. 'A lot of people are concerned for his welfare.'

Brother Bede frowned importantly.

'I'm hoping someone with a good memory might recognise him,' continued Robert. 'He could have turned up pleading special circumstances. For all I know he's here as we speak. I just want to help him face up to his past.'

The old monk was trying to rise from his chair, leaning on thin, bony arms. 'Bede, remember another line in the Rule: a man is recognised as wise when his words are few.'

The Archivist sighed wearily, looking to Robert for understanding. '"*Sapiens verbis innotescit paucis*". Chapter Seven, Verse Sixty-One. It's called the eleventh rung of humility.' He spoke with the long-suffering voice of a man who'd made the ladder himself – a little something knocked together in the atelier of human experience. Taking the photograph, he angled it towards the light as if to examine a recently discovered manuscript. An obscure illustration had baffled lesser minds. Expert opinion was required. He gave it swiftly.

'The face means nothing.'

'You're sure.'

'Absolutely. If he crossed this threshold, he didn't stay for long. I'd have known. Frankly, I remember everything I see. A snapshot gets filed away without my even thinking about it. It's a gift, not a skill. Unfortunately I don't get to use it much round here. In days of yore, when I managed—'

The old Scout had finally come to his feet, elbowing his way between Robert and the proud member of the ARA.

'Who are you?'

Robert had reached the door, leaving the monks bunched like two lost sheep. If they weren't going to answer his questions, he wasn't going to answer theirs.

11

Anselm's intention to dissociate himself from the request of Martin Brandwell was easier said than done. Faced with Dominic and Emily Brandwell in their tidy home towards the end of a quiet road off Nightingale Lane, he couldn't even mention his name. Within minutes of his being ushered into the sitting room – an airy living space with antique maps on the walls, handsome books on the shelves, a stripped-pine floor vanishing beneath a patterned rug and chairs draped in blue linen – Dominic and his wife Emily were articulating their disillusionment with Church and State. Anselm – at least on a first meeting – didn't want to add Family to the list. He sat nodding sympathetically, waiting with dread for the sound of the call from Maisie to say that the monk had failed to turn up.

'Right from the start my brother Justin warned us to keep away from him, but we didn't listen. It only took three meetings to find out we should have listened.'

Anselm guessed Dominic was approaching forty. Like Kester, he'd left vigorous activity behind and had that ample, settled look. The nearest he'd come to a stretching exercise was reaching for a second-hand book in his shop near Leicester Square. He spoke carefully as if choosing the right edition for the right man.

'You see, Justin had a breakdown some while back. He works with the homeless and it all got a bit too much. But he pulled himself together . . . eventually. Set up a charity to help people leave the street. It's called the Bowline. Takes them rock climbing. Boating, too. And cycling. They even go on holiday together. You've never heard of it? No matter. The point is, he spends so much time listening to people wanting a free lunch that he's not the most trusting of chaps, is he, darling?'

Emily, seated in one of the blue chairs, nodded. 'That's why we didn't listen.'

'Justin knows Father Littlemore?' asked Anselm. His eyes latched onto a carved mask on the wall: a distorted face with three open mouths, rural art to scare off demons. It was not the sort of thing you'd want to meet in the dark.

'It seems so,' replied Dominic. 'And well enough for Justin to decide he didn't like him. That's all I know. Justin and I don't talk much. No bad history . . . just difference. And because of that, and the breakdown, I didn't take Justin seriously.'

Emily poured tea. The tray had been prepared before Anselm's arrival. She'd let it brew too long. 'We're so glad you're going to find Littlemore,' she said. 'The whole family has been devastated. But it's not us that matters, is it? It's Harry.' She put the pot down and leaned back in despair. 'He's barely spoken since . . . that awful day . . . he's locked up inside himself and we can't reach him. He won't even look in our direction. It's as though he holds us responsible. He's very angry.'

An invisible charge passed between husband and wife. Dominic said:

'Harry refuses to speak to the police. He won't speak to anyone at all, except Fraser.'

'Who's Fraser?' asked Anselm.

'The gardener,' replied Emily. 'He's wonderful. He's been with us for years. But he's not the right sort of person. I mean, I don't want to sound superior or anything, but he was homeless for

most of his life and I'm not too sure he can even read or write.'
She glanced through a wide arch into the dining room and a
far window onto the back garden. A weathered man was removing
his gloves. Anselm had already seen him on entering the sitting
room. The hunched figure had raised a trowel in salute. He was
packing up, now. Emily began to whisper: 'He's as kind as the
day is long, but what Harry needs is someone who can help him
talk about what happened to him. Do you understand?'

'Completely.'

Dominic was bleak: 'He stays in his room. He barely eats. His
behaviour is changing. He spits, he swears. We know he's smoking.
We have to find someone he might trust.'

Anselm agreed. He wondered about those often important
people on the borderlands of family intimacy. 'Have you thought
of your brother, Justin?'

'We did.'

'And?'

'He got nowhere. Took him rock climbing in Wales. We'd
hoped that, far from home, he might get some perspective and
open up. But he just became even more remote.'

They were quiet, listening to Fraser. He was whistling 'Loch
Lomond'. Then Emily spoke:

'Would you have one last try, Father? Maybe he needs someone
like you to unlock the door . . . tell him that what that man did
was awfully wrong.' She was desperate. 'We don't know why he
won't speak. We're here to support him . . . but he seems to
think he's completely on his own.'

Anselm sat very still. He wondered if a bad death might feel
like this. The triumph of appearances not put right.

'Isn't he at school?' he wondered, clearing his throat.

'No, we kept him at home,' said Dominic, embarrassed, acknowledging a mistake made from weakness. 'He had a stomach ache
. . . It's gone, now.'

'Please, Father,' said Emily, 'we've nowhere else to turn.'

Just then, a wizened head appeared around the door. It was Fraser:

'I'll be off then, if you dinna mind.' The Scottish accent was musical and comforting. 'Back next week. I've given young Harry his orders. Sorry to break your stride there, Father.'

Then he was gone and Dominic and Emily were waiting. Anselm couldn't immediately open his mouth. He was scavenging for the right way to express how he'd found himself beyond the limits of any right code of conduct. His skin was tingling with fresh sweat but then the door opened as if lightly pushed. When it had completed its arc, they all looked at the young boy standing in the corridor as if they'd been caught with their hands in the till.

'I'll be in the back garden,' said Harry Brandwell.

12

Harry waited for Anselm at a small table by a wooden shed. Despite the warmth of early evening, he'd put on a blue duffel coat and his hands were hidden deep in his pockets. His face was tense. Anselm had no choice but to take the initiative.

'I've got a shed like that.' He nodded towards the green door. 'At Larkwood we keep our beehives in a clearing near a grave-yard. Actually, there is no graveyard. There are just trees and crosses and a clearing. And my shed . . . which is where I go to hide from monks like Brother Bede. He knows all the rules and never breaks them. So when I've forgotten to put the car keys back on the hook or left the lights on in the refectory – you know, breached one of the really serious rules that keep a commu-nity on the right side of the road – and I know Bede is on the warpath, I go and hide among my hives. I can see him coming through a crack in the door, red, round and raving, and do you know what, after all these years, he's never once thought of looking in the shed.'

Harry listened to the story intently, his dark brown eyes barely straying from Anselm's face. He seemed to be wondering not whether to cooperate, but how.

'I suppose I should have said I'm a beekeeper.'

Harry was still weighing the odds.

'I make honey, obviously, and swedgers – a kind of sweet – which, if the world were a fair place, would be prize-winning. And I brew mead. Which is a sort of wine. But I imagine you knew that already?'

Harry nodded. Fine lips, like his mother's, parted, but he did not speak. His eyes flicked towards the kitchen to check if they were being watched, and they weren't.

'I'm thinking of making a lip cream for jazz trumpeters but first I want to develop a face lotion for Bede. I'm going to call it "Bede's Balm". You see, when he gets cross, which is pretty much every day, his cheeks go blazing hot, and he could do with something to cool him down. I owe it to him, really. Because, truth be told, Bede is right.'

Anselm was fairly sure that Harry was interested in Bede. He'd sensed that praise for Bede was going to end with a sudden twist, which was true.

'Bede is right because people like me – apparently nice guys who make sweets and non-fizzy drinks – shouldn't be allowed to get away with breaking the rules. Even the small ones. And they shouldn't hide afterwards. The best thing would be for me to come out and listen to what Bede has to say, put the keys back and then turn the lights out on the whole business. That way everyone can start afresh tomorrow. I'm saying that no one should ever hide from what they've done.'

Harry mulled over Anselm's parable and then, as if a decision had been made, he said:

'Father Littlemore's been gone a long time now. The police

don't know where he is. I reckon he's in Spain. Sunning himself. What do you think?'

The poor boy had heard someone rehearse the possible. They'd thought of the Costa del Sol, the bolt-hole for English-born criminals, the sunny refuge where the sheds are villas.

'He's out of reach, I'm sure,' said Harry. 'What do you reckon?'

Harry was appraising Anselm with the same compressed attention that he'd given to the story of Bede's quest for a law-abiding community. When Anselm failed to reply, he seemed to make another decision, but only after another glance towards the house.

'Father, is it always wrong not to tell the truth?'

Anselm couldn't help but squint at the form of the question. He would have expected it to be framed the other way around, in relation to what is right; but Harry had opted for the reverse. He was wondering if it can be right to remain silent. Plato had dealt with this one, somewhere . . . something to do with promises, whether it's wrong to break them when there's a danger of someone being stabbed in the back . . . but Anselm couldn't remember the story; and, given the electric atmosphere that now linked him to Harry, any attempt to recover the memory was an academic diversion. There are instances when moral problems become absolutely incarnate; when, unfortunately, we have to become the Great Mind that knows the answer. Anselm's hesitation was not lost on Harry. It gave him encouragement.

'Does Brother Bede know?' he asked.

'I imagine he does, yes.'

'What would he say?'

'He'd probably tell you that it's always right to tell the truth.'

'And what about you?'

Anselm felt he was hiding in a shed. That he ought to come out and admit that Edmund Littlemore was a long way from Spain; that his refuge was closer to home.

'I've learned never to answer a question about right and wrong without first knowing the facts. The right thing to do, the good thing to do, is best decided after we've looked at what has actually happened. So, shall we start there, Harry, with the facts? If you like, I can help you tell other people what you daren't say by yourself.'

Harry pondered the idea as if Anselm had produced a plate of spinach from behind his back. Despite strenuous objections, he'd been told endlessly that it was good for him.

'Do I have to talk about it?'

'No one can force you to say anything, Harry. You have a choice.'

Anselm had blundered. He should have moved by stages. Instead, he'd bridged the distance between the abstract and the concrete with one giant step. He'd ignored the obvious: that Harry had voiced a theoretical question precisely because the facts were too painful to recount; the boy was trying to handle them on his own, reaching out for the right answer, not wanting to make a wrong move, absolutely convinced that the last thing he could do was discuss the facts with anyone. Harry rose and stepped away from the table.

'Thank you, Father. I'd like to go in now.'

13

Robert drove through the rolling green fields away from Larkwood Priory, the road weaving gently between hedges and low stone walls. On either side were thatched cottages, the odd quaint pub and, peering above the orange tiles or clustered leaves, belfries and steeples. It was a county of ancient churches. He called Crofty on loudspeaker to let him know what he'd found on the balcony: the cuttings, the notes on jazz, the addresses and phone numbers. After a few half-remembered quotations he underlined his most significant discovery: someone was working with Littlemore.

'But who uses fax these days?' asked Robert. 'It's not obsolete . . . but it's way behind email and a scanner.'

'Trace the number. I'm more interested in the message on the postcard. That sounds like an accusation.'

'It does.'

'So maybe Sierra Leone's a part of some bigger picture.' Crofty was thinking out loud. 'You said he ran from the station when they asked about his past?'

'That's right.'

'Okay, find out where he'd been before he moved to London. Hang on a sec.' Crofty paused to take a call from Muriel and then he was back. 'Did you get to question the monk detective?'

'No. He was away.'

'Too convenient.'

'Exactly. Thing is, he didn't know I was coming, did he?'

'Maybe he wasn't away. Maybe you were knocked back when you asked about Littlemore.'

'I didn't mention Littlemore when I asked to see the detective.'

The permutations didn't matter: Littlemore was being protected by the community. The Archivist had lied while the Scout had been unable to hide the frightened flicker of recognition. And if they were prepared to lie or hedge, then one could safely presume that the monk who looked for a rarefied kind of justice was complicit: they were resolved to protect one of their own. Robert said so, knowing this could only add weight to any exclusive, but Muriel was back on line two. Crofty had to go: 'There's still no story because the kid hasn't spoken and Littlemore hasn't been arrested. But get to work. You're onto something. How's the trainee getting along?'

'He's good. What was the point of sending him to Bromley just when we got a break?'

'Didn't he tell you? I'm short-staffed. That's why I gave him a job.'

'Well, it's a pity because he's the one who found the stuff.'

'You should have told me.'

'Didn't he?'

'No. He just said you'd been proved right.'

Robert huffed at the exasperating reticence. 'Where did you find him anyway?'

'At the bottom of a ladder.'

'You've lost me.'

'He cleaned my windows for ten years. Then he got talking to Muriel.'

Robert cut the call and, almost immediately, he felt the gentle touch of intuition. If Father Anselm *wasn't* involved – and he might not be – then whoever had written to Robert did so knowing that when he came to Larkwood looking for Littlemore, the monk-detective wouldn't be there.

Now who might that have been, if not another monk? But how could that monk have known that Robert Sambourne had been in the station when Littlemore came running out? Or that Robert had tracked Littlemore for a week, demanding an interview? All that information was known only to Littlemore himself and potentially someone else, if he'd confided what happened. Could that be the link, then? Did the confidant get in touch with Larkwood Priory, setting in motion the events that had subsequently unfolded?

The phone rang. It was Crofty.

'When I say get to work, I don't mean tonight.'

'Why not?'

'Take a break. Put your feet up. Have one too many. Let yourself grieve.'

14

Anselm didn't notice the heavy traffic. He didn't notice the people walking before his eyes. Somehow he crossed a busy thoroughfare, walking aimlessly onto Clapham Common. On and on he went, heading towards the bandstand, to Anselm's vision a pagoda or carousel without the magical rides that move up and down. He was crossing a still point, vehicles of all shapes and sizes going round and round and round. What was he to do? Edmund Littlemore had sexually abused a boy of eleven.

'Are y'all right there, Father?'

Anselm's eyes flickered. A man had come up quietly from behind. It was Fraser.

'If ye don't mind me sayin' . . . ye dinna look too good.'

'I'm not.'

From a distance Fraser had looked elderly, but close up Anselm judged this thin but strong-looking man to be much younger, perhaps in his fifties. It was difficult to tell because life had turned his skin into a kind of stained parchment. His cheeks were hollowed beneath dark sockets. His forehead was pitted with old scars, those distinctive wounds of life on the street. But the length of a day's kindness was in his brown, boyish eyes. To look into them, you'd think this man had seen beyond all manner of suffering.

'I followed ye, Father. I've been waitin' for ye.'

'Why?'

'I overheard you talkin' there to Mr Dominic and Mrs Emily, okay, and I know you want the best for the wee fella, but I think you might need some help. You're not going to get much of that from his family, you follow?'

'I don't.'

'They're all lookin' in the wrong direction. Do you get me now?'

They'd halted by a bench so Anselm sat down but Fraser remained standing. He didn't want to be seen talking out in the open. Like Harry's glances in the garden, he looked quickly towards the house in that quiet road.

'I've got to know the wee lad, ye know. I see my own boy in his eyes. And I'm worried about him, okay?'

'Of course.'

'And I think you should know he's scared.'

'What about?'

'Speakin' up. Sayin' the truth.'

This much Anselm knew already. But Fraser came close and went further:

'He's scared of someone in particular.'

'Who?'

Fraser ignored the question and in that instant Anselm realised that this once broken man was more than Harry's friend; that he was like a secret presence at the heart of the family; that he knew things he wasn't meant to know. With a shudder, Anselm wondered if Harry had actually confided in him. And then he was sure: the boy had turned to the one person no one would remotely expect of commanding so much trust. As if tracking Anselm's thoughts Fraser quietly said:

'Harry talks to me.'

'I understand.'

'He says things to me he wouldna say to anyone else, okay?'

'Yes.'

'He's been through a big shock, he has.'

'Yes.'

'He's not well in his skin, al'right?'

'Yes.'

'His mammy has already taken him to the police.'

Anselm gave a nod.

'But the wee fella said nothing.'

This Anselm did not know. And he showed it by a look of surprise.

'That's right; his mammy took him for an interview at a hospital and the boy didn't open his mouth, okay?'

Anselm nodded again as Fraser leaned closer still. His brown eyes were aching with concern, emitting a sort of light from their dark sockets.

'But before Harry went down there with his mammy, the granddaddy came to the house.' Fraser waited, wanting to make sure that Anselm was registering what he was saying. 'That's right, his granddaddy had a wee word with him, on his own, just before his mammy took him to the hospital. And then, when he got there, the poor lad couldna speak. D'ye understand what I've just told you, Father? Do ye get ma drift?'

Anselm certainly did. He was effectively saying that Harry's aggressor was his grandfather. The man who'd been to see Carrington after Littlemore disappeared. No wonder Martin Brandwell had spilled his wife's name out as a casualty of any future trial.

'Now I never told you that, al'right?' said Fraser. 'That's for you to find out in your own way and by your own means.'

Anselm said he understood, but he had to ask at least one question. 'Did you know that Harry had been to see Father Littlemore?'

'Who?'

Anselm repeated the name but it was clear Fraser had never heard of him. And that meant that Edmund Littlemore was entirely innocent – assuming that Harry had, in fact, confided in Fraser. But in that case, why did Harry quiz Anselm about Father Littlemore's whereabouts? Why, in the same breath, was he troubled about whether he ought to tell the truth? Why had he come back distressed from that third, fateful interview? Harry's behaviour suggested his relationship with Fraser might not be as simple as the old man liked to think; maybe he hadn't told him everything.

'I've got to go, Father,' said Fraser, narrowing those pained eyes as he scanned the park. 'It's not been easy for me, okay? Justin Brandwell saved my life, he did. I'd had one swally too many and I was lying on the tracks beneath the bridge at Strath Terrace, al'right? A train was coming down the line but Justin got there in time, okay? More than tha', when I'd sobered up, he listened to me . . . someone who'd ne'er been listened to, right? He put me back on my feet. Showed me I had a life worth living. No one else would have bothered. So I owe him. But I can't keep quiet for his sake while that wee laddie suffers. I can't ignore the danger.'

Fraser's voice stopped as if someone had slammed a hand over his mouth. Without saying another word he began walking quickly towards the bandstand, presently disappearing among the nearby trees.

For a very long while Anselm just sat on the bench listening to the traffic going round and round the common: buses, cars, trucks and motorbikes seemingly on the way to nowhere. He didn't want to go back to Larkwood. He didn't want to see John Joe Collins. He didn't want to face Dunstan. He just wanted to remain here while the world went its busy way. But of course, remaining off the carousel was not an option. He had to leave this still point and go home, even if it meant going in the opposite direction to everyone else.

Much later, and looking back, Anselm would think there was a certain irony in what happened next because he stepped off the kerb into the path of a bike courier. The rider was fine, but Anselm was knocked unconscious. Someone called a priest.

15

It was late when Robert got back to London, but not so late he couldn't take the car back to his mother's, rather than have the faff of going round there the next morning. And so he went to Raynes Park directly. As he drove along Coombe Lane his eye latched onto a bulky figure coming out of the Hanabi Japanese restaurant with his arm around a woman. Robert could have sworn it was Crofty and Muriel, but he'd passed them before he could confirm the sighting. Pretty sure it couldn't be, he went to his mother's but couldn't park near the house. He found a slot just big enough some distance away, spending his last atom of patience trying to reverse close enough to the kerb. He then walked back down the street and knocked on his mother's door. There was no reply. After waiting a while and knocking some more he turned to leave, pausing at the gate. Crofty's Audi with the dinted passenger door was parked twenty yards or so further down the road. Robert crossed over. Just as he passed behind a white van, he saw them turning into the street from a short cut by the railway line. Sure enough it was Crofty and Muriel. But they weren't alone. Robert's mother was walking just behind them . . . arm in arm with a man who looked vaguely familiar. They stopped as a group so Robert moved close to the van: he looked through the grimy windows but he couldn't get a clean line of vision onto this other man. Muriel hugged his mother while Crofty put his arm around the man and then Muriel stepped into the road, heading towards the Audi; and at that point Robert could see that she was crying, dabbing her cheeks with a tissue. A moment later, Crofty waddled after her shaking the keys like a bell.

'Your turn, darling.'

'It's always my turn,' she replied.

They were only three vehicles away, so Robert retreated to the rear of the van, peering around the side: the Audi's brake lights flashed and Muriel took the wheel, putting the wipers on full swing, prompting Crofty to lean over and calm things down. The engine barked into life. The headlights came on. With a returning wave, Muriel pulled away. The horn beeped twice.

Robert waited. Then he crept back onto the pavement, walked the length of the van, and looked across the street. His mother was in the arms of the man. They wouldn't let go of each other. Robert screwed his eyes shut and then opened them again. He couldn't believe what he was seeing. The couple stepped apart, holding hands to make a bridge.

'Call me,' said Robert's mother.

'As soon as I get home.'

She stroked his cheek with the back of her hand. 'The future is ours.'

Robert didn't hear the rest because his brain couldn't process the words alongside the visual data. The man who crossed the bridge of linked arms to kiss his mother one more time was the magician's apprentice: Andrew Taylor, the late starter who couldn't come to Larkwood because Crofty had sent him to Bromley. The only further information that registered in Robert's consciousness was as obvious as it was distressing: they, along with Crofty and Muriel, had just celebrated a newfound freedom; a boon, arising from the sudden death by heart failure of Lenny Sambourne, the quiet man who'd loved spending hours pottering about on his allotment.

Part Three

Harry's parents approved of Gutsy. They thought he was a good influence. They thought he might keep Harry on the straight and narrow, especially after they'd found a lighter in Harry's pocket.

'You're not smoking, are you?' his mother had asked, standing close to his father, and Harry hadn't bothered to reply: he'd simply weighed them up as if they were the last two with a chance of being picked for the team. They'd backed off, afraid of the look in his eye; afraid of losing their place in goal. If there was a good side to being abused, it was the power it gave you over your parents.

After the monk had gone, Gutsy came round for a sleepover. He brought some Camel Lights for later.

'Did you tell him what happened with Littlemore?' asked Gutsy.

'No.'

'Why not?'

'Why would I? He's got the same job.'

'Exactly. He's the bloke to tell. He'd understand.'

'Nah.'

'You could've asked his advice. They can't repeat anything you tell them, priests. They'd go to prison before they'd reveal a source.'

'That's journalists.'

They were lying in a bunk bed, Harry on top, Gutsy underneath, voices adrift in the darkness. Gutsy turned over:

'You can't let him get away with it just because he's a vicar.'

'So you keep saying.'

They were quiet.

'Sarah Lawton thinks you get pregnant through your belly-button . . .' said Gutsy, drifting off.

★

Uncle Justin had told his brother Dominic that it was important to get Harry onto a rock face. Forget the box of tissues and the special questions. There's nothing like controlled fear and fresh air to clear the mind. And so a weekend away was organised for the family. This was early November, a month after Uncle Justin had shown Harry how to tie a bowline. While motoring out of London, Harry's father spoke about Fraser: how he'd come back from the dead; how, with the help of people like Justin, he'd found his feet; how he was now helping others find theirs. Harry had heard it all before on television. The only difference was that Uncle Justin had kept himself out of the picture, but he was the one who'd pulled Fraser to safety; he was the one who'd taught him the bowline; he was the one who'd found the job and drummed up the clients.

'Anyone can survive anything,' said Uncle Justin, uncoiling a rope. He looked up. He was trying to sound comforting, but he couldn't hide his own fear. 'You're no exception. All it takes is courage.'

He'd chosen North Wales for Harry's initiation. A light wind funnelled up the valley and across the brown scree to where they were standing at the foot of an outcrop like a protruding bone. In the distance there was a long grey lake, dull as a blind eye. Wisps of cloud played upon its surface. Harry's parents stood back, letting the master do his work.

'Keep your hands low down. Only take one limb off the rock at a time. And remember: there's a rope around your waist: you can't fall.'

After a nod at his brother, Justin turned and began moving up the shin of stone with a name that Harry had been unable to pronounce. They'd all laughed as he got tongue-tied around the fs and ys, and then he'd tired of the family show, as he'd once tired of learning the bowline. When Uncle Justin reached a ledge — a kind of lip sulking on the side of the rock face — he anchored the rope and moments later the slack was taken up and Harry felt a light tug around his waist.

'Climbing,' he called in reply, as he'd been taught.

It wasn't that difficult, actually. Uncle Justin had picked the spot because there were lots of handholds to choose from, lots of fine ridges on which to place the edge of your feet. Up Harry went, thinking this *was nothing, until — after a very short distance indeed — his throat tightened and his chest began to thump against his windbreaker. A new kind of panic entered his life, right there on the cliff face. It expelled the memory of every emotion he'd ever felt before. It was as though he'd been emptied, or perhaps recreated. With each careful upward movement, Harry saw the rope advance ahead of him, but there was always a little slack, leaving him responsible for his next decision. Very gradually the panic subsided.*

The ledge was quite wide. When he reached it, Uncle Justin pulled him to safety, and the two of them sat back, gazing down the valley. There were colourful boats moored in a line on the lake. A winding stream flickered in the sunlight. The clouds stretched across the sky like strips of torn bandage. Down below, Dominic and Emily were hand in hand, their joint gaze sharing awe and terror. And, of course, hope. Hope that Uncle Justin would work a miracle. They were just out of earshot.

'I call this ledge "Speakers' Corner" because it's a good place to talk about everything you've left behind,' said Uncle Justin. 'But you know . . . sometimes I think it's best to let things go . . . act as if they'd never happened. You don't always have to talk about everything; the trick is to know when to be quiet. A priest told me that once. At first, I thought he was wrong, but in the end, he was proved right. It's a beginning, at least.' Uncle Justin filled his lungs with pure mountain air, his eyes dropping onto his anxious brother. 'I've seen it countless times. People don't move forward until they stop looking back. Think about it, Harry.'

Harry didn't respond. He was looking at the boats winking on the lake. But he could feel Uncle Justin's panic as if it was the wind, light now, but threatening to become strong. He let him suffer. At last Uncle Justin whispered as if he was on his knees.

'Don't say anything, will you? Help me keep the family together.'

And like a fallen wizard who'd just uttered his first redundant spell, Uncle Justin edged away and came to his feet. Having tied Harry to a cleat and given him the rope to pay out, Uncle Justin began climbing towards the summit of this low mountain, beloved by many tutors initiating first-timers into the world of mutual trust; the give and take of survival.

'I'm in your hands, Harry,' he said, looking down, those green eyes begging for a new and secret understanding. 'Don't do anything silly.'

When Gutsy woke up the next morning, he began talking where he'd left off. Sarah Lawton really had no idea about the facts of life. Your belly-button? What did she think her parents had done to make her? Just imagine it, the angles involved. You'd need a protractor. And even then, the problem with a belly-button is the depth. You can't—

'I've been thinking,' said Harry, still on that ledge, slowly paying out the rope.

'What? That she's thick?'

Harry had been thinking that with one yank, Uncle Justin would have fallen; only the rope would have come tight before he landed on top of his brother and sister-in-law. Uncle Justin was good at knots. Nothing he tied would ever come undone. That's what Kenny had said in the documentary.

'No. I'm going to spit it out,' replied Harry, his mouth bone dry.

Gutsy took a minute to free his imagination from Sarah Lawton's misunderstandings. 'Are you serious?'

'Yeah.'

'You're going to the police?'

'Yes. I'm going to talk to Sanjay. Maybe it'll make me feel better.'

16

As usual, the editorial conference took place in the Fish Tank
– Crofty's glass-walled office; as usual, he wanted reports on
developing stories while he shuffled a pack of cards, interrupting
a speaker on impulse to pick the queen of spades; as usual he
always got it wrong; unusually Robert couldn't concentrate or
contribute. His attention lay with the man at his side, Andrew
Taylor. Throughout the previous night Robert had tried to make
sense of what he'd witnessed; tried to understand what it might
mean. There was little room for doubt: his mother was in a
relationship with another man. He wasn't simply an acquaintance.
They'd known each other for years. Their intimacy had been
natural, fluid . . . significant. And this was the man who'd made
a sudden appearance as Crofty's trainee, to be mentored by Robert.
That could hardly have been a coincidence . . . which meant
there'd been some sort of plan, conceived – presumably – by
that cabal who'd toasted the future at Hanabi's.

'Okay, people, back to work,' said Crofty, throwing the cards
down, 'bring me the bacon.'

Everyone sidled out. Robert, last in line, had just reached the
door when he turned round to appraise his dad's best friend.
His mother's accomplice. With the sun breaking through the
blinds, Crofty was all orange and striped. His mouth had fallen
open and he looked like a goldfish short of oxygen. Robert
waited until he saw a burst of perspiration on that freckled brow,
then he said:

'Are you all right?'

'Yes. Why?'

'You look a bit green around the gills.'

'Green?'

'Yes, as if you had one too many last night.'

'*Moi? Jamais.* Only at weekends.'

Robert became jocular: 'You've not done anything to be ashamed of, have you?'

'What? At my age?'

Robert mulled over the answer. 'Given time and a bit of practice anything's possible.'

Leaving the Fish Tank, Robert could feel Crofty's troubled eyes upon his back. They almost had fingers, but they dared not touch him. On reaching his workstation, Robert sat down and appraised Andrew. He'd brought coffee and the morning's mail. He was smiling that hopeful let-me-do-the-dishes smile.

'Crofty's waving you back,' he said, pointing.

Robert retraced his steps and placed his head around the door. 'You called?'

'Yes.' Crofty chewed his lip, glanced at Andrew and lost his nerve: 'Don't forget that fax number. Trace it. Whoever sent it did the research. They're the ones who pushed Littlemore to that monastery. They're the ones with all the answers.'

'Sure. Anything else?'

'Yes. The Sierra Leone angle. Find out why someone would send an accusation on a postcard.'

'Okay, but we had this conversation last night. Any fresh thoughts since then? Ideas that came in the night?'

'Yes.' Crofty dabbed his brow. 'You've suffered a huge loss. Your dad was a big man and he's left behind a big hole. Don't fill it up with bad news. Remember what I said, let yourself grieve.'

Robert turned curious. 'With a drink? Maybe one too many?'

'There are worse ways.'

Robert liked that one. Crofty had hit the nail on the head. 'You're right. There's a lot worse, if you put your mind to it.'

Pulling back his chair, Robert sat down, wondering how he was going to relate to Andrew Taylor normally. He felt a flush of confused antagonism. The man was now a part of his life. He was camped on the outskirts of his grief. To avoid his willing glances, Robert opened the letter that had revealed Edmund Littlemore's whereabouts. He read it slowly:

Why have you given up?
Victims always need help to speak out.
Otherwise they get silenced by private agreements.
Don't let that happen.
The American is hiding at Larkwood Priory.
Do not delay. If he leaves, you'll never find him again.

'Are you all right?' asked Taylor. He was no longer Andrew in Robert's mind.

'What do you mean?'

'What I said. I know your dad died recently and I more than understand if you're distracted. Death's a hard one. Not nice. Difficult to find a place on the shelf.'

'What shelf?'

'You know . . . the place for memories. Things you don't want but can't throw away.'

Robert's mind turned misty but he glimpsed the outline of what must be happening: Taylor was making a bid for some kind of affiliation. He was using compassion as a kind of glue. Robert reached for his mug of coffee.

'Thanks, Andrew. That's really thoughtful. You see, he was no ordinary man, my dad. Devoted to my mother. Wonderful with me. More of a friend, as I got older.' Despite himself, Robert became serious; he'd evoked the man. 'As a kid he was always there when I came home, always there when I came running'

– Robert pulled out of the downward spiral – 'I don't think I'll ever get over his passing.'

'Maybe you won't. Maybe you'll just come to—'

'I don't want your advice.'

'I'm sorry.'

'I don't want your sympathy, either.'

'I understand.'

'No, you don't. And stop looking at me like you want to carry the shopping. I don't want your help.'

Robert's mother had held onto this man; she'd kissed him hungrily. She'd sat in her empty house waiting for him to call as soon as he got home. The future was theirs. Robert felt his stomach turn: this sticky attempt to establish a bond must be all part of the plan, the next stage after Taylor had started work on the paper. He'd been assigned to Robert on the day of the funeral . . . which meant the plan itself was conceived beforehand . . . even while his father was waiting to be buried. Robert gazed at Taylor, suddenly sure that he'd been the quick thinker, that the scheme had been his invention. Robert swallowed and said:

'Have you given any thought to the Littlemore story?'

Taylor had. And Robert listened, preparing to mock.

'This is the chronology,' he said, turning over the pages of his reporter's notebook until he came to a neatly written list. 'One: Littlemore attacks an eleven-year-old boy. Two: Littlemore is questioned the same week by the police and he runs from the station. Three: a couple of days later, someone sends research about Father Anselm to Littlemore by fax. Four: three days after that, Littlemore goes to Larkwood Priory. Five: six months later, you receive a letter written on an old-fashioned typewriter telling you to expose Littlemore and where to find him. Six: when you actually get there, Father Anselm is away.'

Robert made a deriding smile. Taylor was frowning importantly, tapping his pad with a pencil.

'My first thought is that whoever sent the fax to Littlemore knows someone at Larkwood Priory.'

Robert had already come to the same conclusion. 'Any second thoughts?'

'Yes. I wonder if three belongs with number five.'

'Sorry, I didn't make an inventory.'

'Is there a link between the fax and the typewriter . . . between fading and obsolete technology? I mean is the person who sent the fax to Littlemore the same person who wrote the letter to you?'

Robert couldn't respond. His mother's special friend was onto something. Taylor spelled out the implications: 'If so, that would mean the person who sent Littlemore to Larkwood is the same person who sent you there to find him.'

Robert had to accept it: Taylor had raised a critical question, because if the fax and letter did belong together, it meant that either Littlemore had been set up, along with Father Anselm and the community — or Littlemore had cooperated in his own capture, deliberately implicating the monk and his brothers . . . and that was inconceivable. Taylor continued his train of thought, not looking up, not daring to provoke another rebuke:

'So it looks like this Father Anselm and his community and Littlemore have all been brought together so that, when you finally expose him, Littlemore will be compromised. He'll be seen to have run away from what he did, seeking shelter among people who ought to have called the police. He'll be convicted when he's brought to trial.'

Robert didn't entirely agree, but he was moving further down the track: why would anyone do that? There was only one answer, and Taylor — maddeningly — was already there:

'Which means that whoever wrote the fax and the letter knows for sure that Littlemore is guilty. And they also know that the boy daren't open his mouth . . . so they've decided to trap Littlemore themselves.'

Robert's disdain couldn't expunge his amazement. Where had this drifter learned to think so cleanly? To see into the mind of someone driven to bring justice to a child who couldn't speak for himself? Where had he learned to second-guess a secret vigilante? In Lusaka? On the London Underground? Behind the bar on a Brittany ferry?

'Whoever they are, they've made a mistake,' said Robert.

'Why?' Taylor closed his pad.

'Because showing Littlemore went into hiding isn't enough to prove he's guilty. The boy will still have to say what happened. Otherwise there'll be no trial . . . and whoever tried to trap him will have wasted their time.'

Swivelling round on his chair to escape Taylor's hangdog expression, Robert rang Stuart Greene, an old school friend at British Telecom who (for a tenner) did odd jobs to promote responsible journalism. Tracing a fax account would be no problem (he said). Robert gave him the number. On finishing the call there was a ring before Robert had even let go of the receiver.

It was Sanjay Kumar.

Robert all but ran to the Fish Tank. Crofty's freckles turned warm and he called the *Guardian* offering them an exclusive – 'You've finally done it, son; you've got a story that's too big for your own paper' – and within the hour Robert was on the phone to the US embassy and the archdiocese of Boston, checking background details while he tapped at his computer, struggling to get the words right, doing his best to be fair. Shortly after he'd sent the article, his inbox went 'ping'. The news editor at the *Guardian* was pleased. In fact, having seen Robert's work before, he suggested a meeting. Perhaps there was 'a conversation we might have'. It was awful, really. Robert was flowering out of dirt. Instinctively, he glanced over to Crofty, the man who'd nurtured and guided his career, even to the point of sacrificing the best scoop his unimportant paper had ever landed.

But his dad's best friend was preoccupied. He was staring at the ground, pretty certain that his star journalist was onto another scandal. Somehow – Crofty was thinking – Robert knows; he's found out about Andrew. He was onto another story of betrayal and shattered trust. A family affair.

17

There'd been nothing to worry about. Nonetheless, and over-ruling Anselm's protestations, the consultant in A&E had insisted on admitting him to a ward for twenty-four hours' observation. 'Consider yourself lucky,' he'd said, not sure Anselm bought into the concept of chance. On arriving back at Larkwood late the next day, the Prior judged Anselm to be fine – a bit too swiftly for Anselm's liking – being more concerned with the well-being of Edmund Littlemore. On hearing of the crime alleged against him the Prior's eyes closed.

'Have you called the police?' he asked, under his breath.

'I was waiting to see you.'

'Why?'

'I thought we ought to have a conversation first.'

The Prior showed his annoyance. 'Prudence takes precedence over propriety.'

They walked into the cloister. The Prior wanted the facts, and quickly.

'Kester Newman is my main source. He's dispassionate. He's observant. He's reliable.'

'What did he say?'

Anselm felt the first stirrings of a headache. 'Edmund Littlemore comes from the States, joins the Lambertines but is then sent to Sierra Leone. It's rumoured that Carrington was shifting a problem character off the map, only it didn't work. Littlemore comes back and is reprimanded. He's then moved to south London, meets the Brandwell family and ends up being accused of a sexual attack. Shortly afterwards he comes to Larkwood.'

'Using a false name.'

Anselm wanted water, but there was none to hand. He sat down between two pillars, listening to the splash of the fountain at the centre of the Garth: 'Upon Littlemore's disappearance, Martin Brandwell visits Carrington. Kester thinks Brandwell has found out that complaints had been made against Littlemore in Boston and Freetown. He's angry because nothing was done and now his grandson has been harmed. They argue because Brandwell is blaming Carrington for failing to act. But it's an odd argument because afterwards neither of them cooperates with the police. Neither of them wants a trial.'

'They made some kind of agreement?'

'It seems so.'

'To conceal Littlemore's past?'

'That's what it looks like.'

'Along with the attack on Harry?'

'That's what Kester thinks.'

The Prior's pacing hadn't strayed beyond the evening shadows thrown by the two pillars. On the turn, and worried, he said, 'And you think differently?'

'I do,' replied Anselm. 'Because afterwards Carrington comes to Larkwood incognito. He takes great pains to say that Littlemore has done nothing wrong. But he wants me to find out *why* he ran away. And that was a very significant request.'

'Why?'

'Because he must have known that the first person I'd ask would be the Lambertine Provincial.'

'Carrington himself?'

'Exactly. He *wanted* me to turn up at Ealing. And when I did, he was waiting for me. But he wouldn't tell me anything. Instead he rebuffs me in the presence of Kester, who'd been kept on hand, waxing a floor for days on end; someone guaranteed to follow me and reveal what I needed to know.'

'But why would Carrington go to such lengths?'

'To get behind the agreement with Martin Brandwell. Regardless of the evidence stacked against him, Carrington is saying Littlemore is innocent; and he's asked me to *help* him, not just *find* him.'

'But why enter into an agreement that frustrates your own objectives?'

'I don't know. But Carrington is obviously trapped. And that's why he came to me in the first place.'

'I can't share your confidence.'

Anselm had to stumble on. The Prior was like a man running away, though he hadn't left the narrow band of fading light between the shadows.

'I have another source. The best kind. Someone with nothing to gain and everything to lose from saying what they know.'

'Who's this?'

'A witness at the heart of the family.'

Anselm explained about Fraser and his intimate connection to the Brandwells, his loyalty to Justin and his devotion to Harry. He leaned forward, animated and sure:

'Harry Brandwell can't speak to his own family, so he's turned to this complete outsider. He's told the person you'd least expect what he can't tell anyone else: that he was assaulted by his own grandfather.'

'Fraser told you this explicitly?'

'Not in so many words, but he left no room for doubt. Harry confides in him. Even his parents said so. And if you want corroboration, it was his grandfather who silenced him before he was interviewed by the police.'

The Prior didn't seem to have heard. He looked trapped. Anselm made a stronger appeal:

'Fraser's there all the time, barely noticed by anyone. They think he's an old fool who can't even spell his name. But he's watching the boy and watching his family. He understands why Harry can't speak and he's frustrated that he can't speak himself. And so he's turned to me. He wants me to find out what he knows to be true but can't reveal.'

'But why would Martin Brandwell want Littlemore to remain in hiding?'

'Because as long as Littlemore is out of the way there's a chance the whole thing becomes history. The family have someone to blame and meanwhile the pressure on Harry to say nothing gets stronger. There's a kind of peace, even for Harry, because everyone leaves him alone. He can begin to forget. The moment Littlemore is found and defends himself, Martin Brandwell is in trouble. People will have to listen to Littlemore. They might believe what he says. And then they start looking for the real culprit.'

The consultant had warned Anselm that headaches might come, but he'd said nothing about their intensity. With flickering eyes Anselm watched the Prior: he'd sat down on a stone bench. His annoyance had turned to dread.

'Leaving aside Kester's assumptions, do you know why Littlemore left the States . . . why he left Sierra Leone?'

'No. Carrington kicked me out before I could ask.'

'Doesn't that suggest there's something to hide?'

'It's possible, yes, but I got the impression I'd met a second persona, someone who couldn't cooperate with me in any way. That's what this strange case is all about.'

'Isn't that worrying in its own right?'

'It could be, yes. But—'

'Shortly after Littlemore came back to England he was, in fact, accused of a serious offence.'

'It seems so . . . though Harry didn't repeat it when interviewed. At this stage we only know—'

The Prior snatched the phrase: 'That Littlemore came to Larkwood after running from a police station.'

'Scared by the allegation.'

'Not so scared to reflect on what happens when you've made a mistake and there's no going back.'

That very idea had tormented Littlemore. Anselm's temples were beating. The Prior continued:

'Have you considered that Martin Brandwell might have been persuaded or even forced by Carrington to enter into an agreement that protects the reputation of an Order over the crime of an individual?'

'I haven't. Because Carrington came to see me. He—'

'Wanted you to believe that Littlemore was innocent, despite the evidence stacked against him.'

The reversal in meaning stumped Anselm. 'But why do that?' he managed.

'Perhaps we've yet to find out. Perhaps we've yet to discover the true scope of this agreement. You know that secrecy arrangements have been entered into before?'

'I do.'

'They've shattered the moral authority of those who conceived them with devastating consequences for those who were silenced. Haven't you considered that in receiving Edmund Littlemore, we may have been drawn into a conspiracy?'

Anselm hadn't. The Prior was relentless:

'So that leaves the intimations of Fraser the gardener, someone you met for five minutes on Clapham Common – someone who you know to have suffered a significant breakdown?'

'It does.'

'He's your best witness?'

The weight of incredulity had gradually accumulated behind the Prior's questioning and now Anselm felt crushed. However, the Prior showed no sign of having finished. He'd simply paused as if to change weapon, causing Anselm to shift closer to a pillar in an attempt to avoid another attack. But there was no escape:

'Assuming you are right and Littlemore is innocent – and I

accept that no formal charge has been made – then why not come to Larkwood the moment he was falsely accused?'

'I don't know.'

'Why become homeless first?' The Prior answered his own question. 'Because – like Dunstan wondered at the outset – it gave him a reason for meeting you.'

It did. There could be no doubt. Only it didn't make sense to Anselm. There were simpler ways of contacting him.

'You've been outmanoeuvred, Anselm,' said the Prior. 'We all have. If Carrington knew about you and your work, so did Littlemore. They've acted together.' The Prior had risen, stepping forward, his round glasses flashing light from the Garth. 'Innocent people seldom plan their escape. They rarely choose a false name. And if they do, they don't linger once their cover has been blown.'

Anselm hadn't followed the last trenchant observation because the Prior held back his explanation, not for effect but to bring all his concentration to bear on the one point that probably explained that look of dread:

'I told Mr Collins yesterday that you'd gone in search of someone called Father Littlemore.'

Anselm thought his head might explode. He struggled to remain attentive as the Prior explained how John Joe Collins had perspired and paled, his eyes flickering like a trapped animal.

'And this is the problem, really,' said the Prior, 'because he must have known that you'd meet the Brandwells. He knew there was a chance you'd speak to Harry. He knew that you would be compromised and that the community would be compromised. And yet, rather than escape while he had the chance, he's remained here, waiting. Perhaps he's paralysed with fear . . . but I'm worried it might be the behaviour of a man who's thought well ahead. He's anticipated this moment, Anselm, even if it's terrified him. He's ready for whatever might happen next. And we aren't.'

Anselm, grimacing with pain, hadn't noticed Wilf's arrival. Larkwood's Guestmaster had a light and timid step and he'd somehow walked the length of the West Walk without making a sound. Even now, he hung back, motionless like a shadow. When the Prior turned in his direction, Wilf coughed:

'I think you'd better come to the reception desk.'

'At this hour?'

'There's a couple of policemen. They've come with a search warrant intending to arrest someone, which is complete nonsense of course, but they insist. They're after someone called Edmund Littlemore and I've told them there's no one here who goes by that name. But they won't listen. They intend to search the place, starting with the guest house. There are some journalists, too . . . all the way from London.'

The Prior nodded slowly to himself and then his eyes rested on Anselm. All the dread had gone. 'Let's see what happens when propriety takes precedence over prudence,' he said.

18

On receiving the message – an incredible message – Anselm suffered a fresh wave of nausea. It was the culminating moment to a long day of unpleasant surprises.

The first arrived on the morning after Edmund Littlemore's arrest. The *Guardian* had run a front-page article about the monastery that had not only hidden a wanted man, but housed a monk who'd tried to silence the victim. 'A minor who can't be named for legal reasons' – as Harry Brandwell was now known – had been approached by 'the monk-detective Father Anselm, ostensibly as part of a search for the missing suspect'. Anselm couldn't read any further. And he didn't want to look either, because there were photographs . . . close-ups of a wanted man blinking by a fire.

Anselm dropped his head and closed his eyes. A journalist had come to Larkwood while he was in London. It was an unfortunate coincidence to say the least. But how had the writer, Robert Sambourne, known that Littlemore was at Larkwood? The only person who knew was Carrington. Did Carrington tell him? There was something strange at work here on any score, because there'd been no need to call the press: contacting the police alone would have sufficed. Involving the *Guardian* had simply elevated Littlemore's case in the public eye. Why had that been deemed necessary?

Anselm made himself read on.

The facts dealt with, Sambourne took a step back, casting his eye towards the United States, Europe, Australia . . . Anselm was horrified: the abuse crisis that had appalled him — a crisis that had always seemed a world away from everything he'd ever known himself — had come to his own door with him as an accomplice. Like someone thrown overboard, he reached out towards random details as if they were floating bits of wood: Harry had given an interview to the police the morning after his discussion with Anselm. And he'd accused *Edmund Littlemore* rather than his *grandfather* . . . which meant that Fraser had either been misled or he'd misunderstood what Harry had wanted to reveal. Or Harry had lied to the police . . . but then why had he been so concerned about telling the truth? Because he was under pressure from his grandfather to blame someone else? Anselm didn't have time to grasp the possible explanations because the second surprise arrived shortly afterwards in the form of a letter from Emily and Dominic Brandwell.

It was a heartfelt expression of gratitude, written just after Harry had given his interview to the police. From their perspective — not knowing that Edmund Littlemore had been living at Larkwood for six months — Anselm had been pivotal in helping Harry to finally open up. They didn't know what he'd said, but they were sure of its effect. He'd succeeded where everyone else had failed. Only (thought Anselm) they hadn't yet seen the *Guardian*. They were yet to revise their understanding of what Anselm had set out to do and what Harry had done as a consequence, in effect rebelling against his scandalous interference.

The third unpleasant moment was not, in fact, a surprise. It was a highly predictable encounter between himself and Bede. They met in the corridor between the calefactory and the kitchen. Bede had come looking for his man.

'You appreciate it is my duty to keep newspaper cuttings on matters that touch upon the life of this community?'

'I do.'

'For my liking you appear too frequently.'

Anselm nodded, wanting to step past the Archivist but like Martin Brandwell he'd blocked any escape.

'Ordinarily your antics are restricted to yourself but this time you've implicated others.' Bede stepped closer. 'We're taxed on how much we knew and why you travelled to London seeking Father Littlemore, who I thought was Mr Collins, when you knew all along he'd been housed within the enclosure.'

'I know, Bede.'

'It doesn't end there. I hold a central place in this tasteless drama. I swore your protégé wasn't here. A photograph on the front page of the *Guardian* shows him working in the orchard.'

'I didn't foresee this, Bede.'

'Foresight has nothing to do with it. As a matter of common decency, you should have told us all who he was and why he'd come to Larkwood. You should have told us what he'd done.'

'I didn't know.'

'But you found out?'

'Only later.'

'Then why on earth did you speak to the boy?'

There was no point in explaining how the mistake had come to pass. Bede was right. Anselm should never have walked into the garden. In fact, he should never have spoken to Martin or

Dominic or Emily. He should have called the police the moment he left Kester . . . only, if he'd done all that – placing prudence over propriety – he'd never have met Fraser; and Fraser had a very different story to tell, if only he could repeat what he'd been told. Bede had been glaring at Anselm and now, deprived of a satisfactory answer, he filled his lungs with rage:

'You've made a big mistake this time "blind pot-holer in the fissures of the human conscience" or whatever claptrap you use to describe your ventures beyond the enclosure. Have you even remotely considered that someone, one day, might just tunnel into your vanity? Do you imagine that blandishments in the press have left your inner life unscathed? What's left of it, after you went public?'

Anselm had never hit a monk before. But he was wondering whether a moment of rapture was upon him. His fingers formed a fist. Unperturbed, Bede angled his head to examine the white knuckles.

'Not a good idea "deep-sea diver in a puddle of moral confusion" – that's one of mine and you can use it as your epitaph because – thank God – you're finished. It's time to face the facts. You've been taken for a ride. The best thing you can do is stand up and take it on the chin. And then read Chapter Seven of the Rule. It's entitled *"De Humilitate"*.'

After Bede had stamped off, Anselm took a winding route to his hives, not daring to meet anyone else. The Brandwell family would all be rightly indignant. The press would all run with a story of mounting censure. Every member of the community already blamed him. Some would harbour strong feelings of resentment. Larkwood's name – its purpose and standing – had been contaminated. And yes, his career was over. Sitting on a weathered pew, distracted, he didn't react to the light touch against his neck until he felt the stab of the sting. He thought things couldn't possibly get worse.

But they did.

And it was this twist in events which gave Anselm that flush of nausea because when he returned to the monastery, summoned by the bell for Vespers, he found the Prior waiting for him in the cloister, standing at the very spot where, only yesterday, he'd outlined Edmund Littlemore's adept manoeuvring.

'The police have just called me,' he said. 'Littlemore won't say a word.'

Anselm was surprised. Silence was not a good defence.

'Apparently, he'll only speak to you.'

'Pardon?'

Like all monks of long experience, the Prior didn't like repeating himself. He showed slight irritation, made extraordinary by his serene forbearance of something rather more serious.

'You're the only man he trusts.'

19

After the telephone call came to its strange and sudden end, Robert held the receiver in the air for a while and then, smiling like a trapper at work, he placed it back on the cradle.

Watched by Taylor, whom he now ignored, Robert had called a certain Rev. Fr George P. Carrington MA (Cantab), Ph.D., Provincial of the Lambertine Order in England. Given Robert's article, Littlemore's superior had expected further press attention and he'd done some homework, trying to cut the interview short by reading a prepared statement. It had taken the usual and expected form – declining to 'discuss matters of substance on the grounds that criminal proceedings were pending and nothing should be said or done to prejudice their outcome'. Father Carrington had evidently been onto a lawyer to get the wording right. But Father Carrington (and his lawyer) hadn't anticipated the actual reason for Robert's call.

'I don't wish to discuss Father Littlemore's dealings with the boy who can't be named,' Robert said, after the Provincial had finished his spiel, quite sure that he'd shut the door to any further embarrassment.

'Then why have you called?'

'Because I'm interested in his dealings with a place that can: Sierra Leone.'

Robert waited and the silence yawned like some black hole sucking in the universe of the known and understood.

'I said Sierra Leone,' Robert repeated. 'West Africa.'

'I know where it is.'

'Just trying to help.'

There was another gaping silence, Robert feeling the Provincial's impulse to slam the phone down, to call the lawyer . . . only maybe that was a closed option, because he couldn't come clean with the lawyer any more than he could come clean with Robert.

'Does the Order have connections to the country?'

And the Rev. Fr George P. Carrington MA (Cantab), Ph.D. began a stammered history, trying to find his feet. Yes, the Order had strong connections with Sierra Leone. Parishes, mainly. And a school that closed in the seventies. St Lambert's Academy. 'The All People's Congress had become the sole legal party . . .' Father Carrington had tiptoed into generalities. Robert broke in:

'Has Father Littlemore worked abroad?'

'I said I couldn't talk about Father Littlemore.'

'No, you said you couldn't talk about Father Littlemore and any pending criminal proceedings. So we can talk . . . unless of course there are proceedings pending in Sierra Leone. Is that the case?'

Father Carrington stalled. 'Proceedings?' he repeated at long last. 'This is all highly speculative and—'

Robert punched harder in the same place: 'Has he ever been to Sierra Leone?'

'I don't understand why you're asking these questions.'

'It's a lot easier just to answer them.'

'I'm afraid I must—'

'Does Father Littlemore understand Krio?'

'I'm sorry?'

The voice dried out. But Father Carrington was also stunned; and being stunned he wasn't able to conceal his desire to know the worst . . . which was why Robert had asked such a precise question. Rather than drop the phone, he listened, no longer breathing.

'I'd like to know if Father Littlemore ever learned the Krio language,' Robert said, gentler this time, coaxing. 'If he did, then I imagine he learned it in situ. Am I right?'

There was no sound.

'Would he understand the odd phrase? A proverb, for example.'

Father Carrington had seemingly vanished . . . and Robert wondered if the line had been cut . . . but then he heard a distant passing siren.

'If you like, I can send you a list of questions,' Robert volunteered.

'That won't be necessary.' The voice was barely audible.

'I'll send them anyway. Do you have a fax number?'

'Fax?' And that was fainter still . . . followed by a soft click.

First thing that morning, Robert had studied once more the notes he'd made from the transcript of Littlemore's interview with the police: 'Birth: Islington, London. Emigration to the US aged two. After school: Ordained into archdiocese of Boston. Fell out with his superior. Came to UK. Joined Order of St Lambert. Sent first to Newcastle then Sierra Leone.' And it had been at this point, when pressed about his return to the UK, that Littlemore had run from the station. The US embassy had already confirmed Littlemore didn't have a criminal record and wasn't wanted for questioning by any police authority. Calls and emails to the archdiocese of Boston had been repeatedly rebuffed.

So Robert had called Carrington, having delayed the move until after the publication of his article. He'd wanted to know if the man in charge had been rattled. Satisfied with the outcome, he now rang the Sierra Leone High Commission. Two extensions and a long pause later, Mrs Sankoh confirmed that Edmund Littlemore was not wanted in relation to any potential criminal proceedings. She wouldn't reveal whether he'd been granted a visa, but she could help about St Lambert's Academy. It had been well known. Someone in the Public Information Unit was an old boy. When Mr Bangura came on the line he was eager to talk. Robert was ready with a pencil: 'Great place. Education and fun. Rigour and vigour. Loss to the country. Two members of the Cabinet went there. Minister of Energy. Minister of Tourism and Culture.' Robert chipped in, hoping to lure his source into admitting that Littlemore had, in fact, been granted a visa: 'Do you know of any mission stations? Somewhere Littlemore might have stayed or worked?' Mr Bangura didn't know but he'd find out and call back.

Flipping shut his pad, Robert checked his watch. It was almost time to vex another troubled soul. He'd invited his mother to a Japanese restaurant.

'I'm chasing down another story,' he said to Taylor, standing up. 'You'll be the first to know if I get anywhere.'

20

The interview room was bare save for a table and two metal chairs bolted to the floor. Anselm sat down, knitting his fingers. Facing him – pallid and drawn – was Edmund Littlemore. His hands were knitted, too. Anyone peering through the reinforced glass panel in the door would have thought the two men had begun with a prayer. Dismayed by the very idea – in these

circumstances and in this place, a Cambridge Police Station –
Anselm quickly folded his arms. Appearances matter, even to the
shamed.

'You've removed the beard,' he observed, managing to compress
all his indignation into a trivial detail.

'That was John Joe Collins.'

'So this is the real you?'

'Yes.'

'Shorn of pretensions?'

Anselm had interviewed many men accused of serious offences.
As a barrister he'd flicked through the court papers, abstracted
from the human cost of the contents, wondering how to build a
strong defence . . . sometimes with an eye on lunch. For the first
time, Anselm was linked to the accused, viscerally aware of what
they were both alleged to have done. On arriving, he'd been
humiliated by the incomprehension engraved upon the faces of
the desk sergeant and the officer in charge of the case, a hard-
looking guy who'd come all the way from London. Reluctantly
– and in clipped phrases – the officer had explained how things
stood; he'd told Anselm how long he could have. Anselm stared
at his would-be accomplice, at the white skin exposed by the
removal of the beard. Unmasked, Littlemore looked ill.

'You turned down the help of a solicitor?'

'I don't need one.'

'You've refused to answer all questions?'

'They asked all the wrong ones.'

'And now you've been charged?'

'It was inevitable.'

There were no windows. Beneath the harsh tube lighting,
Littlemore was barely recognisable, difficult to link with the very
different man who'd split wood wondering if the boomerang of
faith might come back. A distinct lack of emotion marked Anselm's
voice:

'You want to speak to me?'

'And no one else.'

Anselm had thought he knew John Joe Collins. He'd understood his struggle with doubt and the regret. And when he first realised that John Joe Collins was a Lambertine who'd gone missing, he understood the use of a false name and the running away, because people in a crisis often do strange things – foolish moves that can only make matters worse. He'd struggled to make sense of Edmund Littlemore's predicament never quite realising that it wasn't his job to understand anything; that he should have seen things – not for the first time – a little like Bede. He glanced at a bucket in the corner, wondering if crouching to be sick might break the flow of conversation.

'I'm not your confidant,' he said.

'I've nothing to confide.'

'I'm not going to be your confessor.'

'I've nothing to confess.'

Something in Anselm rebelled. He leaned forward, unleashing his disgust. 'I'm warning you, say anything about Harry Brandwell and I'll repeat it to the officer in the case and at trial if so required.'

'That's fine,' said Littlemore, with sudden violence, 'because you can tell them I said I was innocent. And I am.'

Suppressing his emotion, Littlemore set his jaw. He was ready to fight and, seeing that resolve, Anselm suffered a flicker of doubt. Could Harry have lied? Had Martin Brandwell pressured his grandson to blame someone else? After asking those two questions of himself, Edmund Littlemore suddenly looked vulnerable and frightened. His eyes were burning with the terror of a man who'd found himself locked up and questioned by people whose natural repugnance for what he was alleged to have done could not be concealed. Subject to the provisions of the Police and Criminal Evidence Act 1984 and the Codes of Practice (as amended), he'd been treated like a beast. In ancient and simpler jurisdictions, Edmund Littlemore would be dead by now, stoned or burned, depending on local mores.

'I can't help you, Edmund. It's too late for that.'

'No, it isn't. Now is the time.'

Anselm went quite rigid. 'Time for what?'

'The most important legal fight of your life.'

'What do you mean?'

'I need someone who looks beyond the evidence . . . someone who won't be tied down by the limitations of a trial.'

'I don't follow.'

'I want you to represent me in court.'

After a long pause Anselm laughed. 'You're not serious.'

'There's more to this case than you realise,' said Littlemore, whispering. 'There's more at stake. It reaches beyond Harry. He's the accidental key. Crimes have been hidden behind a wall of silence. Someone has to bring it down. That's why I came to you. You can do it through this trial. This is our one chance.'

'*Our* chance?'

Dunstan and the Prior had been right: Littlemore had planned everything from his arrival to this interview. He'd prepared every step. Carrington, his associate, came vividly to mind, the CEO without the backing of his board: *There are people occupying positions of considerable trust and influence who do not want this man to be found . . . Someone, however, must intervene, regardless of such misguided . . . sensitivities.*

But who were these 'people'? Whatever the answer Edmund Littlemore was the central figure in a baroque plot to out-manoeuvre them. And he, in turn, was looking to Anselm.

'If you fail,' said Littlemore, 'then it's not only Harry who'll suffer. There are many others. They are the Silent Ones. They live and die in their own private hell. You can take the first step that might help them find their voice. They've been lied to and cheated. Their goodwill has been exploited. They've said yes to a cover-up when they should have said no. You can do something to change all that.'

Anselm was no longer inclined to laugh: 'Edmund . . . have you lost your mind?'

'No. This is real. I wouldn't have come this far if I thought there was any other way. There isn't. Every ordinary avenue has been blocked. All that's open now is the extraordinary . . . which no one will expect.'

Littlemore was either mad or duplicitous beyond anything Anselm had ever encountered. But what if he was telling the truth? Anselm had to take him seriously, if only to understand what had happened between them: 'Why not approach me directly? All you had to do was pick up the phone.'

'Because you wouldn't have listened. You'd have refused to get involved. The only way to get your attention was to bring you into the problem.'

'Compromise me?'

'I'd say narrow your options. Now you have a choice.'

He was right about the refusal. Faced with a request in like terms six months ago, Anselm would have pointed at the door. Now his attention was rapt.

'Don't you wish you could do something to change the past . . . how we're seen?' asked Littlemore. 'Do something to make up for the abuse and the secrecy on our side of the fence? Claim back some . . . integrity? I know it's easier to turn the other way and thank God it's got nothing to do with you . . . but I've taken that option away. Now you have a chance to get involved and change things for the better.' Littlemore's eyes darted towards the glass panel. There were footsteps in the corridor. Voices. 'From now on I won't say another word, either to you or the court. I'm joining those who've been silenced and it'll put the trial on the front page . . . but only if you represent me. All you have to do is find out why Harry is prepared to blame an innocent man. That's the thread. Follow it. You'll reach the Silent Ones. This is your way – our way – of making a difference.'

Edmund Littlemore stopped talking. The silence in the room was like a kind of darkness and Anselm was left groping for meaning and direction. Just then the interview door opened. An officer leaned inside:

'Time's up.'

In a stupor Anselm rose. On reaching the corridor he turned. 'I can't do what you ask,' he managed. 'It's simply not possible.'

But Littlemore didn't even move. He was like a statue on a grave.

A second officer pointed down the corridor: 'This way, please.'

Once outside, Anselm felt a sudden chill. His brow was wet with anxiety. He walked aimlessly, rehearsing what he'd just been told, not daring to believe it, not daring to disbelieve it. Reaching a junction, he stopped as if he'd struck a lamppost.

He'd forgotten to ask Littlemore why he left Boston.

And he'd forgotten to ask about Sierra Leone.

21

The Scriptorium was cool. A shaft of sunlight fell upon Anselm, joining him to Dunstan's tidy desk. The Prior, head down and seated by the panelled wall, seemed more of an observer than a participant. Having listened to Anselm's report, he'd consulted Dunstan alone. Having listened to Dunstan, he'd convened another conference and this one promised to be as unhelpful as the first.

'Do you believe him?' asked Dunstan, one bony finger resting on the space bar of the typewriter.

'It doesn't matter what I believe.'

Anselm had taken refuge in one certainty: he'd left the Bar; he wouldn't be going back into court. The only practical issue was the restoration of Larkwood's name. A public statement was required to explain how the community had made an error of judgement. He'd prepared a draft text and brought it with him.

'I didn't trust him from the moment I set eyes on him,' said Dunstan, gracelessly. Proved right so far, he wasn't inclined to be magnanimous. He'd chosen a cherry-red cravat for the confrontation. 'It takes years of practice and experience.'

'What does?'

'Seeing through people.'

Anselm sighed. Dunstan seemed to reach for the Angostura bitters:

'I shared an office with Blunt, you know.'

This was a new one. 'Really?'

'Yes. Always knew he was bent.'

The sun had shifted onto Dunstan himself and his glasses had turned almost black. He cut a sad figure. Denied preferment in the post-war Service, he'd gone back to Cambridge to teach Middle English, tapping out monographs on the mysticism of Margery Kempe. While contemporaries – and competitors – were elected as Fellows, appointed Readers and awarded Chairs, Dunstan had remained on the lower rungs of the academic ladder. He'd discovered Larkwood – a cynic might say conveniently – at roughly the hour when the ladder itself had been taken away: enforced retirement had been the door to a late and uneasy vocation. The community had paid dearly for his dashed expectations.

'Cultured man, Blunt,' he went on, pressing the space bar. 'But he helped Stalin. *Les extrêmes se touchent*, I suppose. They covered up the mess until seventy-nine. I'm told the King knew back in forty-eight.'

Anselm sighed again. Dunstan was half smiling.

'You have been seduced,' he said, after another oily thud. 'You've been lured into wondering whether you're the only man alive who can solve this case. He's dangled a subject of immense importance before your eyes, daring you to turn away. You're forgetting this *Arschloch* was shifted around because he's always been a problem. Carrington buried his head in the sand and now it's time to face the consequences.'

Anselm opened the press release and then closed it again.

'Forget the Silent Ones,' advised Dunstan. 'They don't exist. Littlemore's played you like a fiddle. He set out to exploit a weakness.'

'Which is?' asked Anselm.

'A readiness to trust . . . to the point of being—'

'Credulous?' supplied Anselm.

Dunstan savoured the word as if Anselm had fed him medicine with a spoon. Which wasn't entirely surprising. When Anselm had canvassed the possibility with a journalist that goodness could survive beneath any heap of moral wreckage, he'd been called naive. Dunstan had lapped up the entire paragraph.

'Look,' said Dunstan, trying to be patient, 'if Harry Brandwell is just one among many . . . why hasn't Littlemore said that to the police? Why hasn't Carrington?'

Anselm had asked himself the same question. 'Because they either can't prove it or they're trapped in some way, unable to reveal what they know – like Fraser. Which explains why they came to me.'

'All right then, Harry is one among many. Why didn't he say so? He's told the police everything else.'

'Maybe he doesn't know.'

'Why blame Littlemore?'

'To protect someone he daren't accuse.'

Dunstan groaned. 'It's that bang to the head. You're not thinking clearly. Let's take things slowly from the beginning. Littlemore runs from the police. He tells Carrington why. They're both in serious trouble: Littlemore for what he's done, Carrington for what he's failed to do. How do they avoid the fallout?' Dunstan waited, allowing Anselm to focus his mind. 'This plan is the answer. They've turned to the monk who believes in Man. Littlemore told you a story that no one else would believe.'

'But why me?'

'He's chasing a rogue verdict.'

'How?'

'The allure of reputation, dear boy. He seeks to exploit yours.'

'*Reputation?*' Anselm shook his head. 'I'm the corrupt lawyer who tried to silence the defendant's victim. Who'd believe anything I say?'

'You remain the man who's solved cases the courts had left behind. You have a reputation for finding justice in dark places.' Dunstan's glasses glinted as he shifted forward. 'If *you* stand up for Littlemore, there's a chance the *jury* will listen.'

'I doubt it.'

'They might be prepared to look past the evidence.'

'Unlikely.'

'How about trust a trustworthy man? It's happened before.'

'When?'

'Have you forgotten already? When you argued that a vagrant from Boston should be offered a home at Larkwood.'

Dunstan almost smirked, knowing he'd timed the rejoinder perfectly. He looked away, drawing Anselm's irritation to the surface.

'Maybe I am naive but in this instance it doesn't matter. I'm not going back into court. The only outstanding question is our role in the mess to date. I've prepared a statement for the press.'

Anselm held it out towards Dunstan and the Prior but neither of them reacted.

'What's going on?' asked Anselm, uneasily. 'Am I missing something?'

The Prior, until now motionless, nodded gravely.

'You're missing the obvious,' he said, helpfully. 'Just because you've left the Bar doesn't mean you *can't* go back into court. The only question is whether you *ought* to . . . in these particular circumstances.' He let his words crackle between them like burning furniture. 'You can't hide behind monastic conventions or social expectations, though in the present case, I rather wish you could. Larkwood's rules of enclosure protect a way of life but you have a role beyond the enclosure . . . beyond the protection of rules. We made that decision a long time ago. You can't come running home when you find yourself in a dangerous place.'

Anselm fidgeted with his press release. It had been well crafted. It was terse. 'Aren't you going to call Carrington?'

'What will he say to me that Littlemore hasn't said to you?'

'I have to take this request seriously?'

'We all have to. But you're the one who has to make a decision. I can only point from the sidelines.'

'Then point, because I don't know what to do.'

The Prior went to the window as if to get his bearings from the sky. 'If you think that Dunstan is right, then you should withdraw at once. Littlemore and Carrington can find someone else to trick and cheat. On the other hand, if you think Littlemore has told you the truth, then you'll need a good reason to walk away from what has already happened.'

Anselm recalled Clapham Common and how he'd longed to stay there, disengaged from the messiness of decisions, the world going round and round. When he'd tried to step off it he got knocked out. He said to the Prior: 'If I get it wrong, then we'll never recover as a community.'

'No, we won't.'

'Neither will you,' said Dunstan.

The Prior was squinting at the sun. 'Take three days. I'll be waiting between the two pillars after Vespers.'

22

The Geisha Garden was tucked away down a side street off Shaftesbury Avenue. There were orange lanterns above each table. Bamboo screens created intimate compartments. A long ink painting of cypress trees with herons in flight covered one wall.

Calligraphy on silk banners fluttered as the waitress swept silently over the matted floor. She was dressed in a black kimono.

'The obi is tied in the taiko style,' she replied, answering Robert and pointing to the drum of material tied on her back. 'To me it's just a fancy knot, like.'

'Where are you from?' Robert had to ask.

'Manchester.'

It was perfect. The geisha was a Lancashire lass. She looked like one thing but she was another. She was appropriately complex. Like Robert's mother. Robert had been rehearsing the sight of her in Taylor's arms; he'd been picking over their plan to bring Taylor closer to Robert, and, finally, he'd come to accept what had been obvious from the moment he peered from behind that white van: he'd lived a substantial part of his life among false appearances. And with that surrender, a strange insecurity had entered his bloodstream. Nothing was what it seemed. Even simple remembrances were under question, if only to reinstate them. There was anger, too, but not because of any betrayal or breach of trust – that just made him sad and confused – but because of the swiftness to celebrate, coupled to the idea that Taylor or anyone else might seek intimacy by stealth, exploiting Robert's vulnerability in the aftermath of his father's death. The move wasn't simply crass; it failed to take his grief seriously. It reduced his dad's passing to an opportunity.

'I never knew you were interested in things Japanese,' said Robert's mother, smiling woodenly as she sat down. 'You're full of surprises.'

He had been philosophising between the Tube station and the restaurant – how food eaten in its most natural state wasn't just a style of cuisine but an approach to life. No strong spices. No complex sauces. In a way it was simply honest.

'And honesty is important, don't you think?'

'Of course I do, Robert. But you won't stop me eating Indian.'

'Or Italian?'

'No . . . of course not.'

Robert's dad's favourite meal had been lamb chops scottadito. 'Burned fingers'. You ate them with your hands just after they came sizzling out of the pan. Robert sighed, remembering his dad licking his wounds. 'I don't think he'd go for raw fish. What about you?'

'I don't know, darling. Like I said, I've never tried.'

'Have you really *never* been inside a Japanese restaurant?'

'Never.'

'What, never?'

Robert's mother smiled, again woodenly, but there was pain there now. 'Hardly ever.'

Robert's dad had loved that 'What, never? No, never! What, never? Well, hardly ever!' routine from *H.M.S. Pinafore*. He'd adopted it as a trademark question. The formula of reply and counter-reply had driven Robert round the bend, not least because his dad's Australian accent had been utterly incongruous. Robert had stopped using the word *never* just to escape his dad's maddening rejoinder. Now he wanted to murmur *never* again and again, if only it would bring back that sing-song voice from Down Under, with its appeal for a shared understanding.

'I thought you'd have given sushi a try by now,' he said, anger rising at the lie. 'It's pretty commonplace. What about Muriel? Has she taken the plunge?'

'I don't know, Robert, you'd have to ask her yourself. She's always had a preference for vegetables.'

'Yes. Dad's.'

'That's right.'

'From the allotment.'

Janet Sambourne was one of those envied women who looked forever young. At quite an early age, her hair had turned white which – to quote Muriel – had given her the sophistication of middle age without the spread. She'd kept it short, cut fashionably. Black eyeliner gave a striking contrast. Even now in her sixties she was – to quote Muriel – a dish. The only thing that gave her away was her hands, the blue knotted veins. She had old hands.

Robert said, 'Japan is another world. Out there, the big thing is seaweed. Kids take it to school instead of a packet of crisps, can you imagine that?'

'No.'

Robert's dad – on the other hand – had seemed so much older than his years. There'd been deep lines on his face and – in a way that had touched Robert, even as a child – he'd always looked worried. He'd been anxious to please. Careful not to offend. Whether in a shop or a queue he'd been ready to bend to someone else's convenience.

'That's why there's hardly any heart disease,' said Robert.

'Really?'

'So they say. We should have changed Dad's diet years ago. Fed him kelp.'

If there was a single insight that wounded Robert the most, it was this: the appearance of Taylor was not really all that surprising. Relations between his parents had always been subtly strained. If his dad had been quietly worried, his mother had been quietly crisp. Somehow or other, Robert had sensed that his dad hadn't quite lived up to expectations. Perhaps he'd aged too soon. He'd always been retiring and he'd finally retired to his allotment rather than . . . what? Go back to the Wimbledon Light Opera Society where they met? Go back to happier days? The days when the two exiles in the chorus found common ground admiring Crofty and Muriel? The stage lights had faded long before Robert was born. When he'd pored over the old programmes asking questions, it was the wistful principals who churned out the stories. His parents listened as if they hadn't been there.

'Kelp?' said Robert's mother. 'He'd have used it for compost.'

'He'd have wanted to, that's for sure. He loved that heap. What do you do with the peelings now?'

'I throw them out . . . I'm sorry.'

Throughout Robert's youth, his parents had rarely done anything together. In retrospect, it had all been planned very skilfully, so that Robert wouldn't quite notice, but there are some things that can't be completely hidden. By running parallel lives, Robert had become the grass verge in-between. He'd had to look in different directions to find them; he'd felt their separation without teasing out the implications. On a sudden wave of anguish, Robert recognised that his dad had loved hopelessly. He'd always been looking at his wife when her back was turned; he'd tracked her movements, even as she left the room to answer the telephone; somehow – between a performance of *The Sorcerer* and the birth of a late son – he'd lost his wife, living like a man who'd mislaid the key to his own front door. He'd been an outsider, waiting for handouts of affection. He kept up the show, wanting to give Robert the happy home that had never been all that happy. And now he was dead.

'I suppose the allotment will have to be handed back to the—'

'Robert, there's something I have to tell you. We have to talk.'

'About?'

'Me. My future. About what happens next.'

'Fire away. I'm all ears.'

'There's no easy way to say this.' Old fingers fiddled with a pearl necklace.

'Just be honest.'

'I'm always honest.'

'Spit it out then.' Robert's impatience flashed from his mouth like a spark, surprising himself and burning his mother.

'Don't make things difficult, will you? I want to move on . . . but I need your help . . . your permission.'

'Permission?' Robert pondered the word. It wasn't one of his mother's. She must have got it from some self-help book . . . or maybe Taylor. Quite apart from managing the disclosure of a secret relationship, she had to legitimise her association with a man nearly twenty years younger. Robert didn't know which was the stronger reaction, dismay or embarrassment.

'I know you're going to be upset and I don't want that,' she said, reaching over to touch her son's hand. 'But you've guessed, haven't you? You don't want me to sell the house?'

As their skin touched, an unbearable insight came to Robert like a splash of ink on a white shirt. His dad, spring-cleaned out of his own home, had known about Taylor. There'd been no secret between husband and wife. Robert's dad had accepted the existence of this other, younger man. He'd looked the other way.

'It's a big house and I want something smaller,' continued his mother, pleading for understanding. 'I'm not as young as I was, and I need a place I can manage.'

Robert opened the menu as if the subject was closed. 'It's your house. You can do what you like.'

'It's not as simple as that.'

'Really?' Robert raised his eyes in a challenge. He hated himself. He was enjoying this. Grief without an outlet was turning bitter and he liked the taste. It was simple and clean.

'The decision affects you, Robert.'

'Does it? How?'

'Your things,' said his mother as if she was peering through smoke. 'You've left lots of things in your old room. They'll have to go.'

Robert's eyes flickered. He hadn't quite seen what his mother was getting at, but now he did. His dad's death had been such an immense event that Robert hadn't seen beyond the empty bedroom in Raynes Park. With the sale of the house, his own past would be sold off. His memories would be handled by the Halifax. He'd never see his dad's workshop at the end of the garden. He'd never smell the wood or handle the tools. He'd never feel the rush of a train as it shook the timber walls, scaring a boy into those strong, tweedy arms. There were so many 'nevers'. What, never?

'I'm thinking of your boat, for example,' she said, opening her own menu. She looked totally lost. Her idea of daring was vegetarian. 'Do you still want it?'

Robert seemed to feel that thumb on his throat. He couldn't swallow without pain. The geisha from Manchester had fluttered across the matting, alighting by their table.

'I want everything,' said Robert, loosening his collar. 'Including the boat.'

He meant especially the boat.

'There's no rush, darling,' said his mother. 'I didn't mean to upset you . . . the end of the month will do.'

'Is that all you wanted to say?' he asked, longing for her to turn round from the dishwasher or the ironing board or the cooker; to turn round and face him simply and without that crucifying hesitation. In a flash of despair he wanted to salvage something from this sinking relationship. 'Is this the only permission you need?'

'Yes. What else could there be?'

The geisha turned to Robert, sensing his authority. 'Shall I come back later?'

23

Anselm went for long walks in the woods. He ambled through fields. He sat by the Lark. He thought deeply about Bede's assessment that he was vain and Dunstan's that he was naive. But try as he might, he couldn't accept that either characteristic was at play in the present circumstances. On a level deeper than any flaw, he'd been roused by Littlemore's appeal to help make up for the history of abuse and silence. But he feared making a catastrophic mistake. And so Anselm couldn't decide what to do. He was paralysed. On the evening of the third day he returned to Larkwood unable to channel the mounting desperation. He tried to slip past Sylvester but the old man hollered:

'You're late, you goose.' He was pointing at the parlour. 'They've been waiting half an hour.'

Puzzled, Anselm opened the door and there, seated at the table, was Kester Newman, his expression as reproving as it was cold. But the person who seized Anselm's attention was an elderly man dressed in tired black trousers and a white Aran jumper, the sleeves hanging loose after years of wear. His round cheeks were covered in pure white stubble. By his side was an oxygen bottle with a mask sitting on the valves.

'I'm sorry not to have called first,' he wheezed, rising with some difficulty, 'but I have to speak to you. I have to know the truth.'

Dominic Tabley had been a Lambertine for the greater part of his life. His golden jubilee was coming up. At eighty-three he thought his quiet retirement would continue without much worry. How wrong he'd been. The greatest crisis of his life had unfolded and all he could do was watch from an armchair in horror. He was stooped, like a man folding up his tent. His arms were tired and his handshake had been weak. From a lowered and shining head, troubled eyes sought Anselm's understanding.

'I must ask you directly and I'll take you at your word,' he said. 'Did you hide Edmund?'

'No.'

'Did you try and stop Harry talking?'

'No.'

Anselm gave a brief explanation while the old man, trusting absolutely, looked at Kester as if to say, 'I told you so.' Turning back to Anselm, he said, pulling for air: 'I married the Littlemores and baptised Edmund. I know him as a man and he would never harm a child. But I've married and baptised three generations of

114

the Brandwell family and I've known Harry since he was born
and I can't believe he'd ever lie . . . so I don't know what to
think. One of them has done something terribly wrong. That's
why I've come to you. I have to know, you have to tell me . . .
did Edmund do this thing? He must have spoken to you while
he was here.'

'He tells me he is innocent,' said Anselm.

'Did you believe him?'

'I don't know what to believe.'

The old man's voice trembled. 'Why will no one trust Edmund?
Why am I alone?'

Father Tabley had hoped to find an ally. He'd made a mad
dash into the countryside, twisting the arm of a novice to do
the driving because no one else would listen. There'd been no
point. Resigned, he said to Kester what he'd been saying since
Littlemore's arrest. 'I can't accept he's guilty. But I don't know
why Harry would make such an accusation.' He leaned his elbow
on the table, his hand on his brow as if to shield himself from
the sun. 'I never thought I'd live to see this day.'

Anselm left the parlour to make coffee. While in a side-room,
waiting for the kettle to boil, he realised that a visit from someone
who knew both the accused and his alleged victim was fortuitous
to say the least. On returning to the parlour, he seized his
opportunity:

'I have to make an important decision that will affect both
Edmund and Harry,' he said, while pouring. 'I need your help
. . . yours more than anyone else's.'

Father Tabley was nodding with the artless surrender of a boy.
Kester had taken a seat by the wall as if to watch from afar . . .
just as, in another life, he'd watched fools try to hide the numbers.

Anselm went straight to the point: 'Why did Edmund leave
Boston?'

'Hasn't he told you? Can't you guess?' Father Tabley's breathing
was painful to watch. His whole upper body was involved in the

operation, one bony arm locked against the edge of the table. 'He left because of the crisis . . . I would have thought that was obvious.'

The old man explained, telling Anselm what Littlemore had kept to himself. In part, he was already familiar with the context. Edmund was ordained in 2002 just before the child abuse scandal erupted in the archdiocese of Boston. A number of priests were brought to trial. People he'd met, if hardly known. The crimes were inconceivable. But they were real. Children had been exposed repeatedly to known offenders who'd been moved around like pieces on a chessboard. Secrecy had taken precedence over transparency . . . and justice and compassion. But once the secret was out, others found their voice. The problem hadn't been local; and it hadn't been national . . . it had been international. There'd been some lone voices, but it had taken the press and the courts to flush out the poison.

'The whole God-awful business had been covered up,' said Father Tabley, hoarsely. Small wonder then, that Edmund lost confidence in the leadership . . . and colleagues who'd known and said nothing. The decisions made without his knowledge. Friends who admitted afterwards they'd heard rumours. He'd felt like a party to the crime. He'd been ashamed to walk down the street . . . seeing himself as others might see him.

'He wanted to escape . . . get away from the shame about things he hadn't done. He wanted a new start. So he wrote to me.'

Father Tabley paused to catch his breath. Talking was an uphill affair. He waved at Anselm from the incline, telling him not to worry. He managed a troubled wink. Stopping and starting he moved on again, talking of Edmund's mother, a commercial lawyer with an American firm based in London. Skyler had married Jonathon, her manager, and Father Tabley had been a regular in their Islington home, going so far as to warm a bottle when both of them were on the phone dealing with international clients who – sadly – had to be more important than the family; than their son.

'They wanted to cut back on their work, but it's almost impossible in a big firm like that,' said Father Tabley, wondering if Anselm had known the same pressures. 'The partners want your soul. In return, Edmund got three nannies in eighteen months and his parents got a divorce. Which is sad, don't you think?'

Father Tabley did his best to help and he'd have done more, in time, but then Skyler went home to Boston, taking Edmund with her. Fairly shortly afterwards she remarried. An ad man. John Joe Collins. Second-generation Irish. Hadn't taken to the boy who'd found rebel songs vaguely embarrassing.

'I kept in touch with Skyler through letters and calls. We managed to stay friends, and I watched Edmund grow . . . from afar.' He became wistful. 'I'm afraid I never took to the accent . . . it really is something else.'

And so, the absence of *Rs* notwithstanding, it was to Father Tabley that Edmund had turned when he found himself adrift. He called all choked up, wondering what he might do in a situation where nothing could be done.

'I spoke to Owen Murphy, the Provincial, and he agreed to open our doors. We kept the reason quiet to smooth Edmund's way. The last thing he wanted was to be quizzed about his past. To be asked if he'd known anything. He began a probationary year in Newcastle and that was that . . . So you see' – Father Tabley heaved more air – 'Edmund could never have touched Harry. It wouldn't make sense . . . would it?'

Anselm agreed. 'But why did he come back from Sierra Leone?'

'The real question is why send him there at all?' snapped the old man, with a rasp of protest. 'I have to tell you . . . George Carrington is a very different man to Owen Murphy. Owen was old school, flexible, trusting . . . a man who believed in giving someone a second chance. But not George. No . . . I'm afraid George belongs to the new breed . . . the sort who want subcommittees for this and subcommittees for that. George was elected after Owen died, and the first thing he did was to write a mission statement. A *mission statement*. Frightful thing.' Father Tabley reached for his coffee and sipped it using two hands, the sleeves of his Aran jumper falling down to his elbows. He was thoughtful, frowning to himself. 'George doesn't always see the human situation . . . that's why he wants guidelines to tell him what to do. Manuals of Best Practice.'

And of course, guidelines can't cover everything, and there was no manual to deal with Edmund's situation. So George was left with his gut reaction, and, lacking Owen Murphy's compassion, he just didn't like the fact Edmund had been given a fresh start. As far as George was concerned Edmund should have stayed in Boston. Should never have been allowed to walk away from a crisis. He considered that ignoble.

'George's father was in the Paras,' said Father Tabley, as if to explain an obscure moral code. 'Last man down stuff. Third Battalion. Never got over the withdrawal from Suez. That's George's background. So even on first meeting he was unsympathetic to Edmund . . . and as a kind of rebuff, to show him he couldn't just choose his fights, he sent him to West Africa. Gave him a Peace Corps language manual and told him to learn Krio. He'd only been in England six months.'

'But why did he come back? I understand that things didn't go smoothly.'

'Well, of course they didn't,' exclaimed the old man, huskily. 'Edmund had never wanted to go out there in the first place, never mind teach himself a new language. Small wonder he didn't settle down. It had been a *pointed* decision . . . a swipe at Owen Murphy's way of doing things, and a swipe at me, too, because I'd been very close to Owen . . . we'd been students together . . . we'd seen the world change, seen it become a complicated place.'

'And you'd vouched for Edmund,' said Anselm in the melancholic hiatus.

'Yes, I'd do it again.'

Anselm and Father Tabley appraised each other with shared understanding. They'd both paid the price for backing a new beginning.

'Have I helped?' asked Father Tabley, uncertainly.

'Yes.'

Anselm rose and went to the window, as if to watch a mysterious stranger walk quickly away. Carrington had come to Larkwood with the express intention of sending Anselm down a path that would lead to this crisis — perhaps not this meeting, but certainly the request to represent Littlemore. But what was Carrington up to? The hapless man described by Kester was not the bureaucrat described by Father Tabley. And neither of those men compared with the visitor who'd asked for Anselm's help, who'd assured him that Edmund Littlemore had done nothing wrong. Far from being a vexed administrator, he'd been poised and absolutely sure of himself. In turning to Anselm, Carrington had breached every guideline imaginable. And that only made sense if he backed Littlemore's story.

'I'm going to represent Edmund at trial,' said Anselm turning round.

'You?' Kester was accusing. 'But why?'

Anselm couldn't give all the reasons, so he gave the only one that might cause pause for thought: 'Because I've been given the name of someone who might have attacked Harry Brandwell. And it isn't Edmund Littlemore.'

'Who is it?' asked Father Tabley, both hands on the edge of the table.

'I can't say. And the person who told me can't say either.'

'How unfortunate,' muttered Kester.

'That's why they turned to me,' said Anselm, 'as I have turned to you. Because until now, I didn't know what to do.'

'But you have no choice,' exclaimed Father Tabley, a surge of emotion congesting his lungs. 'You must help Edmund . . . and Harry, too. He's been forced to lie . . .'

Father Tabley could no longer speak. He reached for his oxygen mask and Kester came swiftly to his side, helping adjust the strap while Anselm turned on the air. There was a soft hiss and then the old man closed his eyes like a babe in arms.

Anselm walked with his guests to what he thought was their car but turned out to be Father Tabley's classic Triumph motorbike and Watsonian sidecar . . . a wonder in waxed navy blue and polished chrome. He'd used it to weave around the backstreets of Newcastle making house visits. Now, like him, it was a relic, wheeled out to make an impression at a festival. When he'd been safely strapped into his seat, the bottle of oxygen between his legs, Kester closed the canopy and drew Anselm aside, speaking quietly and with purpose:

'He's a good man who refuses to believe anything bad about Skyler Littlemore's neglected child. But he's been fooled, just like you.'

'I'm prepared to take the same risk, that's all,' replied Anselm.

'He's a saint, what's your excuse?' Anselm didn't have one. Kester went on: 'He believes everything you tell him, especially if you cry. He's never questioned Littlemore's story. He's incapable. But you're not.'

Anselm looked at the old man, smiling through the windscreen. His trip hadn't been in vain after all. He was nodding like Aged P in *Great Expectations*, deaf to Kester's warnings, his mind on a toasted sausage when he got back to the warmth of his castle.

'He's picked you because no other lawyer would accept a client who refused to speak,' said Kester, almost despairing. 'By refusing to speak, you can't question him and he doesn't have to explain himself. If he still prays, he'll be on his knees begging the God of surprises that you'll take his case. Don't give him a reason to think that God is on his side.'

Anselm wanted to explain that Harry Brandwell's case might be the tip of something far greater but Kester – like Dunstan – would have found the idea not simply incredible but confirmation that Littlemore was pandering to Anselm's vanity. Instead, Anselm made a plea:

'You once came running after me because you trusted me to do the right thing. Trust me now.' He stepped closer. 'I may need help at some point. Secret help. Can I call on you?'

'That really depends.'

'If I do, it's because I've no other option.'

Even before Anselm had written down the mobile number, Kester was astraddle the Triumph, adjusting his helmet. The engine fired and gravel churned, Father Tabley nodding and waving from his bubble of blissful ignorance.

24

Anselm followed the Prior outside. It was a balmy evening made delicious because it belonged to a time that would shortly be seen as carefree.

'I've spoken to every member of the community,' said the Prior. 'Not many will grant you their support.' He took a narrow path that skirted the Old Abbey ruin, remnants of a fourteenth-century Benedictine foundation that had been harvested for stone during the Reformation. As if paralysed by a vision of splendour the bemused masons had left the arched windows untouched. They were covered in ivy now, with creeper swaying where coloured glass had once captured the sun. When the two monks came to a bench, the Prior sat down. 'You'll be denounced – along with the community – but you mustn't waver. See this through. You have my confidence.' And then, after a pause: 'There's something you ought to know. Dunstan has cancer. They've given him a couple of years.'

'God, no. Whereabouts?'

'Generalised. There's nothing to be done.'

'When did he find out?'

'Late last year. He said he couldn't care less, but he's not been the same since. He might be old but he's not ready to die. It's not easy for him. He's reviewing his life and he doesn't like much of what he sees.'

No one else in the community had been told. This was Dunstan's wish. He didn't want any special treatment or pity: he preferred the honesty of being tolerated from a distance.

'I'm only telling you because it helps explain why he's taken this Littlemore case so personally. Littlemore arrived shortly after the diagnosis. And now he's latched onto him and all he thinks he represents.'

'The betrayal of trust?'

'Yes.'

'Why should that bother him so much?'

'I don't know, but I've never seen him so disturbed.'

After the vote had been taken in Chapter to offer John Joe Collins a job, Dunstan had taken the Prior to one side, warning him that a mistake had been made, asking if he could be involved in any future deliberations. The Prior had agreed. Strange, really, that he'd been right to question the homeless man's intentions. At the time, he'd had nothing to go on, just instinct and ill will.

'Dunstan will never forgive me,' said Anselm.

'I wouldn't be too sure.'

'What do you mean?'

Anselm had never got to know Dunstan. Tolerance had nothing to do with it: he'd disliked him, simply and cleanly, viewing his natural death with an element of quiet anticipation. It was ugly but it was true.

'Dunstan *wants* you to conduct this trial,' said the Prior. 'He didn't say so, of course, but I know him well enough to recognise when he's performing.'

'You're not serious. He wants me to go into court and lose, just so he can say he got it right?'

'So it seems.'

'God, he's twisted.'

'No, there's something else at work; something very human.'

'Which is?'

'The awful longing of a disappointed man to make a difference somewhere in the world before he dies. It's a powerful urge, but it can be blinding.'

Though not always, the Prior seemed to add. The possibility swelled the silence that ensued between them. When it became taut, Anselm began to speak quietly, repeating the speech he'd made ad nauseam to an imaginary audience who simply couldn't understand his decision.

'Maybe Dunstan is right. Maybe Littlemore and Carrington have come up with a plan to pull off an acquittal . . . but having met Father Tabley I don't believe that's what's happening here. Which means everything Littlemore said is true: they came to me because Harry Brandwell isn't the only victim. There are others who need to be found . . . and this trial is the only way to reach them. I can't risk failing them.'

'Anything else?' The Prior was numinous and knowing.

'I don't want to be like Dunstan, incapable of trust. Everything he said just pushed me away from who he's become, towards who I want to be, when I look back on my life. He's nudged me back into court.'

'Anything else?' The Prior had sensed something deeper still. 'Go to the end of your concerns.'

'I recognised what Littlemore described: the sense of guilt by association. It's irrational, but I feel it, too. Like that generation of Germans carrying the weight of atrocities they didn't know about and would never have committed or condoned. Like Littlemore, I wanted to turn away and pretend this awful business had nothing to do with me. But that's no longer possible, because I've met Harry Brandwell. But I've also met Edmund Littlemore and George Carrington, and they seem to have found a way of dealing with the shame they feel. So I'm grateful they came to me, grateful they gave me the chance to be involved, to help make up for the past, to be different . . . to be on the side of the Silent Ones. That's why I'm prepared to take the risk that Dunstan would never countenance . . . for the sake of Dunstan . . . and all the other fractious, difficult men I know who'd die rather than harm a child; all the good and inspiring men who feel they stand in the shadow of what others have done.'

The Prior reflected on Anselm's apologia, then he said, 'When you next look Harry Brandwell in the face, you'll have to call him a liar. That's the cutting edge of the risk. Are you ready to take it?'

'No. I hope to find another way. I left the Bar a long time ago. My methods will be different.'

Anselm didn't fully understand what he'd just said. All he knew was that an unconventional trial would require an unconventional approach. He'd have to improvise.

'Prepare a statement for the press, will you?' said the Prior. 'The sooner the news breaks the better. You don't want an uproar on the first day of the trial.'

Anselm nodded, realising that no form of words would work, that he'd be drafting the terms of his own condemnation. And he looked at the tall windows robbed of glass, thinking of Dunstan under sentence of death, an old man robbed of his self-esteem. He, too, stood condemned, only there was no chance of reprieve. His story had been told. Almost.

25

Within the space of a week every loose end came together: it was an embarrassment of riches. First Stuart Greene called, saying he'd traced the fax number; then Mr Bangura rang with details about Lambertine mission stations in Sierra Leone, making, in the process, an accidental disclosure; and then there was a lunchtime meeting with the news editor of the *Guardian* which began with the offer of a job before the waiter had even come back with the wine list. The last development was all the more significant because it meant Robert would be freed from having to see Andrew Taylor – at least for the time being. He wouldn't have to contain himself, saying thanks for the coffee.

To celebrate, his mother organised a dinner at Raynes Park, aiming to kill two birds with one stone, because she'd already found a buyer for the house. In at least two respects (she'd said, sadly, though thrilled for Robert) it was the end of an era. Robert thought the chain of surprises had come to an end, but then, to top it all, he received a letter that very morning, the day of the meal, from the monk at Larkwood Priory.

'Do you want to talk shop for the last time?' said Robert to Crofty when Muriel had cornered his mother in the kitchen. The feast was over. At Robert's insistence they'd had scottadito. 'Burned fingers'. Everyone had made quick intakes of air, dropping the meaty bones on their plates. No one escaped without a flick of the wrist. Everyone had burned their fingertips. Robert's dad had been there, watching. 'I've got a new angle on the Littlemore case,' explained Robert.

Crofty had wounded Robert deeply. It wasn't the offer of a job to Taylor as such or even the longstanding complicity. The cutting edge was the deceit that comes with any pretence. The dissembling. And Robert had viewed the man as if he was a second father. Hadn't even called him Uncle Alan. He'd been closer and more important than any nod towards attachment by blood. He'd confided in him, and received confidences in return. Knowing, then, that Crofty had kept silent on such an important matter – feigned ignorance, dodged questions, stalled with answers – Robert could only look at him if they talked business. He needed to suppress his disillusionment with the bonhomie of colleagues who didn't really care about each other; professionals whose shared concern was the story. And so Robert opened the French windows and ambled down the flagging that led to his dad's shed. Crofty followed with a bottle of limoncello and two glasses. A train careered along the lines hidden by trees. When the clatter was over, Robert said:

'The fax came from Carrington. He's the account holder.'They sat down on a couple of white plastic chairs, garden furniture to be thrown in with the sale. 'And if Taylor is right – that whoever sent the fax also wrote the letter – then that means Carrington persuaded Littlemore to go to Larkwood and six months later he tipped me off. He set up Littlemore to be caught . . . because Carrington knows he's guilty.'

Crofty filled their glasses, holding them in one hand. 'Which means that Littlemore must have made some sort of confession to his boss.'

'Yep. After he ran from that station.'

'But why admit anything?'

The question brought Robert to the new angle on the story: 'Because he had to explain why he wouldn't cooperate with the police. At the same time, he was silencing Carrington. I'm pretty sure he didn't make any old admission . . . he went to *confession*. That way Carrington couldn't repeat anything. You know, the Seal. It's absolute. So Littlemore told him what he'd done, knowing that afterwards his boss couldn't say a word that might lead the police to even suspect him. It's incredible . . .'

'And that explains how Carrington knew about you,' said Crofty, revolted by the full, sordid picture. 'Littlemore must have told him you were there, at the station . . . that you'd gone after him.'

'Yep. Thing is, he misread Carrington. Didn't imagine that he'd use me to expose him . . . that he wouldn't let him get away with a crime just because he'd been gagged and the victim was too scared to speak.'

Carrington had evidently come up with a plan and it had worked brilliantly. As Taylor had correctly guessed, by persuading Littlemore to hide in a monastery he'd undermined any later denial of guilt; at the same time he'd sent a sort of message to the boy: with Littlemore out of the way you're free to speak without fear . . . which is exactly what happened. Robert drained his glass and told Crofty about Mr Bangura at the Sierra Leone High Commission.

'He called with a list of places where Littlemore might have worked.'

Crofty frowned. 'I thought they refused to comment on whether he'd been granted a visa?'

'They did. But Bangura doesn't work in the visa section. He's Public Information. Gives answers for a living. And he slipped up. Told me that Littlemore's visa had been withdrawn while he was out there.'

'Withdrawn? Why?'

'A complaint was made.'

'Regarding?'

'He didn't know, but it was short of a specific offence. My guess is that it's got something to do with "a bad character can't be hidden for long". Thing is, they kicked him out of the country. This is the past he ran away from.'

Crofty nodded, unscrewing the bottle top. 'So he comes back to the UK?'

'Yep. And nine months later he attacks the kid.' Robert held out his glass. 'Carrington can't do anything about what he knows. So he sets him up to be convicted. To be honest, I misread him. I thought he was trying to protect Littlemore. I hadn't appreciated the difficulty of his position, how much he knew and how little he could do; that his hands were tied. But he found a way, with a little help from the *Guardian*.'

Crofty put the bottle on the ground and leaned back in his chair. 'Why you, though?'

'What do you mean?'

'Why write to you rather than the police? Why seek coverage in the press?'

It was a tantalising question. Robert didn't have an answer, and he didn't much care. Littlemore had been caught, and that was all that mattered. He raised his glass:

'To the reverend George Carrington and his honourable machinations.'

A train rattled by, drowning the clink of cheap crystal. When the quiet returned, Robert looked over to the kitchen. His mother and Muriel were talking earnestly. They'd been looking at a flat together. There'd been talk of curtains and a new bathroom. Where had the grief gone? Had there been any? Or just impatience? Crofty licked his thumb and forefinger and said, with a raised voice, 'Why involve Sister Wendy?'

This time Robert did have an answer. It had come that morning in the form of the letter from Father Anselm Duffy in relation to the pending trial of Edmund Littlemore. Robert's article in the *Guardian* had been fair in spirit – the monk wrote

– but wrong in substance as regards himself, but since it had been fair, he was entrusting him with the enclosed press release.

'He's going to represent him at trial,' said Robert.

Crofty seemed to chew something bitter knowing that he was compelled by good manners to swallow it afterwards. 'You're joking.'

'I'm not.'

'This is the Church protecting their own.' Crofty took a swig as if to wash his mouth out. 'He's not even bothered what things look like. Doesn't he realise that impressions count?'

Robert nearly sputtered his drink all over Crofty's face. Talk about 'out of the mouths of little children'. His hypocrisy was awe-inspiring. 'You're missing the point,' he said, mischievously. 'This is all part of Carrington's plan. He'll have told Littlemore to get the monk to represent him, told him that his reputation for being the hombre on the side of the widow and the orphan will get him off.'

'Will it?'

'Of course not. Carrington knows that Littlemore will have to explain himself. He'll have to make another kind of confession, because this Anselm was a lawyer. He won't take silence for an answer. You watch. There's going to be no trial. Littlemore will plead guilty and the boy will be spared giving evidence.'

Crofty stared into his glass. 'What the hell did Littlemore say to the monk that would make him stick his head on the block?' He reached for the bottle, the aftertaste still in his mouth. 'What if Littlemore won't plead?'

'He's stuffed either way. He's got no defence.'

Another train swept by. The windows rattled in the shed and, for a brief moment, Robert caught the smell of his dad . . . a manly aroma of skin and aftershave . . . spice and surf. He saw his dad's smooth, red cheeks, the whitening hair, those eyes like cups of blue water with flakes of broken glass at the bottom. He felt the brush of soft, worn tweed.

'This Carrington's got some imagination,' said Crofty, checking the label. 'And he's ruthless. To get Littlemore he's risked the good standing of the monk.'

Lenny Sambourne had gone down the line. It was as though Robert had been left behind. He felt stranded in the middle of nowhere. There was no going back to the world as it had once been. And even if he could go back, he wouldn't, because Andrew Taylor was there now. His gaze drifted across the darkness towards the kitchen window. Muriel was laughing, two burned fingers zipping shut her lips. They had a girly secret. Robert blinked and swallowed:

'Maybe the monk will find out he was cheated by those he trusted most.'

'And then what? What can he do except go down with the ship?'

'Nothing, I suppose.' Robert smashed his glass against the wall, making Crofty jump for cover. 'Let's go in. I fancy a sing-song.'

Robert fished out his dad's recording of *The Mikado*, Gilbert and Sullivan's comic take on a fad for things Japanese. When everyone's glasses had been filled, he went straight to the best track, urging all present to sing along. Robert was the only one smiling. Shortly, Donald Adams was making his celebrated, blood-curdling screech before swinging into the jaunty refrain:

> My object all sublime
> I shall achieve in time –
> To let the punishment fit the crime –
> The punishment fit the crime;
> And make each prisoner pent
> Unwillingly represent
> A source of innocent merriment!
> Of innocent merriment!

Robert sang a fraction too loud and he let his eyes rest a little too long on each of his captives. But everyone joined in, tipsy and mock-cheery . . . until Robert's mother began to cry. Only a short while ago the sight of her tears would have distressed him – coming, as they often did, by surprise from behind a shopping list – but not now. With knowledge came confusion. He'd discovered a new and toxic emotion, a mix of guilt and pleasure upon inflicting pain, a pain he felt, too; a binding pain that brought everyone together in a chorus of brute sincerity. Muriel turned off the music, nearly falling off her red high heels. Her eyes were alight with rage, something old, suppressed for God knows how long, but it was coming out now. She pulled Robert into the corridor by an earlobe, whispering.

'You don't know the half of it.'

'Of what?'

'What your mother's been through. Now give her a break. You've had your fun, though God knows why you're making her suffer. Your father would turn in his grave if he could see you now. You owe her everything and yet you treat her like some kind of criminal. He's dead, Robert. It's no one's fault.'

Robert felt like a boy who'd killed a sparrow. He could feel the warmth of departed life in his hands. Muriel stomped away, her ankles weak on their narrow stands:

'Let her turn the page, will you?'

Crofty waddled past, carrying a tray of tinkling glasses. His mother followed, going upstairs. When she came down again, she was carrying the one item of personal property that Robert had left behind when he'd come to collect his stuff: a large wooden ship, painted white.

'I can't look at it, Robert,' she said, her eyeliner smudged into black wounds. 'It makes me think of your father. And even if you have to remember to move on . . . I have to try and forget. Is that so bad? Can't I grieve in my own way?'

★

Robert went home, his arms around the boat. On the Northern Line a little boy stared in wonder at the rows of tiny windows, the yellow funnel in the middle with a black domed top, and the coloured bunting hung from bow to stern. He turned to his dad asking for one just like that, pointing excitedly, but his dad said you couldn't buy such things. They weren't for sale. Even at Harrods. On reaching Tooting Bec, Robert rose from his seat and knelt down, placing the ship in the boy's hands. The high seas were in his wide, unbelieving eyes.

'She's yours, Cap'n.'

And then – as if an alarm had sounded – Robert ran onto the platform, sliding through the corridor and leaping up the escalator. He fled just in case he changed his mind; just in case the father came after him wondering if the thing had been stolen from a museum. On reaching street level, Robert stumbled onto the pavement. His lungs were pumping air and sweat burned his eyes. That thumb was on his throat again, pressing hard. Tearing at his collar, Robert suddenly made a loud, guttural sob. And then he finally broke down, crying like he'd never cried before, crying like he'd never thought was possible, one hand reaching out to his dad who was gone and would never come back.

Part Four

Part Four

Harry and his granddad went for a stroll on Clapham Common. They walked in silence until they reached the bandstand. The orchestra hadn't turned up yet. All the chairs had been laid out for the audience. Harry felt there were thousands of eyes upon them. People secretly watching. Ever since his life had changed . . . or had it ended? . . . Harry felt people were looking at him: in the street, from cars. And now from behind trees. Everybody knew and everybody was whispering about what had happened. They watched Harry and his granddad sit down as if the performance was about to begin. Harry's granddad was nervous. There was a shake in his voice.

'You know what you have to do, don't you?'

Harry nodded. His hands were in his duffel-coat pockets and, being seated, he felt like he was in a straitjacket.

'You've got to stand by what you've said. You've got to be a strong boy. It won't be easy.'

Harry had been sick when Sanjay came round to say he'd arrested Father Eddie. He'd thought Father Eddie was in Spain . . . sunning himself; starting over. That's what Uncle Justin had said. Harry had thrown up right there in the sitting room.

'There's nothing to be frightened about,' said Harry's granddad, quietly. 'You've said it all on video. You won't need to say it again. Remember? Sanjay explained. All you have to do is answer the questions put by Littlemore's barrister. And what does he know? He wasn't there.'

Harry nodded again and sniffed. Father Eddie's barrister was the monk. According to Sanjay − who'd come round again to explain − it was unheard of, scandalous, awful. He couldn't imagine why the monk had agreed to go back into court. But Harry could and it terrified him. Because this was the monk who'd come to the house to find out what Harry knew — and Harry had told him nothing; but then the monk had spoken to Fraser. Harry had watched them through his binoculars.

'And if he wasn't there,' continued Harry's granddad, knitting his fingers to hide the tremble, 'what's there to be frightened about? He can't contradict you.'

But what had Fraser said to the monk? thought Harry. Could he have told him everything? That night — the day he'd seen them talking on this very spot — Harry had taken a cigarette and burned himself. He rolled the hot ash against the top of one hand. The skin had melted and he felt the pain like an awakening: for those few seconds he was intensely alive. When his mother saw the oval blisters the next morning she gaped, speechless and guilt-stricken, as if she'd provided the matches. Harry wanted to reach out to her; he wanted to curl up on her lap and feel her hand stroking his hair . . . like she'd done when he was a child, only he wasn't a child any more. Not after what had happened. He was trapped . . . hating Father Eddie for what he'd done, angry with Uncle Justin for what he hadn't done and frightened of his granddad for what he might yet do. How could he reach over that lot to clutch his parents? Wasn't there someone out there who could reach him? Someone who could find a way to the place where he'd been abandoned?

'I'm only trying to help,' said Harry's granddad. 'I just want to give you some confidence. All right?'

'Yes.'

Musicians had started to arrive, straggling towards the bandstand. They were dressed in rumpled black, carrying scuffed black cases of different sizes. The conductor was at the podium joking with a man heaving a tuba on wheels, a maestro trying to hide last-minute nerves. The people Harry had imagined to be watching him had started to emerge from behind the trees. Families were bagging chairs with hands and coats, wanting to be together. The tuning up began, strangely harmonious, a gust of sound soon to become a tune.

'Do you want to stay?' asked Harry's granddad, hopefully; wanting *to be normal again. But Harry didn't. The performance was over. This lot had missed the show.*

When they got back home Harry went to his bedroom. For the past few months, every time he shut the door he'd thought of the trial that would start next week: he'd found himself at the Old Bailey, waiting for the end of the world. Once, desolate and desperate, he'd reached up to God, wanting to claw him down into his horrible life, a life that was already over, begging him to change things back to what they'd been. But all he'd heard was Father Eddie's voice, coaxing and insistent: 'Ohlman de pan in yon wa-ala . . . It means everyone has his own troubles.'

Father Eddie included.

That had been the key, turned to win a boy's trust. Father Eddie had come down to Harry's level. They'd both got problems that no one else would understand . . . they'd stopped playing chess.

A faint knock came at the door. A timid tapping on the frame.

'Yes?'

Harry's mother came in, seeming to hug the wall. Her eyes were round and frightened, checking Harry's skin for fresh burns or contusions. She was alone on stage without a script.

'I was just wondering if you'd seen the kitchen knife.'

'Which one?'

'The big one . . . with the black handle. It lives in the block with the others by the toaster, but it's gone missing.'

Harry frowned and scratched his nose. The trial was listed for three days. There'd be lots of talking and to and fro but what would that achieve? Something, but not enough. Nothing to compare with what he'd suffered. He shrugged his shoulders. 'What would I want with a knife?'

26

R v. *Littlemore* opened in Court Twelve at the Old Bailey on a Thursday in the first week of August. It was a warm day with clouds drifting carelessly across a cobalt sky. A crowd had gathered in the street behind a row of grey metal barriers. Police officers in fluorescent jackets stood on the pavement, keeping the entrance clear. Seeing the gathering as he approached on foot from Ludgate, Anselm lowered his gaze. For months he'd lived in dread of this moment. Now that it was upon him he wanted to turn round and go back to Larkwood; to deal with his bees and the other simple obligations of a quiet life. The clouds were drifting there, too. Bede's parting words rang hoarsely in his ears:

'Find out what really happened . . .'

Littlemore had been right about one thing. Anselm's decision to represent him had placed the trial at the centre of a media storm. The coverage had been universally negative except for a cautious analysis in the *Guardian* by Robert Sambourne, the journalist who'd first broken the wider story. Reluctant to join the chorus of disapproval, he'd opted to await the jury's verdict. The existence of an ally of sorts had given Anselm some comfort, because the upshot of public debate had been a steady flow of mail, some hateful and abusive but the greater part carefully worded testaments of profound disillusionment. They'd wondered how Anselm could be so insensitive to *appearances*. How, given the scandal of child abuse in the Church, he'd even contemplated giving an impression of solidarity with a perpetrator against his victim. The irony was sharp. It was precisely this impression that Anselm wished to change – and in the most public way possible.

'Prove me wrong,' Dunstan had said, demonstrably insincere. He'd been moved to the infirmary, his illness public now. On a side table stood his old typewriter. It was the only object he'd brought with him. 'I tried to warn you but you wouldn't listen.' Dunstan had grimaced trying to find a comfortable position but the pain had got him cornered. He'd given up. 'You're making a huge mistake.'

Contrary to Dunstan's intentions, these unpleasant declarations had given Anselm a sudden jolt of adrenalin. Leaving the infirmary, he'd abruptly perceived the obvious: he was one step ahead of everyone . . . the police, the courts and even Littlemore himself. Thanks to Fraser, Anselm already knew why Harry might blame an innocent man; and he had a name for the true culprit. All at once, Anselm's objectives had fallen into place: if the evidence emerged, he'd incriminate Martin Brandwell; in the process, he'd look between the lines for the faint shadow of the Silent Ones, those exiles who'd chosen obscurity over their right to justice. It would be without question the most serious case he'd ever conducted.

And the most hopeless.

Having booked a room at Gray's Inn, Anselm had knelt in the nave listening to the traditional Gilbertine prayer for those beginning a voyage: a request that Providence guide his going and coming, and protect him from harm in-between. Then he'd taken the train for London. He'd thrown his tatty wig and torn gown into an old carpet bag, along with the trial papers and a copy of *Archbold*, the bible of criminal procedure, borrowed from Roddy Kemble QC, his old Head of Chambers. He'd also brought Larkwood's copy of the *Code of Canon Law* . . . he'd marked a number of paragraphs that had stirred his imagination.

'No other decision was possible,' Bede had huffed, out of breath. He'd driven Anselm to the station enclosed in a reproving silence; he'd dropped him off and pulled away without a parting word; but then he came back, running onto the platform, hot and bothered. 'The moment you went into that garden and spoke to the boy, there was no turning back. Now you have to finish the job . . . find out what really happened. For his sake, and ours.'

27

Anselm's heart was racing. He felt sick. On reaching the court entrance, he'd raised his eyes to see a couple holding a banner with a message for him: 'What you hear in the dark, you must speak in the light.' There had been a shout of indignation from a man gripping the barrier: 'Shame on you.' Now, sitting in court, Anselm was sweating with primal anxiety. He'd never known such a feeling, because he'd never been in such a position before: advocate and client were in the dock. He appraised his surroundings.

Littlemore sat with eyes closed, flanked by guards, the three of them dwarfed behind a high glass wall. Along the bar, prosecuting counsel – Laurence Grainger – was pouring himself a glass of water. Beyond him, across the aisle, sat the press, bunched and expectant. Above them, in the public gallery, Martin Brandwell was staring at Anselm. There was hate in his eyes, and knowledge . . . or was it fear? Behind him sat Fraser, hunched and alone. He gave the slightest nod to Anselm, urging him on.

Find out what really happened.

At exactly 10 a.m. Mr Justice Keating came onto the bench. Anselm had warned the court that a preliminary matter required his lordship's attention.

★

'He will not speak?'

'No, my lord,' confirmed Anselm.

'Because he can't or because he won't?'

'The latter, my lord.'

'Will he at least answer arraignment?'

'No, my lord.'

Mr Justice Keating smiled without humour. The controversial character of *R* v. *Littlemore* knew no bounds and he didn't seem altogether pleased. The court's dignity was not something to be toyed with – either by a priest returning to the Bar, or another priest scorning due procedure, and certainly not by two of them acting in concert. His little finger smoothed a white eyebrow.

'I've never come across a like circumstance. Have you, Mr Grainger?'

'No, my lord.'

The two men spoke like inquisitors troubled by an emerging heresy.

'I'm going to need your guidance, Mr Duffy – or do I call you "Father"?'

That question, too, smacked of a new and suspect doctrine. Grainger was quick to intervene:

'I suspect your lordship might well think that the use of any title which affords the defence special dignity in the eyes of the jury would be quite improper. Conventional language should prevail.'

'That has to be right.'

'I'm grateful.'

'Mr Duffy? Do you agree?'

'I do. My learned friend is far-sighted.'

'Good. I'm not. Could you now help me with this peculiar silence? Or is it holy indifference?'

'No, my lord. It's merely a fact that falls to be examined.' Anselm reached for *Archbold*. 'The matter is dealt with at paragraph four-two-two-two-eight. *R* v. *Schleter*. I quote: "Where the defendant stands mute, the court cannot of itself determine whether he is mute of malice or by visitation of God but must direct a jury to be forthwith empanelled and sworn to try the issue." Notwithstanding such a—'

Mr Justice Keating raised a halting hand. 'This is a grave case, Mr Duffy. I want to be fair to you and your client . . . but is this some kind of joke?'

'No, my lord.'

'Then explain the meaning of "mute by visitation of God"?'

'When a person is deaf and dumb or so deaf he cannot hear the indictment when read.'

'I see. Might I ask if God has made a visit to Father Littlemore?'

'Put like that, my lord, no, he hasn't. Which is to say the defendant is perfectly capable of hearing the charges laid against him and responding to them.'

'And what is "malice" in this context? Ill will?'

'No, my lord, simply an intention to remain silent.'

'So where do we go from here? You want a hearing to determine what we already know to be the case?'

'No, my lord. Notwithstanding *Schleter*, there's no need to empanel a jury. I formally admit that my client is mute by malice and the jury can be informed accordingly. Not Guilty pleas can be entered on his behalf upon your lordship's direction.'

'Mr Grainger?'

'As your lordship observed, this is a most serious case. I wouldn't seek to trivialise matters any further by insisting on a pointless hearing.'

Mr Justice Keating nodded and turned his attention to Anselm. 'Mr Duffy . . . I don't know what your client hopes to achieve by this refusal to participate in his own trial, or what you hope to achieve by representing him without instructions, but let me make something absolutely clear: I will not allow either of you to diminish the authority and reach of this court. Do you understand?'

Anselm reddened. He'd never been warned in such terms before. 'Yes, my lord.'

The jury was called and sworn in. The clerk stood and began to read out the three counts on the indictment, charging Edmund Steven Littlemore with . . . something in Anselm closed down. He didn't want to hear the details, not again. They appalled him. If Harry Brandwell had told the truth, there could be no hope of complete recovery. Upon conviction, Littlemore would face a substantial period of imprisonment.

But he claimed to be innocent.

Find out why Harry is prepared to blame an innocent man. That's the thread. Follow it. You'll reach the Silent Ones. This is your way – our way – of making a difference.

Anselm turned to the public gallery. The charges had been put. Not guilty pleas had been entered on the court record. Grainger was on his feet, ready to open the case to the jury. And Martin Brandwell had his eyes tight shut, like a man seeking help from the God of surprises.

28

Martin Brandwell opened his eyes and gazed down into the courtroom. Was this to be the moment of unravelling? Was this the end of things: a stripping down in public, after so much had been done in private?

Dear God, how did I ever come to this? I've spent my life trying to cure disease and I'm the one who's sick.

Martin was as weary as he was frightened. But would exposure be so bad? Wouldn't it be better for everyone? Better for him at least? He was too old to carry the weight much longer. For a mad, majestic moment, Martin nearly stood up, ready to shout to the world what he'd done, seeking neither judgement nor mercy, just relief. But Mr Grainger got there first, and the jury were absolutely concentrated.

'All abuse involves exploitation,' he began, quietly, as if he was telling a secret. 'It involves the strong exploiting the weak. The weak find themselves charmed, flattered and eventually won over until, to their alarm, they find they're also snared. Usually by fear but often, also, by respect. Respect for someone's reputation. The weak become victims who dare not speak out. These elements are invariably found when an older person preys upon someone much younger than themselves. However, to better understand the Crown's case against the defendant, you will have to appreciate that this man took the principle of exploitation to new and extraordinary lengths. For – we say – he not only exploited his victim, he exploited his family; he exploited the relationships within that family; and in particular, he exploited the good name of someone valued by that family: Father Dominic Tabley. You will shortly see how this defendant used this elderly man's reputation as a means of gaining access to his dearest friends, and their children and grandchildren, one of whom was an eleven-year-old boy . . . Harry Brandwell, who'll tell you how he was charmed, flattered and won over until he finds himself here today, betrayed and abused, a witness to his own ordeal, a brave victim who has refused to remain silent on account of anyone's reputation.'

Martin looked into the long glass-walled dock. Littlemore was sitting alone like the last pawn on the board – nothing to fight for and nothing to fight with. Would he keep his promise? Or had he spoken to the monk when he was hiding at that priory? Had he compromised everything? Martin's worried eyes drifted back across the empty benches to Littlemore's counsel . . . and he caught his breath: the monk was looking directly at him. And with pity. Or was it the last-minute hesitation of an executioner?

Christ, I want all this to end. Let me die, here and now.

'In effect, ladies and gentlemen,' said Grainger, leaning back, his voice stronger now, 'this defendant devised a most unusual modus operandi. By insinuating himself into a family close to Father Tabley he sought to minimise the chances of exposure should his later offending come to light. You cannot for one moment underestimate the cynicism involved in this man's forward planning . . . his long-sighted preparation . . . his intention to exploit every element in someone's character and their surrounding relationships. Even those rooted in faith. For you see, ladies and gentlemen, this defendant belongs to the same Order as Father Tabley. When he targeted Harry Brandwell he did so knowing that if Harry was to make any complaint, it would be to his parents; and his parents, in turn, would be compelled to speak to Harry's grandparents . . . and the family, as a whole, would then be confronted with a dilemma: the only way they could expose the defendant would be to bring disgrace upon Father Tabley by associating his name with the abuse that had taken place – abuse that had only happened because his name was used like a key to effect a first and fateful meeting. In effect, the defendant was exploiting a tenet central to the faith they were meant to share . . . the readiness to forgive not seven times, but seventy times seven.'

Grainger turned to look at Littlemore. He paused, eyes narrowed as if to focus on a distant, ruined landscape – a place that had once been sunny. Sure now of what he could see, he continued:

'The Crown says this defendant gambled on the willingness of a family to forgive him rather than shame their Church and blight the remaining years of a renowned and failing friend. You may think that such a scheme would never work, ladies and gentlemen. But people of good faith will always be tempted to protect the message by forgiving the messenger. As for renown . . . well, it's the most prized flower in the garden. We all admire it. No one wants to see it harmed. And, as you shall see, Father Tabley is no ordinary man. There was a perverse logic to the

146

defendant's thinking. But, being perverse, he failed to gauge the integrity of the Brandwells . . . and the strength of Harry's character. If there's light to be found in this dark and disturbing case, it is the refusal of a family to be blackmailed into silence . . . their belief that there can be no forgiveness without justice.'

Martin instinctively looked at Father Anselm. The monk had obtained copies of Harry's school reports by court order . . . reports in which Harry's strength of character had been discussed in less than flattering terms. He'd been in trouble with Mr Whitefield, the headteacher, for lying. At the time, Martin had exploded, shocking Maisie, Dominic and Emily and terrifying Harry.

'You must always tell the truth,' he'd shouted. 'And I mean *always.*'

Martin's secret hypocrisy had been stomach-turning . . . Grainger paused. He became wistful:

'Anyone who spends time with children knows they're full of mischief. But they're innocent. It's there, plain to be seen, like a ship-in-a-bottle. How it got there we just don't know; but seeing it, we're amazed . . . and sometimes moved. We handle it with great care. *This* defendant threw it against a wall. *This* trial is the nearest Harry will get to picking up the pieces.'

The ground in the court seemed to open up and Martin lost his bearings, the atoms of his very self falling into the ditch that led to the hell of his own making. He almost wept. But there were no tears for these particular circumstances. Neither God nor nature had ever thought they might be necessary.

29

For a moment Robert was transfixed. Mr Grainger was holding both hands in the air as if he was showing that ship-in-a-bottle to the jury. Everyone was staring into the space between his outstretched fingers. He was holding tragedy up to the light and it was awful. Without searching his memory, Robert found himself a child again, aged ten.

He was crying. Paul Wilson had been mocking him again. Saying his dad's face had more wrinkles than a sultana. And Sharon Hogan had sniggered. Robert was in love with Sharon Hogan. Arriving home from school, he heard this slow grating sound coming from the shed. He tiptoed to the end of the garden and peeped around the door. Sunshine poured through the windows onto the tools and wood. There was a smell of fresh sawdust. His dad was bent over his worktable, sleeves rolled to the elbow, a saw in his hand. A train thundered by sending a burst of wind into the trees. When the branches were still and the clatter of the wheels was fading, Robert's dad spoke. He didn't look up.

'Has my boy been crying again?'

'Yes.'

'Because of that Wilson lad?'

'Yes. He said you looked old so I hit him in the face and then Sharon Hogan whacked me with a ruler.'

'Don't, Robert. Find another way. You don't want to be hitting anyone.'

'Why not?'

'Because it only makes things worse.' He paused, keeping the saw in position. 'Remember the koala? Nothing disturbs him. Sleeps for twenty hours and only moves for four minutes, and that's while he chews a leaf. The world could end and he'd still reach out for another mouthful. That's the way to deal with Paul Wilson, matey. Turn away and make yourself a bacon sandwich. There's nothing like a bacon sandwich.'

Robert would have done anything to have had his dad's childhood. At night he told Robert stories – true stories about life in Queensland. How he'd raced cane toads in the school swimming pool. 'Borrowed' pineapples from a neighbour's plantation.

Tried to count the stars in the night sky – 'more stars than you could ever imagine, mate' – after bunking down in the outback. How he'd been frightened of dingoes when he got lost in the mulga. Robert would listen, forgetting everything, even a toothache. He longed to go to bed, just to be transported to this magical, faraway kingdom.

'What are you doing, Dad?' asked Robert. He touched one of the strips of wood soaking in a tub of water. 'What have you done that for?'

'To make the wood soft so it'll bend. I'm making a ship. An ocean-going liner.'

'For me?'

'Who else? Paul Wilson?' And those soft, green eyes turned their tide upon him. 'Help me, will you? Give me a hand.'

Robert took the saw. Guided by a stronger arm, he followed the line drawn upon the wood. Back and forth they went, hand in hand, quietly working.

'What shall we call her?' asked Robert.

His dad didn't reply for a while. Then he said, 'How about the *King Andrew*? It's a good, strong name for a ship that's going to battle with the high seas. Are we agreed?'

'Yes.'

'The *King Andrew* she is, then. May a fair wind guide her way. And you, her captain.'

'I love you, Dad.'

'And I love you, skipper.' All at once, Robert's dad stopped work and he turned to check the wood in the tub. 'I don't know about you, mate, but I could do with a sandwich.'

The shed quivered and the windows rattled as another train swept by. The sun caught the dust shaken from the rafters. Silence returned like a cat through a half-open door.

Robert blinked. His eyes were wet. A journalist from the *Daily Telegraph* was looking at him wryly – after all, it's not every day a fellow hack is moved to tears. The misreading brought Robert sharply back into the present. There were greater misunderstandings unfolding before his eyes, for both the prosecution and the defence.

First, Mr Grainger had no idea that Littlemore had been expelled from Sierra Leone. And why should he? No offence had been committed that ought to be brought to his attention. But Robert wasn't convinced. He'd been chasing down the contacts disclosed by Mr Bangura. Significantly, those who'd met Littlemore had been reluctant to speak, but finally – and off the record – Robert had been given the name of someone who might: George Timbo, a former civil servant and president of SLAOBA, the St Lambert's Academy Old Boys' Association. To date, he'd returned none of Robert's calls. The point was this: it seemed pretty certain that Harry Brandwell wasn't Littlemore's only victim. There had to be more . . . at home and abroad. It had been this realisation that gave Robert the answer to Crofty's tantalising question: why had Carrington written anonymously to him rather than the police?

'He's after more than a conviction,' Robert had said in the Fish Tank, sipping Scotch after his leaving party. Taylor had tried to tag along but Robert had swung round and told him to go home. 'He wants maximum publicity.'

'To what end?' Crofty had opened a packet of digestive biscuits.

'He's making a public appeal for other victims to come forward.'

'You're stretching things there.'

'I'm not. It's exactly what happened in the States even though it wasn't planned. The *Boston Globe* covered the trials of five priests back in 2002. That's what brought everything out into the open. The spotlight drew everyone's attention to what had been done to these kids and what hadn't been done with the perpetrators. Others came forward telling the same story. That's what began the landslide . . . throughout the US, everywhere. And I think Carrington wrote to me because he knew I cared;

he knew I'd chased Littlemore . . . and he gave me the story that brought me to the *Guardian*, because he wants national coverage . . . for a national problem in his Order. Maybe something way beyond Littlemore.'

Crofty, unsettled by beer, wine and spirits, had become lightly patronising. 'You're running away with yourself. Don't get me wrong, you did good, Robert, you did good. But you're not Bob Woodward yet.'

Robert had snatched the biscuits, his voice raised with the embarrassing aggression of a drunk in a public park. 'You'll see . . . Harry Brandwell is just the first to speak. There'll be more. Many more.'

Something the sober Mr Grainger couldn't possibly appreciate.

The second misunderstanding caused Robert considerable disquiet because he felt, in part, responsible. He'd expected Littlemore – pushed by Father Anselm – to plead guilty . . . only that hadn't happened. The trial had begun . . . and Father Anselm couldn't know he'd been used by Carrington. He knew nothing of the cuttings, the fax and the letter. And the only way he could have been enticed back into court was if Littlemore – nudged by Carrington – convinced him it was morally necessary. Whatever they'd come up with, he'd been gravely misled.

This was the great irony of the trial and the one flaw in Carrington's ruthless plan: Father Anselm had been deceived as much as Littlemore. They would both go down. Father Anselm would simply be a casualty of the operation; collateral damage . . . a price worth paying to see Littlemore brought to justice. The question for Robert was this: do I tell him? Do I show him what I found on that balcony? But it was impossible. The journalist who'd exposed Littlemore could hardly befriend his counsel.

Or could he?

Robert let the question hang in the air. A woman had entered court and taken the stand. She turned to the public gallery as if to get her bearings and then she faced Grainger.

30

Anselm turned a page in his notebook. So this was the woman Martin Brandwell had kept out of his reach. Unlike her husband, she was frail. Her arms were thin and her head leaned forward as if she was walking into the wind. Perhaps she was nervous on, this day of all days, but Anselm got the impression she was an anxious woman; someone who plodded on plagued by small worries. An image came to his mind, clashing violently with the delicate woman in the dock: a horse wearing blinkers.

'How old were you when you first met Father Dominic Tabley?' asked Grainger.

'Nineteen.'

'He introduced you to the man you would later marry, a student of medicine?'

'That's right.'

'He played Cupid?'

'Oh no, Mr Grainger, it was a joint operation. We trapped him together.'

Anselm smiled. She was delightful. An artist, according to her statement. She wore large jewellery and pastel shades of linen and silk. Her wrist bones were fine; the sort that break easily.

'He married you in due course?'

'Yes, and baptised our children.'

'And they are?'

'Justin and Dominic Brandwell . . . we named Dominic after Father Tabley. He also married Dominic and Emily and baptised Harry.'

'Your only grandchild?'

'That's right. I've hinted we'd like more, Mr Grainger, but it doesn't go down very well.'

Anselm listened to the prosecutor at work with approval. With short questions prompting longer answers, he began painting a picture of a family and their friend.

Father Tabley had been known as 'the Chief'. And the Chief had been a part of the Brandwell family from the outset: as Maisie said, he'd been part of the sting that brought Martin to room 256 at the London School of Hygiene and Tropical Medicine for a talk on vector-borne diseases. Only Maisie turned up because the actual event had been organised for the following month. By then, Maisie and Martin had become an item. The significance of Father Tabley, who'd given Martin the wrong day, never diminished. After the marriage, when Martin's research into malaria took him to Asia and Africa for months at a time, the Chief was on hand, like an uncle to the growing family; only he was more than an uncle. As a man of wise words, he was there – alongside Maisie and Martin – to help Justin and Dominic construct a moral framework for themselves and a conscience towards the world. He made the whole business of right and wrong accessible and real. Funny, too. They holidayed together in the summer. They shared the Christmas season. Then, twenty years after that first meeting, Father Tabley was transferred to Wallsend in Newcastle.

'Justin was thirteen and Dominic was eleven,' said Maisie. 'It was a time of change for us all, really . . . Martin had just got a post at the Dreadnought Unit at St Thomas's Hospital in Lambeth and I'd dropped the evening classes for a day job.'

'You remained in close contact?' asked Grainger.

'Oh yes, but it was never quite the same as before. Father Tabley was far too busy.'

Finding himself in the old docklands by the River Tyne, he'd come across old shipyard workers who'd never been members of a union. Some of them didn't bother going to a doctor either, until they'd no choice. They'd been dying from asbestosis, lung cancer and mesothelioma, thinking they were on their own. He set up an advice centre, contacting solicitors to progress claims for damages. He went to the press with their stories. He helped them face a terrible death, making sure the families were supported day and night. In time, he opened a project to assist parents with disabled children, a home-help service with free meals for the elderly, an employment training scheme for youths released from young offender institutions.

'He turned down an MBE,' said Maisie. 'Didn't even want it mentioned that he'd been on the list. What mattered was the work, and he did it non-stop until he retired seven years ago. He's a hermit now.'

'You see him?'

'Never. You know what a hermit is, Mr Grainger? He's out of circulation. But we've kept the memories . . . along with the impact he had on our family.'

Justin in particular was deeply influenced. On leaving school he worked with various voluntary organisations offering help to the homeless. After years of experience, he founded his own project . . . the Bowline. Mr Justice Keating nodded. He knew it well. And he'd seen the BBC documentary. Various members of the jury nodded too, smiling at Maisie's evident pride.

'And now I'd like to turn to Father Littlemore,' said Grainger.

Technically speaking, Anselm was impressed. By that one announcement, Grainger had compared light with dark. The jury seemed to have fallen under a shadow.

'How did you come to meet him?'

'He called us out of the blue, asking for an interview. He said he was an old friend of Father Tabley's and a member of the same Order.'

'He came at Father Tabley's behest?'

'No, quite the opposite. He said Father Tabley wasn't to know. No one was to know. It was a secret.'

Father Littlemore had said he was preparing a memoir about

Father Tabley's life and he wanted to gather stories and recollections from those who'd known him well. The idea was to give him the bound volume on the day of his Golden Jubilee.

'How long did this interview last?'

'Oh, an hour and half, maybe more.'

'Did he listen carefully to what you said?'

'Heavens, yes . . . he took lots of notes . . . checked the details . . . names, places, dates. The spelling. He seemed very thorough.'

Mr Grainger paused. 'Was there anything striking about his questions?'

'Yes . . . he was very interested in our children . . . what they were like and so on. At the time I thought he was just being sociable but now . . . well, I see things very differently.'

'Why?'

'Because this is the information he used to make contact with my son Dominic and eventually Harry.'

Grainger nodded as if the idea was new to him. 'Have you been shown a draft of your account?'

'No.'

'Were you contacted subsequently to confirm any details?'

'No. He left saying this had to be kept absolutely secret and that he'd be in touch. I never saw him again.'

'Thank you, Mrs Brandwell.'

Grainger sat down and Anselm rose, recalling his visit to Dominic and Emily's house near Clapham Common. Dominic's regret was that he hadn't listened to his fragile brother. They were separated by difference. And something far more nuanced. Justin had travelled a very particular voyage, from breakdown to recovery. Like the prodigal son, who'd then got the fatted calf of his father's attention.

'Do you know which of your sons the defendant made contact with first?'

'Yes. It was Justin.'

'Who has no children?'

'I've made heavy hints, Father. But he's found his own place in life. His family are the people the rest of us forget.'

Anselm stressed his point: 'The defendant gave priority to someone who had no children as opposed to someone who had. Do you know why?'

'I don't . . . but forgive me, Father, I can't see why it matters.'

'Well, if your aim is to approach and befriend children, why get to know someone who hasn't got any?'

'Look, Father, if he'd left Justin out of his planning, Mr Grainger would've had a field day showing just that, wouldn't he? And you'd've had nothing to say, would you?'

'A lot less, certainly. But can you help me a little further? Did Justin and the defendant develop any kind of association? Something approaching friendship? One that might have soured?'

'I really don't know, Father.'

'Haven't you spoken about this terrible business as a family?'

'Of course we have.'

'Well, haven't you discussed with Justin how and when he met the defendant?'

'I know they met because of me, that's all. You ought to ask Justin.'

'I'd like to Mrs Brandwell, but he hasn't provided a statement in this case. Like your husband.'

Anselm began to sit down, his cross-examination finished, but then he stalled.

'You said Father Tabley was known as "the Chief"?'

'That's right.'

'Why?'

'Because he's a real chief.'

'Tribal?' quipped Anselm.

'Yes. You see, Father Tabley was a missionary once. The people wanted to thank him for all he'd done . . . so they made him a chief.'

'Which country are we talking about?'

'Sierra Leone.'

'Intriguing. Where was he based?'

'Freetown. A school. St Lambert's Academy.'

'The Chief was a teacher?'

'Yes.'

'Subject?'

'Biology. He was absolutely fascinated by living things. Even mosquitoes.'

'How long was he out there?'

'Seven years.'

Anselm noted the replies and then paused to join some mental dots. 'So you first met Father Tabley after he came back from Freetown?'

'That's right, yes. The same year.'

'Did he open any community projects in London or anywhere else during the two decades you knew him . . . before he went to Newcastle?'

'No, all that came later. For those twenty years Father Tabley did his ordinary work in an extraordinary way, but he was changed dramatically by what happened when he got to the North-East. Can I tell everyone?'

'Please do. But first could you tell us how long Father Tabley was in Newcastle.'

'Another twenty years.'

Anselm made a note and Maisie took a sip of water. Then she said:

'It began with an old woman at the fish market in North Shields who kept coughing and no one knew why. Even the doctors.' Maisie was addressing the judge; she wanted high authority to know the story. 'But it was Father Tabley who found out that forty years earlier her husband had been a lagger on the docks and that he used to come home covered in white powder, and that she used to wash his overalls in the sink. She'd been contaminated by asbestos dust. After she died – and it was

horrible and drawn out – Father Tabley set up an advice centre
in her name. The Dorothy Newman Centre. In a way, he'd rescued
her from a meaningless death. Everything he did flowed from
that poor woman's story.' Maisie paused. It was as though she'd
removed her blinkers and the wind had dropped. Raising her
height, she turned towards the dock. 'You don't belong under
the same roof as such a man. That you used his name to get to
children he would have saved from harm is unforgivable.'

Anselm seemed to ponder the remark. 'Thank you, Mrs
Brandwell.'

After lunch, Grainger called two further witnesses, a representa-
tive sample of five couples with identical testimony. They'd all
been close friends of Father Tabley. They'd all been contacted by
the defendant in relation to the preparation of a jubilee memoir.
They'd all told their personal stories. The defendant had made
copious notes. He'd been interested in their children. He'd asked
them to keep his visit and purpose a shared secret. They'd never
seen him since.

'The memoir itself has never materialised,' said Grainger,
replying to the judge's query. 'Despite a careful search of the
defendant's premises, no documentation of any kind was found
– either the original notes or a composite text.'

'Thank you, Mr Grainger.'

Anselm accepted the evidence but clarified two points. First,
that in each of the five families there were three generations: the
grandparents who'd first met Father Tabley, their children, and
finally the grandchildren. Second, in *each* case the defendant had
made contact with every child mentioned, but in *no* case – save
that of Harry Brandwell – had there been any contact with a
grandchild. An unexpected picture was emerging in Anselm's
mind – drawn without intention by Grainger . . . a secondary
image behind the representation of planned abuse. It was like a
mirage. It mightn't, in fact, be real. But one element had stopped

shimmering. It had come into focus as Maisie left the witness stand: Anselm was sure that in those early years Martin had felt displaced by Father Tabley. While he'd been getting stung to death by mosquitoes in a swamp by the Mekong River, Father Tabley had been wiping the dishes. Martin had come home to hear Maisie applaud the man who'd held out a cure deeper than his for the sickness of this world. At the heart of this treasured friendship lay an understandable envy. Perhaps that's why Martin had declined to provide a statement.

'Given the time, I don't propose to call any further witnesses, your lordship,' said Grainger. 'Tomorrow I'll move onto the substantive issues in the case: the defendant's dealings with Harry Brandwell.'

'Very well. Ten o'clock, ladies and gentlemen.'

31

'The defendant contacted you?'

'Yes,' replied Dominic Brandwell, the next morning, after he'd been summoned and sworn.

'The object of his call?'

'He was preparing a memoir.'

An arrangement had been made for Sunday lunch. He'd brought flowers. A box of Thorntons. They'd discussed childhood memories about the Chief until late evening. Other invitations followed.

'And gifts?'

'Yes.'

Grainger looked up. 'For you and your wife alone?'

'No, he brought a ship-in-a-bottle for Harry.'

'Anything else?'

'A pencil case.'

'How old was he?'

'Eleven.'

The adults had gradually become friends, the attachment woven from similar interests. Father Littlemore had been fascinated by Dominic's collection of antique maps, showing an impressive knowledge of seventeenth-century Dutch cartography. He'd shared his wife's enthusiasm for West End musicals, knowing most of the words to most of the songs.

'Could I now take you towards the end of the same year. What came to pass?'

'We'd been on holiday in Ireland for three weeks. The whole family. Cycling round the Ring of Kerry. We'd rented these bikes—'

'A little later, please.'

'You mean September? The beginning of term?'

'Yes.'

'I'm sorry.'

'Don't apologise. Just tell the jury what happened.'

On the first day a tragedy occurred. A boy went running out of the school gates into the path of a car. His body had been dragged down the street, where he died. The boy – Neil Harding – was in Harry's class. They'd known each other since nursery. They'd literally learned to talk together.

'What was Harry's reaction?'

'He folded up.'

'Could you elaborate, please?'

'He vanished inwards and wouldn't come out. The school provided counselling but he wouldn't talk to anyone . . . not to me, not to his mum and not to any of the professionals.'

He stopped working or playing and couldn't sleep at night. He'd lie between his parents, eyes wide open, staring at the ceiling. And then, one morning, he just stopped talking. Wouldn't utter a word. And then Emily, Dominic's wife, thought of Father Littlemore. She'd seen Harry looking unhappily at the ship-in-a-bottle as if he wanted to sail far away from his childhood. It was devastating. She called Father Littlemore and he came round the same day.

'He crouched down in front of Harry and asked him if he knew how to play chess.'

'Chess?'

'That's right. He asked him if he knew the rules and Harry just looked at the carpet, and then Father Littlemore asked if he'd like to learn some secret moves known only to Bobby Fischer. Harry had never heard of Bobby Fischer and Father Littlemore said he'd have to come along to find out . . . but that he wouldn't have to say anything . . . Father Littlemore would do all the talking. And then Harry spoke. He just said, "Yes." It was the first time he'd opened his mouth in three weeks.'

A meeting was arranged at the defendant's premises in Mitcham. Two further meetings took place, making three in all.

'Could you describe Harry's demeanour after each encounter?'

'He was progressively . . . agitated. But after the third, it was obvious something had happened.'

'Why?'

'He came barging into the house and ran upstairs. He was sick . . . locked the bathroom door and wouldn't open it. He had a shower . . . which he's never done before, not in the middle of the day . . . and he's not been the same since.'

Grainger waited while Dominic composed himself. Then he said: 'Did he speak about what had taken place?'

'No. He's never spoken about it.'

'Did he do anything?'

'Yes. Later that evening he came downstairs carrying the ship-in-a-bottle . . . he looked sort of ill with anger . . . and he threw it against the wall . . . right over our heads.'

Since that day, Harry had displayed numerous signs of profound psychological disturbance. Apart from rarely speaking, he'd begun to bed-wet. His behaviour deteriorated . . . swearing, lying, smoking. There were burns on his skin consistent with non-accidental injury. No one could reach him.

'It's as though we've lost our son,' said Dominic. 'We're hoping this trial will help bring him back home.'

Grainger sat down and Anselm slowly came to his feet. For a long while he stared at his own hurried notes and the lines he'd drawn in the margin. He was deeply conscious that Dominic had turned to him as a measure of last resort and that he now felt betrayed. And now he wouldn't understand the point of Anselm's questions any more than he'd understood why he came to Clapham. Anselm was destined to disappoint him.

'How long did you know the defendant?'

'About a year.'

'During that time did he ever show an interest in Dixieland Jazz?'

'I beg your pardon?'

'Dixieland. Hot Jazz. Early Jazz. Did the defendant ever show a liking for the style?'

Dominic turned involuntarily towards Anselm. He was angry and confused. 'No.'

'Did he ever mention Bobby Hackett?'

'No . . . never. He said his thing was West End shows – *Les Misérables*, *Billy Elliot*, *Blood Brothers*. That sort of thing.'

Matters would have to be left there. The jury was bemused and Anselm could feel the cold stare of Mr Justice Keating. He turned back a page in his notes. Harry's school reports had furnished Anselm with a glimpse into Harry's world and apart from the recent history of fibbing he'd found something else that was potentially significant. The headteacher Mr Whitefield had come to a similar conclusion, though for his own reasons. Anselm advanced, feeling his way:

'When did you come back from your summer holiday?'

'Sorry?'

'After cycling around the Ring of Kerry. What was the date of your return?'

'The end of August . . . the thirty-first.'

'You went by car?'

'Yes.'

'When did you get home?'

'Late in the evening.'

'Did Harry eat anything on the way?'

'Pardon?'

'Food. Nourishment. Did Harry eat?'

'I can't recall.'

'Please try.'

Dominic closed his washed-out eyes, rehearsing the incidentals of that homeward journey. 'No, he didn't.'

'He went to school the next morning?'

'Yes.'

'Did he want any breakfast?'

'I'm sorry I just don't remember. And how could it possibly matter? A boy met his death, for heaven's sake. Who cares what Harry ate beforehand? Harry was shattered afterwards.'

'Did he want to stay at home that morning?'

'Of course he did. What do you expect? He was upset the holiday was over.'

'Did he say as much?'

'No, but it was obvious.' Dominic's impatience flared. 'And he went to school and by the end of the day his life had changed. Have you forgotten that?'

'Far from it, Mr Brandwell.'

It seemed that Anselm's intuition had been confirmed, but he decided to leave the subject for the moment; he'd return to it with Emily in due course. Instead he opted to remind Dominic of another lapse of memory.

'You said Harry refused to talk to you, your wife or any professional.'

'Yes.'

'What about your brother, Justin?'

'Oh yes, I'm sorry . . . he tried too. He took Harry rock climbing in North Wales.'

'You were present?'

'Yes, with Emily. We watched them climb to a ledge that Justin calls "Speakers' Corner". He often goes there with people from the Bowline.'

'Do you know why?'

'He says when people get perspective, they can speak. You always need some distance. And up there, you can look down on the world as if it was made yesterday. For some people it's a key.'

Anselm was roused by the symmetry of place and purpose. 'Did it turn for Harry?'

'No.'

'What about your brother? Did it turn for him?'

'I assume so.'

'Do you know what he said?'

'I don't.'

'Did he give you any advice afterwards?'

'Yes . . . he said don't ask Harry any more questions. He said leave him alone.'

Anselm nodded to himself; then he reached for a handhold that might not be there. 'Keys turn in two directions, of course. Have you considered that your brother might have turned it the other way? Not to open but to shut?'

'Don't be ridiculous. You weren't there.'

'Neither were you.'

Anselm sat down, feeling the chill of that Welsh mountain air. The next person to question Harry Brandwell after that climb in Wales had been Anselm. In the boy's back garden. By then he'd concluded that Littlemore was somewhere in Spain – a very adult reflection. Out of reach. Sunning himself.

32

Martin Brandwell left the public gallery. He went quickly down the stairs, through security, and out of the Old Bailey, heading east along Ludgate Hill towards St Paul's Cathedral. Nipping down a side street he pushed open the door of a small café. Justin was waiting, sitting at a table in a far corner.

'There's nothing to worry about,' said Martin, sitting down, already lying.

A waiter brought coffee and then withdrew. Justin was handling a glass salt cellar, turning it round and round, watching the white crystals fall. There were grains of rice, too.

'They look like maggots,' he said, giving the cellar another shake.

'I said there's nothing to worry about.'

Justin looked up. His eyes were red, his skin white as plaster. Martin's heart almost stopped: his boy was falling apart once more. If inner filth could bleed, Justin's blood would be spreading like a dark pool, reaching for the door and the outside world. Martin placed his hands around his son's, bringing them together around the salt pot. He kept them there as if to keep a wound closed.

'He's cross-examined Maisie and Dominic,' said Martin. 'He knows nothing, I promise you. Littlemore has remained silent . . . no one is going to know. This will be over soon. Hold yourself together . . . please, my boy.'

Justin had been like this before the breakdown. He'd started twitching around the mouth, laughing suddenly, crying quickly, laughing some more and then he'd fallen on his knees, his chest heaving in silence. An hour or so later he'd been all smiles, absolutely carefree . . . just like a kid about to go on holiday . . . excited and silly . . . and that night he'd taken an overdose. Heroin. To this day Maisie thought it had been sleeping tablets. The guilt and shame had finally burst out, like an abscess at the centre of his conscience. Martin had hoped for healing but now he realised how foolish he'd been: how do you heal a sickness for which there's no cure?

'Your mother will never find out, Justin,' breathed Martin, as if he'd climbed to Speakers' Corner. 'She's going to live out her years without knowing . . . if that is what you want.'

'There's no other way.'

'Are you really so sure?'

Justin barked, neck bent, face lifted: 'Yes.'

Martin raised his hands and cradled his son's head. But Justin wouldn't look at him. He tried to pull away, closing his eyes, but Martin wouldn't release him.

'Are you clean?' asked Martin, quietly.

'Yes.'

'Truthfully?'

'Yes, honestly.' Justin was crying; he leaned back, and Martin had to let go. The world seem to slip from his fingers. 'I'm just so tired, Dad . . . I can't get away. I can't escape . . . I can't shake off who I am . . . what I've become. What I've done.' Tears of exhaustion ran down his cheek. 'I can't get clean in the way that matters most . . .'

'Let me talk to your mother. Let's get everything out into the open.'

Justin was hopeless. 'It wouldn't make any difference. I remain the same. So what's the point?'

'Because you wouldn't remain the same. Even you can change.' Martin was desperate. He'd been using shining phrases for seven years now. A small table had never felt so large. He couldn't even reach the other side. 'There's hope for everyone, no matter what they've done. A fresh start is always possible.'

'Who told you that? The Chief?'

'No, you did. You founded the Bowline. You, too, can get help, but you have to speak.'

'Speaking doesn't always work, Dad. It can't work for me, you know that . . .' Justin's voice trailed off. He dried his face with a sleeve and nodded at the waiter for another coffee. They were quiet, Justin twirling the salt cellar, Martin handling the pepper.

'You promised to support me,' said Justin.

'I have done. And I always will. But the harm is ongoing . . . I didn't imagine what might happen to Harry. That secrets breed secrets.'

Justin's lip and cheek quivered with a sort of electric jolt. 'Mum isn't to know . . . and that's final, okay?'

Martin nodded obediently. The cost of the secret was his subordination. It kept Justin clean, even as it dirtied his father. The waiter came and went. Justin reached for the sugar. His face was still now.

'You should have kept away from Littlemore,' said Martin, quietly.

'I tried. But he wouldn't leave me be; he knew what he was after. I couldn't pretend I didn't know what he wanted.'

Martin put the pepper pot down.

'Littlemore will be convicted.'

Justin tasted his coffee. He didn't seem to have heard.

'And then we help Harry face the future,' said Martin, forced to move on.

Justin's eyes were glazed.

'This can be your way of—'

Martin stopped because Justin had raised a finger of warning. He'd always done that when his dad threatened to go off limits. Over the years, Martin had come to sense where the boundaries lay in Justin's mind. If he strayed, Justin would give the signal. A sort of tension came between them, like the hum of an electric fence. Hearing it now, Martin retreated.

'I'd better get back to court.' He hesitated, wanting to heave Justin out of the pit he'd dug for himself. But it was too deep, too dark. He was somewhere out of sight, at the bottom. 'I'm with you, son,' he managed.

'No, Dad,' replied Justin. His cheek quivered and he laughed. 'I once thought you could share this with me, but you can't. I'm on my own.'

As Martin left the café, he stifled a spasm of grief. The weight of guilt for his collusion was nothing compared with the unbearable sight of Justin damaged and damaging, the evil running deep and wide, eating away the relationships that ought to bring him fulfilment and happiness. His own son was like a disease. Martin almost stumbled into the gutter. For the first time in his life, he wished his wife was dead.

On righting himself, he looked across the road. A man was walking away but there was no doubt. It was Fraser . . . but the fear roused at seeing him was quickly followed by a deeper, more primitive reaction. Martin was scalded by jealousy and guilt. This was the man who'd won Harry's confidence; this was the man he trusted more than anyone, including his grandfather. Could any indictment be worse?

33

Even as Emily was speaking – upset by Anselm's interest in the marginal – Anselm realised he'd uncovered potentially significant evidence. Evidence that might yet harden into a defence. First, however, he'd picked at the lining of Grainger's case.

After taking the stand, Emily had confirmed her husband's

account of Harry's behaviour; she'd stressed, under Grainger's careful direction, that the defendant had suggested after the first meeting that he see Harry alone and that Emily had not been present in the building thereafter, and that Harry had come out of the third encounter so distressed he couldn't relate what had happened to him; she'd then explained how she called the police and how, during the subsequent video interview, Harry was unable to open his mouth. Cross-examined by Anselm, she admitted that Harry hadn't in fact accused Littlemore . . . that *she* had suggested Littlemore's name . . . *after* Harry had thrown the ship-in-a-bottle against the wall. Harry had simply agreed to his mother's inferences, nodding, but still not speaking. While this was an important concession, it wasn't out of the ordinary: victims often need such promptings. Thanks to Fraser's disclosure, Anselm had also brought to light another potentially telling detail: Martin Brandwell had spoken in private to his grandson immediately before the recording. Questioned about the relationship between her father-in-law and Harry, she'd agreed that Martin Brandwell could be intimidating, that Harry had sometimes been frightened of him.

'You can't be suggesting that Harry's grandfather persuaded him not to speak?' Emily said, astonished.

Anselm then flipped the argument upside down, scoring a small point in Littlemore's favour. 'Perhaps he told him to tell the truth . . . and that's why Harry couldn't open his mouth.'

These were small victories, something for a floundering defence advocate to hang onto when it came to making a speech. However, it was only after returning to territory already tentatively explored with Dominic that Anselm made a significant discovery.

Potentially significant.

When reading Harry's school reports, Anselm had underlined an interesting entry from the pen of Mr Whitefield. Apart from a history of 'prevarication' – a nice word for lying when it suited him – Harry had fought with Neil Harding. Twice. They might have learned to talk together in nursery but they weren't on speaking terms by the time they got to secondary school. And while the young boy's death was unquestionably shocking, Emily confirmed that Harry wasn't a witness; he didn't see the body; he didn't see the stains on the tarmac; he didn't meet hysterical classmates running from the accident site. In a vital sense, he'd been cushioned from all that was traumatising for a bystander. He was told about it by a friend who hadn't seen anything either. Anselm was edging towards the proposition that Harry's disturbing behaviour might have another explanation – antecedent to Neil Harding's death. Which is why he'd asked Dominic about the holiday that ended the night before term began. Anselm now returned to the subject with Emily:

'Does it strike you as odd that Harry didn't eat on the way home? That he didn't want any breakfast the next day? That he wanted to stay at home?'

'Not especially. We'd had a wonderful holiday.'

'Did Harry say it was wonderful?'

'He didn't need to . . . we'd *done* wonderful things.'

'Did you ask Harry why he wasn't eating?'

'Yes.'

'What did you say?'

'I asked him if he was sad to be going back to school and he said, "Yes".'

'So it was you that mentioned school as the reason? It didn't come from him?'

'Father, if you had children you wouldn't ask questions like that. You *know* what's bothering your child.'

'Like you *knew* it was Father Littlemore who assaulted Harry?'

Emily sighed and looked to the jury. There had to be parents in the box who'd understand what she was trying to say. You have to help children along, and you do that by showing them you understand what they're feeling. You don't wait for them to tell you.

'Who went on this holiday to Ireland?' asked Anselm. His intuition was stirring.

'My husband, Harry, my in-laws – Martin and Maisie – and myself.'

'A cycling venture around the Ring of Kerry?'

'That's right.'

Anselm thought for a moment. 'The trip home to London. By car, that's twelve or thirteen hours, isn't it? If you take the ferry from Rosslare to Fishguard in South Wales?'

'Yes, but we took a longer route, crossing from Dun Laoghaire to Holyhead.'

'That's way to the north.'

'Yes, but we were staying the night in Harlech. Splitting the journey into two days. You see Justin has a cottage just outside the town, overlooking Tremadog Bay. He'd been climbing in Snowdonia and we'd arranged to meet up for the evening.'

While Emily was upset by this excursion into irrelevance, Anselm teased out the detail, his pulse beginning to run. They booked a hotel in the town. They arrived at about two in the afternoon. At six, Harry went to fetch Justin. On his own. A ten-minute stroll. Along the beach. He was back, with his uncle, by eight.

'Two hours later?'

'Harry adores his uncle, Father. They spent some time together while the grown-ups had a lie-down.'

'Did you discuss what they did to pass the time?'

'Of course not . . . or if we did I can't remember.'

'How did your brother-in-law appear that evening?'

'I don't know what you mean.'

'What was his manner? Was he stressed or flustered in any way?'

'No. He'd been climbing . . . got lost . . . fallen and cut his hands and face . . . but that's all normal for Justin.'

'Did Harry eat that evening?'

'No. He went straight to bed. The poor thing was exhausted. So we had some adult time.'

Anselm slowed with the cold impulse of a hunter. 'Are you aware that loss of appetite is itself a symptom of some significance?'

'It can be, but there was nothing wrong with Harry. We'd spent two weeks pedalling up and down hills and he'd left us all behind.'

'Could you confirm the following for me, please? Harry didn't eat that night?'

'No.'

'Nor the next day on the way home?'

'No.'

'Nor that night when you got there?'

'No.'

'And not the next morning when he got up?'

'That's right. And I don't know why you keep going on about eating, it's—'

'Thirty-six hours without any kind of nourishment . . . and all because he didn't want to go back to school?'

Emily was upset and confused. She felt criticised by Anselm, and the humiliation was intense. She thought he was implying that she hadn't looked after her son properly; that it was her fault terrible things had happened to him. She wasn't able to imagine what Anselm was pointing towards. But Mr Justice Keating, after years of being ambushed by the unexpected, was more than capable. He put his pen down with a forbidding glance at Grainger. He'd glimpsed part of that foreign land that may or may not be real. Unable to reply, Emily pulled out a tissue and Anselm sat down. He had to control his emotions and his mind. But it wasn't easy. There was a chance that Littlemore was innocent, because Anselm didn't credit a trauma in Harlech followed by another in London, with Justin Brandwell and Edmund Littlemore as assailants standing in line. And that meant Harry had lied to

Fraser with one story (blaming his grandfather) and lied to the court with another (blaming Father Eddie). It meant that Martin had wanted to avoid this trial to protect Maisie from learning that their son, the survivor who'd come back from the brink to save others, had destroyed Harry's childhood, that Harry was the living sacrifice to that end, and that Littlemore was just driftwood for the pyre . . . though why Harry had thrown that ship-in-a-bottle against the wall remained a deeply troubling question.

But there was much more on the line. If Littlemore was innocent, then the Silent Ones were real, and his and Carrington's scheme to reach them became critically important. Anselm *had* to find them. By the same token, if there were no Silent Ones, Littlemore was guilty. He'd brought Anselm on side to conjure a defence out of nothing: to kick up enough dust to cause a doubt in the jury's mind. The outstanding questions were vital, urgent and decisive: who were the Silent Ones? Why had they chosen obscurity? And how were they connected to Justin Brandwell?

Mr Justice Keating closed his red notebook. 'We'll adjourn for lunch. Who is your next witness, Mr Grainger?'

'Father George Carrington, my lord.'

34

And of course, if anyone knew the answers to all the questions it was the Provincial of the Lambertines, who'd come to Anselm incognito knowing that he would shortly be exposed as Littlemore's superior. He'd hoped that one day he and Anselm would be in a courtroom together. That seemingly impossible moment had now arrived.

There are vested interests, he'd said.

Carrington entered the witness box and swore to tell the truth.

The formula was short, but Anselm watched him closely, noting every inflection of feeling, plotting the curve of every nuance, every gesture, trying to determine if this man was a friend or a fraud. If Carrington was an honourable man, there was a secret bond between them; and an exchange would presently take place before everyone's eyes, its significance unseen – a sleight of hand in the interests of justice. Anselm turned to the public gallery, just to make sure an important witness was there: and he was; Kester Newman was sitting on the back row by the door, ready to listen to his master's voice.

There are people occupying positions of considerable trust and influence who do not want this man to be found. Someone, however, must intervene, regardless of such misguided . . . sensitivities.

Grainger covered the evidence quickly. Yes, the Lambertines had a manual of child protection procedures. They'd been drafted by Carrington himself, in consultation with expert opinion. Amendments were made in keeping with the developments of best practice. All members of the Order had studied the provisions in detail. Yes, Father Littlemore had been given a copy. Yes, he'd examined them. Yes, he was aware that under no circumstances should he permit himself to be alone in a building with a minor. Grainger underlined the point and then he shifted ground:

'Father Tabley will be celebrating his Golden Jubilee shortly.'

'He will, yes.'

'Did you ask the defendant to prepare a memoir to mark the event?'

'No.'

'Did anyone else?'

'Not that I know of.'

'Were you aware that the defendant had set himself the task?'

'No.'

'That he was visiting families with children on that understanding?'

174

'Absolutely not. Had I known I would have forbidden it.'

'Why?'

Carrington became sententious: 'I can't imagine anything that Father Tabley would want less.'

Grainger gave a light flick to his gown. 'Thank you, Father. Please answer my learned friend's questions.'

Anselm reached for the *Code of Canon Law*. Its provisions had no application in this particular court, of course, but Anselm had underlined some important passages that just might help him find people like Harry, forced to lie and to live a lie.

If, indeed, he had lied. If, indeed, there were other people waiting to be found.

'Father Carrington, I assume the Lambertine Order has an archive system consistent with the dictates of Canon Law?'

'It does, yes.' Carrington had recognised the open volume in Anselm's hands. 'We follow the same procedures for any diocese.'

'Would you confirm, then – pursuant to Canon four–eight–six – that the archive is in a safe place?'

'It is.'

'That "written documents pertaining to the spiritual and temporal affairs" of the Order "are safeguarded there, after being properly filed and diligently secured"?'

'They are.'

'Canon four–eight–seven . . . the archive is locked?'

'Correct.'

'You retain the key?'

'I do, in common with my deputy, the Vice-Provincial.'

'Where is the archive?'

'In a room adjacent to my office.'

'Canon four–eight–nine, paragraph one: "There is also to be a secret archive, or at least in the common archive there is to be a safe or cabinet, completely closed and locked, which cannot be removed".' Anselm appraised Carrington as if they were in the parlour at Larkwood. 'You have such a secret archive?'

'Yes.'

'Where is it located?'

'In the basement of the building where I live.'

'The basement door is locked?'

'It is. But the key is to hand to comply with fire safety regulations.'

'Where is it?'

'On a board in my office. Each key is clearly labelled.'

Anselm resumed his reading: 'Paragraph two: "Each year documents of criminal cases in matters of morals, in which the accused parties have died or ten years have elapsed from the condemnatory sentence, are to be destroyed. A brief summary of what occurred along with the text of the definitive sentence is to be retained."' Anselm looked up. 'The Order has complied with these requirements?'

'No.'

'Why not?'

'There have been no criminal cases. Not one in our one-hundred-and-seventy-year history in these islands. Had there been, then the relevant records would have been dealt with as prescribed.'

Anselm showed curiosity: 'What about cases that didn't come to trial? I'm talking about allegations against an individual that have not led to any criminal proceedings. Are relevant documents retained? Correspondence, minutes of meetings, records of interviews?'

'All such material is preserved.'

'In the secret archive.'

'Yes.'

'Subject to the provisions for destruction?'

'No, the types of document you mentioned are kept in perpetuity.'

Anselm made a puzzled frown. 'Why?'

'Because there's been no criminal case. It is the criminal case that entitles someone to have information about them destroyed after a reasonable period of time.'

'So nothing is shredded? Each allegation and accusation remains on file?'

'Indeed. Along with the response of the accused and any documents produced during any internal enquiry.'

'Including agreements between the Order and a given individual? Agreements which resolve a dispute that never ended in a trial and a definitive sentence? Assuming, of course, that such agreements might exist.'

'That's quite correct . . . assuming such agreements might exist.'

'For completeness, and continuing the assumption, would those records include details of any compensation payments made under mutual terms of strict confidentiality?'

'They would, yes, though you must appreciate I am merely endorsing your hypothesis. I'm not in a position to confirm or deny that complaints have, in fact, been resolved in this manner, because to do so would undermine the principle of secrecy that protects both parties. Without the consent of a specific individual, I can only speak hypothetically; and speaking hypothetically, I can only assure you that each and every record would be properly and safely conserved.'

'How, exactly?'

'The relevant records of a given complaint would be placed in a brown envelope and then sealed with the date of closure and the names of the parties involved written on the outside.'

'"Closure" isn't quite the right word, is it?'

'Not in a moral sense, no. Such things can never be closed.'

'But envelopes can; and, once closed, they would then be placed in the secret archive in perpetuity?'

'Yes.'

'What happens when a new leader of the Order is elected? How is the principle of secrecy preserved, given that the individual concerned was not a party to the original agreement, but, of necessity, only comes to learn of its existence after the fact? How is he bound by something he might otherwise not countenance?'

Carrington obviously thought the question to be penetrating. He said, 'They are sworn to secrecy on the day of their election.'

'Before they are permitted access to the archive?'

'Precisely.'

'At which point he might examine the relevant records?'

'No. He would need the permission of a consenting party.'

'In effect, then, you are an ignorant custodian?'

'Not quite. I know they are there; I just don't know exactly why they are there.'

Anselm glanced at the jury as if to take any questions, then he said, 'Would you accept that a natural consequence of this arrangement is that you evade the obligation to report a crime?'

'I can't evade what I don't know about.'

'But this swearing to secrecy in advance is inimical to transparency. It has to be.'

'Which is why, having taken the oath, my first act as Provincial was to abandon the practice and forbid its reinstatement.'

Anselm noted the reply and then moved on. 'And what of complaints against an individual that were not settled by an agreement of some kind?'

'Those records are kept separately in the secret archive. They are not sealed. And as to what they contain, if they relate to a potential criminal offence, then – pursuant to the system of mandatory reporting that I implemented following my election – the proper authorities will have been informed.'

Anselm's finger moved down the page. 'Canon four-nine-zero, paragraph one: "Only the bishop is to have the key to the secret archive." You are not a bishop, but you are the Provincial. Do you possess the key?'

Carrington smiled gently. 'It's a safe. But the combination is known only to me.'

'Would you write the number down for his lordship, please?'

The court clerk provided a chit of paper and Carrington took out a fountain pen, slowly unscrewing the cap. In a charged

178

silence, the number was shown to Mr Justice Keating, Grainger and finally Anselm: '1-7-1-5-1-3 moving clockwise from the digit 1 and back again.' The combination memorised, Anselm handed the chit back to the clerk.

'Same Canon, paragraph three: "Documents are not to be removed from the secret archive or safe." Accepting that you can only speak for your stewardship, have any documents been removed from the safe?'

'None whatsoever.'

Anselm closed the volume and placed it to one side. 'Father Carrington, does the secret archive hold a file on Edmund Littlemore?'

'It does.'

'Have you disclosed it to the police?'

'Yes. And I've sworn an affidavit attesting that no other documents of relevance have been retained in any manner of archive.'

Grainger gave a confirming nod to Mr Justice Keating. Anselm continued:

'Am I right in saying the file contains absolutely nothing except correspondence between the prosecuting authorities and yourself regarding this one case, along with notes made by you after a single meeting in which the defendant protested his innocence?'

'That is correct.'

'Would you confirm please, that this insistence on innocence was given to you by the defendant on the day following Harry Brandwell's first video interview?'

'It was.'

'When, as the court has heard, Harry failed to repeat the allegation reported to the police by his mother?'

'That's right, yes.'

Grainger confirmed the timings for the court record and, his cross-examination complete, Anselm resumed his seat. In doing so, he turned to the public gallery. Kester Newman was on his feet making ready to leave and meet Carrington who'd already left the witness box. Their eyes met briefly and Anselm prayed that the former accountant had been listening carefully; that the restive student kept on his knees to wax a corridor and meet Anselm would now think long and hard about the contents of that secret archive and whether or not he'd be prepared to open the safe, if asked; should Anselm find it necessary to go that far.

Anselm felt a light brush of air. Grainger was at his side, leaning down to whisper:

'I'm sorry, I don't have any choice. You've brought this on yourself.' Returning to his place he addressed the bench, 'My lord, I apply to call my learned friend, Father Anselm Duffy.'

35

A soft gasp filled the courtroom and Martin stopped breathing. Grainger was addressing the bench but Martin couldn't hear the words. He pushed past the knees of excited spectators, stumbling towards the door held open by a scolding official trained to handle misfits and distressed relatives, not a father crippled by shame. He pulled at his collar, loosening the tie, taking quick steps down the stairs that led to the public entrance.

Had Littlemore said anything to the monk? Would it all come out, now, under oath? Martin reached the swing door and pushed it open; he went up Warwick Lane, whimpering like a child: a man infantilised by fear and weakness and, yes, love. Above all, love. Ever since he'd lied to the doctors and lied to the police and lied to his wife and lied to the world and himself – and all out of love – he'd ceased to be a man. He'd been stripped of dignity and self-respect and moral authority. He'd become a child again, but without innocence. He was burdened with knowledge.

Littlemore had promised to say nothing. He'd given his word.

Martin thought he might be sick. He stopped to lean on a wall, head down. At his feet were flattened fag ends, a tissue smudged with lipstick and a torn paper cup. Looking up, out of breath, he saw clouds changing their shape like milk dispersed in water. The sky behind was a shining, majestic blue . . . there was no escaping the appalling beauty of this ruined world. A breeze tugged his hair. He could almost taste brine.

'Dad, I'm not normal,' said Justin. 'I'm not like other people.'

A gentle wind came off the sea. There were boats leaning into the waves. A boy in bright red trunks was standing ankle deep in the surf, staring down at his toes. His skin was white and he was shivering with delight. Other children skipped over low breakers. The long beach swept towards a lonely headland.

'You're a doctor, Dad.' said Justin. 'Is there a cure?'

Martin didn't know. He thought not. But it wasn't his field. And he was still devastated by Justin's confession. Martin's own world – the world he'd known and loved – had collapsed. The foundations had been rotten. After Justin tried to take his life, Martin had begged him to explain why . . . and Justin, drugged and weak, had told him. They'd come to Harlech as soon as he was discharged. There were things to talk about, though God knows Martin had no idea what he might say in reply. He said:

'The best thing is to speak to a specialist. Someone who knows what can be done, and what can't be done.'

Martin's own father had been a great talker. He'd put great emphasis on sitting down and talking out a problem. Martin had taught Justin to do the same, only, without Martin realising it, Justin had held back everything worth saying.

'I can't, Dad. I've told you and I can't tell anyone else. I don't want anyone else to know. Can't you understand that?'

Martin could. He stopped walking, bringing them both to a halt. Unable to reply honestly, he turned to look at his son, but his eye snagged on the little boy in red trunks, bending down to reach the water. He was trying to catch the foam. He was learning one of life's difficult lessons: there are some things you just can't keep for ever. Martin's focus shifted to Justin. His son was gazing at him, as vulnerable as the day he'd been born, looking to the one person in the world who might even begin to want to understand his problem. Only it wasn't a problem. It was an affliction. Martin could think of none that was deeper.

'I don't even want to look at a girl, Dad.'

Martin nodded.

'I've tried walking across the room, you know; but I end up walking for the door. I'm just not at ease. I don't belong. I'm different.' Justin dragged a hand through his tangled hair. 'Mum keeps asking why I don't have a girlfriend, why I don't want to get married, why I don't want children. What can I say?' He stared out to sea, at the boats lilting in the wind. 'She'd never understand. It would kill her.'

Martin agreed. Maisie would probably die. Some illness would take her away, summoned into being because she couldn't face another morning. Justin was gazing at him once more: at the person he hoped would live and share his secret.

'Will you help me, Dad?'

'How?'

'Just treat me like I'm normal. Be the only one who understands what it must be like. Don't turn away from me.'

But Martin wanted to turn away; and he didn't understand what it must be like. He didn't recognise his own son any more. On the day of Justin's birth, he'd been late getting to the hospital, trapped in traffic, arriving at the very moment of delivery. He'd held the child in his arms, looking into the strangely aged face of the newborn, overwhelmed by the divine aroma of new life, and those impossibly deep eyes . . . wide, watery and searching for understanding. Perhaps asking the first question ever. Where had that wonderful boy gone? The foam had passed through Martin's fingers.

'Stay with me,' begged Justin. 'Don't leave me to handle this on my own. I tried and I can't. If you accept me, then maybe I can change. Will you share the weight?'

Martin felt his entire life come into focus. This moment, this twisted and twisting question was decisive, for all that would happen hereafter. Suddenly he reached out and pulled Justin towards him. Martin wanted his son back . . . the one he'd held in hospital; and this was the only way. He'd have to start lying. He'd have to hide what he knew should be exposed. Hope and confidence? The belief in change? The possibility of a better tomorrow? Fresh starts? He'd have to cling onto the phrases knowing they'd lost their meaning; he'd have to use them if Justin began to sink again into that swamp of inner filth; cite the lines to bring him back to the surface, knowing they'd have no effect. But at least Justin wouldn't be alone. They'd sink hand in hand. How could it be otherwise? Martin could no more let go of this man than he could have let go of that baby.

'Allow me one decision,' said Justin, crying into Martin's shoulder, holding onto his dad as if he might disappear. 'Don't tell Mum, will you?'

'I promise.'

The pact was made. There would need to be another meeting, at least, to discuss the anatomy of secrecy, but for now they walked on, Justin set free by this redeeming deceit. He began talking quickly. How he'd been thinking about starting a project for homeless people at the very bottom of the ladder, people who really thought their lives were over. He'd already thought of a name: the Bowline. He was going to take people out of the cracks in the pavement and let them see the world from a different vantage point: a ledge, an outcrop, a summit. 'It's what I do, Dad, and it works. I'm a different man up there.'

He spoke as if he was trying to make amends, expiate the guilt that had pushed him towards that first, controlled shot of heroin. And Martin grieved some more, because he knew it wouldn't work. Maybe for others, but not for Justin. Because Justin would go up the mountain and he'd come down again and nothing would be any different. Save Martin would be there, waiting with his empty phrases.

'What do you think, Dad?'

He sounded excited. He'd found a way out of his predicament.

'It's inspired.'

Martin went home, where Maisie sat in an old spattered gown before her easel, cleaning a brush. Without turning around, she told him not to worry; that the trial would soon be over. She'd seen how stressed he'd become. Right from the start, she'd advised him to keep away and work in the garden. Prune his roses. Martin stood by the open door surveying the African figurines lined up on a shelf: elegant women carrying water; then he watched Maisie paint: that's how she carried the stress these days. She'd painted non-stop for weeks, rarely looking out of the window, her eyes fixed on an imaginary landscape: a beautiful valley with a winding stream, birds high in the air and a shepherd lying on the grass. It was nauseating. And Maisie was smiling, her face lit by a sun that didn't exist.

36

Robert was on the edge of his seat, taking swift notes, his eyes on Grainger. The prosecutor apologised for the lack of warning, but in the exceptional circumstances of the case where a defendant, having refused to speak, then instructs as defence counsel a man complicit in his attempt to evade justice, he'd had no choice.

'I accept that any conversations between my learned friend and the defendant are privileged but on his own account none have taken place. My interest lies rather in those discussions that might have occurred when the defendant was hiding at his monastery, before my learned friend became his advocate. These are not privileged and they never were. With respect to the police officers involved in this case, I'm afraid my learned friend ought to have been arrested and questioned at the same time as the defendant. Since no such steps were taken, I propose to examine my learned friend now, in open court. I see no alternative.'

'Mr Duffy?' It was evident Mr Justice Keating agreed.

'I have no objection. But if I am to give evidence, I do so as a monk, not a lawyer.'

And with that, Father Anselm removed his wig and bands, and finally his gown. The jury watched, like the press, spellbound, wondering why the monk had made the distinction at all.

Before Grainger could get into his stride, he was corrected:

'We didn't know the defendant was a member of a religious order. He came to us as a homeless man. He used a false name and gave no account of himself. So we weren't hiding anyone. We were misled.'

Grainger seemed off balance for a moment, because his surprise witness had just volunteered a number of damaging admissions. At a stroke, the monk's candour was laid before the jury; at a stroke, he'd taken control of the questioning.

'You were his confidant at the monastery?' asked Grainger.

'Yes, I suppose I was, though we didn't talk much. Monasteries are like that.'

'Did he go to confession?'

'Not to me.'

'Did he mention the Brandwell family?'

'No.'

'Harry Brandwell?'

'No.'

'Did he make any reference to the circumstances that had made him putatively homeless?'

'Not directly, no. But two conversations took place which seemed to me significant.' The monk almost ignored Grainger. He was speaking to the jury, as if sharing a twin conundrum. 'The first was about faith. He asked me if I'd ever thrown mine away. Which is an odd way to phrase it, really: "lose", yes, "throw away", no. That made me think of some mistake, rather than a thought-out decision. Like one might "throw away" a marriage by outbursts of violence or whatever.'

'The second conversation?' Grainger asked, like a prompt.

'It seemed linked. The defendant wondered what would happen if you made a mistake and it couldn't be rectified. He said, "You're left with what you've done."'

Grainger – like Robert – watched Mr Justice Keating's red pen as he slowly underlined these critically important words, astonished that the monk had chosen to reveal them. When the judge looked up, Grainger moved – with deference – to bring down his witness:

'Knowing what you now know, Father, would you accept that the defendant was almost certainly referring to what the Crown say happened between himself and Harry Brandwell?'

The monk's head was angled as if he was trying to make sense of a rune. 'No, Mr Grainger, I'm afraid I wouldn't.'

'And why not?'

'Because I got the very strong impression he was talking about someone else.'

The court fell absolutely silent. Uttered like that, in this place, after Grainger had called a charlatan to the stand intending to disgrace him, the monk's searching declaration had the quiet ring of truth. And there was no one to gainsay it. Robert couldn't believe what was happening . . . the direction of the trial was shifting in Littlemore's favour. Despite all the evidence against him, the monk had established some doubt . . . and nothing more was required for a shock acquittal. Robert flicked over the page of his notebook. But what was he to write? That Carrington, in trying to ensure Littlemore's conviction, had gone to the wrong man; that he'd gone to the one man who might just win the case? Grainger proceeded like a rambler who'd spied strong ground. But Robert sensed more sand; it was going to give way as soon as Grainger stepped forward:

'Why did you speak to the victim in this case?'

'Because his parents asked me to.'

'And why did you visit his parents?'

'Because I was on the trail of a man who'd used a false name. I'd left home wanting to find out why. Fortunately, I did.'

'Why fortunately?'

'Because Harry asked me, is it always wrong not to tell the truth? And I didn't know what to say. Now I've got the chance to ask him the same question.'

Grainger had undoubtedly planned the end of his cross-examination. He'd have spent an inordinate amount of time getting the wording just right, his aim to elicit a reply that would conclude the monk's evidence with a crowning disgrace. But he'd now decided to back away. Robert could feel it in the air. Grainger had lost his nerve.

'I'm grateful, my lord.'

The monk left the witness box and shambled back to his place at the bar, seemingly oblivious to the eyes focused upon him.

'It's been a long day, ladies and gentlemen,' said Mr Justice Keating. He spoke watching Father Anselm gather up his wig and gown. 'We'll meet again on Monday. I've another matter in the morning, so we'll meet at two o'clock. Have a good weekend.'

Robert ignored the hubbub among his colleagues and quickly left the court. Once outside he didn't know where to turn because he didn't know what to do. The monk was going to pull off Littlemore's acquittal. Littlemore was going to walk free. Only, his counsel didn't know about Carrington's plan, framed because Carrington knew Littlemore was guilty. He didn't know about George Timbo from Freetown who'd finally returned Robert's calls. He didn't know why Littlemore had been kicked out of Sierra Leone. Robert hailed a passing taxi. He was going to do what he should have done the day he borrowed those house keys from Sanjay – something he would have done, if his dad hadn't died; if he hadn't been disorientated by his mother's cheap bid for a more exciting life.

37

Anselm called Kester Newman as soon as he reached the robing room. He didn't bother with any preliminaries and went straight to the point.

'Bring me to Father Tabley. I need his help one last time.'

An arrangement was made and Anselm took a Tube to Ealing Broadway where, after a ten-minute walk, he was back at the Edwardian manor, only this time skirting a boundary wall until he came to a lodge by the back entrance. In the old days, servants would have lived here, thought Anselm. They'd have shared secrets about their elders and betters. It had been another era; long before the main building had been bought to house an Order's government.

And its archives.

The lodge was now a hermitage, of course. And Father Tabley had the place to himself, subject to unwanted visits from Carrington and Kester – the high and the low of Lambertine life – who kept a watchful eye on the old man's health. Ordinarily, Anselm would have teased stories out of the shrunken figure lodged in an armchair, but there were pressing matters to deal with. Two in fact; and both of them were likely to be distressing.

'I can't cushion what I'm going to say,' said Anselm. 'If Edmund

Littlemore didn't harm Harry, then the person who did – I'd been told – was Martin. Yes. It's inconceivable. But I had a reliable source. I now think Martin is innocent. And it seems that Edmund might be, too.'

Father Tabley had aged dramatically since their last meeting. Sand in the timer runs fastest towards the end and Anselm could sense the fear of death: as with Dunstan, life was running through the old man's fingers. His loose white Aran jumper seemed to hang on a frame of wire. But there was more at work here, more than natural decline: the trial had ravaged him. If Dunstan was going to die through illness, Father Tabley was going to die through choice.

'Everyone has thought that Harry suffered a shock at school and that Edmund exploited a request for help. But it seems something happened at the end of the summer holidays. Something traumatic that preceded the shock at school by a couple of days. This is the focus of my attention. And without my explaining why, I can tell you that the person likely to be responsible is Justin.'

Father Tabley shook his head, his mouth slightly open. Anselm proceeded, watching the old man's features very carefully:

'You helped Justin as a child; you can help him now. Why did he suffer a breakdown? I need to know what happened . . . because if I'm right he's going to need specialised treatment, not simply justice.'

Father Tabley turned from Anselm towards his oxygen bottle. He was just checking; making sure the mask was on hand. A frail hand covered his face as he began to speak.

'He was such a creative child. If you'd asked me back then where he'd end up, I'd have said on the cover of a book. He simply loved stories. He was always inventing adventures . . .' Father Tabley was almost overwhelmed at the recollection. 'I was amazed at the depth of his imagination. He would reach for his sword and shield, lost to this world.'

189

'And then?' Anselm felt like a warden in a dark corridor.

'He began wanting to escape.'

'His imagination?'

Father Tabley's voice was hoarse and would have been grating if it hadn't been so quiet: 'Himself.'

He became ill at ease in the presence of other people. He began to climb trees – not like other boys, for danger or the thrill of conquest . . . but to get away from who he was, when he stopped to think . . . when he looked at others and then looked back at himself. He retreated from ordinary company. He stopped telling stories. It was as though he had nothing else to say; nothing anyone would want to listen to.

'I didn't follow his development because I moved to Newcastle.'

He'd been thirteen. Anselm said, 'Adolescence,' more as a question than a comment, but Father Tabley simply agreed. He wondered how many fun-loving boys changed at that unsettling juncture between innocence and responsibility. Justin had been one of them. Anselm gave a nod, watching Father Tabley closely.

'Maisie told me he became increasingly quiet. There was some-thing on his mind . . . something he wanted to talk about.'

Anselm couldn't escape a backward glance, for the darker preoccupations of adolescence trouble everyone. He'd found German terms for his own, elevating them to the realms of transcendental philosophy. It can be a confusing time when no one quite understands what you're talking about. But Justin's situation was different. He'd grown into confusion and stayed there.

'Martin was deep in his work, and I don't think Maisie quite noticed what was happening . . .' Father Tabley shifted in his armchair; like Dunstan, he was uncomfortable in his body. 'She'd taken on a day job, if I remember rightly . . .'

'Yes,' said Anselm. 'She'd given up the evening classes.'

'That's right. But this is the very time when parents feel they must take a step back and stop asking those questions which drive their children mad; they begin to leave someone they've loved and led to find their own way. It's right and natural . . .'

What had Maisie said in court? That Justin was one of life's loners? She'd watched her boy grow into a man she didn't fully understand: it had been painful, no doubt. She'd watched him shift from trees to mountains, thinking he was just one of those people who, like an artist, occupy the margins of society.

'Justin lost himself in other people's problems,' said Father Tabley, his chest beginning to heave. 'He worked with down-and-outs, drinkers, rent boys, prostitutes . . . I mean kids of thirteen, fourteen, on the street with nothing but their bodies. These people became Justin's family. He did his best to find them a home.'

There is remorse, here, thought Anselm, feeling a slight chill. Self-hatred. Self-disgust. Consuming shame. Emotions whose shadows fell even now upon the face of Father Tabley . . . for having gone to Newcastle? For having kept quiet when Justin first turned inwards? It was difficult to know: the man's engagement with the family had been exceptionally close; Justin's confusion will have roused complex and varied reactions in those who'd known him, from powerlessness to responsibility.

'There's an old expression,' wheezed Father Tabley. '"Everyone has their own troubles." And at some point they have to be faced. It doesn't really matter how they got there. Either you choose to do something about them, or they do something to you.'

In Justin's case, he'd taken a syringe and taunted death in a purple haze.

'When was this?'

'Seven years ago. Just before my retirement.' Father Tabley returned Anselm's gaze uneasily. 'He recovered . . . and the Bowline was the result. I'd thought he'd left the shadows in his past behind.'

But he evidently hadn't. Anselm mused upon the outcome, his attention drifting involuntarily around the spare room. The old man lived simply, under the eye of an icon, far from the misery and anxiety he'd tried to displace in Newcastle. But something of that world – the world of unresolved harm – had come back to haunt him. He was troubled and distressed by a confusion of memories. Anselm thought he'd better leave, but he couldn't go without raising his final question. It had been nagging at him all summer and during Grainger's careful handling of his evidence. He said:

'You've followed the trial?'

'Yes.'

'You know the case against Edmund?'

He nodded, panting, a hand on his chest.

'Well, if Edmund is innocent, then it follows everything he's done has an innocent explanation.'

Father Tabley continued nodding.

'Can you tell me why he'd prepare a memoir that you wouldn't want and which doesn't appear to exist?'

Father Tabley was bewildered. The police had asked the same question and he just didn't know. Couldn't imagine why. His eyes swam with tears.

'I'm struck, too, that Edmund didn't go to Newcastle,' said Anselm, watching from afar, 'where people would have a lot to say; instead he restricted himself to London. Do you know why?'

'No.'

'I just wonder if he was looking for a different kind of story.'

'I think you'd better leave.'

Kester had spoken. He'd picked up Anselm's overcoat and opened the door. If Father Tabley hadn't reached out to shake Anselm's hand, Anselm was fairly sure Kester would have pulled him out by force.

They stood on the gravel path that led away from the lodge. Kester regretted his manner, wanting to make a kind of peace. He produced a packet of Benson and Hedges. The hypnotist had told him if he so much as lit up once he'd be finished for ever.

Back to forty a day. Striking a match, he cupped his hands to hide his defeat. A gust of smoke shot through the night air.

'You remember Dorothy Newman? The woman who washed her husband's overalls in the sink?' he said. 'Well, she was my grandmother. My grandfather died of natural causes, but she's the one who got asbestosis. Father Tabley helped her make sense of that one. Day after day. From the moment she was diagnosed to the moment she died. I was there.'

And it's partly why you're here, thought Anselm.

'I'm going to help him die, do you understand?' Kester filled his lungs and let the blue smoke slowly escape. 'I'm going to help him get past this trial and face death with some peace of mind. Peace that Littlemore took away by contaminating his name.'

Anselm understood the impulse. He wanted a cigarette but he resisted. (There'd been no hypnotist in his case. The Prior just gave an order.) 'You still think Littlemore is guilty?'

'I keep things simple. I've put my faith in the one witness who ought to be listened to most: Harry Brandwell.'

Anselm kicked a few pebbles, wondering how to make his request. There was no easy way. An ambulance flashed by without its siren blaring. Help on the way in silence.

'I'd like you to open the secret archive.'

'I knew you were going to say that.'

'I need to know what it contains. You might not believe this, but there may be a link between this trial and historical complaints against members of your Order.'

'You're insane.'

'No, I'm merely feeling my way. I'm on the trail of a cover-up – the sort of thing you tried to leave behind.'

'Where did you get that from?'

Anselm couldn't say: if Littlemore was innocent, then so was Carrington; and Carrington wanted Anselm to work in the dark. He'd have his reasons.

'Here's the combination,' said Anselm, holding out a folded piece of paper. 'You want to keep things simple? You trust Harry Brandwell? I'll accept that. But you accept this: if Harry sticks to his story on Monday, throw that paper in the bin. But if he retracts his evidence, open that safe. And you can do it for the sake of men like Dominic Tabley.'

38

Anselm got back to Larkwood late that night having left Kester to struggle with his conscience. He was exhausted by so many things: the trial, the substance of the trial, the obligation to unsettle people who would otherwise look to him for under-standing, the effort involved in maintaining confidence in Edmund Littlemore; and more. Kester had unnerved him: he'd kept things simple, believing a child's credible allegations. Anselm was out on a limb, believing a man with a complex history and an implausible explanation. On pushing open the arched door at reception, he made a deep sigh of relief. There was a very partic-ular aroma at Larkwood, impossible to describe or name, but unforgettable: a blend of incense, warm wax, flowers, old wood, fresh air, bleach and history; the history of men on their knees: that too, left a certain something in the air. On opening his eyes, he saw Sylvester. He was in his dressing gown – a tattered thing from his youth without a belt, held in place by frayed garden twine.

'You've got a visitor.'

'Now?'

'I didn't like him at first. But he's a good lad. Knows his knots. He's got something to show you. This time the Weaver's gone too far.'

★

Anselm wouldn't have called Robert Sambourne a lad, any more than he'd have called Carrington shifty. He was a serious and composed young man. Perhaps Anselm had been looking at the Brandwells for too long, but he also detected suppressed sorrow. It marks the mouth and eyes.

'You're about to get Littlemore off this charge,' he said. 'He's played this very cleverly – the not-talking routine. He's outwitted you . . . and Carrington.'

The journalist had taken a folder out of his rucksack. Opening it he removed a letter and began to read: '"Why have you given up? Victims always need help to speak out. Otherwise they get silenced by private agreements. Don't let that happen. The American is hiding at Larkwood Priory. Do not delay. If he leaves, you'll never find him again."' Robert passed over the single sheet of paper. 'That's the original. I've made a copy for you.'

Anselm studied the indentations more than the words: the misaligned stamp of an old typewriter. Like Dunstan's. Anselm handed the letter back, declining the duplicate. Its contents had been etched into his memory.

'I'm fairly sure Carrington wrote it,' said Robert. 'He certainly sent Littlemore these.'

Robert produced a number of enlarged photographs: pictures of news cuttings. Anselm glanced at a marked passage: *I venture to call him naive and he agrees, almost happily. I ask why help the perpetrator? Sadly, our conversation ended there.* And then another: *I wonder if his capacity to trust is almost blinding.* Over the page: *A disciple of the fifties trad jazz revival . . . a horror of mobile phones.* Further down: *A sort of guestmaster for the homeless.*

'There's a page of notes on jazz history, too.' Robert leaned back. 'I imagine he researched West End musicals to get near Emily Brandwell. He learned the words to the songs.'

'Where did you get these?' Anselm was barely able to speak. He was staring at the cuttings.

'They were hidden at Littlemore's place. You've been targeted.'

Robert explained: Littlemore must have confessed to Carrington, aiming to use the sacrament as a shield. Carrington, finding himself silenced, sent Littlemore to Larkwood planning to expose him afterwards. Littlemore? He must have thought Carrington was helping him to protect the Order's reputation. But he also . . .

Anselm had ceased to listen. He was totally absorbed by the cuttings. Or, to be precise, the border. He recognised the album in which they'd been preserved. It was shelved in the library downstairs. For a long while he just stared at Bede's handiwork. Robert's voice finally broke through:

'. . . so Carrington used me to get maximum press coverage and he used you to make sure Littlemore went down. Unfortunately, you've—'

'The letter was written by Dunstan.'

'Sorry?'

Anselm looked up. 'I know who wrote the letter. He's a member of my community. He's dying thirty yards or so from where we're sitting.'

'Postmarked Glasgow?'

Anselm nodded. 'His brother Evelyn lives there. He sent the cuttings, too – I assume to Carrington who then faxed them to Littlemore. There's no other explanation. Carrington must have contacted Dunstan . . . told him about Littlemore and then asked his advice.'

'Told him he was guilty?' ventured Robert. 'Broke the Seal?'

'No.'

'How then?'

'There are ways of saying you've got a problem on your hands; ways of asking for help.'

But Carrington had told Dunstan enough to get his warped imagination going. This entire scheme was evidently Dunstan's invention.

'How does this Dunstan know Carrington?' asked Robert.

'I've absolutely no idea.'

And it didn't matter: the evidence was there on the table before Anselm; it was there, in his memory, recalling Dunstan's performance in the Scriptorium. He'd urged Anselm not to take the trial in the full knowledge that Anselm would do the opposite; knowing that Anselm didn't want to be like him, unable to trust. Anselm felt a fool. And naive, only this time he wasn't happy about it. Robert cleared Anselm's mind by returning to the trial.

'Littlemore is going to walk free. You've found someone else to blame.'

'No. I've found evidence.' Agitated, Anselm came to his feet and began pacing the room. 'Something happened to Harry Brandwell in North Wales before he got home. He was with his uncle. And that uncle—'

'Haven't you considered that Littlemore and Justin could be in this together?'

Anselm had explicitly rejected the possibility. With uncharacteristic petulance, he snapped back: 'What do you mean?'

'I followed your cross-examination; and I agree: Harry was attacked at Harlech by his uncle. But these people often work in groups. They help each other. And it looks like the uncle passed his nephew on to Littlemore six months later.'

Anselm was shaking his head. Perhaps he was out of his depth. Perhaps he'd been out of court too long. But he refused to accept what Robert was saying: it was unimaginable . . . and it would mean that Littlemore's plea for the Silent Ones, all that stuff about 'changing how we're seen', his longing to claim back some integrity – it would mean that the entire speech had been a cynical move to lure Anselm on side.

'I've been contacted by a man called George Timbo,' said Robert.

'Who?' Anselm felt like a man who'd tried to run away only to find that the door was locked. He sat down.

'He's a career civil servant from Sierra Leone. I traced him because I found out that Littlemore had been kicked out of the country. I wanted to know why and he told me.'

'And?'

Robert produced another glossy sheet: this time a print of a postcard. It showed children dancing in the sea. Anselm couldn't make sense of the writing and he didn't try.

'It's Krio,' said Robert. 'It's an accusation. Basically it means you can't hide who you are for ever. It'll come out eventually.' He took back the picture. 'Littlemore didn't get the chance to commit an offence because they stopped him first. He was travelling around, playing the same game he played here in England, getting near children he had no cause to meet or know. They put him on a plane. Didn't take any chances.'

Anselm glanced at a copied cutting, saved reluctantly by Bede: *For a man who has confronted extreme evil he remains surprisingly buoyant about the human condition.*

'What was I thinking?' he murmured.

'The best of people, I imagine,' said Robert. He collected his papers and put the folder back in his rucksack. Then, rising to his feet, he placed his business card on the table. 'If there's anything you think I can do, give me a call. I'll let myself out.'

Anselm didn't move: his memory was turning back the pages. He'd sat like this, numbed, after Carrington had gone; he'd been thinking about John Joe Collins the wanderer from Boston, Massachusetts. Eventually, he'd left the parlour concluding that his life was about to become a little complicated. His naivety had been stratospheric. Humiliated, Anselm switched off the light. Rather than retire to his cell, he went to the infirmary.

Dunstan lay perfectly still in bed, his thin arms lying on the white top sheet and tartan blanket. His dark glasses were on a side table. His eyes were closed. The sockets were black. His chest rose slowly and fell again. He was a few steps ahead of Father

Tabley: the sand had almost gone from the timer. It was slowing now, as it does, just before the end. Anselm sat down on a chair.

'Why not tell me, Dunstan?' he said to the sleeping man. 'Why make a fool of me – if only in your eyes? Couldn't you have told me what you knew? Wouldn't that have been a better way to die – to have worked with me, rather than against me? We could have handled Littlemore together, openly, simply, decisively. Now, I've raised a doubt in the jury's mind.'

Anselm stood and opened the door. But as the handle turned, Dunstan made a sigh, and then he spoke in his sleep, his face creased with pain.

'I shared an office with Blunt, you know,' he whispered. 'Always knew he was bent.'

39

The Prior informed the community of Robert Sambourne's disclosure the next morning and the upshot was astonishment at Dunstan's eccentric interference and unqualified support for Anselm; at last they rallied around a single flag: pity for the fool who should have known better. They passed him in the cloister, strangely polite. Benedict and Jerome offered to take his turn washing the refectory floor. No one had any idea how Anselm might extricate himself from his predicament: he would return to court knowing his client was guilty but obliged to discredit his victim. Only Sylvester had words for the moment, disclosed on Monday morning:

'Be prepared.'

For what? Anselm thought, walking slowly along Holborn. The unexpected? That had already happened; and Anselm hadn't been prepared. There was nothing he could do to resolve the situation. If Littlemore was convicted, that left Justin Brandwell free; if Littlemore was acquitted, the two of them would remain at large, all the wiser, far more careful, incapable of truly recognising the scale of harm they'd caused and might well cause again. The two of them plagued by a perverse, self-affirming guilt that would never lead to change. A narcissistic guilt, very close to pleasure, that fed on continual offending. Anselm could have wept. And not just for Harry. That phrase 'the Silent Ones' had captured his indignation and sense of purpose. It had brought within reach the silent suffering he'd known about but had never encountered. And it had all been a mirage, an alluring distraction to draw Anselm away from the awful truth. It had brought him on side to help the very people who thrived on silence.

'Canna have a minute of yer time, Father?'

Anselm stopped and turned. Standing in a closed shop doorway was a wiry, hunched figure, head shaven, hollow-cheeked, the forehead scarred above brown, childlike eyes. It was Fraser.

'You need to know something, okay?'

Another unwanted revelation? thought Anselm. He waited, already wearied.

'I think you should know that there's something passin' between the granddaddy, Martin, and his son . . . Justin. I dunna know wha' it is . . . but I'm sure it's important, al'right? And I dinna like tellin' ye, but I've got to think of the wee fella.'

Anselm, of course, was hardly surprised; he didn't need to be told, but he waited some more.

'I followed Martin to a café where he met Justin.'

Anselm nodded.

'And Justin was all upset – cryin' and that, and I'm a startin' to think maybes he's not the man I thought he was, you get ma meanin'?'

Anselm did; he nodded sympathetically. Fraser's hero and saviour was turning out to be the kind of man that had put people like Fraser on the street in the first place. His soft brown eyes were misting with a refusal to think that far, but he couldn't stop his mouth:

'I think summat might have happened to the wee fella on that holiday . . . I heard what you were sayin' in court and I caught your drift, okay . . . and I just thought ye should know that the granddaddy seems to know already. I followed him to a café . . .'

What could Anselm say? He went for phrases he'd often used at the Bar to calm those distraught relatives who couldn't face an emerging truth about one of their kin:

'A great deal can still happen. Everything can change its appearance. The trial is never over until the jury comes back with a verdict. Until then, try not to come to any conclusions.'

With those words, he left Fraser wringing a flat cap as if it were a dish-cloth. Anselm was almost distraught himself: a broken man's reconstructed world was about to be dismantled again, and this time there wouldn't be much chance of building something new afterwards.

Anselm turned into Old Bailey. He could see the court ahead and the group of steadfast protesters. He could see the banner held in silence by two people who'd used scripture to speak for them: 'What you hear in the dark, you must speak in the light.' But Anselm had heard nothing. He'd been in the dark and now he was approaching the light. What else could he do, except to cross-examine Harry Brandwell?

40

Robert wondered what the monk was going to do. Withdraw from the case? Pursue the line of attack upon Justin Brandwell? Or what? He could hardly contradict Harry Brandwell, not after what Robert had told him. The court clerk appeared. Mr Justice Keating came onto the bench. Grainger stood up, so did the monk, but he said nothing, resuming his seat to place his head in his hands, leaving Grainger to call his child witness.

The TV monitors flickered into life, joining the court to the link room. Harry Brandwell appeared like the winner of a children's competition, only his expression said he wished he'd lost. Robert had seen happier rabbits in his headlights. Harry took the oath. The live transmission cut and Grainger asked for the first video recording to be played. Moments later Harry appeared again, only this time younger. The evidence was fresh in Robert's mind: Harry's initial 'complaint' had been made to his mother by nodding at her questions. The police had been called. This interview had been the result.

Robert watched intently: Harry sat there, staring towards the ground, ignoring the questions from Sanjay. He was like someone trained to resist a hostile interrogation, only Sanjay couldn't have been nicer. The tape ended and Grainger asked for the second recording to be played.

This time a very different boy appeared on screen: Sanjay barely had to ask any questions because Harry had heard them before; this time he was giving the answers . . . beginning from the moment 'Father Eddie' had lured him into the presbytery by a promise of chess stardom.

Robert glanced over at Father Anselm. His head was still in his hands. He was listening rather than watching – or was he thinking, wondering what to do? Harry's voice was loud and clear, flowing without hesitation. Sanjay teased out some detail, but with very little effort. Harry's only impediment, it seemed, was natural embarrassment. There was no fear or anxiety. As if making the same observation the monk suddenly looked up and stared at the screen, this time appearing to watch rather than listen. Robert stared too, wondering what the monk was noting, because Harry was utterly convincing: this boy was telling the truth. There was a slight, trembling relief in his voice, as if the words spoken out loud were creaks in an opening gate, and he could see a new world on the other side of silence. And as Harry finished, he smiled . . . an unforgettable smile, because to Robert's eyes – and no doubt to those of the jurors – he was a simple boy again; he'd retrieved something of his innocence, the unexpected gift that comes with absolute honesty. At a signal from Grainger, the recording ended and Harry appeared on the screen, sitting in the link room. He looked helpless and exposed. It was time to be cross-examined.

'The Ring of Kerry is just incredible, isn't it?' Father Anselm had removed his wig. He was seated, looking at the small screen in front of him.

Harry nodded.

'Admit it, though, you pushed your bike up the hills?'

Harry nodded again.

'Me, too. Did you see Kate Kearney's Cottage? The Blue Pool? And those incredible beehive cells on Skellig Michael?'

Harry was nodding all the time.

'How about Ladies View? Do you know why it's called Ladies View?'

'Because of Queen Victoria's ladies-in-waiting. They liked the view.'

'Exactly.'

Harry smiled nervously and Father Anselm turned whimsical: 'I can't think of anywhere in the world to compare with that little corner of south-west Ireland. What do you think?'

'It's really something else.'

'Close to paradise . . . when it doesn't rain?'

'Yes.'

'And I suppose in the evenings it was all DVDs and chocolate because – let's face facts – you deserved some reward for putting up with all those castles and churches?'

'No, it was pizzas.'

'Eating in front of the screen?'

'Yes.'

'Nothing better. Unfortunately my Prior won't hear of it.' The transition from irrelevance to pertinence was so smooth that Father Anselm hardly seemed to shift direction: 'When you gave that first video interview where was Father Eddie?'

'At home, I suppose.'

'And where would that be?'

'Here in London.'

'Not far away from where you lived in Clapham?'

Harry nodded.

'Just down the road in Mitcham? A few stops on the Tube?'

'Yes.'

'Did you say nothing because you were worried Father Eddie might say you were lying?'

Harry didn't reply, so Father Anselm came from another angle: 'Your grandfather spoke to you before you were interviewed, didn't he?'

Harry nodded.

'You have great respect for your granddad, don't you?'

'Yes.'

'Because he can be strict. He's got high standards. And I'm one of those people who think boys like someone who draws a line and makes it clear you can't cross it. Am I right?'

Harry nodded again and Father Anselm added, even as the boy was agreeing with him, 'Did your granddad urge you to tell the truth? When you saw him on your own, did he say, "Harry, you must always tell the truth"?'

Harry didn't react. For a moment he looked like the boy in the first video interview, but then, very quietly, he said, 'Yes. That's exactly what he said.'

Robert edged forward, his pen noting not just Harry's admission, but the reaction of the jury. Father Anselm was nodding at Harry, as if they'd come to a deep understanding; one they could build upon. He proceeded in a voice suggesting that he, too, was going to make an admission:

'Now, I met you for the first time the night before you gave the second video interview. Do you remember?'

'Yes.'

'We were in the garden. And you wondered where Father Eddie might be. I couldn't tell you he was at Larkwood because I'd got all tangled up. I couldn't speak honestly, so I didn't say anything at all. But you did. Do you remember where you thought he might be?'

'I thought he might have gone to Spain.'

'That's right. You said, "He's out of reach".'

Harry nodded. Father Anselm continued:

'And then you asked me, "Is it always wrong not to tell the truth?", and I didn't know what to say, did I? I'm still not so sure, but I reckon you already knew the answer because your granddad had told you once before. You just didn't like what he'd said. Because it was too simple. It was kids' stuff. Am I right?'

Harry nodded with a kind of relief. At last someone was putting words into his mouth that were true.

'My guess, Harry, is that when I left that garden you decided to answer the question yourself, feeling sure that you'd never see Father Eddie again, because Father Eddie was far off on a beach in Spain getting a suntan.'

Harry's relief had subsided; he was frowning now, head slightly angled as if ready to push back.

'Is that why you gave an interview the next day?' asked Father Anselm.

Harry's expression said he wasn't going to reply. But Father Anselm had drawn a line, too, and he wasn't going to let it be ignored. He wanted the truth:

'When you told your mum you wanted to talk to Sanjay, is it because you thought no one would ever find Father Eddie?'

Harry was staring at his questioner.

'Did you think you could say anything you liked, because Father Eddie couldn't answer back?'

Still no response. Father Anselm seemed to relent:

'Did you think it didn't matter what you said because Father Eddie wouldn't get into trouble? Because he was on the Costa del Sol where even famous criminals can live the good life without worrying about the police in Britain?'

There was a long pause as Harry looked towards what Robert assumed was the door out of the link room and the court clerk sitting on a chair. There was no escape. Harry's eyes came back to the screen.

'Father Eddie was never in Spain,' said Father Anselm, after waiting for Harry's attention to return. 'I knew. You didn't. But what neither you nor I could ever have known was that Father Eddie, if and when he was found, would refuse to speak: that he would keep his promise to you. So, what you say is very important. No one is going to contradict—'

'What happened to me happened.' Harry was angry with a tearless, voice-cracking rage. 'Everything I said is true . . . everything . . . it all happened, only it wasn't Father Eddie, it was someone else. I just wish—'

'Pause there, Harry,' said Father Anselm, raising his hand in a gesture of calm. 'You can't run away from this trial by telling me what I want to hear. You've tried that with your mum and Sanjay, maybe, and it doesn't work, does it? The need to tell the truth keeps chasing after you, and I'm sorry, but it is very important. Your granddad, in this instance, is absolutely right.'

'Father Eddie was really kind,' said Harry. 'He made me laugh and he taught me the King's Indian Defence. He only tried to help me. I said I'd speak if we were alone, if my mum wasn't in the building, it had to be just me and him and no one else, and he could never repeat what I said, and after I'd told him, he said he'd have to talk to my mum and dad, he said he'd have to speak to the police and that's when I ran away and that's when my mum started asking questions and—'

Again Father Anselm had raised a friendly hand. 'Let's take

this a little more slowly. Is that why you threw the ship-in-a-bottle against the wall? Because you felt betrayed?'

'Yes, he said it would all be between us, and then he said he'd have to tell someone else. He'd promised to say nothing. I'd said I'd only speak if he made the promise and he made the promise. I'd tried to tell the counsellor at school. She was kind, too, but she said a door had to be left open and she wouldn't make the promise and Father Eddie was the only one who understood and then he went and let me down.'

Father Anselm was smiling very sadly. 'I wonder if he was asking himself a similar question to the one that bothered you. Is it always wrong to break a promise? Maybe Father Eddie was as troubled as you were about whether it's always wrong not to tell the truth?'

Harry agreed with his eyes. He looked exhausted. And alone . . . criminally alone. There was something grotesque happening in the court: an abandoned child was on screen and no one could reach him, no one could help him. Not his family, not the police and not the courts.

'Harry, this is the judge speaking.' Mr Justice Keating, formidable and stern had become the Old Bailey's nodding grandfather. 'I want you to relax now, all right? I want you to take a glass of water and calm down. You've been a very brave young man. But I've got a few questions for you.'

Harry drank some water offered by the clerk in the link room.

'Why have you not told someone in your family about this before?'

Harry held onto the glass, blinking at the screen. 'I was hoping someone else would explain what had happened. I was hoping they wouldn't let Father Eddie get into trouble for something he didn't do.'

'Someone else?'

'Yes.'

'Who?'

'I can't say.'

'Is this what you've been waiting for, since Father Eddie was arrested?'

'Yes.'

'And all through this trial?'

'Yes. Every day I've hoped they'd go to the police, but they haven't done. They left me here to explain.'

Mr Justice Keating nodded, sad like Father Anselm. Sad like Robert and everyone watching. This young boy had been forced to grow into a world of deceit where the truth is flushed out by pressure. He'd tried and failed.

'Harry, were you assaulted at Harlech?'

Harry simply looked at the judge; yet something in the boy's manner suggested he'd turned aside.

'Who was responsible? Have no fear. This court is here to protect you.'

But Harry was frightened and the court couldn't protect him. And Robert knew the boy was right: no court can protect someone from the consequences of speaking the truth about their family. The roof comes down. Relationships are destroyed for ever. Against themselves, those who love you blame you, too, never wanting to reveal their disappointment, their preference for a world of familiar, warming illusions. Robert felt the bitterness in his mouth. If he hadn't been in court, he'd have spat on the floor.

'There are people here who can help you, Harry,' said Mr Justice Keating.

'I'd like to go now,' he replied. Before the court's eyes – or Robert's, at least – a barricade was under construction that would cut Harry off from the outside world. Built from his own fear and the incapacity of anyone to reach him, the thing was rising by the second. Like the Berlin Wall, it would be finished by morning. There was a hint of early cheek, too, from behind the wire, because Harry hadn't waited for permission. He'd already gone towards the door.

'Well, Mr Grainger, it's difficult to imagine a more complete retraction of the case against this defendant.'

'No, my lord.'

'In those circumstances . . .'

Robert didn't wait for the formalities to be completed. He, too, wanted to escape. Only he felt a total amateur at self-protection. Maybe it was because he'd grown up, but he couldn't build that defensive wall. Maybe the skill evaporated as you got older – a strange mercy that meant as an adult you had to face facts. But what of Harry Brandwell, who was still a child? The hack from the *Telegraph* had turned to Robert and said, 'What a lying little bastard.' A tabloid trainee had gone considerably further. No wonder Harry hadn't dared to speak at the beginning: to be believed, there could be no half-measures; there was no room for hesitation; you had to go the distance; and in his young mind, Harry had known this. He'd known that if he faltered only once, his universe would split right open, dividing those who were still prepared to listen from those who'd never listen again, leaving him to flounder between the two. And so he'd made his choice. And it had been horrifying. He'd turned his back on the lot of them. From now on he was lost to everyone. He'd chosen silence. He'd grow up safely enclosed, never learning those other vital skills that bring fulfilment and happiness, only acquired when you reach out and trust someone.

When Robert got outside, he paused to watch the camera crews and photographers. They'd got wind of something interesting and were jostling at the barriers. They'd have something decent to broadcast; something worthwhile to write about. Robert moved off, wearied of his chosen profession. But most of all he was confused: what had Littlemore been up to? He'd fled from the States and been kicked out of Sierra Leone. And more urgently, what was Father Anselm going to do about Justin Brandwell? Letting his imagination wander, he thought of the Wall. It wasn't finished, yet. If there was a chance to save Harry from himself and his family, it was in the monk's hands and no one else's.

You've got till morning, he thought. After that, you can forget it.

41

Cornered in the robing room, Anselm could only nod while Grainger lamented the outcome, lamented the investigation and lamented modern youth. Softening, he lamented sex cases in general. They were so damned delicate. So bloody unpredictable. Then, with a sigh, he apologised for any unfounded imputations: 'All part of the job, I'm afraid . . . but if I was that boy's father I'd string him to the ceiling.' Thus reconciled, Grainger let Anselm pass. Taking his bag, he went straight to Court Twelve to find Littlemore, only he was Edmund now, because he was innocent. The distance between them had vanished. Many questions remained to be answered, but some were more urgent than others. They left the Old Bailey, nudging their way through the photographers and news crews, away from the couple with their accusing banner, and made for the Viaduct Tavern on Newgate Street, the pub that had once been a prison. A boy on the far side of the road followed them for a while, giving up when he realised they weren't that famous. Anselm ordered a couple of whiskies and went straight to a small round table in a far corner. Sitting down, he said:

'What's going on, Edmund?'

'I can't tell you. I've made promises.'

'You don't always have to keep them.'

'These aren't that kind.'

Anselm took a large mouthful, leaned back, groaned and closed his eyes. 'Have you been silenced by your Order? Has Carrington?'

'I've made promises.'

'Did Carrington inherit a nightmare from Murphy?'

'I've made promises.'

'How the hell do you know Dunstan?'

'I don't.'

'Carrington?'

'Dunstan was his tutor at Cambridge. Pushed him towards a career in the Foreign Office but he joined the Lambertines instead. Dunstan remained a guide. Irascible, I'm told . . . frequently unpleasant, often insulting, unpredictable, but above all a friend to anyone whose life has fallen apart.'

So, in this confusing drama, Carrington was the first to have been compromised. He'd turned to the one man likely to understand, an embittered, disappointed outsider with a fertile imagination. Anselm could still hardly believe it: Edmund's coming to Larkwood had been dreamed up by Dunstan. But it hadn't been to trap Edmund. He'd known Edmund was innocent all along. So who'd been his target? Who was the man he wanted to trap . . . for himself and for Carrington?

'You're almost there,' murmured Edmund, leaning over the small table. 'You've found out everything you need to know . . . at one point, I thought you'd cracked it there and then, in court . . . the answers are all within your grasp. Just reach out.'

'Why did you track down Justin Brandwell? Why did you try to become his friend?'

Edmund shook his head. This was the territory of promises again. He, like Carrington, had been compromised. They'd both been silenced.

'Why did you collect all those reminiscences on Father Tabley?'

Another shake.

'Does the memoir exist?'

Edmund leaned forward, elbows on the table: 'Yes.'

'Can I see it?'

'It'll tell you nothing you don't know already. It's a book of stories.'

'What were you doing in Sierra Leone?'

'The same thing I was doing in England.'

Anselm couldn't join the dots. He couldn't make the connection between Justin Brandwell and . . . these others, like Harry. People who'd chosen silence, or had silence imposed upon them, somehow . . . because they'd made promises. What was the point of contact between Justin and the Lambertines? There had to be one, otherwise Carrington wouldn't have turned to Dunstan and Dunstan wouldn't have devised his crazy scheme. Anselm felt like giving up. 'Where do all the roads meet? What's the one answer to all the questions?'

Anselm all but saw Dunstan rise from his deathbed, hollowed eyes wide, a hand clutching at Anselm's sleeve before those final grains landed at the bottom of the hourglass. '*Les extrêmes se touchent,*' he gasped. And then the vision was gone. Anselm was blinking at Edmund who, seeing the fright in Anselm's face, had been unnerved, too.

'Go to Larkwood and wait for me there,' said Anselm. 'Bring George Carrington with you.'

'Do you now see what's happened?'

'Not fully, no. Ask me again after I've spoken to Justin Brandwell.'

Edmund nodded with exhausted satisfaction. It was as though the end was almost near. His work almost done. For a brief second, Anselm thought Edmund might break down: the strain had finally got too much; but he didn't. And Anselm knew why: because his concern was for the others . . . who were now, at last, within reach.

On leaving the Viaduct Tavern Anselm stopped in his tracks. On the far side of Newgate Street stood the boy who'd followed Anselm and Edmund from court. He was watching the pub entrance and now, seeing Anselm emerge, he beckoned with his hand like a pupil trying to attract the attention of a teacher. He had something important to say. He had the troubled look of someone about to break a promise.

Part Five

Part Five

Harry kept his head down. His eyes roved, recognising everyone's foot-wear: his father's suede shoes, his mother's blue ankle boots, his grand-mother's heeled sandals and his grandfather's black brogues. Everyone's but Uncle Justin's, because Uncle Justin wasn't there. Not surprisingly, he hadn't dared show his face since the collapse of the trial. They'd come home to Clapham, filing into the sitting room, no one capable of speaking, no one able to frame the right question for the boy who'd lied from the word go. Rather than break the ice, they went in and out of the room, whispering in the kitchen or corridor, returning to sit down or walk to the window. Harry just watched their shoes moving across the wooden floorboards.

He knew what they were thinking.

They were all thinking about that report from Mr Whitefield. The one about Harry telling lies to Mrs Quirke about the broken window and to Mr Elliot about the chocolate bar. They were all asking themselves if he'd lied at school and lied to his parents and lied to Sanjay . . . then maybe he'd lied in court. They were all feeling sick: maybe nothing had happened to Harry at all. The boy had caused a storm out of nothing, to steal some attention roused by Neil Harding's death.

But that's not all they were thinking. There was something else.

They were rehearsing the monk's insinuations about Uncle Justin. Those pointed questions about the key and Harlech. They were wondering if anything had occurred during those two hours that Harry had been away. They were asking themselves the inconceivable: was it possible that Justin could have . . . but that's how they found the assurance they needed, making sighs of relief whenever they left the room: it was just inconceivable. Ludicrous. Justin was his grandparents' son, his father's brother and Harry's uncle. He'd founded the Bowline. So if Justin had done nothing wrong, what did that leave?

'We need to talk,' said Harry's mother, her boot heels squeaking against each other. 'Remember what Mr Whitefield said about lying? That it only leads to more lies? Well, we have to know what happened . . . if anything happened.'

'The time to speak is now,' added his father.

His grandmother joined in: 'We'll believe anything you say as long as it's true.'

Only Harry's grandfather had the sense to keep quiet. He'd told Harry he must always tell the truth while secretly hoping he'd lie. They'd looked at each other, both of them grieving, both of them knowing something terrible had just happened; that they'd never be the same; that their relationship was secretly over.

'Gran's right,' said Harry's mother. 'We'll believe anything, but it has to be true.'

Harry felt the knot tighten in his stomach. He didn't belong here. Not in this room, not with these people. A flush of sweat made his scalp tingle. He felt suddenly cold. They didn't even realise it, but they were against him: they didn't want to believe a truth that didn't bear thinking about.

'You don't want to know,' said Harry.

'Sorry, darling?' asked his mother.

'None of you want to know, not really.'

'That's not fair, Harry,' complained his mother, lovingly.

Harry looked up from the spread of shoes to appraise each harrowed face: his grandfather turned away as if accused; his grandmother blinked slowly, waiting for Harry to say something she was prepared to believe; his mother bit her lip; his father stared back, ready to defend his absent brother; the brother he hardly knew. They all looked absolutely shattered. But most of all they were embarrassed. Mortified. Wondering what the neighbours and Mr Whitefield were going to say. Harry couldn't stomach the sight of them any longer.

'I want to be alone for a while,' he said. 'Is that all right?'

His father spoke for everyone. 'Of course. But think about what Gran said, okay? This can't go on.'

Harry went to his bedroom, leaving them to argue. He'd made a decision that morning, before going to court, and it was almost time to make a move. The only person who understood what Harry was going through and what he'd been through was Fraser. And Fraser was leaving. He'd told him yesterday while they were in the garden.

'I'm goin' home, laddie,' said Fraser on his knees, pulling out small weeds with weak roots. 'I'm goin' back to Scotland. That's where I belong.'

Harry felt a surge of confusion; it would mean they'd never be together again.

'I havna told your parents because they wouldna understand. They'd only try and make me stay and make a fuss, so I think it's best if I just up and go.'

Harry watched Fraser stroke the heads of the flowers. He seemed to be making sure they looked clean and smart before he went away. He spoke quietly of the Western Isles. That's where he was heading. A croft on the Isle of Barra. Near Castlebay. His grandfather's birthplace. A cottage in a dip of land facing the Atlantic. A wild place. A wonderful place. He should have gone there years ago rather than come down to London. Though if he'd done that, he'd never have met Harry.

'I want to thank ye for what ye've done, okay? For not treating me like dirt on the pavement.' Fraser leaned back on his heels and took a long, slow breath. 'You're the only one who knows why I left Glasgow, al'right? I never told anyone else, okay? Not even your Uncle Justin. No one. Just yourself.'

Harry thought of Ryan, Katie and little Ellie. Fraser had brought them up on his own after their mother took the bus back to her mother in Kilmarnock. He'd worked for the council cleaning the streets, coming home to cook and wash and iron and clean. And he 'hadna minded because I'd been left with three angels'. But one night he agreed to meet some friends at the Duke of Argyll. Just for an hour. Three minutes away. Round the corner. 'Only the babysitter hadna turned up, Harry. I called ma pals and they says, haway man, come down anyway, just *for a wee swally.' So he took a chance. He left the children alone, locking them in to keep them safe. While he was out, Ryan got up and jammed some bread in the toaster. The toaster was near a curtain. Within ten minutes the whole flat was in flames. 'The poor laddie tried to put out the fire all by himself.' Meanwhile Fraser heard a siren – he even mentioned it to his pals – and then he carried on watching Celtic v. Rangers.*

'I told you, Harry, because, to be honest, you remind me o' ma wee boy. And I've never been able to beg his forgiveness. Say I'm sorry. Never been able to thank him for tryin' to save his sisters, ma girls. For tryin' to do what I shoulda been there to do.'

Harry had found faces for the names. Fraser had given brief, hurried descriptions, but Harry had added all sorts of detail. He could see Ryan's freckles, Katie's golden bunches, and little Ellie's pixie nose. He could see Ryan running frantically around the flat in his pyjamas throwing cups of water at the flames. He could see Katie and little Ellie fast asleep in the same, small room. Fraser reached for one last weed.

'I was hoping you'd do me a favour after I'm gone, Harry.'

Harry nodded and so Fraser explained. He said he'd made a memorial. He'd put three plants on the bridge spanning the tracks where Justin had saved his life. 'He told me to think o' someone I loved and to live for them.' Now there were three pots standing close together on the pavement. No one had ever taken them away or damaged them. But they needed looking after every now and again.

'I can tell you where they are or I can show you,' said Fraser. 'I dinna mind. All I want you to do is to keep your eye on them, okay? Keep 'em tidy. Keep 'em bonnie. Would you do that for me?'

Harry thought for a long while, watching Fraser's gentle hands touch the heads of the flowers. And he thought of the Western Isles, far from London. It was almost like Spain. A new life without much sun. But a new life all the same. 'I'd like you to show them to me,' he said, at last.

They'd agreed to meet at the bandstand on the common the next day, so, after checking the time, Harry put on his coat and picked up his sports bag. He tiptoed across the room and slowly opened the window. When he was sure there'd been no pause in the quarrel downstairs, he climbed out onto the flat roof over the kitchen, dropping into the driveway of Mr McGregor, the next-door neighbour. Within minutes he'd scaled a wall and was walking quickly along a cycle path that ran behind a line of houses.

Harry had learned a long time ago how to control his feelings. He'd trained himself to function like a tap, so he could let out the pressure as and when circumstances would allow. Between times, he'd felt nothing, save when he took the time to burn his skin. But now, leaving behind those who would love him, he could almost feel the pain in his hands as he tightened the hot and cold, knowing in some deep part of himself that he'd never be able to open them again.

42

Robert drifted aimlessly along Cheapside. He didn't want to go back to the office and he didn't want to go home. There was no escaping it: leaving aside the tragedy of Harry Brandwell, he'd failed. The big story about the abusing priest hidden by a monastery and a celebrity monk had collapsed. The idea that Robert had been used to attract the attention of the press to help expose a larger scandal was pure imagination. Father Anselm had been approached simply because no one else would have cooperated with Littlemore's silence, which had been no stratagem, just a means of keeping his promise to Harry Brandwell. The two of them had been waiting for Justin Brandwell to declare himself. Robert's only role had been to maximise the pressure. There'd been no conspiracy. Crofty was right. Robert had made a fool of himself. Not that anyone on the *Guardian* would blame him. But secretly, his judgement and instinct would be questioned. The story that had brought him onto the paper had been no story at all.

In fact – and the irony was bitter – it had been *Andrew Taylor* who misunderstood the connection between the fax and the letter; it had been *Andrew Taylor* who first misread the data, finding a scheme to ensure Littlemore's conviction. Robert had been knocked off course by a trainee who'd cuckolded his father.

Was this the sort of thing you just had to accept? You had to sit back while a gigolo tried to worm his way into your life?

No, it wasn't. But Robert *had*. He'd kept quiet, contenting himself with infantile protestations, snide remarks here, a knowing glance there: the whole sorry package of a coward's hesitation; not having the guts to push open a door and say what you really think. Robert thought of Harry, compelled to follow a parallel road: he'd finally been taken from home to the Old Bailey, and there, before the eyes of a judge and jury – people charged to find the truth – Harry had shown Robert what happens when you settle for half-measures and hesitation. You get walled up while everyone else walks free.

In a blush of resentment Robert thought of his mother. The remaining links between them had almost lost their meaning. He hadn't even seen her for months, not since he burned her fingers and made her sing, 'My object all sublime'. Not since he gave his boat away and wept for his dad. They'd only spoken on the phone, never referring to the conversation in the corridor, when she'd asked to grieve in her own way. The most recent call had been a week ago to say the sale of the house had fallen through . . .

Coming to Threadneedle Street, Robert slowed, frowning.

She'd also asked about his workload and what it was like on the *Guardian* and then, as if it hardly mattered, she wondered if he'd be covering the Littlemore trial, whether he'd be in court to watch the monk go back to the Bar? Whether he'd be forced to work at night? It was a conversation that stumbled between their injured feelings. Polite and anguished . . . but planned.

Robert began striding, turning into Lombard Street.

Had she been covering her back all these months? Almost every conversation had run along similar lines: enquiries about his whereabouts and intended movements . . . when he'd be here and when he'd be there.

He started running along King William Street, dodging between the suited bankers and tight-skirted secretaries, disbelief growing as he moved faster and faster. His mother had certainly been grieving over the breach between them, and she might well have been interested in what he was doing on the day to day, but above all she'd been securing her life from outside interference . . . making sure he couldn't suddenly turn up at the door, even to be reconciled.

She'd been blocking out her diary.

Reaching Monument, Robert took the Tube to Embankment and the overground to Raynes Park. This time he wouldn't hide behind a van. He wouldn't even knock on the door.

43

Anselm took a taxi to Clapham urging speed whenever possible. On passing the common he could have sworn he saw Fraser walking towards the bandstand but then the driver slammed on the brakes, jerked to the left and squeezed past a dump truck. When he looked towards the grass again Anselm's line of vision was obscured. Reaching Dominic and Emily's house, he threw some notes at the driver and ran to the front door, ringing the bell and knocking in quick succession.

The door was opened by a man Anselm hardly recognised but knew: Martin Brandwell. He looked broken-hearted.

'What do you want?' he whispered.

'I must see Justin.'

'You can't.'

'It's urgent.'

Martin's face twisted with pain. He'd thought Littlemore was guilty. But he'd been innocent. He daren't think of the implications. 'He's not here.'

'Then I have to find him.' Anselm reached into his bag and took out a kitchen knife. 'Harry intended to do something very silly. His best friend saved him from himself. Now it's our turn to save him from everyone else.'

Maisie appeared behind her husband. 'Oh dear God, what's going on?'

Frustration and anger made Anselm raise his voice, appealing to those out of view: 'Let me in. We have to speak about the trial. It's not over. And it will never be over until a jury brings home a verdict.'

Anselm had placed the knife in the middle of the dining table. They'd all wanted Harry brought downstairs to explain himself, only Anselm stopped them, insisting that they talk first. He pointed at the chairs, wanting formality to help contain any eruption of feeling. They sat down, made submissive by the sight of the blade.

'This is what things have come to,' said Anselm. 'Now help me bring them to an end.'

He glanced around the table. In one of those rare and deeply unnerving moments of insight Anselm felt certain this family was enmeshed in something profoundly harmful and beyond their control. They were confused, dejected and frightened. And – to quote Athanasius, cited prophetically by Sylvester – there was enmity towards ascetics. He could feel it like heat from a fire.

'Gutsy Mitchell found the knife by accident, looking for a tennis ball in Harry's sports bag,' he said. 'He took it without Harry knowing. You heard what Harry said in court. He's been waiting for the person who assaulted him to make an admission. That didn't happen. It seems he's prepared his next move.'

'Save your fairy tales for the Old Bailey,' murmured Dominic. His voice grew louder: 'He stole it, for God's sake . . . like he stole the matches and the cigarettes and whatever else that took his fancy. He's wound us all round his little finger . . . he's had us all running after him like fools, bowing and scraping, not daring to contradict him.'

'Never, never, never,' said Emily, quietly, looking at the ceiling. 'He'd never do anything so . . .' But she couldn't finish the sentence, because Harry had already done the unimaginable: he'd accused an innocent man of something that might not have happened. She covered her face and began to cry: 'Where has my boy gone? What's happened to him? What did we do wrong?'

'We can't trust him, Emily,' said Dominic, being strong, saying what he didn't want to believe. 'Our son is a thief and a compulsive liar. And to think' – he laughed bitterly – 'we told Mr Whitefield he was overreacting. We told him Harry meant no harm, that he'd only fibbed to protect a friend.' Dominic turned on Anselm. 'And my brother is a good man, a noble man. He's given his life to help people worse off than himself and you dragged his name into the gutter with your disgusting insinuations. You found a few loose ends in the evidence and you tied them together to make him look like a beast. That wasn't necessary. You could've defended Littlemore without smearing Justin. But you had to find a culprit, didn't you? You had to find someone to blame, anyone at all, but you chose Justin. Why not me? Why not my father? God almighty, why not Emily? I'll tell you why: because you know dirt sticks to a good name. Now get out of my house. I don't know why I let you through the door. You come in here and tell me to sit down at my own table? Just leave, now, before—'

'No, Dominic, not just yet,' said Maisie, raising herself in her seat. 'I've got something to say. When Justin was a boy he told me he wanted to help the poor. And there were tears in his eyes. He was only thirteen. He'd seen this man without any shoes and—'

'Stop, no more,' said Martin. 'Not another damned, stupid word.'

Martin had been seated with his chin on his chest but on speaking he looked up, rising from his chair.

'I've heard enough.'

Grasping the knife, he raised it high in the air and stabbed the middle of the table . . . not once, but over and over again, grunting and spitting through bared teeth. Anselm threw himself backwards, stumbling for balance as his chair tipped over. Dominic lurched to one side, pulling Emily towards him. Maisie shrieked but Martin carried on, ignoring the cry of terror, bringing the blade up and down. The tip had broken so he was chopping into the wood, getting slower and slower until he lost strength, until the knife grew heavy. When he'd finished, he threw the weapon aside, staggering backwards. All eyes were on the table as if it was covered in blood.

'Now sit down, all of you,' he said, picking up the fallen chairs. 'Sit down and listen, for once. Harry's told you all he can. I know how he feels, because I've been silenced too.' He glared at them one by one. 'I said sit down.' Nobody dared move, Anselm included. They were all paralysed with fear. Martin walked over to Maisie and put his arm around her shoulder. 'Come on, darling, take a seat. Listen to Father Anselm . . . I'll make some tea. You've got some Earl Grey, haven't you, Dominic?'

'Dad, what are you talking about?'

'I said I'll make tea. Milk and sugar, Father?'

Anselm looked from the knife to the table to Martin, and then said he'd take it with lemon. He sat down fairly sure no group of people had ever listened to what he might say with such bristling concentration. This was heat from a very different fire. Their world was in flames and they could only watch and listen while Grandpa fiddled about in the kitchen trying to find a lemon. The only exception was Maisie. Her eyes were glazed as she mouthed her husband's confession: *I've been silenced too.*

'None of this confusion and fear and anger is your fault.' Anselm spoke just above a whisper. 'You've all been trapped in a wider, hidden tragedy. But Harry has been abused, abandoned and betrayed. He's been failed. He's been isolated in such a way that no one can reach him. So he's floundered on his own in the dark, holding onto what is right – the need to tell the truth – but

226

forced to tell a lie. He was breathtaking in court today. He looked embarrassment and shame in the face for having blamed an innocent man and he didn't flinch, he didn't turn away; he accepted the consequences. You should be proud of him. He's halfway there. He's on his way home. But he's trying to survive by himself. He's trying to remain . . . a good boy.' Anselm addressed Dominic and Emily. 'He's still a child. He needs you more than ever.'

The water in the kettle began to complain. A cupboard door opened and closed. Crockery tinkled. The tug at the fridge produced a sigh.

'What do you mean? A hidden tragedy?' asked Dominic. He'd blanched.

Anselm glanced at Maisie. She wasn't entirely present. She didn't seem to be listening. Her eyelids twitched.

'I've been feeling my way forward,' said Anselm, 'trying to understand why Harry would have to lie. Why someone would make him lie. And I've come to believe that Harry is not, in fact, alone. There are others. And somehow, in a way that I'm yet to understand, Harry's trial has brought them within reach. But I need to find the connection between the evidence that unfolded before our eyes and their . . . invisibility.'

'I just don't understand.' Emily moved fallen strands of black hair behind an ear. She, too, had paled. 'There might be others?'

Anselm was now sure that Justin knew about the Silent Ones, because Martin's murderous outburst had cleared his mind of any doubts, even as it raised further questions. He advanced tentatively. 'There's some connection between the memoir compiled by Edmund Littlemore and a group of people who've chosen silence . . . rather than follow Harry's example, rather than speak out about what happened to them . . . only, of course, Harry only made it halfway: there's still some distance to go. The rest haven't even begun the journey.'

'Memoir?' said Maisie, her blinkers seeming to appear whenever her gaze hardened. 'It doesn't exist.'

'I'm afraid it does. And the key question is how those stories are linked to the people I'm trying to find. I believe Justin knows the answer.'

'Nonsense,' she scoffed. 'What makes you think he'd know anything?'

'Because he didn't provide a statement for the trial.'

'So what?'

'It meant I couldn't ask him any questions. It meant he didn't have to say anything.'

'Neither did my husband. I made a statement instead.'

'Maybe you don't know anything, Maisie,' said Anselm, gently.

On hearing the remark, Maisie flinched as if blinded, and then the kettle began to whistle, rising to a shrill scream. Just as suddenly, the sound began to fade and Dominic's confusion became uncontainable: 'Who silenced my dad?'

'I don't know,' said Anselm. 'But everyone has to speak for themselves. It's not just Harry who has to find the courage.'

'Why do you think Justin could make any sense of this memoir?' Dominic was looking over Anselm's shoulder towards the sitting room window. His shoulders had squared.

'Because he's the one that Edmund Littlemore went to see first. And afterwards Justin tried to stop you from meeting him. I'd like to know why.'

'Well, you can ask him right now.'

Dominic left the room as the front doorbell rang. He returned, standing behind his brother like a prison guard. Halting suddenly, Justin scanned the expectant faces, his tormented stare finally alighting upon the splintered table. While he tried to interpret the atmosphere and the damage, Martin sidled past him carrying a tray. He'd repositioned his maroon tie. He was smart and silvered again, only the hardness had gone. He even seemed younger. But he didn't acknowledge his son. Not because he didn't love him. On the contrary, he did – he must do, thought Anselm. Rather it was the outcome of a decision made while he looked for the

Earl Grey in the kitchen: the refusal to resuscitate a once sacred lie. An arrangement between father and son had been slain.

'Sorry, Father, I can't find a lemon. Have you ever tried lime?'

44

Anselm had hoped to find Justin and speak to him privately about Harlech and about the memoir: he'd hoped to find the link between the two because, while Anselm had exposed Justin as Harry's attacker, he couldn't picture how Justin was implicated in a wider scandal involving the Lambertine Order or how that scandal might involve the Bowline, if, indeed, there were any connections at all. These were the remaining, critical questions and only Justin knew the answers. Carrington, Littlemore and Martin Brandwell had all been silenced. Getting Justin to speak was therefore vital. If needs be, he would have to be broken down . . . gently and kindly so he didn't clam up and refuse to cooperate. And now was the moment to do it, in the aftermath of the trial, when he was weak and frightened. But Anselm had lost control of the encounter. He'd lost control of the entire meeting. Dominic was in charge.

'My son stole a knife, Justin. The eight-inch kitchen variety. It seems he planned to stick it in your back. Any idea why?'

'I'm going to see Harry,' said Emily, unable to take the strain. 'He'll have heard all the noise and I want to tell him everything's fine.' Her eyes were almost closed as she made for the door.

'Would you like some tea, Justin?' said Maisie but Dominic silenced her with a punch to the door.

'Tea isn't always the answer, Mum. It might have been when we were kids, but it isn't any more.' He turned on Justin. 'Dad said he's been silenced. What the hell does that mean? For once look me in the eye for longer than a second and tell me if—'

Anselm intervened. 'This isn't the way to proceed, Dominic. Trust me. Let's just—'

'You're out of your depth, Father. You don't know what it is to have a child. You don't know what it is to have a son. You don't know what it is to go upstairs and smell his burning skin. If you did, you wouldn't be sitting there with your arms folded. You'd feel something here' – he stabbed his gut – 'you wouldn't sleep at night. You wouldn't eat. You wouldn't give a second thought to—'

'Harry? Harry?' Emily was opening doors, walking along a corridor. 'Harry? Where are you?' She came halfway down the stairs. 'He's not in his room.' But Dominic wasn't going to be sidetracked. He'd moved from the doorway towards his brother. The quiet guy with the books and maps was capable of the outdoor stuff too.

'Don't worry. Harry probably went out for a walk while his granddad was wrecking the table. He'll be talking to Fraser because he can't talk to me. So, let's find out why. Tell me, Justin, what did you say on "Speakers' Corner"? Did you tell him to—'

'He's not with Fraser,' said Justin, one fist locked into his hair. There was a twist to his mouth and his green eyes were squinting. 'You won't be seeing Fraser again. He's gone back to Scotland. I put him on the train this morning.'

'Who gives a stuff about Fraser? I want to know about you. I want to know how—'

Anselm stood up. His mind couldn't move quickly enough. 'Fraser was not on that train. I saw him half an hour ago on the common.'

'You can't have done,' whispered Justin.

'But I did.'

Justin looked wildly at the ground. Emily's voice came loud and shrill. She'd gone back upstairs. 'He's taken his sports bag.'

'Fraser's going to kill him,' said Justin.

Dominic gaped at his brother. Martin collapsed on his knees, shocked like Anselm. 'What are you talking about?'

'Fraser. Fraser's going to.' Justin ran to the door, then he stopped and turned. 'Stay here. Leave this to me. I'll bring Harry home, I promise.'

Anselm chased after Justin, climbing into the dinted Volvo even as it pulled away from the pavement. They didn't speak as Justin, leaning forward, drove round the common, Anselm staring anxiously at anyone walking with a boy, trying to spot that loping walk of the trusted gardener. Not finding them, Justin accelerated along Battersea Rise, swinging into a side street that lead to a housing estate. 'Fraser lives here,' he muttered, pulling up; but Anselm, on the turn, had seen the outline of a man and boy on a bridge. Leaving the car door wide open, he ran towards them, followed by Justin. Coming closer, they slowed. Fraser was on his knees in front of some flowers in pots, clustered on the pavement in the middle of the bridge. He was talking, while Harry stood behind him, one hand searching through his sports bag.

'Fraser,' called Justin, 'what are you doing? You promised. You said you'd leave town.'

Harry turned. Recognising his uncle, he dropped his bag, but he didn't move.

'Come here, Harry,' said Justin, edging forward, arms open. 'Just get over here, now.'

After hesitating, Harry began walking . . . but not towards Justin. He came towards Anselm, his face folding inwards, his mouth plunging horribly at the corners as he began to cry. And then, as if set free, he ran. Instinctively Anselm raised his hands as if to catch a life thrown away and then Harry was sobbing against him. After a moment, Anselm lowered a hand onto the boy's head. 'Don't worry, Harry,' he said. 'Everything's going to be fine. You're safe now.'

Fraser, still on his knees, was watching with a narrowed eye, his fingers still smoothing the plants. His attention flicked onto Justin. 'You've told him, haven't ye?'

'I swear I've said nothing.'

'But he knows' – Fraser made a tilt towards Anselm – 'I can tell. He's lookin' at me like he once looked at your father and like he probably looked at you. It's not very nice, frankly. You broke your word, Justin. You went and ruined things. We were sorted, you and me.'

A train rattled beneath the bridge heading towards Clapham Junction. Fraser stood up, watching the carriages pass, shaking his head. He was muttering to himself. When the rumble and clatter had stopped, Justin made a plea:

'Keep your side of the agreement, please. I promise, I've kept mine. We can still walk away from this.'

Fraser turned from the empty tracks, one eye closing. 'You came a runnin' here, didn' ya? The two o' ye? You're both a-lookin' *worried* . . . you didna think I was goin' to *harm* the wee laddie, did ye?' He was astonished and reproving. 'You didna think I'd go and *hurt* the boy . . . that I'd *injure* him?' He laughed indignantly, unable to comprehend his accusers. '*Me?* I wouldna touch a hair on his head. I only wanted to say *goodbye*. I was goin' to *leave*, like I said I would . . .' He turned again to look down the line. A train was approaching the bridge at St John's Hill, heading towards them, gathering speed, the rattle getting louder. Fraser watched it coming, shaking his head. Suddenly, he began to smile, his lips stretching over large, yellow teeth.

'You're a fool, ye know that?' There was delight in his eyes: the first twitch of a coming ecstasy. 'A numpty. Did you *really* believe *anyone* coulda touched *me?*'

'You're still a victim,' said Justin, edging forward once more. 'No matter what you did afterwards, you remain a victim. And—'

'*Victim?*' Fraser's breath caught in his throat. 'I made it up, laddie. Cos I *know* what goes on, don't I? Just like you. We've both of us had a lot of experience, haven't we?'

Justin froze.

'Yes . . . that's right . . .' And Fraser suffered a squirt of joy. 'I made it up . . . and you . . . you *believed* me.' After a low sigh he looked down the tracks, wistfully. His pleasures had always been short-lived. 'You know, I really thought we were sorted, you and me. I wonder where I went wrong?'

Anselm's hand locked onto Harry's head so he couldn't move, because Fraser had swung a leg onto the bridge wall. Within seconds he was on the far side, with Justin running forward, yelling, 'No, no, no,' but Fraser only grimaced, dropping backwards, arms extended, the horn from the train sounding, the brakes screaming . . . so much noise, come too late to make a difference.

45

Robert lost courage as soon as he reached Raynes Park. He'd moved purposefully along the path by the railway line, intending to come through the garden gate, but when he got there he backed off, feeling his chest tighten. He retraced his steps to take refuge in the George Rayne, a free house not that far from Hanabi's. After a few pints of Abbot Ale his heart slowed. He chewed nuts, his mouth hanging open as he made imaginary speeches in his mind. When he'd boiled off the froth − when his indignation had subsided and cooled to something hard − he went back down the narrow path. He rattled open the lock, pausing by his dad's shed as a train swept by, and then, moved by a gust of memories, he quietly turned the handle of the back door.

A soft yellow light escaped from the dining room. There was music . . . Dean Martin. Old records belonging to his mother. She had Sinatra, too; and Brenda Lee. Never played and never replaced by CDs. Robert hung his coat on a kitchen chair and then walked in as if he'd been invited.

'Sorry I'm late' – he paused to listen to Dean – 'I prefer "That's Amore", but this one's great too' – and he joined in – '"Everybody loves somebody sometime – dum-be-dum – everybody falls in love somehow – dum-bah-dee-dah – something in your kiss just told me – yum – my sometime is now" . . . What a voice. Good evening, Andrew, it's been a while. How are you?'

Robert's mother stared at Andrew, and Andrew stared at Robert's mother. The curtains had been drawn. There were two candles between them. The white tablecloth was starched. The green napkins lay open. Judging from the near empty plates, the main course had just been finished.

'You've surprised me,' he said, pulling up a chair and sitting down. 'I'd have thought you'd keep away from things Italian. If I'm not mistaken, that's saltimbocca alla Romana. Dad used to make it with turkey breasts beaten flat, do you remember? I bet you had veal. No half-measures. No cheap substitutes.'

Robert's mother was dressed casually, but he could spot the effort: the eyeliner, the pearl earrings, the heavy bracelet of mixed precious stones. His grandmother's jewellery. Not the stuff his dad had bought when they were younger. Hell, no. She *never* wore that lot. What, *never*? Hardly ever!

'As you know I'm discovering things Japanese. But I don't mean restaurants. I mean family honour. Shrines. Respect for your ancestors. Thing is, I can't imagine the right kind of shrine for my dad – something we could all go to, do you know what I mean? I think we discussed this way back, Andrew. Remember? We wondered what to do with those memories that don't quite fit on the shelf. And now we've gone and got some more.'

Andrew hadn't looked at Robert since they'd shaken hands. He'd gone for a pink shirt and navy blue jacket with flat silver buttons. Boat club style. Only Andrew wasn't the boating type, if you left out the ferries. The yacht people had money. They didn't clean windows or break into old cars with a coat hanger.

'How's Crofty these days?' asked Robert. 'Still sending you to Bromley whenever I might go to my mother's?'

Andrew angled his head to one side to deflect the ridicule.

'I suppose Muriel introduced you? Or was it Crofty?' Robert waited, eyeing the guilty parties. 'Is this where it all began, with Andrew cleaning my dad's windows? Come on. You'll have to tell me sometime. Now's as good a time as any.'

'You're drunk,' said his mother.

'No. I'm upset. To be precise, I'm grieving . . . but I get the impression I'm on my own.'

'You've been following us, haven't you? Alan warned me.'

Alan was his mother's name for Crofty. She'd never bought into the boyish banter between his dad and his best friend. She hadn't bought into very much at all.

'No, I saw you by accident. Once. And that was enough. Do you mind if I turn off this music? It's beginning to annoy me.'

Robert rose and stubbed the button with his finger, cutting 'Gentle On My Mind' mid-stream. The silence came like a hole waiting to be filled.

'I'm going,' said Andrew. 'I'll give you a call.'

'No, stay.' Robert's mother leaned over the table, placing a hand on Andrew's sleeve. 'Robert is right. Now is as good a time as any. There'll never be a good time. There never was a good time. For any of us.'

'At last, you've said something that's true.' Robert was doing a slow hand-clap. '*Bravissimo*, as Dad used to say. And speaking of Dad – because someone has to speak for him – couldn't you have waited a little longer before carrying on as you did before? A short break would have been decent. Just long enough to acknowledge that a good man's life was over.' Robert looked at his mother coldly. One of his Abbot Ale speeches sprang to mind: 'He never failed you. He never turned his back on you.

He never hurt you. And he accepted what you were doing . . . for me. Didn't that slow you down? Aren't either of you ashamed by the scale of his . . . sacrifice?'

Robert's mother turned white; and for a long while she barely moved. 'Sacrifice?' she repeated at last, rising like a fighter hearing the bell. 'You speak of *sacrifice?*'

'No, don't,' pleaded Andrew as if the roof might cave in. 'It's just not worth it; I'll go.'

'You'll stay,' she seethed, 'and you'll never leave again; never, ever again' – and as she spoke, Robert's mother's charm and poise and dignity disappeared; she turned with shocking speed into the fragmenting woman Robert had seen in the kitchen clinging onto Muriel. She rounded on Robert, the black eyeliner beginning to loosen. 'You dare to talk to me about decency, about respect, about *grieving.* You don't know the meaning of the word. You don't know what you've lost. But I do. I know what I lost so that *you* could have a *life* that belonged to *someone else.*'

Robert had never seen his mother like this before. She'd gone beyond the breakdown witnessed from the garden. She was on her feet, standing in the middle of the room like one of those wrestlers waiting to grapple with some fat, tattooed beast in a pair of swimming trunks; the ridiculousness of her posture made her menace all the more frightening. Robert was her opponent and the fight was going to be ugly and brutal and vulgar.

'He used to hit me, you know? Grabbed my hair and threw me across the room. You didn't know that, did you? Well, you've been protected. But I was scared of him. So scared I daren't run away. And when I wanted to, when it was all planned, when I'd found another life far from this house, from this room, my son ran away. Did you hear what I said? *My son ran away.* Because he was scared, too. Frightened of being hit again. And he'd gone. And do you know why? Because I'd done nothing to stop his father. I left it too late. I'd listened too often to his apologies and his promises and explanations . . . and because of me, as

236

much as because of him, my son ran away.' Robert's mother was blinking wildly, black streaks running like blood from her eyes, the shock of white hair disarranged. She moved to one side, still half-crouching, fingers curled. 'I couldn't find him anywhere, not in London, Manchester, Liverpool, Edinburgh, I went everywhere looking for him but he'd vanished, and it was only then that the big man finally realised what he'd done, finally realised what happens when you fill a room with your temper. He had a breakdown. Can you imagine that? *He* had a *breakdown*. Not me, no. *I* had to keep going. *I* had to get up in the morning and smile. *I* had to fill your bottle, change your nappy, sing nursery rhymes, pretend nothing had happened. *He* was on his knees, head in his hands, wanting to turn the clock back. But that wasn't possible, was it? His boy had gone and we had another child to look after.'

'That's enough,' said Andrew. He'd come round from his side of the table like a referee knowing the contest was unequal; that someone might get seriously injured if the fight wasn't stopped. He put his arm around her, drawing her away. She gave up, turning into him, overwhelmed. 'I'm sorry . . . I'm so very sorry.'

'Stop, we've been over this.'

'No, I should never have allowed you to remain away.'

Robert pressed himself against the dresser, trying to keep back from the emotional conflagration. He'd been blinded by the image of his mother being thrown across the room, unable to connect the revelation with the man who'd apparently done it; the man who'd made the ship; the man who'd gone to his allotment because he could no longer remain at home. The man who'd drawn a moral from the eating habits of the koala bear.

'Have I got a brother?' he asked, his tone trembling with apology and confusion.

Robert's mother seemed to leave the ring. She patted Andrew's lapels and moved in front of a wall mirror, taking out a handkerchief to wipe the smudges off her cheeks. Standing closer, she tidied up the corners of her mouth, removing the smears of lipstick. Stepping back, she checked her appearance and then came to Robert and took him by the hand.

'Come with me.'

46

Anselm left Justin on the bridge waiting for the police like a lost child, while Anselm took Harry, a child found, back home. A passer-by, pulling up on seeing Harry's distress, offered to get them away from the accident site immediately. Even before the car had finally stopped, Harry ran to the opening front door and into the arms of his mother: she'd got her boy back. Dominic appeared, drawing them into the safety of the house; Maisie was fussing; Martin stood at the end of the corridor, watching like a man condemned, horrified – it seemed – by the consequences of his silence. Anselm hesitated, wondering whether to leave, but Harry freed himself, turning round to say, 'I want to tell you what happened.'

Everyone realised that it was too late to gather evidence. There could be no future trial. But there was an overwhelming and shared recognition that Harry's decision to speak was vitally important and that whatever he might say ought to be preserved. So Sanjay Kumar brought video equipment. The curtains were drawn. Doors were closed. The camera light flashed green. Harry began.

That Fraser was dead – that he'd fallen to a horrific and mutilating end – was almost an incidental detail. The shock worked more like a key, turning this time to open rather than close. Harry was like a hostage, freed at last from his captor. There was no pity, just relief. And he needed to talk. He needed to explain what had been done to him. He needed the world to know. But – and this cut Anselm to the quick – he wasn't addressing his parents, his grandparents, the police or anyone else, just yet. His first confidant, the person who would first receive his story was Anselm, the man who'd seen things that no one else had been able to see, who'd heard things that no one else had been able to hear.

'I went along the beach in Harlech and, when I reached the cottage, I saw the front door was open, just a couple of inches, and I assumed Uncle Justin was inside, that he'd left it like that for me, but I was wrong because, when I pushed it open, I saw Fraser inside wearing a dressing gown.'

'Fraser?' Maisie had positioned herself near her grandson on a hard chair to better hear whatever he might say, but Harry wasn't really aware of her. His eyes were on Anselm.

'He'd gone on holiday with Justin and three others, and the others had gone back that morning by train but Fraser had lost his ticket, so Uncle Justin was going to bring him by car. He'd had a bath or something.'

Anselm raised a hand. Harry didn't need to say any more. He'd spoken twice already: on video and in the courtroom. The pause allowed the boy to step past the initial rising of memory, a skill he'd learned during his long, imposed silence. After a moment, he began to speak of things he'd never said in court, the preliminaries; those accidental touchings, first apologised for, and then repeated. The pattern was agonisingly predictable. The violation of intimacy had moved hand in hand with the creation of a seemingly innocent – and hidden – interdependence. Fraser had told him things he'd never told anyone else. He'd relied on him. He'd been kind. And Anselm, listening sadly, thought: how much wrongdoing and compromise begins with pity – and a secret.

'He was really kind to my mum and dad too and said he'd do anything for them. He brought them cuttings from a friend at Kew Gardens and he kept his eye out for bargains at the market, things my mum didn't want but it showed he was thinking of her.'

Without allowing his attention to shift, Anselm was acutely aware of everyone else in the room: Sanjay near the wall beside the camera; Dominic and Emily sitting on either side of their son on the sofa, close, but not restricting; Maisie to one side on the hard chair; Martin far away, standing alone by the window in the dining room, listening but in exile, never having imagined where secrecy and silence might lead; and looking down on them, the strangely unnerving mask: the carved face with three large mouths.

'I said nothing because I felt sorry for Fraser and I didn't want him to get into trouble. He'd lost his three children and Uncle Justin had saved him and I didn't want to be the one to upset everything. The BBC were making that film and then afterwards Kenny drowned in the canal and Jock stole that woman's handbag and that left Fraser. He was the only one left who'd been inter-viewed and I didn't want to be the one to mess things up.'

Anselm, in effect, resumed his cross-examination. He isolated the detail and then quickly moved on. These touchings had gone on for three years, beginning when Harry was nine. He'd said nothing to anybody. He'd been too frightened to ask Fraser to stop. He'd thought Fraser would deny it and get angry and tell his mum and dad. He'd hoped Fraser would go away one day.

'Did you know Fraser and the others were going on holiday with Uncle Justin?'

'No. If I had of done, I'd have stayed with my mum and dad.'

'Of course you would. Was Justin in the cottage?'

'No. He'd gone climbing on his own.'

'Did you get the impression Fraser knew you'd be coming?'

'Yes, he did.'

'That he knew when Justin would be back?'

'Yes.'

'And he did come back, didn't he?'

'Yes.'

And Harry hadn't needed to say anything to his uncle. It was obvious that something had happened because Harry was crying, and Fraser was trying to calm him down, telling him to shush. Harry couldn't remember exactly what Uncle Justin shouted, but he dragged Fraser outside and beat him up. He came back inside about ten minutes later. His face was cut and scratched.

'He asked me to say nothing and he promised me it would never happen again. He said that Fraser was very sorry—'

'To say *nothing*?' Maisie was unbelieving and this time Harry spoke to her directly:

'That's right, Gran. He told me to keep quiet because it was the only way to hold the family together.'

'The family together?'

'Yes, and that it was better for me. That talking about it would only make things worse.'

'But why would Justin say such things?' Maisie was looking round the room for support, but she was isolated in her doubt. No one else questioned Harry's account. Harry turned back to Anselm.

'He said the same thing on "Speakers' Corner". He asked me to say nothing. To help keep the family together. And he said a priest had once told him you don't always have to talk about everything . . . that the trick was to know when to be quiet.'

Anselm pondered the phrase. It sounded like the endpoint of more pity and another secret. 'Did he say which one?'

'No.'

'A *priest*?' Maisie turned instinctively to find Martin, only she then cringed, remembering his madness with the knife and the bizarre confession; and Anselm couldn't help her, not just yet. He kept his attention on Harry who was changing before his eyes, becoming a kid again: 'Returning to Harlech, when your uncle first asked for your help, where was Fraser?'

'Still outside.'

'They'd had a fight . . . but not for ten minutes. Ten minutes is a very long time. I learned that lesson at a village fair when

241

I did a three-minute round in a boxing ring. It felt like a lifetime. What else did they do, if they didn't fight?'

They talked; and for much longer than they'd fought. But Harry hadn't heard anything. Fraser was the one speaking, his distinctive voice for once harsh and threatening. Threatening what? mused Anselm. Yet again pity and secrets were involved – Anselm knew it – and out of their insidious relationship an agreement had been made, forced by Fraser. Anselm saw again his leering face, the stretched lips . . .

'I tried to tell the counsellor at school but she thought I was on about Neil Harding. Only Father Eddie understood what I needed, that's why he shut the door and promised not to tell. I told him there's no way I'd say anything unless we were alone, but he was thinking of Neil Harding, too. He didn't expect me to talk about Fraser.'

'Did you tell him about Uncle Justin?'

'Yes. And he said he'd have to speak to him and that's when I ran from the room because the BBC were all excited and they were talking to Fraser and the others and then my mum started asking questions and I just didn't know what to say; I didn't want to pull the family apart, so I nodded at my mum and said nothing to Sanjay, and I just hoped Uncle Justin would change his mind and come and help me. The worse it got, with the police coming round and me making videos and all that, I thought he'd speak up and I don't know why he didn't. I don't understand why he let me face all the questions when he had all the answers.'

'Thank you, Harry,' said Anselm, leaning back. His cross-examination was over.

'I'm sorry. I'm sorry for what I did to Father Eddie. I'm sorry he got into so much trouble.'

Anselm was reassuring. 'You might find this hard to believe, but Father Eddie is very glad you did what you did. Because it gave him an opportunity that would otherwise never have come his way. He wanted to bring your family back together. And through you, many others.'

No one understood Anselm . . . except, perhaps, Martin who'd turned from the window to gaze at his divided family; Martin, who'd been silenced too – though Anselm was yet to find out why and how. And by whom. He was staring with immense sadness, because they would all have to start another impossible journey: to understand Justin and whatever had compelled him to protect Fraser. It was inevitable. The time of secrets was almost over and there was relief in Martin's face. But not Maisie's. She was appraising him with absolute incredulity. He knew something she didn't. She rose from her chair, unsteady on her feet, the flat of one hand pointing at the camera, not wanting her confusion to be captured on film.

'Martin, tell me, what's all this about?' But Martin was shaking a soft, silvery head at his strong and implacable wife. 'No, darling,' she ordered. 'You have to tell me. What is going on? What's all this about our family needing to be brought back together? We did a good job, didn't we? We're all close, aren't we? Until this dreadful business happened with Father Littlemore, everything was fine, wasn't it?'

'No, my love, it wasn't,' said Martin, quietly, not budging from the far end of the dining room.

'Am I a fool, then?' Her voice had risen, threatening to become shrill.

Anselm was so focused on this tragic broken couple that he didn't hear the doorbell ring. He only surmised its having rung because Justin appeared in the doorway, with Sanjay standing behind him. Maisie, hearing the movement of feet, swivelled slowly away from her husband, placing one hand on the back of a chair for support.

'Justin, is this true? Is it true, this nonsense about Fraser?'

Justin nodded. He looked even more like a boy than when Anselm had left him on the bridge. He was standing as if he'd been summoned to see Mr Whitefield. Anselm had never seen such a devastated expression upon a man's face in his life. He'd seen killers and rapists and thieves break down, but none had looked like this.

'But it can't be,' sighed Maisie.

'Mum . . .' It was Dominic, rising from the sofa. 'Let's make some tea.'

'But Harry *spoke* to you,' whispered Maisie. 'He *turned* to you. He *trusted* you. He thought that you of all people would *help* him . . . and you didn't . . . Why?' She waited and swallowed. 'Why didn't you tell us about Fraser?' She raised her voice. 'Why?'

Justin didn't answer. His head had sunk lower and lower until his back had begun to bend. Maisie looked upon him, eyes flickering uncontrollably; and then she reached down and picked up her bag — a canvas thing for fruit and vegetables, with a big sunflower printed on the side. She walked past her son, pausing to say, very quietly, 'You must never come into my house again, do you understand?' And she waited, not moving, until Justin gave another nod. 'Thank you.' She set off, her voice coming softly from the corridor: 'You should have turned to me, not your father. I'd never have let this happen. Never.'

'Mum, come back. I said nothing to Dad about Fraser . . . absolutely nothing, honestly.'

But she was gone, her final word spoken. As the front door shut behind her, Anselm beckoned Sanjay outside, into the garden.

One of the problems about hating mobile phones is that you don't appreciate their vital importance until circumstances arise where nothing else will do. And Anselm wanted to make a private call. Standing by the small table where Harry had once grappled with truth-telling, Anselm rang Kester Newman. Insofar as making an urgent appeal went, he needn't have bothered. Kester had already opened the secret archive. He didn't have much to say and most of it came as no surprise to Anselm. Among the pile of brown envelopes were the names of the five individuals whose parents had given statements to the police during the Littlemore investigation. But there was one other name that Anselm recognised, one victim that he hadn't expected to find, and the presence of that one name among the others changed the appearance of everything. Kester's surprise lay elsewhere, with the identity of the perpetrator: the only name repeated on every envelope. His final remark was thrown out like a cry for help:

'I was eleven when he came to Newcastle.'

47

As a boy Anselm had tried to understand the night sky. He'd had a real job finding the asterisms, despite his father pointing them out repeatedly, his patience fraying. Sagittarius, the archer, had been the hardest, but he'd seen it eventually, once he stopped trying too hard. Anselm thought of that wondrous moment of seeing now as he went back towards the house. But he opened the door without the wonder; he felt no wonder.

Sanjay took his phone and said goodbye. Harry was in his bedroom talking to his mother. That left Martin in one armchair, Dominic in another and Justin on the sofa. This was the Brandwell family as they'd been when the boys were children, Maisie somewhere else making tea. Anselm appraised their surroundings: the framed maps of a world misunderstood by mariners too close to see the truth; the shelves of novels: old, embedded culture. Dickens, Thackeray, Austin. French classics, too: Hugo, Flaubert, Daudet. *Les extrêmes se touchent.* Once more. Evil could find a footing anywhere. In pride of place above the mantelpiece was the carved, wooden mask. At Larkwood it would have been an icon.

'Those three mouths make me shiver,' said Anselm, addressing Dominic, his eyes on Justin. 'Where's it from?'

'Sierra Leone.'

'A gift from the Chief?'

'Yes.' Dominic looked past his brother at the carved face with its oval eyes and gaping lips. 'The Chief used it to scare us when we were kids. Chase us round the garden. We used to ask him to do it. Play the monster.'

'A gift to your parents?' confirmed Anselm.

'Yes. He thought my mother would like it. Local art.'

Justin was sitting on the edge of the sofa as if he was on a ledge without a rope. He was leaning forward, looking down between his legs, as if to measure the drop. An almost cruel compassion drove Anselm forward because now was the time to break Justin – and he had to be broken, because he'd lost the ability to break out. Paradoxically, it wouldn't take much. All Anselm had to do was show that he was already inside Justin's mind. That he'd already seen the dirt he was hiding.

'"You don't always have to talk about everything",' quoted Anselm. 'Is that how it goes, Justin? Was that another frightening gift from the Chief? Just for you and no one else? Did he teach you the trick of when to be quiet?'

Perhaps that was one of the deeper reasons for Justin's later cooperation, for why he'd allowed his name to be written on that brown envelope – the name that had surprised Anselm. He'd already learned to disregard his own suffering.

'He said it was better for me. Better for my mum. Better for my dad.'

'Better for him?' Anselm wasn't being wry; he wanted to know if Tabley had dared to bring himself into the equation.

'He didn't say.'

Justin hadn't shaved; he was scratching his jaw as if he might claw the bristles out. His eyes were on the imaginary scree far below. The rocks where his life was lived out. Where he crouched and hid and cut himself. He seemed to be looking at Fraser's dismembered body.

'How old were you?' asked Anselm.

'Eleven.' Justin sniffed, embarrassed.

'Why didn't you say anything?'

'How could I? His photo was on the wall. He'd married my parents. My little brother was named after him.'

Dominic raised his eyes as if his father had picked up that knife again. Justin didn't need any more prompting. He was already talking about the now familiar pattern of accidents, apologies and power. It could have been Harry speaking, but it was Justin. He was unravelling their shared history. Nothing would be left but the loom. And Anselm leaned back, exhausted, knowing this was the moment Edmund Littlemore and George Carrington had been waiting for. This was the end result of Dunstan's dying bid to catch a kind of war criminal. Anselm barely listened. He absented himself, thinking of the night sky, because Justin wasn't really speaking to him; he wasn't even speaking to his father; he was speaking to his brother, the one who'd been spared a lifetime's self-disgust, and so much more. The one who'd met Emily and settled down. The one who'd grown to enjoy a good book in the evening.

'He started becoming really friendly with you,' said Justin, as if angling to see behind one of those sharp stones. 'And I just knew it was a warning so I said, "Please don't touch him."'

And with that plea, a boy had come to an unspoken agreement with a man of God: that he could do whatever he liked to Justin, as long as he left Dominic alone.

'He'd say sorry,' said Justin, sniffing again. 'Sorry for what he'd done and for what he'd made me do. He'd cry, but he couldn't bring himself to look at me. Because I was disgusting . . . but he'd be holding onto my hand. That's how I knew he'd be back. We both knew he'd be back.'

That's when he started wearing the mask from Sierra Leone. While Maisie was out giving evening classes and Martin was in Saigon and Dominic was asleep next door, the Chief would come into Justin's room as if they'd been playing in the garden. It wasn't Tabley, not really; and it wasn't Justin either. In time the

Chief stopped saying sorry. It was as though neither of them was involved.

Anselm came to Justin's assistance because there was too much to say, too much for Dominic to understand. It would take time; an awful lot of time. 'When did it come to an end, Justin?'

'When Tabley was transferred to Newcastle.' At last he looked up. 'I was fourteen.'

'Three years?'

'Yes. And then he shook my hand.'

'Shook your hand?' echoed Dominic.

'Yeah. As if we'd been through hell together. Said he'd asked to be moved as far away from London as possible. Said he wanted a fresh start. Said you didn't always have to talk about everything.'

In fairness, Sagittarius is one of the harder ones to find, thought Anselm. You have to look for a 'teapot', with the Milky Way coming out of the spout – the Milky Way is the steam – and once you see it, the whole sky takes on a new meaning. But it's not easy. There's no obvious link between an archer and a teapot. For a long time Anselm had seen nothing but the steam.

'Why didn't you say something to me?' asked Dominic.

'You were only eight. It didn't seem right. And anyway, I think you've forgotten.'

'Forgotten what?'

'I kept telling you to stop asking Tabley to play the monster in the garden. You were the only one who liked it.'

Dominic had to move. He stood up as if there were insects crawling over his skin. He plucked at his shirt and jerked his head, listening to Justin talk as he'd never talked before. He could have been describing the weather. How he'd tried to escape the guilt until, twenty odd years later, somewhere between narcotic rapture and prescribed medication, he'd told his father enough of what had happened to make any further hiding a waste of time.

'Heroin?' repeated Dominic, leaning his head against the wall.

'You never get over what's happened,' said Justin. 'It's there all the time. It surfaces when you least expect it, when you're about to have a great time, when you've met someone special, when you're sitting in the dark. It comes back. Like a pointing finger. Kitchener's. Only it's not "Your Country Needs You". It's "You Are Dirt". "You're shop-soiled".'

Dominic couldn't turn away from the wall. Justin was explaining how, having told his dad, he thought things would be different. He'd shifted some of the weight by sharing the secret. He'd started the Bowline. But that had been a distraction, really, something that took him outside of himself. A finger can't point at you when you're too busy to walk slowly down the street; too busy to read a good book; too busy to meet someone special. He'd tried to salvage something from the experience: he'd used it, once or twice, to reach people who couldn't be reached. People like Fraser.

'He told me I should have left him lying on the tracks . . . so I told him my story, told him I knew what it was like to die and stay alive. And then he told me he'd been abused, too. That he'd been handed round the staff in a care home. I believed him . . . I thought I understood him better than anyone . . .' For a moment Justin's eyes glazed; and Anselm knew he was back on the bridge, being taunted. He'd faced his worst night-mare. Fraser had farmed the experience of his victims to give himself credibility . . . taken their tears and resistance to kindle some pity; and Justin, quick to believe and slow to question, hadn't only been fooled, he'd given him another opportunity. He'd placed him at the heart of his own family.

'I can't imagine what you've been through,' whispered Dominic, his forehead still against the wall. 'I can't begin to understand what you've felt all these years . . . but you brought Fraser into my home.'

'I thought he could be trusted . . . I thought he was a—'

'You did nothing, Justin. Harry told you what that bastard had done to him and you did nothing. Why didn't you at least get rid of him?'

'I tried, but he wouldn't leave. He refused. He was keeping an eye on Harry, making sure he didn't speak—'

'But you're the one who told Harry to keep quiet. Why? For the sake of the family? It doesn't make any sense. You've pulled the family apart.'

Justin glanced at his father, and Martin's hands rose as if to cover his mouth. His intimations were taking shape. 'I can't help you any more, son. You have to explain yourself. Too many people have been hurt. We don't understand . . . Why didn't you expose Fraser?'

'After I'd kicked his teeth in he vowed it would never happen again.'

'So what?' snapped Dominic, coming away from the wall.

'He said if I didn't keep quiet . . . if I didn't help him keep Harry quiet . . . then he'd tell the BBC, he'd tell everybody in the street, he'd tell the police, he'd—'

'I don't give a damn who he threatened to tell. *I'd* tell the BBC. *I'd* go to the police.'

'That's not what stopped me, Dominic. He threatened to tell Mum.'

Dominic frowned. 'You're joking, aren't you? You put your hand over Harry's mouth because you didn't want Mum to know about Tabley?' He moved to the chair vacated by Maisie, sitting on the edge, glaring at his brother. 'That's what you call keeping us together? Putting my son through hell? Because Mum adored Tabley?'

'No, Dominic. I don't. It's what I call being trapped, doing what you don't want to do because you're so confused you can't see straight, because you can't sleep at night, because you daren't get up in the morning, because if Fraser had said anything, it wasn't only about Tabley and it wasn't only about me. It was about Mum herself.'

'What do you mean?'

Justin faltered – and in that instant, Anselm realised that Justin had lied. And with great skill. He'd said he couldn't speak out because of Tabley's standing: his photo was on the wall, he'd married his parents . . . Dominic had been named after him. But under Dominic's questioning this unchallenged explanation now crumbled. Justin showed a spark of protest but then – amazingly – it simply vanished, like a blown-out flame. He spoke through a kind of haze: 'I told her, Dominic. Right at the start. I told her everything. Dad was in Cambodia and I went to Mum and I told her what had happened and I asked her to stop him. But she didn't believe me. I'd told all this to Fraser. He was threatening to tell her she was to blame . . . tell everyone. Not just family. The press. The police. The court. Anyone who'd listen.'

Dominic was shaking his head, smiling insanely. Martin's arms had dropped apart and he was looking at the ceiling as if he'd been crucified.

'You told Mum?' echoed Dominic. 'What did she say?'

'Nothing.'

'That's not possible. She must have said something.'

'She didn't.'

Dominic tried again. 'She must have reacted . . . She must have done something.'

Justin seemed to look back at that now distant moment. And for a second or so, he turned into that frightened, trusting boy. 'You're right, I'm sorry. I forgot. She went into the kitchen and made some tea.'

48

Robert's mother had left the flickering candles behind and brought Robert into the sitting room. She'd turned on a lamp stand, sat down on the sofa and patted the cushion beside her.

'Come on, sit down.'

Robert had obeyed and his mother had reached over and taken a hand to hold in her lap. She'd been calm, stroking his skin. A memory of childhood had returned to Robert like a delicious smell: he'd been wounded by Sharon Hogan and his mother had smoothed away the pain with her own stories of heartbreak; how girls only hurt the ones they love.

'I want you to be brave, Robert,' she'd said. 'I want you to try and understand that very complicated situations can arise in life and we don't necessarily know how to handle them; all we can do is our best, and our best can never be good enough.'

Robert had accepted the preamble. By the time she'd finished chapter and verse, so to speak, his universe had changed irrevocably. For better or for worse? He sat by the lamp stand, arguing the merits.

'I'd planned to leave,' she said, running her thumb along a vein in Robert's hand.

'I'd arranged to go to Bristol. The police had got reports of someone looking like Andrew, so I'd found a flat and a job and I'd bought a railway ticket. A couple of days before I was due to go a young girl came to the door. She was lovely. Dark brown eyes the size of saucers. Long auburn hair with a braid. But she was very confused. Far too young to be a mother. You see, in her arms was a baby. A little boy.' Her thumb pressed hard into Robert's skin. 'She wanted to keep him but she couldn't. She was still at school, she had no support at home, and she hadn't seen Andrew for months. Hadn't told him that she was expecting because she hadn't known herself. Social Services were involved and they'd talked of adoption. But the beautiful girl with the auburn hair had another idea.'

Robert closed his eyes, feeling his other hand being taken and pressed on top of the other. She'd done that, too, when he was small. She'd clasped his two hands together between hers, like she was doing now. He'd always thought it was her way of trying to hold all of him at once.

'I'm not your mother, Robert. I'm your grandmother. And the man you deeply loved was not your father. He was your grandfather. Your father is Andrew. And he came back looking for you when he found out about your birth. But it was too late, by then . . . at least, that's what we'd thought. Because you'd grown. Your grandfather had changed – he really had; he wasn't the same man; he was a gentle, good and a sorry man. And you adored him. You ran to him whenever you saw him. You brought him stones off the ground and shells off the beach. He'd been to you what he'd longed to be with his own son. You were twelve.' Robert's grandmother released her grip, but he didn't pull away. She was touching him lightly, accepting that he was grown now, that she had no hold on him. 'Andrew went to Muriel using a false name. Cleaned her windows for years. And when he got to know her, he told her who he really was. Muriel came to me. We met secretly. And then we told Alan. But we couldn't think of a way to tell you. Because Andrew couldn't *replace* the man you thought was your father . . . your dad . . . he could only destroy what had grown slowly over the years between you – and so he let you go so that you could have what he longed to give you himself, what he'd never had . . . a happy childhood.'

Robert lost track of his grandmother's words. Because, in a strange way, he knew the rest. He knew so much. He knew why his 'mother' had been crisp with her husband. He knew why his 'father' had always looked vaguely worried and anxious to please. He knew – especially because his grandmother hadn't said it – that the great transformation had come too late for them as a couple: that she'd probably forgiven him, or tried to – seeing him so changed – only to find she could never love him again; she'd lost too much; love had gone its way trying to find Andrew.

'I sent him photographs of you, school reports, everything. He knows you as well as anyone. He came to school plays, sports days, concerts. You've never noticed him because he's always been there. Never too close, never too far away. He's got a collection of cuttings – everything you've ever written in the *Chronicle* and the *Guardian*. He's often followed you from work, or passed you in the street on your way home. He's stood in queues. He's waited in the rain never knowing if you'd turn up where you sometimes go. You've never been out of his mind since the day he found Sandra, your mother, and she told him where you were.' His grandmother ran a hand through his hair. 'He knows you as if he'd never been away. After your grandfather died, Alan gave him a job on the *Chronicle*. The idea was that he'd get to know you just like he'd got to know Muriel, to build something without the burden of the past, without any shocks or confusion . . . something natural and normal. To bridge the distance slowly until the time was right . . . but within a week you got the job on the *Guardian*.' Robert's grandmother smiled gently, at home in her new role. 'Get to know him, Robert. He'll help you come to understand your grandfather. And he'll help you understand yourself, too, because that's part of what it is to have a father . . . They know and understand things that no one else can.'

Yet again, she'd left herself out of the reckoning. Robert took his hands back. He wasn't simply disorientated, he was deeply ashamed. For most of his life he'd judged this incredible woman to be remote, never appreciating the sacrifice she'd made. He'd punished her, even as a boy, calling her 'Mother' rather than 'Mum'. As a man, he'd taunted her. He'd wounded her. He'd made her pay. He'd rewarded his 'dad'.

'I'm sorry.' He didn't know what to call her. 'Mum' was off the menu.

'So am I, Robert. Let's accept each other's mistakes, however grave, however stupid, however thoughtless. There is no other way forward.'

After standing up, she smoothed her skirt and went back to join her son. She'd made some pitte dolci di Pasqua. Sweet Easter turnovers. Robert's favourite. He'd seen them on a plate by a bottle of moscato.

Robert thought he might just leave. He could step outside and they wouldn't even know he'd gone until they heard the door clip shut. He could head back to Tooting and get smashed. He could take his time to get used to this new and frightening world. Or he could go and join his family for dessert. That was the long and the short of it. He gazed around the room. All trace of his grandfather had gone. Nothing remained. Save the memory of a man who'd loved him. And even he was strangely remote, like a retreating ghost. When Robert felt quite alone, he took a deep breath and turned off the light. His dad was waiting for him — on the other side of a half-open door.

49

Martin found the bottle of Bunratty potcheen, bought during the fateful holiday in Kerry and never opened. According to the gnarled vendor, it was 'the treasured spirit of life and a cure for all ills'. He'd winked and laughed, wrapping the ancient medicine in old newspaper. Martin filled four small glasses and then retired to a corner chair, listening — like Anselm — to Justin's continued unravelling. Ultimately, Anselm thought the process completely mysterious. After thirty years of silence, you'd have thought the weave would be too tight; that there'd be a need for tugging and tearing; but no: paradoxically, the threads were loose. All it had taken was for the most important one to snap.

Dominic couldn't understand his brother's experience, how he'd managed to conceal what had happened, and Justin tried to explain: how silence gets more and more powerful over time; how it becomes almost physically impossible to open your mouth;

how showing what you feel – an ordinary response for Dominic – was a forbidding and dangerous task for Justin. You learned to live in a prison, in solitary, where you can't cause any harm. And by the time Justin cracked up in his early thirties, there was no way out of the building, because, by then, Tabley was a household name: he'd become a sort of Mother Teresa around the docklands. Maisie had considered him a saint. She'd lobbied for the MBE. She'd written to the cardinal saying Tabley should be made a papal knight. How on earth could Justin stand up against all that? Who was he to bring an admired man down for something that had happened twenty years before?

'But you must have done something?' Dominic was looking at his father; but his father just closed his eyes: this was Justin's moment.

'I did. We went to see Tabley's superior. Owen Murphy. A sort of desk clerk who'd found himself running the bank.'

Murphy was completely stunned: he had known Tabley since their student days. At first he refused to believe it, *couldn't* believe it, but then Tabley admitted everything in writing, apologising without reservation. Another meeting was called, but the desk clerk was speechless. There were no protocols to fall back on, no guidance save past reported practice elsewhere – and that had been to move a man on, but Tabley – as a man – *had* moved on. So what was the point? Apologising on behalf of the Order, Murphy had put his head in his hands wondering how he was going to break the news to the multitude who'd been inspired by Tabley's charitable work. He apologised again to Justin, because the subsequent publicity would inevitably engulf him, along with his family and friends. In the meantime, he said, something had to be done. Compensation would of course be offered, but Justin cut him short. He wasn't interested in money and he certainly didn't want an outcry. And so Murphy proposed a novel solution: Tabley was to retire from public life and become a hermit – an outcome that would acknowledge the wrongdoing while protecting people like Maisie who'd invested part of their life's meaning in the man's presumed character and example.

'I couldn't tell her, Dominic,' said Justin. 'If I told her what had happened, well, she'd have fallen to pieces. I didn't want that. Not then and not now.'

Dominic couldn't believe what he was hearing. 'What are you on about? You'd already told her. At the time. And she turned away.'

Justin nodded. An eyelid flickered as if there was dirt on a lash.

'She didn't protect you. She didn't believe her own son . . . Where the hell is your anger?'

Justin didn't react, save to pull at the lash.

'Aren't you angry?' Dominic was like a paramedic trying to find a pulse: it had to be there; and Justin nodded again, with irritation, but the older, more vital emotion was way out of reach, buried deep in the past . . . beneath strata of shame and denial and confusion, a boy's desperate attempt to keep home life normal, with a mum and dad and a little brother, sharing happy times . . . watching *Only Fools and Horses* . . . eating chestnuts round the Christmas fire – the stuff of other people's memories.

'It was my choice, Dominic,' said Justin, his eyelid no longer moving. 'It's what I wanted.'

And so Justin, Martin and Murphy had all sworn to keep the matter secret. For the common good. There'd even been a strange kind of ceremony, using the Bible. They'd brought God into the arrangement, as witness and protector. Anselm, roused by dismay, had to interject: 'At whose suggestion?'

'Murphy's.'

Anselm sank back into himself; and Justin explained how the matter seemed to have been concluded. He got on with the Bowline. Tabley moved to a kind of prison cell in London. He was – to quote Maisie – out of circulation. But then Littlemore came along.

'He started asking questions and I realised straight away that

257

he knew everything. But I couldn't work out who'd told him because Murphy was dead and Littlemore hadn't known him . . . He only knew the new guy, Carrington, and he'd had nothing to do with the arrangement.'

And Littlemore wouldn't give up. He kept returning. But in a way that was *compassionate*. He'd been like Justin chasing after one of the hardened drinkers milling around Charing Cross. He'd refused to back off. He'd been extending a helping hand. Wouldn't take no for an answer.

'So we had another meeting. With Carrington and Littlemore. They wanted to call in the police. Get me counselling. Meet all costs, pay compensation and I told them to forget it. I told them this was my decision. I wanted privacy. I said—'

'You *turned down* treatment?' asked Dominic, but Justin pushed on, ignoring the question as if it was a passing siren.

'I said they didn't have the right to change the ground rules that made living possible for me. I said they *owed* me. And this time it was me who reached for the Bible. I told them to swear on it.'

Dominic was wooden. 'And?'

'They refused. But they gave me their word. I accepted it.'

So Justin had thought he was safe, that there would be no more digging in the burial ground, but then – and this had been like a ghastly miracle – Harry falsely accused Littlemore. The police called him in and Justin's heart almost stopped beating. He feared that Littlemore would reveal what he knew about Tabley, a fear that only grew more insistent after Littlemore sought refuge at Larkwood Priory. By then, of course, Justin had been brought to his knees by Fraser's threat to enlighten the world about Maisie. That was the whole, sorry story.

'No, it isn't, Justin,' said Dominic, his voice hoarse from the moonshine. 'You silenced Harry. You did to him what you'd done to yourself.'

'I know.'

'It's unpardonable.'

'Don't say that, please.'

'But it is. It's as unpardonable as what was done to you. And you can't cover this kind of stuff up . . . not for anyone. Not for the Church, not for yourself and not for Mum. You should never have spared her, Justin. You should never have let pity get in the way. Pity just brings bad fruit out of bad fruit. It's all rotten. Don't you realise, it was pity that brought Fraser into this damned house?' Dominic's anger became white hot. 'And that's not all. You went along with his blackmail . . . and not just because you wanted to protect Mum . . . You did as you were told because it suited you. You liked being the saviour of the Embankment. And just like Tabley you wanted to keep things nice and clean. You had the Bowline and he had Newcastle. New lives. But neither of you were interested in reality . . . the full, grubby picture. That's why you silenced Harry, Justin. It was good for you.'

Anselm flinched. If there was any truth to Dominic's words – that there was a top layer of self-interest to cap the strata of shame and confusion – then Justin couldn't absorb it . . . any more than he could break through the rock to his anger, or recognise the need for treatment. All he knew was that he'd done something profoundly wrong. He was swinging back and forth saying he was sorry; and Anselm watched the pleading as he'd watched Tabley in his cell: closely and with a mixture of anger and that very delicate commodity, pity. Poor, abused Justin. His childhood had been ruined; and now he stood condemned as a man because he'd failed to handle the consequences.

'Harry's situation is over,' said Dominic, cutting short the flow of apologies. He came to his feet, reached for the bottle and filled everyone's glass. He wasn't offering, he was imposing. Another binding ritual was underway; a pledge with the treasured spirit of life. 'Yours isn't.' He was standing over Justin. 'And we're going to sort it out now. I'm going to call Mum and get her back here. Then we all go to the police. I'll do the talking.'

'No, Dominic, no. Impossible.'

'You've no choice.'

'I do. It's the one thing left to me. I do have a choice.' And before Dominic could answer back, Justin looked up, beseeching and crushed. 'You don't know what I live with. You can't imagine it, and I don't want you to. But I can't talk about it . . . and you can't speak for me. No one can. I could never go into a court-room, even with anonymity. I can only hold things together if I keep some . . . *dignity*.' Justin all but smiled as he used the word. As if dignity didn't really belong to him, but he could at least pretend, as he'd pretended all sorts of impossible things as a child. 'Tabley can keep his reputation. Mum can keep his photograph. And I can keep some dignity. Some self-respect. Allow me that, please? Tabley will be dead soon. I was the only one . . . Can't we just let it go?'

Dominic slumped into his chair. Nobody spoke. Nobody could speak. Justin seemed to have a single coin in his outstretched hand: the authority of a victim to choose his future. Anselm appeared to weigh its worth and then coughed, lightly.

'You weren't,' he said.

'Sorry?' Justin had dropped his hand.

'You weren't the only one. Edmund Littlemore called them "the Silent Ones". He couldn't reach them because they'd all made promises, like you; they'd all preferred silence, like you; they've all lived thinking they were the only one. But you were all deceived.'

The effect of this quiet declaration was roughly equivalent to Martin's command after he'd thrown the knife aside, when he'd told everyone to sit down and listen. Only this time Martin himself was rigid with attention. The poor man had kept faith in the first awful secret and it wasn't what it had seemed.

'I imagine none of them want to go into a courtroom,' said Anselm, swishing his glass, looking at the almost pure spirit. It had burned his mouth and set his heart racing. 'None of them want their wider families to know what was done to them. They all want to keep their dignity, and I imagine they all think that one day Tabley will be dead and it will all be over, only, of course, it won't. You know that, don't you, Justin? You must say something very similar to the old boys on the street who are just living out their days after learning that bad things don't just go away. You tell them they can get past their demons. But they have to talk, don't they? Strange, isn't it, the importance of *speaking*?'

'I'm not the only one?'

'No.'

'How did Littlemore find out about these others?'

'I really don't know. He kept his promise to you like he kept it to Harry. But he did something else, something completely extraordinary. He used Harry's trial to showcase the evidence against Tabley without saying what it meant. He let the prosecution show the world that he'd been involved in a private investigation into Tabley. In effect, by vanishing, he'd sent the police to all the victims, asking them about Littlemore while he was hoping they'd all speak about Tabley, but they didn't. He hoped I'd get the message. I was a little slow.'

'How can you be so sure?' Martin placed his glass on the table. He was a clever man, and he knew a final and foundational disillusionment was approaching.

'Because, without violating the terms of secrecy entered into between individuals and the Lambertine Order, I've managed to discover the contents of the secret archive. There are nine sealed brown envelopes all carrying the name of Dominic Tabley and someone else. You are number four, Justin. I shouldn't have told you about the others; and I'd ask you to continue the secrecy – not for the sake of Tabley or his Order, but because – for now – it remains the choice of the victim concerned. We can't ignore that, can we, Justin?'

Martin stood up as if to get some height, some perspective on his own involvement, only he'd shrivelled up: his shoulders had fallen. His arms were hanging down. 'You mean that when

I spoke to Murphy all those years ago, he knew about three other victims?'

'Yes. He may well have known of more . . . people whose cases were in the process of being resolved.' Anselm's anger and pity had cooled; he was pondering, now: like Dunstan on Blunt. 'Murphy received most of the complaints after Tabley had been in Newcastle for years. In all probability they came forward in later life when, like you, Justin, they finally cracked. For all sorts of reasons – though I suspect they are very close to yours – they all chose silence. They all think they're on their own. They all want to keep their dignity.'

'And this Murphy put his hand on a Bible and sealed an envelope and banged it away in a safe?' Dominic asked. 'And then he called the next one and did it again? Playing out the surprise? Playing out the shock?'

'Something like that. Perhaps exactly like that.'

'These sorts of damned archive exist?' Dominic wasn't really asking; he just couldn't believe that Carrington's hypothetical evidence had any footing in the real world. It had sounded like one of Justin's stories, the invention of a child's adventurous mind.

'I'm afraid so.' Anselm felt compelled to enlighten those present. 'When it comes to handling sensitive information, the Church is not that different from a government and an Order not that different from a department. They've all got secrets they don't want. They've all got ways of hiding them so that confidence isn't shaken in the scheme of things. They've all got ways of holding back what can't be revealed without causing more harm; perhaps irreparable harm. And there's always someone somewhere behind a desk, an elected official who didn't know what they were letting themselves in for, who hopes against hope that time will redeem them from the responsibility of having to disclose the truth.'

'But you are meant to be different,' said Dominic.

'Yes, we are.'

Anselm finished his potcheen. 'Mountain dew' it was called in

Ireland. What a wonderful world that would be, he thought: the spirit of life shining on every blade of grass, there to be touched and tasted. He sighed and addressed Justin. 'You can be different.'

Justin didn't understand. He looked to his father as if he might help.

'You can lead the way,' said Anselm. 'There are eight people out there who need a leader. There may be more. They need someone to show them that courage is possible. They need you to show them the meaning of Edmund Littlemore's evidence.'

'But Tabley is dying. There's no point.'

Anselm put his glass on a table and walked across the room. Throughout Justin's stripping down, he'd waited, wondering if anyone would actually remember that the thing was there on the wall. The mask – and its fatalism – had so insinuated itself into the Brandwell family that they didn't notice it was still watching over them. Only Justin had been aware of it, avoiding sight of its triple grimace; and even he had said nothing because accepting it was part of the scheme of things. It still had power over him. It could still command his obedience.

'He isn't dying,' said Anselm, taking the mask off the wall. He turned around keeping the monstrosity behind his back. 'He wants to die, and that is a very different condition.'

50

By the time Dominic dropped Anselm at the property in Ealing, it was dark. The sky was clear and the stars were splendid, though Anselm, looking up, didn't try to find the Plough or Pegasus or any other existing pattern. He invented his own, joining nine twinkling lights to make the Silent Ones. Perhaps there were more. Perhaps they filled the night sky. And perhaps Anselm's imagination was veering out of control but he was nonetheless convinced that, joined together and elevated by a name, these lonely stars received a kind of glory. Kester was standing outside, smoking. The ash flared red as Anselm came near.

'He's waiting.'

What am I to say? thought Anselm, leaving his carpet bag in the vestibule. Do I speak for his victims? Speak for the Church? Speak for myself? Do I try to understand him? Condemn him? There was too much to be said, and the right to articulate anything belonged to those who'd been betrayed and abandoned. Anselm's task was merely to bring about that encounter. But not behind closed doors, sealed by an oath and hidden in a safe.

'I'm not here to judge you,' said Anselm, walking into the sitting room. 'I'm here to make a request.'

Through the corner of his eye he could see that Father Tabley was seated in an armchair with his oxygen bottle at his side, the mask in position over his mouth and nose. A soft whisper of air flowed through the tube. Upon impulse, Anselm looked over to the icon on the wall: it showed Lazarus, wrapped in bandages, emerging from his tomb. He'd been brought back from the dead to live once more. His family were weeping with wonder and joy.

'I know you've apologised,' said Anselm, unable to face Father Tabley. 'But something is missing from the . . . resolution of things.'

Father Tabley had gone to Newcastle wanting to get away from who he'd been and what he'd done. He'd been overwhelmed, no doubt, by the death of Dorothy Newman, but the real engine for all that selfless work was regret. He spent twenty years atoning for his past without seeming to realise that a crime is a very public concern. You can't hide it away. You can't escape the consequences – any more than the shipping companies on the Tyne could escape liability for harming their employees. Did Father Tabley arrange meetings between dying men and lawyers never once thinking that something similar ought to have been done in relation to his own criminality? Did he contact doctors and specialists never thinking that someone ought to have done the same thing for Justin and his eight companions? Did he really think you could move on and leave so much behind? If he'd truly come to visualise the depth of injury he caused, could he seriously believe that secret settlements were justified by the need to protect people like Maisie or Kester, all those admirers who had a vested interest in his reputation? Perhaps there was something Anselm might say after all. He spoke while looking at Lazarus and listening to the whisper of air.

'Justin hasn't moved on. He's trapped by secrecy. He doesn't know how to handle his own story. He doesn't know how to ask for help. There's something I don't understand, but it's true: compensation payments are important; so are abject apologies; but without a public acknowledgement of responsibility, without a trial and a judgement and a sentence, victims can remain chained to their past. It's another crime.'

Anselm didn't know what to do with the mask. He was holding it behind his back. He'd removed it from the Brandwells' intending to return it to Father Tabley, but now that he was with the old man, the gesture seemed inappropriate; perhaps even wrong.

'Do you remember what you did after Dorothy died? You went to the press. You went from house to house finding those people who were quietly dying. You became their voice. You set up an advice centre. Well, something similar has to happen again, only this time it is out of your hands. The people you harmed need to know they aren't alone. There is only one thing you can do, and that is why I'm here. I've come to ask you to stay alive. You cannot die. Not yet. You have to give living its full measure. You know the passage. There's a time for weeping, a time for dancing, a time for living and a time for dying. Once the Silent Ones have been brought together, once they've been vindicated, then you can go.'

Anselm walked to the door, keeping the carved face out of view.

'The Silent Ones?' Father Tabley had pulled off his mask. There was confusion in his voice.

'Edmund's name for those who made the Dorothy Newman Centre possible,' replied Anselm, turning the handle. 'Their silence was central to her rescue and everything that happened afterwards.'

Father Tabley thought for a while, struggling, it seemed, with uncontrollable shame, wanting to make some kind of reply.

'I changed,' he said at last. 'I'm not that man any more. I don't recognise the man I was . . . I hate the man I was. Tell Edmund, will you? Tell him I changed. I want him to know.'

Anselm could just see Kester outside. His cigarette blazed, sending a glow of faint light upon his face. He could very well have been the next victim. But he hadn't been.

'I did change,' repeated Father Tabley.

Cautiously Anselm moved into the darkness of the vestibule, hands outstretched feeling for the walls. 'Changing was never enough . . . because remorse doesn't end with change. It ends with justice.'

A moment later he was standing outside where Kester had once vowed to help an old man die with some peace of mind. He'd been bullish and sure. An ambulance had flashed by. Now they were joined by the darkness and silence.

'What am I to do?' asked Kester, breaking out of a reverie.

'Keep him alive.'

'What for?'

'His trial. That's where his story ends and all the others begin. That's our goal, Kester: a new beginning for those who didn't think it was possible.'

Kester still had the mobile phone he'd used at PwC. It was no longer state of the art, but it worked; and Anselm used it to make one last important call. A woman he didn't know answered. She was evidently in tears. And notwithstanding Anselm's gentle and polite remonstrations, she refused to put him onto the person he needed to contact. Finally, he said:

'May I ask . . . has something bad happened?'

'No, something good,' she replied, with one of those sniffing laughs. 'Something very good.'

With that happy concession she agreed to allow a meeting. But there was no rush; Anselm was to take his time. And so, after throwing the wooden mask into a refuse truck lurching along Uxbridge Road, Anselm hailed a cab and asked the driver to meander south of the river. They chatted about a scandal at Westminster but Anselm's attention was riveted on a picture in his mind: Lazarus with shining eyes, restored to his family, children pinching at his skin to see if he was real.

51

The conversation between Robert and his father flowed easily. And that was because Andrew's innocent deception had worked: they already knew each other. Best of all, they'd already reached the depth proper to a father and son relationship because Andrew's misreading of the Littlemore case – the conspiracy that never was – had played a significant role in damaging Robert's career with the *Guardian*. They'd kicked off their association with the sort of mixed baggage that ordinarily takes years to accumulate. It was nigh on perfect. They'd put their coats on and were sitting outside on the decking, hunched in garden chairs.

'I don't understand how he could have been one man to you and another man to me,' said Robert, hands thrust into his pockets. They'd discussed almost everything else, slowly approaching the dividing line between them. 'Was he two people at the same time? Or did he change? And if he changed, does it matter?'

Robert's mind was teeming with questions – cold analytical questions – that seemed to have no bearing on the man he'd known and loved. The Lenny Sambourne who was 'Dad' had been a wonderful, irreplaceable presence in Robert's life. The image of his 'mother' screaming in fear was simply unreal. This other man could not have been responsible for the nightmare; but he was.

'For a long time, I just didn't care,' said Andrew, from behind an upturned collar. 'If I wanted to know anything, it was why. Why had he been so out of control? Why couldn't he relate normally? Why had he kept exploding? There had to be an explanation.'

Andrew discovered the reason by chance, after a friend in Zambia invited him to spend a couple of weeks bartending in Brisbane. He stayed on and hitchhiked north to Mackay, knowing his father had worked on a sugar cane plantation near Bakers Creek. He made enquiries, finally meeting a boozy fisherman who remembered Big Lenny Sambourne. And then came a totally unexpected revelation. Big Lenny was no native Aussie. He'd been born in Sheffield, coming to Australia aged eight with his twin sister. His parents? They'd died. The sister? Hadn't seen her since they arrived in Melbourne. Never said how they got parted. And as for Big Lenny, well, he was a strange kind of raw prawn, because, having said all that, which wasn't much, he went back to Britain in the sixties to find his parents after convincing himself they were still alive.

'It's taken me time to piece things together,' said Andrew. 'I spent years trying to trace his past. And now I know a little of what my father and your grandfather kept to himself.'

Leonard Andrew Sambourne and his twin Margaret Lucy were brought into the care of the state by court order. Two years later, they were included in the child migration scheme that sent 150,000 children from Britain to different parts of the empire, 7000 of them to Australia.

'It was a way of saving money as much as anything else,' said

Andrew. 'They deported vulnerable kids overseas and then looked the other way.'

If similar cases were a guide – and it seemed that they were – Lenny and his sister were told their parents were dead, and the parents were told that their children had been adopted. Without any documents linking them to their past or each other, they were separated on the quayside upon disembarking and taken to different institutions where – and again surmise had to take the place of established fact – Lenny was subjected to grave and prolonged abuse.

'Many kids were sent to loving homes and decent schools, but a lot weren't. They were seen as cheap labour. And other things. My dad – your grandfather – was one of them. He had no childhood memories. He never spoke of playing in the backyard or swimming in the sea. I only realised this recently, after I began to remember him without anger. But he only talked about animals. Never people. He spoke about koalas and dingoes and wallabies and cane toads but never people. He'd lost faith in people.'

Andrew had been helped by the Child Migrants Trust in Nottingham. But the absence of records – the erasure of identity – meant that without an oral account from a victim only a sketch of the possible was within reach. But this much was certain: Lenny had run away from a brutal regime and gone looking for his sister. He failed, it seemed. But he also came to believe that he'd been misled about the fate of his parents. Crofty had remembered Lenny as a young man ostensibly researching his ancestors, joking that they'd been sent to Van Diemen's Land on a prison ship. He got nowhere, he'd said. Which must have been true, because there was no way of linking him to any surviving relatives in England. Government departments and the relevant charitable agencies only kept closed archives. Lenny will have had no realistic chance of retrieving any information. Years later, and helped by the Trust, Andrew finally traced a Barnardo's file and the identity of Lenny and Margaret's parents. Further research demonstrated that they died while he was in Australia. He came home too late.

'I don't know what happened to him in that children's home,' said Andrew, 'but I can work backwards from how he behaved with me. I can see that he was damaged. That he'd tried to cope on his own and couldn't. He was harmed and then he went on to harm the people closest to him. He'd tried to live a normal life with Mum, only it fell apart when I came along. Maybe the sight of me brought back his own childhood and everything that had happened. I don't know.' Andrew shifted deeper behind his collar. 'It doesn't have to be that way. Many people suffered the same type of abuse as my dad and they didn't go on to hurt anyone else. But my dad did. That's his story. He never let the anger out. He never told anyone what had been done to him.'

Unlike Andrew, who'd spent years running away from himself until he met that barely coherent fisherman. He was saved by an irony, because, in asking questions about his father, he was confronted with the antecedents to his own story.

'I think it helps to know why someone behaved in the way that they did,' said Andrew. 'It's made a difference to me. Did he change? Yes, he did. Does it matter? Yes, I believe it does. You knew someone completely different to me. Keep what you can out of your own experience. No one should take that away from you . . . or from him. It's yours and it's real.'

'But what about you?' Robert wasn't sure he'd be able to cherish a memory in isolation from his father's experience; it, too, was real.

Andrew was feeling the cold. He was hugging himself, blowing warm air through pursed lips. 'It's no different for me. No matter what's happened, nine times out of ten, there's something worth keeping. I've looked at my experience. I've taken what I can, and I value it.' He paused to let a train go past. 'I just wish you'd kept that ship. I'd have liked that ship.' They listened to the fading rumble. 'Because the ship you describe was the *Arcadia*. It left Tilbury in February 1953 and took him to Melbourne. It took him away from who he might have been, and me. It took him away from me. Do you fancy a bacon sandwich? There's nothing like a bacon sandwich.'

On entering the kitchen Robert's grandmother put her arms around her son and grandson, drawing them to her and together. They were all too tired to speak. She'd been crying and her stained cheeks provoked more tears, this time from her brood, but then the doorbell rang. Robert pulled away, wiping his eyes. Moments later he was taken aback. There, on the front step, was the monk, Father Anselm. He looked exhausted, too.

'Is this a good time or a bad time?' he asked, uneasily.

'A good time,' said Robert, with a laugh. 'A very good time. Come on in. I'd like you to meet my dad.'

52

The last time Anselm had tasted a bacon sandwich he'd been significantly inebriated after a night out with Roddy Kemble QC. They'd narrowly escaped arrest. Then, as now, he'd been struck by the mysteriously calming effect of sliced white bread – the soft, spongy variety that no self-respecting nutritionist would ever recommend. It was the cornerstone rejected by the builders, said Anselm. Absolutely, replied Andrew. Agreed, said Robert. The woman who'd taken Anselm's call – Robert's numinous grandmother – was smiling to herself at the stove, shaking the pan. Presently she left and closed the door behind her.

'Dunstan picked you for a very specific job,' said Anselm, in the pause. 'You thought that you'd been tipped off. You thought that your role was to publicise the Littlemore trial to draw more victims into the open. You thought there'd been a conspiracy with members of the Church hiding one of their own at the expense of the abused and betrayed.'

'I did and I was wrong.'

'No, you were right.'

'What? About Littlemore?'

Anselm shook his head. 'Dunstan's target was someone else. Helped by Littlemore and Carrington. I missed the signs and you weren't to know, but make no mistake about it, we are dealing with hidden victims and a conspiracy of silence, and it's your task to reach them. It's your task to help them speak.'

Robert turned to his father in astonishment, but his father was almost scolding. 'Didn't you see this coming?'

'Me? How could I?'

'You should have taken a closer look at the evidence.'

'Why?'

'Because of that letter. It spoke about *victims* needing help to speak out. In the plural. Remember?'

Anselm was amused: they were like tag wrestlers, fighting but on the same side. Robert seemed to speak for them both: 'Who was the target, then?'

'Dominic Tabley.'

Robert frowned. 'The hermit?'

'Exactly.'

Understandably Robert couldn't make any of the necessary connections. 'Why target one of the good guys?'

If the answer to that question had been simple, then maybe Anselm would have picked up one or two of the signs during Edmund's trial. As it is, a kind of protocol stopped him from offering any further explanation. Only the victims were entitled to speak about what had happened to them. The nearest Anselm could go to making a disclosure was now, as he gave a forewarning:

'Justin Brandwell is going to contact you. Listen to what he says and take it from there.'

Robert's questions tumbled out, one after the other, but Anselm only shook his head. There was nothing else he could say. To clear up some of the confusion he recounted Harry's disclosure concerning Fraser – leaving out the death because that would only distract from the matter in hand – stressing that, for present purposes, the Littlemore trial had been a window onto another secret landscape.

'Justin will explain everything. He'll take you there.'

Robert capitulated. He was content to wait for some future meeting. Turning to his father, he recalled those reports in the *Boston Globe*. They'd exposed a secret landscape, too, he said. Sad, wasn't it (he added), that these hidden worlds kept recreating themselves in institutions of every kind . . . including the family. There was a perpetual need for intervention.

'May I give you some advice?' said Anselm, rising. His thoughts were on home.

'Sure.'

'Your father is right. Go back to the wording of Dunstan's letter. Victims need help to find their voice. Your primary goal isn't to report on a scandal or damn an institution or bring the instigators to account. All that is going to happen anyway. You've got a different objective. It's to persuade. To encourage. To re-assure. There are people out there who'll never speak as long as they think they're just fodder for a headline. Make them feel that in coming forward they'll recover some—'

'Dignity.' Robert's father had spoken quietly.

'Yes,' said Anselm, with a smile. 'Precisely.'

On opening the front door Robert said he had to ask one last question. 'Did that old monk really meet Baden-Powell?'

'Oh yes. Shook his hand at Olympia. What did he drill you to the floor with? Scouting in the Matobo Hills? The Siege of Mafeking?'

'No. King Dinizulu's necklace. Do you think he'd give me an interview?'

Anselm didn't quite know how to explain the paradox. 'Not

a cat's chance in hell. He's old school. Doesn't believe in talking. Thinks we should never have dropped the sign language.'

Anselm caught a late train to Cambridge where Bede was waiting in the community's aging Fiat. They trundled along the empty lanes to Larkwood, Bede complaining in advance that the press would go too far in their praise of the detective recluse; that he'd keep the more moderate examples, out of obedience, but the rest would be used to light the fire. I'm home, thought Anselm. But he wasn't, not quite. Robert was yet to do his work and Anselm's own understanding of events was not yet complete. He understood almost everything, save the beginning; the great beginning that had sent Edmund Littlemore into the past of a man who'd watched over him like an absent father. He'd shortly find out because Edmund and George Carrington were waiting for him, probably with Dunstan, eager to know the upshot of their extraordinary bid for transparency and justice.

Part Six

The investigation into Fraser's death wasn't carried out by Sanjay, but it was Sanjay who came round to disclose the results. After he'd finished his explanation, Harry felt the eyes of his family upon him. No one spoke. They were as shocked as he was, only there was pity too. Pity for Harry.

'I'd like to be on my own, if you don't mind,' he said, rising.

His mother began to fuss but his father said let him go; let the lad get some fresh air. His grandfather agreed. Only Uncle Justin stared into space, barely seeing Harry as he crossed before his eyes on the way to the door. Once outside, Harry walked slowly to Strath Terrace, the road between Battersea Rise and St John's Hill; the road with a bridge and a shrine to three dead children. When he got there, he noticed that more flowers had been laid on the ground. People had been adding their own tributes. There were small cards with messages. The heap of affection and compassion took up half the pavement. Before long the police would have to remove it, or at least reduce its size. Harry stood looking down at the three plants he recognised: Fraser had chosen yellow for Ryan, green for Katie and blue for Ellie. Tears began to run down Harry's cheeks. He'd come to know these children. He'd seen the freckles, the bunches and the pixie nose. He'd found a place for them inside himself, something to make sense of what their father had done to him; something to give a meaning to his silence. Sanjay's voice seemed to come on a light wind.

'Fraser never intended to go the Western Isles, Harry, because his grandfather never had a croft on the Isle of Barra. That was all invention, to send us in the wrong direction if you ever decided to speak out after he'd gone.' The police officer's voice was drowned by a passing dump truck; then he continued, more quietly. 'Fraser had no children, Harry. That was all invention, too. They didn't exist. He was never married.

He'd never been a street cleaner in Glasgow. There'd been no house fire. This was all a world he invented to win your sympathy; to keep you quiet. I'm sorry.'

Harry still couldn't believe it. He'd spoken to Ryan, seeing him try to put out that fire. He'd shared the panic and terror. He'd closed his eyes like Katie and Ellie as if to sleep through a nightmare. They'd all been so real. They were still real.

'The poor man killed himself,' said an old woman, appearing in Harry's line of vision. 'He did my garden and he fixed my washing machine. You'd never have known he was so unhappy.' Then she was gone, a bunch of white roses laid on the pile.

Harry didn't know what to think. He'd rebuffed his grandfather and Uncle Justin. They'd both come to him almost on their knees begging for forgiveness and he'd looked past them into the garden, trying not to blink until the two of them had gone. He hadn't offered them a glance or a word; and he'd almost enjoyed their hopeless pleading. But looking at this shrine, this mountain of lies and manipulation, Harry felt something very different in the warmth of a dawning light. He saw the two men again, heads bowed. They'd been trapped. Like Harry, they'd been exploited and twisted into doing things they would never have wanted to do. The three of them had been forced into the one invisible prison, kept apart and set against each other. In their case, for the sake of his grandma and her belief in Father Tabley. In Harry's case, for the sake of a would-be father, broken by the loss of children he'd never had.

Staring at the mound of flowers, the warming light grew stronger still: it was for the sake of Ryan and Katie and Ellie, because of the real experiences that Harry had shared with them, that Harry would try and forgive his relatives. If he could never understand the actions of Fraser, he could totally understand the mistakes of his uncle and grandfather. There was something he could save from the tangle of betrayal and coercion because there was something they'd shared in common. Sanjay had named it as he'd closed his folder.

'You've all been victims. And victims have to stick together.'

★

Harry went home making a number of resolutions. The New Year's kind. Sincere and easily broken because they were secret. But it was a beginning. First, he'd ask to go back to 'Speakers' Corner' with his Uncle Justin. Second, he'd suggest going to a concert at the bandstand with his granddad. And third, he'd say sorry to Gutsy for having lied. He'd broken the golden rule between blood brothers; and they were halfway there now, because Gutsy had gone and cut himself on the kitchen knife.

53

Father Dominic Tabley was arrested on the same day that Justin Brandwell made a complaint of historical abuse to the police. He admitted everything. Writing in the *Guardian*, Robert revisited evidence adduced in the Littlemore trial, covering the allegations in great detail. Other papers followed suit. A public discussion was underway as people who'd known the great man in Newcastle made sense of the monster who'd terrorised a boy in London. One question arose with sickening inevitability: were there others, like Justin, who'd felt unable to contact the police? Robert followed up his report with a series of essays exploring the anatomy of abuse, the allure of secrecy, and the inner devastation that always came with silence. He spoke to survivors – of violence, exploitation, torture and kidnap – observing that redemption always began with talking. Closing the paper on the final article, Anselm found himself waiting with quiet if melancholic anticipation. Would the others follow Justin's example? Would those who needed a trial to find closure actually find the confidence to come forward?

Only time would tell.

In the meantime there was a hiatus. And Larkwood's Prior decided to fill it. Given the sophistication (not to mention the deceit) involved in Dunstan's plan – his use of Anselm and Larkwood in the hands of others to expose Dominic Tabley – the Prior organised a meeting of the entire community, to be addressed by the two protagonists, Edmund Littlemore and George

Carrington. There was a need for a great gathering in. There were many questions to be answered. And so everyone assembled in the circular Chapter Room. A candle was lit on a central stand behind the chairs of the invited speakers. Anselm, seated in his recess in the wall, listened intently.

'I don't suppose I'll ever forget the day of my election,' said Carrington. 'First I took the oath of secrecy regarding the contents of the secret archive, then there was a celebratory meal, and later I spent the evening reading a monograph on Ruusbroec, but I couldn't concentrate. Shortly before he died, Owen Murphy got blind drunk. I found him crying, inconsolable, and all he'd say was that if he could have his time again he'd never have allowed himself to be elected Provincial. I don't know why, but I threw the article aside and went straight to the safe. On opening the door I saw a pile of brown envelopes. Dominic Tabley's name was written on them all.'

Carrington had come to a swift, if assumed, conclusion. Sailing close to the wind, he'd called two of the named parties inviting them to contribute funds to one of Tabley's social projects. The icy refusals had confirmed his suspicions. The legendary hermit had a buried past.

'Given my oath of secrecy,' said Carrington, 'I was powerless to act. However, I'd noticed that all the named parties were resident in England. There were no . . . arrangements between Father Tabley and anyone in Sierra Leone.'

Given the recurring nature of the crime, Carrington refused to believe that Tabley's offending had been confined to his time in London. And so he saw a way forward: if he could unearth an offending history in Sierra Leone, then criminal proceedings might be possible over there, which would pave the way for an investigation here in England. The problem was how to get someone onto Tabley's past without telling them what they were actually doing.

'I was the solution,' said Edmund, wryly. 'George sent me to

Freetown. Told me to find anyone who remembered Father Tabley and remind them his jubilee was approaching. Extend invitations. Suggest they contribute to the celebration.'

In this way Carrington had sent Edmund towards potential victims whose experiences had not been brought to the attention of the Order. The scheme worked. Summoned to meet a dying man, Edmund found himself at the beside of a tormented witness, a one-time school janitor whose later preferment had been bought with silence. In tears, he revealed a history of abuse at St Lambert's Academy that had never been openly addressed. The school had simply been closed and the perpetrators brought back to England, Dominic Tabley chief among them. Literally. But that status, linked to the fact that the officials who'd negotiated the closure were now distinguished public figures, meant that powerful people had a vested interest in keeping a hidden scandal hidden. No sooner had Edmund begun asking questions than vague but damaging accusations were made against him and his visa was promptly withdrawn – almost certainly by the same people who stood to face censure if Edmund's enquiries continued.

'I was annoyed with George,' confessed Edmund. 'I'd come to England to get away from one scandal and he'd sent me towards another. I said just that, on the day I got back to London. I made a lot of noise. And then he pointed out that I'd left England at the age of two. That if my parents had stayed together in London, I could have grown to be one of the victims – which shut me up because he was right. Father Tabley had been very close to my mother, more than just a friend. He'd done the same thing in Freetown. Made himself part of the family. Displaced a few fathers. The man had a system.'

The recognition of his good fortune transformed Edmund's understanding of why he'd come to England. All the more so because, shortly afterwards, he received a message on a postcard from the widow of the man who'd died plagued by guilt. There'd been no accusation. Just a stark warning that Dominic Tabley couldn't have changed. A warning that couldn't be ignored. Under the pretext of compiling a secret memoir, Edmund set out to find the children he might have harmed. It had become a very personal project, watched with seeming detachment by Carrington. Edmund, of course, could not have known about the secret archive, or its contents.

'After tracing Justin Brandwell I was certain that he was a burdened man. I pursued him, hoping he'd be the one to speak out first, making it that little bit easier for any others, but he refused. He bound me to silence, along with George, and I thought the project had foundered. But then – and I don't want to be misunderstood, because the experience has been awful – I had the good fortune to be falsely accused.'

The ensuing nightmare put Edmund right at the centre of the secrets which crippled the Brandwell family; secrets linking Harry Brandwell to Justin and Justin to Dominic Tabley. Although that's not how Edmund saw it at the time. He'd gone to George Carrington who sat frozen with shock for something like five minutes before he lifted the phone and said, 'I know an extremely unpleasant man who'll know what to do . . . if there's anything that can be done.'

That man was, of course, Father Dunstan Hartley-Wilkinson, Carrington's former tutor at Cambridge. He'd listened in disgruntled silence and then hung up. The next morning, he called back. Carrington's recollection of the exchange was so vivid, Anselm almost felt he'd been there, gripping a second receiver.

'There's only one solution,' said Dunstan. 'It probably won't work but it's worth a shot. Do as I say, for once.'

'Of course.'

'This Littlemore, has he got any guts?'

'I really don't know. But he cares.'

'Caring is not enough. He'll need something like hate or anger if he's to survive. Love betrayed would be ideal, but a man can't choose his wounds.'

'Survive what?'

'You'll receive some cuttings after this call. They're character assessments of Anselm. You've heard of him. He's ideal for this operation. Give them to Littlemore. Tell him to study them carefully.'

'Right.'

'I don't require interjections. Just make notes. He must go homeless for a month, turn up at Larkwood using a false name, befriend Anselm and contrive to remain here. After six months I'll write to the journalist and expose him. You must come here at the same time and ask Anselm to find Littlemore. We'll liaise. Hopefully their paths will cross and then we'll all be damned in the public eye. That will raise the profile of the coming trial.'

'What trial? The boy hasn't spoken.'

'Arrange for Anselm to meet the Brandwells. He'll be stumped. He won't say that Littlemore is at Larkwood because Littlemore isn't wanted by the police. But if he meets the boy – and we have to pray that he does – he'll tell him to speak out. And this is the weakest point; it could all fall apart here, because we have to pray that the boy sticks to his story. There's a chance. He's lied once so he might lie again, especially if he thinks Littlemore is out of reach. Are you noting this?'

'Yes.'

'Some indication would be helpful. Next. After his arrest, Littlemore is to say nothing to the police. He can only speak to Anselm, and when he does, it is to ask him to defend him; that by defending him, he'll reach the Silent Ones.'

'Who?'

'The Silent Ones. Use that exact phrase. It will draw Anselm back into court. Thereafter, everything should fall into place. Here and abroad.'

Carrington didn't know what to say. He looked at the receiver as if he'd been connected to Wonderland.

'You doubt me?' called Dunstan, sounding mad. 'Think it

through and you'll see there's no other way to help the people who need to be helped and to expose those who need to be exposed.'

Carrington had put the phone down thinking he'd wasted his time. But his mind kept returning to the elements of Dunstan's so-called operation, and the more he did so, the more he became convinced that it might actually work . . . that it showed a certain genius.

'He'd built something extraordinary around Edmund's failed investigation. While it was outlandish, if successful it would over-come every complication in the case, meet every difficulty, respect every sensitivity. I was astounded at his intellectual and moral daring.'

Carrington embellished his point by explaining the restrictions inherent to his circumstances. He couldn't go to the police because there was no crime to report – not that he actually knew of. He'd been sworn to secrecy in respect of confidentiality agree-ments made before his election and he couldn't go behind them: the individuals concerned had a right to anonymity and he had to respect their elected silence. For that very reason he couldn't confront Tabley himself. At the same time, Carrington suspected that each individual had almost certainly thought they'd been an isolated case, but he couldn't take the initiative to disabuse them, since that would involve not only breaking his oath, but violating the secrecy attached to each separate agreement. Moreover – and critically – with each victim compartmentalised, they'd lost any sense of a greater identity, along with any conse-quent sense of solidarity, shared power and mutual authority. Each of them would have thought that in exposing Dominic Tabley – by then an acclaimed figure – they would be assuming all the responsibility for any scandal.

'And then I realised what Dunstan was trying to do in using the press,' said Carrington. 'It wasn't to provoke outrage. He saw publicity as the only means to reach the people who were lost to the public eye, but who formed the public eye . . . the people who quietly read the papers and watched the television and listened to the radio, thinking that their story was their own story and no one else's. A story best left untold.'

Dunstan had evidently realised that, if Anselm went back into court, he'd be faced with the evidence collected by Edmund. He'd have to try and make sense of the fact that Edmund had been investigating Tabley. All he'd have to do is find out why Harry Brandwell had been silenced and that would lead him to Justin's great secret.

'This is why I decided to endorse the scheme,' said Carrington. 'Because I recognised that Dunstan was right: there was no other way to save Edmund, no other way to save Justin and no other way to save Harry. And no other way to reach the Silent Ones. He'd devised a means of not only flushing out the crimes of Dominic Tabley and the mistakes of my Order, but also exposing the well-intentioned secrets that were crippling the Brandwell family, a family that stood as a symbol for all the others. And he'd done that by convoking not the police, whom he couldn't approach in any event, but representatives of the very institution that had failed the victims in the first place. I have to admit, I was awed by the breadth of his vision. And moved . . . because the prospects of success rested not upon his planning or Edmund's daring . . . but two short prayers.' Carrington looked around the room, taking his time to make eye contact with every member of the community. Reaching Anselm he stopped, and said, 'I apologise without reservation for the duplicity involved. I hope it was justified by the seriousness of our purpose and, I dare say, the obedience of a pupil to an obnoxious teacher who wouldn't take no for an answer.'

The Prior thanked the two speakers and then asked the question that was on Anselm's mind: 'What's happening about Sierra Leone?'

'This, too, is part of Dunstan's programme,' replied Carrington. 'If you like, we've turned full circle. I'd hoped people would come forward in Freetown prompting revelations here in London. Now it's the other way around. We can only wait. It is a deeply private and personal decision. Our objective has simply been to create the conditions in which a free and fearless choice can be made.'

At the conclusion of the meeting Anselm thanked his collaborators and then quickly retired to his cell. The 'gathering in' had exhausted him. While Carrington had maintained the fretful detachment of an agent handler, Anselm (like Edmund) had relived the anxiety of the man on the ground who'd taken significant risks, not knowing if his stumbling in the dark would lead anywhere. He'd been worn out by the recollection of trusting Edmund against the odds, trying to reach Harry Brandwell, accepting the dismay of his parents, struggling to interpret Justin's behaviour, invigilating the disintegration of flawed relationships . . . the sheer mechanics of aiming to bring a true and lasting resolution to the problems of a gravely damaged family. As a kind of animated backdrop, playing constantly even as Carrington joked about Dunstan, he kept seeing Fraser tip backwards, arms extended, eyes closed. In the split-second coldness of the moment, no part of Anselm had wanted to reach forward to save him. A callous disregard for a ruined life had emerged just as Harry came running towards him. And now he felt a peculiar species of guilt. That recollection was exhausting too. All this had flowed from Dunstan's plan, crafted overnight in a cell ten yards from his own. Turning off the light, Anselm thought of the old man, confined now to the infirmary. He'd never liked him, and he still didn't like him, though he now had a grudging admiration. Most of all, however – and for the first time – he wanted to *understand* him. Being twisted and embittered didn't explain Dunstan's feverish desire to unmask Dominic Tabley. There had to be another reason. Something like hate or anger. Or love betrayed.

54

The Silent Ones grew day by day. Some openly, some anonymously. A special kind of voice was taking shape, gathering depth
and colour. Its volume was growing. Police officers, using the
memoir collated by Edmund, were able to approach individuals
and sensitively explore the past, opening the door for a voluntary
disclosure. Some took the opportunity; others did not. They'd
been given the choice. Articles in the *Guardian* and other papers
brought these testimonies together, creating a bond between
people who'd never met one another. Among those who found
the courage to speak was Maisie Brandwell. But not in public.
She came to Larkwood by appointment to see Anselm.

'I've a confession to make,' she said, leaving Martin to pick
some plums.

They sat at a table beneath a wellingtonia tree in an enclosed
herb garden. Limes and chestnuts gave shade to the flowers and
weeds that grew by the surrounding white fence. Small fish
nipped the surface of a large green pond in the centre.

'I think I was in love with him,' said Maisie. 'Awful, isn't it?
I was a married woman with children. I used to imagine that if
anything terrible happened to Martin while he was out in
Cambodia then maybe Dominic would leave his Order. It was
all nonsense, of course. All in the mind. But it's what I used to
think. One of those dreams that you'd never take seriously. But
you keep returning to it.'

It seemed to Anselm that Maisie had fragmented. She spoke coherently, but moving around, like someone stepping from one stone to another, leaving behind what she'd just said. She'd lost her blinkers and couldn't see straight.

'Justin used to tell the most wonderful stories. You couldn't work out where fact began and fiction took over. Even when he was very small, he was away with his imagination. I remember once driving the car and I nearly had a crash because I could see Justin in the rear-view mirror, with his hands in the air, sort of pulling at something, and I asked him what he was doing, and do you know what he said? He said he was in the jungle. He was climbing a creeper after a monkey. Isn't that extraordinary?'

Anselm said it was. Maisie thought for a moment.

'He always looked after his brother. I remember once when Justin nearly lost an eye. He'd fired an arrow straight into the air and then looked up as it came down. Missed his eye by an inch. There was blood all over his face but do you know what he was doing? He was comforting Dominic, because Dominic was in such a state. He just didn't think of himself. We named Dominic after Father Tabley. Did you know that?'

Anselm said he did. Maisie seemed to step back.

'Justin once dressed up with his sword and shield and made himself some sandwiches. He spent ages looking for his gloves and then he went upstairs and walked inside the wardrobe. He was *desperate* to go to Narnia. Absolutely desperate. Inconsolable when I told him he couldn't get there. Can you imagine that?'

Anselm said he could. He'd tried himself.

'The thing I can't get over is this: Justin came to me. He began to tell me what had happened and I stopped him. I just wouldn't listen. I think I put the kettle on. I remember it now. I thought he'd reached the age when boys start exploring this sort of thing, you know, and Justin being Justin, he'd let his mind go where it shouldn't. And do you know something, Father? He never mentioned the subject again. Not once.'

Taking Maisie at her word, Anselm could only pity her. If she'd entertained any fears, they'd have been smoothed away by the passing weeks and months. Because if there was any truth to Justin's story, then he'd have returned – and he hadn't done. Taking Maisie at her word, she'd missed her one opportunity. It had come and gone before she even reached the kettle.

But Anselm hadn't taken Maisie at her word. Her son had said things no parent would dare to leave unexplored. And she had done. Because she loved Tabley? Partly. Because she didn't want to believe Justin? Probably. Because Tabley's 'system' – to quote Edmund – was bewitching? Almost certainly.

'I share the blame,' she said, as if reading out loud. 'Dominic is right. I should be ashamed of myself.'

Her guilt was mechanical, and not because she didn't care; in fact, it was probably because she cared beyond measure; but like Justin she was cut off from her deepest reactions. Like Justin, she daren't reach into herself. The cost of doing so was incalculable. She, too, needed help.

'We get older but we don't get any wiser, do we?' she said, moving to another stone.

Anselm agreed.

'I said to Harry that I was prepared to believe him as long as he told the truth. Isn't that an odd thing to say?'

Anselm's sympathy was without qualification. Deciding in advance what you're prepared to believe was a distinctively human foible. Lord Denning had made a similar mistake when dismissing an appeal by the Birmingham Six. Faced with a cover-up of unthinkable proportions – alleged police brutality, perjury, involuntary confessions and erroneous convictions – he'd considered the vista so appalling that he thought it couldn't possibly be true. In his own way, he, too, had put the kettle on.

'He made Justin think he was interested in his brother,' said Maisie, scratching lichen off the table with a beautifully rounded nail. 'That was all nonsense. He picked Justin because he told tall stories. It wasn't a mistake, something that happened on impulse. It was a calculated decision. Awful, isn't it?'

Anselm said it was; but he watched Maisie carefully now, because her nail was sinking into the soft wood of the table. There'd been no confession so far, he realised, feeling ill at ease. Maisie was crossing to another stepping stone. She had the air of someone who might lose her balance and fall.

'I slept with him, you know,' she said, quietly, frowning at her broken nail. 'Only once. That's why he said he was going to Newcastle. Isn't this absolutely dreadful, but until very recently, I've never regretted it. I felt guilty of course. I knew it was wrong. But it happened so . . . naturally; so accidentally. It was difficult to feel entirely bad about it; I didn't want to feel bad about it.' She pulled at the split nail with her teeth. 'It had been important to me.'

Maisie stopped there. With a tissue she wiped the blood from where the quick had been torn. She, like Anselm, was thinking about Dominic Tabley. Had he loved Maisie, too, and made a serious mistake? Or had he been smoothing over his departure from Justin's broken life, tying Maisie down with secret, shared sin? Dark chocolate; the kind that's eaten in silence? When Dominic Tabley had driven his gleaming, classic Triumph to Newcastle, he must have been fairly sure Maisie wouldn't be mentioning his name too often.

'I've never told that to anyone before, Father,' said Maisie. 'But I wanted you to know. I wanted you to understand how I could have failed Justin so completely.'

Anselm had barely spoken so far, and when he opened his mouth, now, Maisie stood up, still preoccupied with that damaged nail. She wrapped the tissue around the end of her finger, wincing at the pain.

'I won't be wanting absolution, Father,' she said, rather like a shopper at the market. 'And it's not because I don't think I need it . . . or need *something*, anyway. The problem is, I don't know *what* I need at the moment. I wouldn't mind a new life. Have you got one of those on the shelf?'

Maisie began the walk out of the garden and back to Larkwood. Anselm kept to her side, not presuming to deal with her last question. When they reached the monastery car park – a stretch of gravel beneath plum trees – Martin opened the door to their gleaming Rover. Like Martin it was silvery and conspicuously clean. He reached for Maisie's seatbelt, clipped the buckle into position and checked she was comfortable. Then, after shaking Anselm's hand, he quickly occupied the driver's seat as if he didn't want to leave his wife alone too long. Seeing Anselm's unease, Maisie pressed a button and the window came down.

'He's not what it's all about, Maisie,' said Anselm, stumbling for some kind of blanket response to the many painful questions.

'Oh, you're wrong there, Father,' she replied, eyes shining with childlike confusion. 'He's exactly what it's all about. Because he changed. He really did. Didn't you know that? He said sorry with absolute sincerity. And that means he gets a clean slate in the eyes of God. He might even be a saint. I'm not sure I can accept that. What do you think, Father?'

She kept those eyes on Anselm as the window moved slowly up its groove. The engine began to purr and then the vehicle moved away, swinging towards the monastery gates. Instinctively – and almost recoiling – Anselm recalled Dominic Tabley in his Watsonian sidecar, the bottle of oxygen between his legs. He'd nodded and waved in a bubble of blissful ignorance.

But something else was bothering him. And it was only much later in the absolute silence of the night that Anselm had an appalling thought. He was so struck with conviction that he had to get up. After pacing his room, he threw open the window, seeking the companionship of a sound in the trees.

At the Bar, Anselm had always had a problem deciphering his rushed notes of evidence. Fortunately, his memory seemed to select seemingly unimportant details and put them to one side for later consideration. And there were four such items that now came to mind: Edmund's father, when traced, hadn't liked his son's Boston accent. Father Tabley hadn't liked it either. Anselm shuddered because, during Edmund's presentation to the community, he'd stated something that Anselm had found ever so slightly unconvincing, and this was the third item: he'd said that his understanding of why he'd come to England had been transformed when Carrington pointed out that Edmund was fortunate not to have been one of Tabley's victims. It had been a good point. A rousing point. But not a point that would explain what subsequently happened: Edmund's single-minded attempt to expose his mother's one-time friend and guide. After his arrest, he'd been the object of widespread loathing. How had he survived the ordeal? Through anger? Hate? Love betrayed?

Anselm listened to Larkwood's owl. In all his years at the monastery he'd never actually seen it. Yet each of them knew the other was there. Rather like Edmund and Dominic Tabley.

It hadn't always been thus. Tabley had once warmed bottles for Edmund and fed him. In those days he'd been part of the family, a very young family that would shortly be sundered by divorce . . . Anselm could scarcely believe the conclusion to which he'd been drawn. But it seemed unavoidable because, speaking to Anselm as John Joe Collins, Edmund had let slip an important truth that he'd shared with no one else, not even Dominic Tabley. And that was the fourth item on the shelf: he'd crossed the Atlantic to find his father.

55

If it was remarkable that the accused had chosen to stay alive, it was outright astonishing that his adversary, Dunstan, refused to die. As if to scorn medical authority, he simply wouldn't go. The consultant had never seen anything like it. The old man was hanging on for the trial. Only, towards the end of Lent, he finally began to lose his grip. The Prior, being generous, said he was like Moses. He was going to die without having reached the Promised Land, though why Tabley's appointment with a court should have so preoccupied him remained a mystery. Anselm paid frequent unwanted visits, only to be bitten or bruised, because Dunstan's spleen wasn't simply intact, it was expanding. Only his body was shrinking. A mysteriously unhappy man would shortly steal away and everyone would breathe an open sigh of relief. Things turned suddenly for the worse on a Friday night. Brother Aelred, the Infirmarian, knocked on Anselm's door.

'He wants to see you.'

'Me?'

'Just go, will you? Or he'll throw the bedpan at me.'

Anselm strode quickly to the infirmary where he found Dunstan propped up in bed. Electric light hurt his eyes, so a plate of candles had been lit. The soft glow gave a yellowy sheen to his skin. He was withered, now. The bones in his arms were visible, his cheeks scooped hollow. Determined to die in style, he'd chosen a lime-green cravat.

'You've never quite taken me seriously, have you?' opined Dunstan, as Anselm sat down. 'You think I'm all mouth and no trousers.'

'No, I don't.'

'Spare a dying man false pity. All I want is your attention.'

Dunstan angled himself towards Anselm and then, in a surprising gesture of submission, he removed his glasses. The lights of his eyes were barely flickering, but all at once they grew strong, as when wax spills and the flame eats the exposed wick.

'Immediately after the war I was sent to Lower Saxony. Drab place. No *jeunes filles*. Absolute hole. I felt like *eine Scheiße* passing through . . .'

★

An official in Whitehall had prepared a file of photographs to help Dunstan and his peers find monsters masquerading as nobodies. At the top of the list was 'Hitler, A.' After a couple of months he got bored to death. Everyone he interviewed had been picked up because they looked like Goebbels – 'and he was already dead' – or Goering, 'who'd already been arrested'. A lot of people were imprisoned because of mistakes and grudges. Files were mislaid. The photographs weren't always linked to names. Allegations floated free, anchored to neither a name nor a face, and the damned Americans weren't cooperating. Running their own show in Berlin. One day a young woman was brought to Dunstan's office. There was no file, no allegation and no photo. The paperwork was 'on its way' from some *Urinflasche* in Hamburg. The woman had asked to be interviewed.

'She was tearful. *Awfully* polite. Couldn't explain why the brute had thrown her in the back of his van, and all I could say was that there are no brutes in the British Army. Couldn't trace the bugger anyway. No damned paperwork. She was Bavarian . . . and that's where it all began . . . with an accent. They have a way of talking, you know . . .'

Dunstan had wondered what she was doing in the far north-west, when she came from the far south-east. Nursing, she said, pointing at her uniform, with more tears. All she wanted to do was go back home . . . to a place near Grassau in the mountains.

'A farm or something with a mill and a brook,' recalled Dunstan, his breathing becoming shallow. He grimaced and pushed on. 'You know, milk churns and national dress. She was the lovely maid of the mill. Have you read Müller? Don't bother. Well, it was the world she'd loved and lost, and all because of Wagner. I hummed some Schubert. A song about a brook . . . *War es also gemeint, mein rauschender Freund*? But then she sang it and I almost blacked out. I could hear the damned river talking. This was the language before the Nazis used it for shouting. Couldn't take the sound. The *beauty*. I had to send her back to prison.'

Dunstan didn't speak for a while. He closed his eyes and his chest rose and fell slowly. Then, just when Anselm thought he might have drifted off, he swore and said, 'I couldn't get her out of my mind.'

But without a file, he had no questions. Without questions he had no reason to see her. So he summoned her anyway and they talked. She'd wanted to go to the Staatliche Akademie der Tonkunst in Munich. But then the war happened.

'And I'd wanted to be a poet. Only I couldn't blame the Reich. I'd no talent.' They talked of those twin dashed hopes, encouraging one another to have another go. 'Nothing brings two people together better than disappointment. I just didn't see what was happening. When I called the guard it felt like I was ordering a war crime.'

Dunstan had been haunted by her face and voice.

'I found reasons to see her. Apologised for the delay. The conditions. I lent her books. And then, one morning, I woke up and I was changed. Felt like I'd been floored. Took me a while to find out what the hell was wrong but then I worked it out. Love's like that, don't you think? Hides itself in the making and then takes you down when it's too late to get out of the way. Clever girl. Patient girl. All she'd done was sing a song.'

In the absence of the file and no prospect of its appearing, Dunstan made a bold decision.

'Do you see this typewriter?'

Anselm said, 'Yes.'

'I used it to write to that halfwit Sambourne.'

'He's not a halfwit.'

'Well, I was, because I also used it to authorise her release. She promised to write and send a photograph. I must have been crazy . . . I actually imagined a life in the mountains. A family. *Kinder*. Milk, fresh from the churn.' Dunstan's face creased and his chest made a soft rattle. 'I'd even practised the *Schuhplattler*.'

Anselm asked: 'Did she write?'

'No. The file arrived instead. A beige thing with a green tag at the corner.'

On opening it, Dunstan discovered that the girl who'd loved Schubert had never been a nurse. She'd never helped the sick or wounded. In fact, obtaining witness statements from the sick and wounded had been the primary explanation for the delay in obtaining the file. Evidence had only hardened into sustainable allegations with their recovery.

'She'd been a camp guard. Belsen. Not much poetry there; not much music.'

Dunstan sighed as if he'd come to a plateau. His head fell to one side, and Anselm wondered if he ought to call Aelred, but then Dunstan reached towards him. A cold bony hand hooked itself into the sleeve of his habit.

'She was never caught,' he whispered. 'She got away. Maybe she's still alive. Propped up in bed. Someone will think she's wonderful. A nice old lady. Backbone to the church choir. And they'll be right. But they'll be wrong too, because you can't just drive round the corner and change your clothes. I was there, Anselm. I went into Belsen. April the fifteenth, 1945. There were bodies everywhere . . . *everywhere*' – Dunstan covered his face with his other hand, speaking hoarsely through his fingers – 'I let her go. I'd seen the bodies and I let her go.'

Dunstan's mouth fell open and a soft gust of air came out.

'I'll get the Prior.'

'No, stay with me. Don't go. I'm frightened, Anselm. I don't want to die.'

Dunstan's grip on his arm had suddenly weakened. But he didn't pull away. Anselm took his hand.

'Don't say anything,' murmured Dunstan. 'I don't want any last-minute crap.'

'All right.'

'Just don't let go.'

'I won't.'

'Oh God, I'm scared. What if there's nothing?'

'There's something.'

'How the hell do you know? Tell everyone I'm sorry for being such a bastard.'

'Okay.'

'You can have my typewriter.'

'Thanks.'

Dunstan frowned in pain. 'I don't want to meet her victims. I daren't see her victims. What do I say? That I loved her?'

Anselm didn't make any suggestions because Dunstan made another soft, low exhalation and then his hand lost its tremble. Suddenly, he raised his head and turned to Anselm looking strangely surprised, as if he'd just woken from a bad dream. Then he smiled, sank back, and the faint light in his eyes disappeared behind the rising mist.

Anselm didn't move for a long time. He kept hold of Dunstan's hand, not wanting to lay it flat on the tartan blanket, wanting to keep something that it might contain, something offered, but it was empty. And then, quite suddenly, he was ambushed by a depth of affection that he could never have believed was there. A candle guttered and spat; then its flame grew tall.

56

The received wisdom is that difficult people must have a background story which explains the rudeness, the hard edges, the outbursts of temper. Something appropriately dramatic. The only question is whether we ever find it out. On that basis, Anselm felt he now understood Dunstan's fractured character. However, after meeting his brother, Evelyn, Anselm realised a more sophisticated theory would have to be framed, because he was as objectionable and quick-tempered as the firstborn of the

Hartley-Wilkinson line. The rest of the family weren't that different. Their redeeming feature was a certain eccentricity, because Evelyn, irrevocably English but kilted with the vanity of Rob Roy, insisted on playing the bagpipes by the graveside. Warned in advance by the Prior, Anselm thought the spectacle would be utterly excruciating. In fact, it was deeply moving. The low drone gripped his throat and then 'Amazing Grace' emerged, echoing through the trees; for Larkwood's dead lie in a grove of aspens. When Evelyn had finished, everyone drifted away, picking their way towards the sunlight.

The burial was nonetheless a sad affair. It soon became clear that no one in the family knew anything about Dunstan's experience of Belsen. Neither, of course, did anyone in the community. All those hints at self-importance as an interrogator had been intimations of shame and failure. But no one could have had the slightest idea. And they still didn't, because Anselm knew he was the bearer of a secret that Dunstan wanted taken to his grave.

'He never forgave the Service for denying him a career after the war,' said Evelyn, knowledgeably, making ready to leave in the car park. 'That's where his disappointments began. He was a bloody awkward sod.'

They were evidently a plain-speaking family because a number of bystanders nodded in agreement. A spade was a spade. But they couldn't have known that Dunstan had been exiled from the Service because of a mistake, robbing him of the chance to make amends; that C's underlings had kept the wound open by retaining him as a talent spotter; that they'd probably scotched any chance he might have had of becoming a Fellow – they couldn't have him sipping sherry in one of their Alma Maters. All of which, if true, would have made Kafka blink, because while punishing Dunstan, they'd recruited former SS officers to help fight the Russians.

'He urged me to join the Service,' said Carrington to Evelyn. 'But he warned me that the place was jam-packed with – I'm sorry, but I have to quote him – "masons, arseholes, pimps and peers". He meant no harm, I'm sure. I joined the Lambertines instead.'

The supposed asymmetry brought a smile to Anselm's face. Carrington wasn't simply a man of principle, he had a devilish sense of humour which, linked to Dunstan's acid wit, must have made tutorials on mysticism an unforgettable experience. Strange to think that it was there, in a Cambridge don's rooms discussing Margery Kempe, that a friendship had been forged that would one day generate a plan to secure Dominic Tabley's arrest.

The gathering was sad in other respects. Dunstan had so effaced himself in the plan to expose Dominic Tabley that none of his victims could possibly have known that an obscure monk was the architect of the scheme; or that there had even been a scheme. Had Robert Sambourne not stumbled upon the faxed cuttings, no one save Carrington and Littlemore would ever have known at all. As a result, to Anselm's mind, there was a group missing from the graveside: the Silent Ones. None of them had come – none of them could come – to pay their respects, to thank him for what he'd done: he'd ensured his own invisibility from the outset. For the same reason, there were no representatives of the Brandwell family. If they thanked anyone it was Edmund Littlemore and Anselm. Even Carrington hadn't made the list.

'You'll return to London?' Anselm was speaking to Edmund as Evelyn was driven away, arguing with a nephew twice-removed who'd said the pipes were out of tune.

'No, I'm going home.'

'To Boston?'

'It's where I belong; it's where I've always belonged. I should never have run away. I should never have pretended I had nothing to do with changing the future. George taught me that lesson.'

You're an accomplished liar, thought Anselm. Like Justin, you've learned to hide what you know, along with who you are; like Justin, your wounds are hidden wounds, but having your own you were able to see his. No one would ever know that in coming to England you were vindicating your mother, bringing your own father to justice, and doing what could be done to help his other victims. And to think . . . everyone thought you'd run away from a scandal. No one would ever know your true motives.

You don't always have to talk about everything.

It was a subtle truth that Tabley had twisted to his advantage; Edmund had made it something noble. They shook hands, promising to keep in touch. There's a thing called Skype, said Edmund. There are things called pens and paper, replied Anselm. In certain important respects (which Anselm wouldn't wish to change) Larkwood had remained embedded in the early thirteenth century.

'London awaits you,' said Anselm, turning to Carrington.

'Yes.'

There was nothing else to add. Both of them understood the implications of Anselm's observation. Carrington would return to deal with the legacy of Dominic Tabley. He'd already been pilloried in the press, simply because he was the man in charge. It was relentless. His evidence in the Littlemore trial had been minutely re-examined. Commentators had judged him – by turns – to be prevaricating, evasive, ambiguous and slippery. He'd been damned as a casuist. A politician. A career cleric. They can't have known that he'd also sent a message across the courtroom to Anselm. As with Dunstan, his true contribution had remained hidden from view.

'Why not tell everyone about Dunstan's plan, and your place in it?' asked Anselm. 'I'll support you. People ought to know.'

Carrington didn't agree. 'I have an important role to play in the resolution of things. Someone has to be accountable for what the Order did, for elevating Tabley above his victims. Someone has to be there, physically present, to receive and accept the anger, the outrage, the suffering. I can't point to Murphy's grave. I'm the one who was elected. I'm the one who opened the secret archive. I'm the one who has to answer for what I found.'

Anselm was amazed. Perhaps it was the lawyer in him. Perhaps it was the coward. Perhaps it was the sophist that would stress truth-telling without regard to timing. But his first instinct would have been to defend himself. He'd have dodged the avalanche of condemnation. Carrington had done the opposite. He must have known, right at the beginning when he first came to Larkwood, that if Anselm succeeded in his mission, he would be damned. People would point at him as if he was Tabley. He'd always accepted the outcome. He'd welcomed it. And he, like the Silent Ones before him, would have to wait for some future time before he could be vindicated.

'Dunstan foresaw this, didn't he?' said Anselm.

Carrington paused, no doubt recalling the language used. 'He warned me, yes. But I didn't really have a choice. He was telling me what had to happen.'

After waving goodbye to Carrington and Edmund, Anselm returned to Dunstan's grave. He looked at the mound of fresh earth and the simple white wooden cross that bore his name. It was already leaning slightly to one side. He'd lived with Dunstan for years. At no point in that long, shared history had he ever remotely felt an attachment to the man. And now, from nothing, he'd moved to a deep and abiding gratitude. He felt immensely privileged to have been involved in his scheme to bring dignity to those who'd been thrown aside.

'I hope you found something rather than nothing,' he said, honouring Dunstan's last scuffle with doubt. But what's your epitaph? he wondered. What have you left behind that everyone knows about and for which you'll always be remembered? What single detail would surface when time had softened the harshest recollections?

Anselm laughed quietly. Dunstan had dealt with that one, too.

He'd left clear instructions with Aelred. As a result it could safely be said that Dunstan Hartley-Wilkinson was the only monk in the history of Christendom to have been buried wearing a pink silk cravat.

57

Dominic Tabley pleaded guilty to all counts on the indictment – and there were many. Following the preparation of reports for the court he was sentenced to eighteen years in prison, the final figure made up of consecutive and concurrent terms, balanced against each other by Mr Justice Keating in a hopeless attempt – his words – to reflect the overall gravity of the case. In effect, of course, it was a life sentence. Dominic Tabley would die behind bars. Or, more likely, in the hospital wing, cared for by people who could no more understand his crimes than his victims could understand his supposed change of character, stressed by counsel during his speech in mitigation.

'Help me clean out Dunstan's cell,' said the Prior.

They'd left his room untouched until the Tabley matter had been dealt with. It was a way of keeping him around until the very end. Anselm opened a window and the spring air brushed against his face. Down below, Bruno was beating dust out of a rug with a cricket bat. Aelred was talking to a wayfarer. Wilf was cleaning the guest-house windows. Life went on. As for Dunstan's effects, there was nothing to sort out, really. A few clothes in a cupboard. Some books on a shelf. Worn-out boots in the corner. A walking stick. A cloak on a hook. Anselm sat down on the blue striped mattress and looked at a facing desk where Dunstan had devised his plan. There was a shoebox behind the typewriter. The Prior lifted the lid.

'It's not just about perpetrators,' said Anselm, suddenly. He didn't know where to begin. 'It's about the people who cover up. It's about the people who spend time wondering how best to manage a crisis. It's about the decisions they make.'

'What is "it"?' The Prior was leafing through some folded papers.

'The scandal. Maybe I'm going too far, but I wonder if the people who organise the smoothing over are as culpable as the perpetrators. Whether, in doing what they do, they take on themselves all the filth they tried to hide, and more. I'm thinking of Owen Murphy. He's committed a crime too, but it doesn't even exist in the statute book. He's hardly been mentioned in any of the discussions about what's happened. Just passing references. The fact that he's dead. But what he did was unconscionable.'

The Prior was frowning at the shoebox. Putting the lid back, he seated himself against the edge of the table and Anselm let loose the thoughts that had been plaguing him since Dunstan's funeral when Carrington had accepted the opprobrium due to his predecessor. He'd been rehearsing that throwaway line of Justin Brandwell's, that Murphy had been a desk clerk who found himself running the bank. The phrase had jarred with Anselm because, in using it, Justin had pitied Murphy himself and his hapless attempt to deal with Tabley's crimes. But Anselm had come to view him very differently indeed:

'He turned that secret archive into a burial ground of unsolved crime, enduring a troubled conscience as if it was the kind of martyrdom that comes with high office.'

By resolving matters with an agreement, by enjoining the parties to secrecy on a voluntary basis, Murphy had exploited the consent of the victims – if consent was the right word to describe the assent of people like Justin Brandwell. He'd drawn him and others into an arrangement whereby he could protect Tabley. If ever quizzed about his own silence, he could only point – respectfully and with compunction – to the expressed wishes of those most intimately involved. But the desired outcome was this: Tabley was protected from any criminal investigation. And Murphy could hide behind the victims' silence as if he had a moral obligation to do so. As could Tabley. This is what had set him free . . . to change . . . in complete isolation from the true and paramount needs of the people he'd left behind.

'When Tabley moved to protect himself he told people, "You don't always have to talk about everything",' said Anselm. 'And that has been the ongoing trick. It's the central plank to all these horrendous confidentiality agreements. What Tabley said in fear, Murphy turned into a kind of law. It served no one except Tabley and the Order. And that puts them both on the same moral plane as Fraser . . . They were all exploiting people's compassion, their readiness to forgive.'

Had Murphy known about Tabley's child? Had Skyler been to see him? Had the Order – a charitable organisation funded by voluntary donations for prescribed legal purposes – contributed to Edmund's upkeep? Or – and Anselm instinctively felt this to be the case – had Skyler just turned her back on the lot of them and flown back to Boston, rejected by her husband? Anselm had to close his eyes: Tabley had brought unimaginable devastation into the lives of decent people, simply because they'd believed him to be more decent than they were. That must have been part of the wayward attraction. Handling the fallout, in every and all respects, was now Carrington's life's work. The man who'd drafted the child protection procedures would have to pick his way through the moral ruins of the past. The same man, by cooperating with Dunstan, had made the secret archive public. The contents had been literally emptied onto the street – if discarded newspapers could be taken as a proxy. What else could be expected of the poor fellow?

'You remain troubled,' observed the Prior. He knew the darker corners of Anselm's mind. 'You've told yourself that Dominic Tabley could never be truly rehabilitated until he publicly acknowledged his crimes. You've wondered if he enjoyed his reformed life, depriving his victims of justice because he wanted to keep his reputation for goodness. And you've wondered if he only stopped offending because self-control had become easier – which it does, with age. You've whittled away at what you can, but one thing won't go away, will it? He did, in fact, change. He did a great deal of good. However imperfectly, he tried to make amends. It would have been easier, wouldn't it, if he'd remained a monster?'

Maisie was struggling with that very question, though she'd gone further, straining to imagine the appalling vista of a mercy without any kind of limitation. For Anselm, however, the problem was slightly different. It was just as familiar, only the familiarity didn't especially help, because every time he encountered it – as he had done with Justin and Maisie and Martin and everyone affected by the outpouring of harm – the freshness of the problem scalded him.

'You're right. I've thought everything you said. But I'm troubled more by the possibility that, while he changed, his victims can't. Or have lost the chance to change. Or will change, but only at immense cost. It's hard to hold the two together – his transformation, if there was one, and their ongoing devastation; what he gained set against what they lost. It's a heartbreaking outcome.'

The Prior nodded, watching Anselm closely. Bruno was giving that rug a pasting. During a pause, the Prior said, 'Dunstan never used to confide much, not in me, not in anyone. Not with his family and not with his friends. But he once turned to me in the cloister after Compline, as if he was going to share some great secret. And all he said was this: "The world is a tragic place." Then he walked off.'

Anselm could almost hear the old man's polished vowels. One had to get on with things. Face the morrow. Do your best. Help those who couldn't cope.

'What's in the shoebox?' asked Anselm, rising.

'Letters. From the forties onwards.' The Prior was baffled. 'They're about war crimes.'

Everything was in chronological order. They all dealt with the same subject: Dunstan's enquiries in relation to a certain Helga Brüning. He'd written to the War Office, the Foreign Office, the United Nations War Crimes Commission, embassies, consulates, here and abroad . . . and these were the replies. Most of them were rather terse, acknowledging his enquiry and refusing proffered assistance. The matter was being dealt with by the proper authorities. He was referred to previous correspondence. At the bottom of the box was a postcard. The Prior gave it to Anselm. It showed a brook and a mill. Written on the back by a wavering hand was a single line in German: *War es also gemeint, mein rauschender Freund?*

Anselm translated: 'Was this what you meant, my rushing friend?'

The Prior squinted, angling his glasses. Dunstan's tiny writing was in the corner. He'd dated the card in pencil.

'Two years ago,' he murmured.

It had been an eventful time in the old man's life, recalled Anselm. He'd got cancer, which hadn't troubled him in the least; but then he'd been contacted by Carrington, and he'd received a message from Helga. She'd kept her promise to write after all. Listening to Bruno flog the rug, Anselm wondered in what order the blows might have come.

'I don't understand any of this,' said the Prior, putting the lid back on the box. 'We'd better hand it over to Bede for the archives. He can find out what it all means.'

'No,' said Anselm, abruptly. 'Burn the lot. It's what Dunstan would have wanted.'

The Prior slowed, regarding Anselm with arched misgiving. To forestall any questioning, Anselm took the initiative.

'Dunstan said I could have the typewriter.'

The Prior looked like he'd dropped a catch. 'Anything you'd like to add?'

'Not really, but thanks for asking.'

After sweeping the cell, the window and door were left open to create a draught. The books went to the library, the stick to Sylvester, the cloak to the vestiary, the boots and clothes to the bin. Anselm then went to the common room and, standing on the rug beaten clean by Bruno, he threw the shoebox on the fire. After a moment of resistance, the cardboard buckled into flame. The letters curled. The mill and the stream vanished, along with the poetry.

Anselm put the typewriter on a table by the window in his cell. He sat down and pressed a few keys. The arms swung up, banged and fell back again. He jabbed the space bar and the carriage jolted along. He slapped the silver lever and the roller gave a turn. It was a beautiful machine. It had been used for a quite astonishing range of purposes, for good and for ill. While giving it a shine with the sleeve of his habit, Anselm had a flash of insight.

Dunstan's real target hadn't been Dominic Tabley. His sharp and jaundiced eye had been on someone else: Owen Murphy, and all he'd done to suppress the truth. When Dunstan wrote to Robert Sambourne his intention was to retrieve every word and phrase that had been hidden away. It was a nuanced insight – obvious, perhaps, given what had subsequently transpired – but it sharpened Anselm's view of Dunstan's legacy: the man who'd said nothing about his own history had given his dying days to those who'd been silenced.

Anselm looked at the worn keys, thinking of Dunstan's fingers, hammering away year after year, forever reminded of that one fatal mistake. He thought of all he'd written afterwards. Why had he given the thing to Anselm? Because it represented the man more than the cravat? Probably, yes; but Anselm had another twinkling insight. He'd have to use it one day to write something important. Something Dunstan would have written if he'd not been arrested just this side of the Promised Land.

Epilogue

The Brandwells were not a family who would find it easy to accept help. Each of them, in different ways, had been let down by the people they'd trusted most. People they'd loved. So it was not surprising that they retreated among themselves where, according to Sanjay Kumar, no one looked to anyone else. They didn't know where to begin. They didn't know how they wanted it to finish. Too much had happened. There were too many different kinds of pain and betrayal. They each knew a journey lay before them – called the next day – but none of them could even begin to think how they might move forward together. A letter of thanks from Harry Brandwell gave Anselm an idea.

It had been written on a computer and printed off on thin paper. There were no spelling mistakes, because the spellcheck was infallible. The grammar was correct, but slightly odd because the computer's suggested amendments hadn't taken into account the fresh and direct manner of speech proper to a youth struggling to say difficult things. Something had been lost, there. The paper was smooth, without a single indentation. Harry had been climbing again with his uncle. He'd been to a concert with his grandfather. He'd gone bowling with his parents and Gutsy. But despite best intentions, everyone remained confused. They couldn't get back to where they'd once been: known territory. They were stranded somewhere new. 'Would you come and talk to them?' he'd tapped. He meant turn up without invitation. He meant would he walk through the door and start bringing his family across the various divides. Help them find the words.

Anselm couldn't do it. The task was too delicate. But he knew someone who could. Using Dunstan's typewriter, Anselm banged out a letter on thick paper to Dr Clare Hawks, an old friend from way back. Even before she'd trained as a clinical psychologist, she'd had a certain eye for foundational questions. Not one to trouble with small talk, she'd sit down with a cup of tea and say, 'Now, Anselm, tell me about your mother.' Anyone who made tea before settling down to business would get on famously with Maisie Brandwell. And so Clare went to Clapham and she went to Leyborne Park. But only after chasing Justin first, because Justin more than anyone was likely to surrender to someone who wouldn't give up; someone whose opening question would tickle him pink. Of course, Clare couldn't tell Anselm how things were developing but he knew she remained involved. And that meant the family were talking. Clare was doing what she did best: joining people together; helping them find a narrative.

On something of a roll, Anselm wrote to Kester Newman. He'd left the Lambertines and gone back to PwC. Anselm had noted an appealing connection between Kester and Edmund. Edmund had confronted the bad in Dominic Tabley; Kester had only known the good. Anselm suggested they keep in touch. In fact . . . it was Clare's idea. While they hadn't even met, she thought they might help each other make sense of their different experiences; help each other come to some kind of global assessment, extending the narrative.

Having posted the letter, Anselm returned to his cell. He hit a few keys. He whacked the return lever. He nudged the space bar. Who else could he write to? He was enjoying this. And then, struck by a bright idea of his own, Anselm fed a fresh sheet of paper into the roller. He'd written two important letters, but there was a third to be knocked out, and anonymously. Just like Dunstan's. With a similar intention.

Carrington's hope was that, following the trial in London, people would come forward in Freetown. Something slightly different had happened. Since Tabley had admitted to the offending in West Africa during his interviews, questions had been asked at a very high level. The suppression of a scandal in the 1970s had become the subject of widespread and painful scrutiny. And the person who had to handle the onslaught of questions was, of course, George Carrington. But — thought Anselm, punching the keys — there was a need for greater transparency. Another investigation was required to throw a fresh light on the man whose morality and probity had been shredded like so much waste paper. There was a story to be told, too, about a dead monk who'd once written an anonymous letter to a journalist. And who better to undertake both tasks than Robert Sambourne?

But when Anselm got to the post office he stared across the counter and couldn't let go of the brown envelope. This was the last thing Dunstan would have wanted. It was the last thing Carrington wanted. Blenching, Anselm said to himself, 'You don't always have to talk about everything.' He backed away, stunned to acknowledge that he was to be the final and solitary holder of all the untold secrets. Moved by a humbling sense of privilege and responsibility, Anselm binned the letter and went back to Dunstan's resting place among the aspens. Evening was falling. For a while he listened to the breeze in the branches overhead.

'Everything that ought to be said has been said,' Anselm confided. 'Nothing remains hidden that ought to be brought into the light.'

Anselm listened to the leaves, and then he moved on. He could almost hear the sweet sound of the pipes. A tune about a wretch saved by grace.